ROGUE'S PARADISE

COVENANT OF THORNS #3

BY

JEFFE KENNEDY

<u>Credits</u>
Cover: Ravven (www.ravven.com)

Faerie, the land of blood, magic, and betrayal...

At last, the fae lord, Rogue, has won everything. He has me in his home, his bed, and I'm desperately in love with him despite my best efforts and better judgment.

Did I mention I'm pregnant?

As our child grows inside me, the one I'm pledged to give to him, I still have no idea what will happen after the birth. Though Rogue is attentive in every way a woman could wish for, bringing me delirious pleasure and gifts beyond price, he still won't—or can't—tell me what game he's playing. Or what the viciously sadistic Queen Titania has to do with our many bargains.

I'm most afraid that, if he betrays us, I'll never be able to forgive him. Even though I can't stop loving him.

As war threatens everything we've built, as my body swells with the enchanted pregnancy, I become more certain with every day that the true enemy lurks within our castle walls. And that the man I've vowed eternal commitment to, may be the last person I can trust...

DEDICATION

To all the wonderful readers out there who love Rogue too.
Despite everything.

ACKNOWLEDGEMENTS

Many thanks, as always, to critique partners Marcella Burnard and Carolyn Crane. They listen to my angst, never give me grief for my bad choices and read on short notice. All the love to you gals.

Special thanks to Grace Draven for beta reading this book. I owe you one!

Also thanks to C.J. Lemire for attempting a beta read under short time constraints and getting me comments on the beginning.

One more time, thanks to Has and E at The Book Pushers, for discovering this series, pushing it and asking for more. Many thanks to Amy Remus at So Many Reads and L.E. Olteano at Butterfly-o-Meter, for checking in with me regularly. You gals brighten my days.

I'm grateful for my Twitter friends, who are ready to step up and cheerlead me through those black moments in the story. I think you all know who you are. (I sure hope so, because I forgot to write everyone down. Oops.)

Gratitude to my editor, Deb Nemeth, and the entire Carina Press team, for seeing this trilogy into the world and giving it that special shine.

A big hug to agent Pam van Hylckama Vlieg, for reading *Rogue's Pawn* and believing in me from there. And for saying all the right things when I ask what happens if I'm not done yet.

Credit to Patricia McKillip, who invented the Liralen, and whose book, *The Forgotten Beasts of Eld,* will live forever in my heart.

Much love to David, who understands.

A NOTE FROM THE AUTHOR

This book is a new edition, one I republished when I received the rights back to the Covenant of Thorns trilogy (and the seven other books I did with Carina Press) in 2022. As I noted in the new editions of books one and two, Rogue's Pawn and Rogue's Possession, very little has changed *inside* the book.

In this one, I changed a conversation between Rogue and Gwynn to better reflect my decade-later change in perspective.

I've left the original dedication and acknowledgements, as they reflect my personal history at the time. Some of those relationships have changed or faded away. Others remain strong. I'd like to add some thanks here, especially to my current agent, Sarah Younger of Nancy Yost Literary Agency, who helped me regain the rights to these books even though she won't benefit directly from them. Also, many thanks to my amazing assistant, Carien, who commenced a re-read of these books for me, so I wouldn't have to. Finally, immense gratitude to my cover artist, Ravven, who came up with the concept for these covers. These are the covers I always wished for. Finally, I have them and they are everything.

Welcome to the second edition of Rogue's Paradise! We can even call it the 10th Anniversary Edition.

ROGUE'S PARADISE

PART 1

REVISITING THE ORIGINAL HYPOTHESIS

CHAPTER I

IN WHICH I AM ATTACKED BY FLYING MONKEYS

֍

The only thing the stories seemed to agree on was that the fae were capricious beings who delighted in disrupting human lives, awarding their magical favors according to a system of ethics known only to them.

~Big Book of Fairyland, "Flora and Fauna"

THE FLYING MONKEYS attacked just before sunset.

Swear to God, that's exactly what they looked like. I even looked for a smoke trail warning "Surrender Dorothy!"

"I have no idea what that means." Rogue, as usual, had read my thoughts as clearly as if I'd shouted them. "But now would be an excellent time for you to focus and possibly assist."

I struggled to clear my fatigued brain and sit straighter on his lap—not easy on horseback, with our steed Felicity breaking into a panicked run over the glassy black rocks as the sky overhead darkened with throngs of winged primates.

"I thought you said we'd have some time before the Queen

Bitch would be strong enough to come after us." I gasped as
the mare whipped around a narrow curve.

Fortunately Rogue needed no reins, guiding her with the
grip of his muscular thighs and likely his mind, leaving his
hands free to hold me tight against him. As a fae noble, Rogue
possessed many skills, and apparently superb horsemanship
ranked high among them.

"What makes you think it's her?" He sounded arrogant—
something that once would have grated on me—but I felt his
anxiety beneath. Rogue had suffered far more at Queen
Titania's hands than I. We hadn't discussed yet what had
happened to him as her puppet and slave, largely because he'd
been letting me sleep off the exhaustion from battling her.

Also, Rogue was far from the type to confide. He might
never tell me.

His gorgeous face was tense, creased with the torment of
his captivity, the winding black lines that covered the left side
of his face and body stark against his skin. Apparently even
immortals could look the worse for wear.

I wasn't in much better shape, perilously drained of my
magic reserves, my hands a crippled mess—and unfortunately
pregnant, just to top it all off.

Neither of us was fit to fight. Nor could we afford to be
recaptured by Titania.

We barreled into a narrower canyon that forced Felicity to
slow her headlong rush and fortunately limited the angles the
monkeys could come at us.

"Whether or not this is Titania's doing," Rogue said, "these
creatures are more like guard dogs. It wouldn't require much
of someone to send them. However, it may require much for

us to deal with them."

"What do you want me to do?" I asked.

"How much power do you have?"

I wished I knew how to answer that. Rogue had been teaching me more about my abilities to work magic and how to draw energy from outside myself, but we hadn't gotten far before Titania snatched him. It was a bad sign that he, the ever-and-all-powerful—far more magical than I, though I hated to admit it—had to ask me for help.

"Some. I don't suppose you have my crystal staff tied to the saddle?"

Rogue looked grimly amused. Then ducked when a flying monkey, clawed fingers outstretched, dive-bombed his head. Monkeys shouldn't have curved talons, but pretty much anything goes in Faerie. A burst of magic from Rogue, his signature feral black and blue, whooshed past me, and the monster chimp dissolved in a puff of sparks.

"Your girl, Athena, took it. She seemed to think you couldn't be trusted with it."

And Athena had ridden ahead with the others, since Rogue had been burdened with unconscious me. Annoying of her as the thing would augment my abilities, even if it was dangerously addictive. Compared to my current alternate fate, that sounded like giving up caffeine when starving to death.

"You can't nuke them all, like with that one?"

"No. Not enough power for so many." He hated admitting it too. Quite the pair we were.

"Tell me what you want and I'll do my best." How little power was "not enough"? No delicate way to pose the question so it wouldn't impugn his male ego. Asking Rogue if he had no magic left and no access to those outside resources he'd bragged of seemed akin to asking a guy whether he thought he could get it up or if he was done for the night.

A trio of monkeys swarmed us, a talon raking Felicity's hide. The horse screeched and put her head down, bucking with terror, which Rogue barely managed to control, his steely strength keeping me from being thrown. My cat Familiar, Darling Hercules, riding behind Rogue on his special saddle pad, sent me a startled image of him digging in claws and holding on for dear life.

Whatever we were going to do, we needed to do it fast. The trio of monkeys wheeled back on us. One went up in sparks, but the other two seemed only singed around the edges and one managed to sink talons into Rogue's shoulder before he got it on the second try. Not a good sign.

Darling Hercules let out a yowling wail and swiped at one of the monkeys that tried to grab him. To all appearances a humble tabby cat, he had grandiose ideas about his size and battle readiness.

"*Goliath,*" he nudged into my head, insistent on his new battle name.

"*Later,*" I answered. "I suppose wishing them away won't work?"

Grimly, Rogue shook his head. "Too many. They'll just keep coming."

Already the evening sky looked dark as night with their bat-winged bodies blocking the last of the light. Only the narrowness of the canyon we were tearing down kept them from simply dropping on us like an immense cloud of hairy locusts. As it was, they came at us singly or in small groups, scratching a cheek here or slicing an arm there, before Rogue could blast them.

"However, if—" Rogue's words came in puffed bursts of effort. "If I can pull power from you...I have an idea. So I need to know how much you have."

I couldn't answer that—not as if I had a little gauge warning me I was at less than 20 percent battery—but I did know how to charge myself up pretty fast. Just lucky that my favorite catalyst happened to be holding me in his arms.

"Ow—dammit!" I screeched as a talon tangled in my hair, taking some of my scalp with it. "Can you keep them off of me? And slow Felicity down, if at all possible."

"For a time, yes. Be sure to hold on." He freed one arm and his gleaming blue-platinum sword appeared in his hand. A major magic for me, a parlor trick for him. Apparently easier than frying monkeys, however. The monkeys came thicker as Felicity slowed, but they stayed farther back, wary of that sharp edge.

Turning myself around in the saddle wasn't easy by any stretch, but I trusted Rogue, even one-armed, and his uncanny long-limbed strength to keep me from tumbling off. I maneuvered to straddle Rogue's lean hips, while Darling Hercules complained bitterly in my head that I'd better not kick him. I told him to make himself useful and deaden the agony flaring up from my fingers as I clumsily slid my bandaged hands behind Rogue's neck. Thankfully the cat did, removing the pain with his oh-so-useful gift of magical anesthesia.

"Gwynn, what in Titania's name are you doing?" Rogue flicked his sword and a monkey fell in two pieces, spraying white blood on the black rocks.

"Kiss me." I pressed my groin against his, the sure rise of his cock making me giddy with a flood of strength and the hope that this might work.

With a grunt, Rogue split another diving monkey and glared at me. "After all this time of dreaming that you'd finally ask me for that, *this* is the moment you choose, contrary Gwynn?"

"You want power from me. You're the one who pointed out that sex energy is my shortcut. So shut up, pucker up and keep an eye on those monkeys."

He barked out a laugh, but wasted no more time. That seductive mouth of his fastened on mine with a ferocity that belied his weariness. His deep blue eyes stayed open and I felt the contractions of his chest as he swung the sword. Holding me pressed against him, he kissed me with all the fierce desire I could wish for. My own longing for him welled up, hot and needy—all the more so for our long separation—so ready for him. A monkey raked claws down my arm, and I flinched but focused on the kiss.

Not sure how to do it, I tried linking with him as we'd done once before, mentally putting myself in his hands and pouring the energy into him. Rogue hummed deep in his throat and pushed the hard ridge of his erection against me, sending a bolt of electricity through me that ricocheted between us. The sexual heat built between us, the magic wild and potent, overwhelming in its intensity. He ran his hands over my back, cupping my bottom and pulling me even closer to the lean length of his body while he stroked his hips, driving me into frenzy.

Wait—both hands?

I became aware that Felicity had stopped and stood head down, breathing in great gusts. Starting to pull back, I gasped when Rogue nipped my lower lip. "No, don't stop, lovely Gwynn."

I managed to tear my mouth away. The skies were clear, if rapidly deepening into an ultraviolet dusk. A luminous silver behind the edge of one canyon wall hinted at moonrise. A few early stars, spinning with kaleidoscopic color, pierced through, like wormholes to other worlds. For all I knew, they were.

"What happened to the flying monkeys?"

"They're gone." He cupped the back of my neck, tilting my head so he could nibble the sensitive underside of my jaw. I melted, moaning a little. "You are delicious, powerful Gwynn. That was far more than I needed. I'm glutted with you."

With a flick of a disgusted thought, Darling Hercules jumped down from the saddle, mentally muttering about there being no mice in this prey-forsaken place.

"What did you do? How do we know they won't keep coming?" I asked, my breath coming unevenly.

"I...reversed them in a way. Instead of finding us, they go backwards."

"Clever."

"I'm flattered you think so." He found my mouth again, kissing me long and sweet and deep, rocking against me.

So help me, I wanted him like nothing I'd felt before. As if all the months of buildup, all that teasing and torment, had layered on, fueling my desire just a bit more with every encounter. This close to him, to his deeper thoughts and emotions, I knew Rogue felt it too. The unbearable need to bury ourselves in the other.

"Gwynn," Rogue murmured. "Say it can be now."

All those times I'd said no. All those arguments and my determined resistance. I might have paid my life debt to Rogue by promising to bear his child, but I'd at least been able to forestall those consequences by refusing his seduction. All come to nothing.

I'd never agreed and I'd still lost that battle. I hadn't quite assimilated that I was truly pregnant. Titania had forced us—tricked, manipulated, however you wanted to split the hairs—into doing the deed, but then she'd removed the memory afterward. It had happened weeks ago. Or months, as time in Faerie flowed in a different way. Titania had restored the memories and informed me of the pregnancy in a neat double whammy meant to lay me low. I was still reeling from the rawness and violation of the rape. Technically I'd done it to Rogue, but I counted Titania as our true rapist, as she'd pulled the strings.

I could let that go now. No more defending myself from the embryo I already carried. I could say yes, finally.

"If you say no again, it might kill me," he growled, biting my lip again, then laving it with his tongue.

"Even though you're immortal?" I teased.

"Even so."

"Then yes."

Something inside me released at that moment, old scar tissue breaking open, finally yielding up that tight, binding pain. A rush of gladness followed. I didn't have to fight this anymore.

Not letting me go, raining kisses on my upturned face, Rogue swung down from Felicity, in a feat of strength and grace that had me gasping. He smiled, the fanged lines around his beautiful mouth twisting with the movement, loving that he'd impressed me.

His magic swirled and he laid me down on a bed of velvet he'd wished into existence, stretching himself beside me.

"Doing magic left and right now?" I asked him in an arch tone.

"Yes. I am overflowing with you. And still you feed me more. Let me have more."

"It's yours."

With a choking sound and some incoherent emotion I couldn't discern, he fell on me, fingers twining into my hair, holding me in place while he kissed me in that drugging way that swept all thought aside.

I meant it too. For the time being, at least, I just wanted to enjoy him. Savor the moment without worrying how much I might lose to his magnetic personality. He'd said he loved me and, though it might not mean to him what it did to me, I wanted to believe in that. Even if it had been in the heat of battle and the crushing aftermath. I only wished that I could touch him in turn. At least loosen the band that tied back his hair.

But I couldn't use my hands. Thanks to the handy anesthetic magic of Darling Hercules Goliath—I was trying to remember, though the name chain was getting ridiculous—I mostly didn't feel anything. The makeshift bandages swaddling my hands, however, both mittened me and hid from view the lethal claws that had made a ruin of my fingers. The feline spirit that had recently taken up occupation in my soul had helped defeat Titania, but it also wanted out and needed my flesh to do it.

Nothing to do about it at the moment. Rogue had promised we'd fix it and we would. For now I wanted not to think
about it, to simply seize the moment and savor Rogue.

Besides, I had other means at my disposal. A lowly scientist
in my previous mundane life as a university professor, I'd
become a sometimes distressingly powerful sorceress, with
even my least notion coming true until I learned to control it.
A hair tie was far more easily dealt with than, say, an army of
flying monkeys. I vanished it, and the black silk cloak of
Rogue's hair fell around us.

"I am looking forward to the moment," he commented in
a wry tone, "when I manage to sweep your thoughts away in
truth."

"You'll just have to work harder."

"Oh, sweet Gwynn, I fully intend to." He untangled his
hand from my own hair and put it on my bare leg, raising my
skirt. I stared into his fulminous eyes, riveted.

At last.

"Oh no!" Starling's startled exclamation shattered the moment. "Turn around, you guys."

Athena's and Larch's voices protested. Rogue and I stared
at each other, sharing the same frustrated annoyance. For once
we were in perfect sync. His hand flexed on my thigh, as if
unwilling to let me go, then relaxed and smoothed my skirt
back down. He sat up, drawing me with him.

Larch, Athena and Starling stood a short distance away,
black-and-silver shapes in the moonlight, Starling wringing her
hands together and clearly kicking herself for the interruption.
My half-fae, half-human maidservant and friend had been

hoping so hard for me to give in to Rogue that she no doubt deeply felt the irony of interrupting us. Larch, a Brownie stolid as the blue fireplug he resembled, looked into the distance. Only Athena, a petite fairy girl with a diabolical brain, seemed unperturbed, spinning her glinting dagger in her fingers, a salacious grin on her face. Darling wound around their feet in greeting and I glared at him. He could have warned us they were close.

"*Goliath,*" he replied in a grumpy mental tone, tinged with more than a little jealousy. Great.

"Looks like you're feeling better, Gwynn," Athena observed. "We thought we'd better come check on you two to see how you fared against those nasty chimps, but you seem to be doing quite fine without us. Brilliantly, in fact."

"We should go!" Starling announced. "Come on, everyone. Back on your horses. We can, um, go find a place to camp."

"No, don't go." I levered myself to my feet awkwardly, Rogue assisting me after a moment's hesitation. Dark and broody irritation rolled off him, but I could hardly dismiss the people who'd accompanied me on this quest—and who probably were the making of it. Especially with another attack possible. What had I been thinking? About sex, clearly. "Are you guys okay? No one is hurt?"

"A pair of those things grabbed Larch and nearly carried him off, but Athena threw her dagger and hurt one, so they dropped him," Starling said, looking between me and Rogue. She produced a bright smile. "So we're fine! We'll just see you and Lord Rogue in the morning."

With night truly fallen, and without Rogue's intense body

heat to warm me, I shivered. He slipped an arm around my waist and drew me against him, a casual intimacy I'd never before been able to allow and I leaned my cheek against his chest. The 3/4 rhythm of his heart pounded under my ear, reflecting all that aroused desire I sensed, but didn't show on his impassive face.

"There should be no stopping for the night," he declared. "It's likely only a matter of time until something worse is sent after us. More distance is better."

"That's not what you said a few minutes ago," I said for his sharp ears only.

He looked down at me, eyes bright as if lit from within, and cupped my face, thumb running over my cheekbone. "I lost my head."

I leaned in to the touch, impossibly moved by that simple declaration.

"I'd tell you two to get a room," Athena cracked, "but I don't think there *are* any for leagues in any direction—besides Titania's castle, that is."

I laughed, amused that the idiom existed in the fae culture, too, but Starling rounded on the petite fairy girl. "You will not speak to Lord Rogue and Lady Gwynn that way!"

Athena spun her dagger for a moment, eyeing Starling. "Why don't you make yourself useful and get Gwynn's cloak for her?"

"Oh!" Starling took the bait immediately and dashed to the saddlebags, rummaging wildly, as if to make up for her lapse with speed. I would have told her not to worry, but having the cloak sounded really good. The cold seemed to be eating into me.

Starling brought it over and Rogue took it from her.

"Allow me." He shook it out and held it for me to step into, his long fingers brushing my neck as he settled it over my shoulders. Fastening the green silk frogs at my throat, he bent down and whispered in my ear. "I'd planned to have you naked by now, not wearing more clothes. You owe me."

Owing Rogue anything generally led to very bad bargains for me, but this time the demand rocketed through me, full of sensual promise. The cloak felt heavenly—hopefully it would soon warm me up.

A hound bayed, the bone-chilling sound eerie in the night, quickly joined by more wolfish howls and shrieks from humanoid throats. Horses thundered in silhouette across the face of the moon.

"Another excellent reason not to be caught sleeping. The Wild Hunt rides—and they appear to have slipped their leash," Rogue said in a dry tone. "Let's be on our way. My Lady Gwynn?"

At least he made a semblance of asking before he swung me up in his arms and strode toward Felicity, who'd managed to find a few tufts of grass growing between the black rocks. Mounting with no hands and the same fluid grace, he continued to hold me, like a bride carried over the threshold.

"I can sit astride," I protested.

"This way you can sleep. Your mortal flesh needs it."

"Starling is half-human—she needs rest too."

"Lady Starling," he called out, and the others clopped up to join us. "Shall I bespell you to stay in your saddle, so you can sleep without fear of falling off?"

"Oh, Lord Rogue, that would be lovely, but I fear I

couldn't pay for such a generous gift."

"On the contrary," he replied. "I am in your debt, for your great services in rescuing me."

She fluttered, embarrassed and pleased, then agreed. Athena and Larch, fueled by magic, could continue indefinitely. Larch never even rode, just ran beside us, his squat, Brownie body moving at uncanny speeds. We set off down the canyon, moonlight bouncing off the opaque glassy surfaces of the rocks.

"You could have spelled me to stay in the saddle. Hell, I could have done that, too," I said.

He adjusted his arms around me, my hip pressed against the hard line of his cock, obvious even through my thick cloak. "Indulge me. If I can't have everything yet, I can at least enjoy the feel of you in my arms."

"You could also let me ride Felicity and you could poof yourself elsewhere, like you do. You have enough power now, I'll bet."

"True." He sounded thoughtful. "But you are forgetting something. I'm not leaving you behind, ever again, my Gwynn."

His words had the power of a vow. Not lightly done in Faerie, where crazy-ass goddess and queen Titania played enforcer and executioner. "You're being awfully sweet and romantic. Prison changed you, man." I reached for the joke, shying away from the intensity of it all, but Rogue went still, pulling his thoughts deep where I couldn't hear them.

"Yes," he finally said. "Yes, it did."

CHAPTER 2

IN WHICH I ASK FOR SOMETHING

In some ways, Faerie contains all the classic elements mentioned in fairy tales, with many of its denizens matching storybook descriptions. But there are other fragments, too, such as the flying monkeys and the Wild Hunt, which derive from other types of stories. It's as if human imagination were smashed into pieces and reassembled like Frankenstein's monster. Which I shall no doubt encounter next.

~Big Book of Fairyland, "General Observations"

B Y MORNING, I had a raging fever.

I shouldn't have been surprised. The last I'd seen, the claws had torn my fingers apart. I doubted they could heal much without further attention. Likely the open wounds had become infected and festered. I really needed to inspect my hands, but with both bandaged, I couldn't do it by myself.

Oh wait—yes, I could, with some judicious magic and some time alone, so I could make the assessment first, before worrying the others unnecessarily. Which might be hoping for a bit much, as the odds were that my prognosis would not be promising.

Still, neither Rogue nor any of the others seemed to have noticed anything amiss with me and I disliked being the whiner enough that I didn't say anything. But when Fergus came galloping up, for a moment I feared I'd started hallucinating.

"Top o' the morning to ye all!" he called out, sweeping off a battered felt cap. He swayed a little in the saddle, clearly already drunk. Where he'd managed to find alcohol in this forsaken landscape, I didn't know. Maybe he had a portable version of his magic drink-cart, forever refilled with his favorite poison. He was in squidgy mode, complete with stubbled chin and bloodshot eyes. Perched atop his prancing hero's battle horse with a sword reminiscent of Excalibur strapped to the pommel, he made an incongruous sight.

"Daddy?" Starling sounded surprised to see him too. We'd last seen him—in full Prince Charming mode—battling the Wild Hunt in Titania's courtyard. Another human immigrant from my old world, he couldn't work magic like I could. Instead, the magic worked him, transforming him into the undefeatable hero of the old tales. However, as with my wishes, it seemed to function in a situation-specific way. When heroics weren't needed, he reverted to drunken Irishman.

"No kiss for your old da, Little Bit?" The question was apparently rhetorical, given that they were both on horseback and Fergus had his gaze fixed on me and Rogue. "So, there's himself, the recently rescued Lord Rogue."

"Fergus," Rogue greeted him in a cool tone.

Starling rode closer, a frown line between her brows. "I thought you were staying back to look for Baby Brody."

Fergus had been on a quest since his son, Brody, disappeared as a baby. Another half-human, half-fae firstborn child.

Another cautionary tale for me.

"We-ell." Fergus drew out the word, digging at his ear with a gnarled finger. In a nonmagical world, I would have put him in his early sixties, but I estimated he'd come through the Veil from the 1700s or thereabouts. Some people did, just as in the old stories. Fergus, consistently cliché, had fallen asleep drunk on a mound and woke up in Faerie. Nobody, so far as I could tell, managed to go back the other direction. I'd tried. "I've it in mind to go after your mother," he finally said, surprising us all.

"You mean," I inserted, "that you think Blackbird's journey sailing over the Endless Sea will be more likely to get you to Brody than searching the Queen Bitch's palace."

Far from offended, Fergus grinned at me. "That may be true. Besides, I don't know what you did to that one, but the place is in quite the uproar. Lots o' folks being called into her presence and not coming back. I thought it best to make meself scarcelike."

I shivered, not wanting to contemplate what Titania might be doing to heal herself, my hallucination-inclined brain all too willing to embroider on some horrific images. "So why bother to find us now?"

Starling gave me an unhappy look, but she knew as well as I that Fergus had been a terrible father. Paternal love hadn't sent him our way and I had no patience for him glomming on to us.

"I recalled how you used yon scepter to scry. Thought mebbe you could tell me where Blackbird might be. Save me a bit of trouble. And since you owe me for helping rescue himself."

"Scrying?" Rogue asked.

"You didn't wonder how I found you? Athena, give me the scepter, please." I didn't owe Fergus a damn thing since he'd attached himself to us out of self-interest, but Blackbird and I had a history, not just because she was Starling's mother.

Athena, however, narrowed her eyes at me, the stubborn skepticism in them belying their doelike lavender prettiness. "No. I don't think I will."

"Dammit, Athena. Just for a minute—it won't take much."

"Your liege lady gave you an order, girl," Rogue said, at his most imperious.

Athena seemed far from impressed. "That liege lady nearly killed herself using the scepter before. You're an idiot if you think I'll let her have it in her current condition."

Rogue gave her his most disdainful cobalt glare. "You may have come up in the world since last we met—"

"And you may owe me the same debt as you avowed Starling," Athena interrupted.

He frowned at her, taken aback. She looked like the simpleminded fairy she'd been when Rogue and I first encountered her, with her girlish frame, violet eyes and powder-blue hair. Unlike the ringlets most of her kind sported, she'd hacked at hers with a knife, so it stood up in short spikes. The boots and brown leather fighter's gear, with the short dagger strapped to her waist, made her look like a punk pixie.

"She's more than what she was," I told him, raising my eyebrows meaningfully. I didn't know how much Athena understood that I had "tweaked" her brain during one of his lessons for me. Playing God scared me on a visceral level and I'd wanted to at least help her instead of harming her. But I'd still yanked her from a fairly blissful existence of playful ignorance, awaking a restless and fiercely intelligent spirit in her. Blessing or curse remained to be seen. "That said, I feel like I owe Blackbird the favor of sending Fergus her way, since I can."

"I'll do it," Rogue said. "It will discharge my debt to Fergus for his role in the rescue. If that's agreeable to you."

"Agreed," Fergus cheerfully replied.

"I'm not going to be dependent on you," I interrupted.

"No," Rogue said to Athena, ignoring me and stopping her from unstrapping the scepter, "I don't need that." His hand absently tightened on my waist as his magic gathered around him and he focused his gaze into the far distance. A trick I'd love to learn. "She is on the Pink Candy Islands."

"Much obliged," Fergus tipped his hat and turned a bit of a wistful gaze on Starling. "Care to come with me, Little Bit?"

She shook her head immediately, the thick paintbrush sweep of her blond hair swinging with the vigorous motion. "No, Daddy. Give Mother my love. My place is with Lady Sorceress Gwynn."

"At least I'll know where to find ye. Fare you all well!" And he galloped off.

"I suppose we might as well eat, since we're stopped," Starling said and Larch began unpacking picnic supplies. Darling Hercules jumped down to explore and, as soon as he moved away, my hands began throbbing with fierce and disconcerting pain.

Time to see just how bad they were.

I claimed the excuse of answering the call of nature and took myself off into the woods. Being on my own two feet again, I wobbled, brain-stunned from the fever, my legs weak.

Alone, I settled my back against a tree, wearied from the short walk, also a bad sign, and sat with my mittened hands in my lap. I really didn't want to look, especially with my head pounding and stomach queasy. The fae seemed to have something of an idea of infection, but they never disinfected anything. Of course, they also never seemed to become ill, and some of the higher fae were even immortal, so it likely just plagued us fragile humans.

Screwing up my courage, I made a careful wish for the bandages to relocate to the leaf litter next to me. Easier to wish them back on again that way. I let myself close my eyes until I was ready.

Then I looked.

And swallowed hard on the bulge of nausea.

Damn. They were bad. The feline claws, curved and with a razor inner edge, extended from the second knuckle, seemingly made of some metal. I would have called it platinum, if that wasn't physically impossible. Nothing remained of my fingertips, except shreds of flesh, blood-caked and oozing pus. Only this pus glowed an unnatural green, like antifreeze. I imagined whatever opportunistic microorganisms existed in Faerie would curdle my blood if viewed under a microscope. My immune system stood little chance against them.

The great drawback of magical anesthesia: the vague and transient pain had let me procrastinate far too long and gangrene had set in. Worse, telltale red streaks of blood poisoning ran up past my wrists.

Miserable, pitiful and afraid, too weak to hold my shit together, I started to cry.

No no no. I choked the tears back as best I could. I needed to concentrate and try to wish the infection away. I'd done a bit of healing on minor wounds I incurred before. Surely I could fix this myself.

Trying to form a coherent wish for this seemed beyond my reach. I needed to be very precise. No blanket wishes like wanting my hands to be as they were before. I'd risk having two appendages that appeared to be hands but didn't have the internal structure. Sure, I'd trained in physiology and had been a professor of neuroscience, but details from anatomy classes had blurred over time. Carpals, metacarpals and phalanges. Mainly I remembered that our hands were the most intricately and densely innervated parts of our bodies.

I really didn't want to fuck mine up.

More than they already were.

Despair and terror didn't foster clear thinking. Unbidden, an image rose in my mind of Lavinia in *Titus Andronicus*, with her hands cut off, bleeding freely from the wrists. Not a productive idea.

One of the terrifying truisms of Faerie, always be careful what you wish for—even as a passing thought.

Not thinking about things in the first place was an excellent preventative measure, and I was trying to wrestle that one down when I heard footsteps in the dry and fallen leaves.

Rogue, walking toward me through the trees. His black cloak streamed around him, inky hair lifted by the breeze. But for his inhumanly long limbs and that alien thorny pattern climbing over the left side of his face, he could be the hero from some gothic novel.

He sank down, straddling my outstretched legs, and took my face in his hands. "Gwynn." His voice was stern. "I heard you loudly from the clearing. You must get a hold of yourself. Don't you dare spin out of control. You know the consequences."

To my utter horror, I burst fully into tears.

I'd always hated how easily I cried, and being sick just made it worse. I sobbed, all the grief, worry and pain pouring out of me, running down my face, and I couldn't even wipe it away. Rogue had seen me weep before—and had always seemed vaguely perplexed by it—but nothing compared to this complete meltdown. That I did not do often or easily.

Once he'd tasted my tears and pronounced them bitter.

This time, he sat beside me and pulled me onto his lap, careful of my awful hands, and just held me, stroking my hair, whispering words of comfort. Gradually my shudders subsided, the rhythm of his alien heart more soothing and familiar than it should be.

"I'm sorry," I finally got out. "I don't know what's wrong with me."

"You've gone through more than most humans could bear. Don't apologize for that."

"Do remember the first time we met, when my throat was injured?"

"How could I forget?" he replied in a wry tone, slipping the image into my mind of me, bound in silver to the bed in his castle, looking like a hot mess. "You were brave then too."

"I was terrified. And you were an ass."

"And yet you survived both. You'll survive this too."

I surely hoped so. "Can you heal my hands—even a little?"

"No. The damage is too great and that is, as you know, the least of my skills. Lady Healer is still in residence at my castle, and she will be able to."

I decided not to comment on my feelings about the fae noblewoman who'd healed me that time, when I'd been bound to that bed, and who then exacted an extraordinarily high price for it. I hated to think what I'd have to pay this time. Good thing my firstborn child had already been bargained away. I would have to deal, if I wanted to survive this. Pride goeth before amputation, after all. "How far is that, at our current pace?"

"Days, I imagine. I never go by horseback."

"I think we need to find a healer sooner than that."

"Why? Are you in pain? Darling Hercules Goliath can—"

"No, it's not that. I'm sick, Rogue."

I sat up so I could look into his face. His eyes were intent, concern swirling in the depths. Absurdly I wanted to kiss him. Because I could, I did kiss him—something I'd rarely, if ever, done of my own accord. And more for comfort than for anything else.

He hummed in his throat, returning the kiss with interest, then pulled away, frowning. "Your skin is very hot."

I nodded. "Fever. It means infection. See the red streaks going up my wrists? That's a...poison from the infection traveling inward. If it gets too far, I'll die."

He looked stricken, the lines on his face shimmering, nearly coiling on their own, as they did when he was upset. "I won't allow that to happen."

My favorite megalomaniac. I forged on, hoping that his fervent determination came at least partially from care for me and not just the embryo growing inside me, that selfsame firstborn child he'd won rights to in a complicated exchange.

"I know you can't take me with you when you poof yourself, but maybe you could go and find someone—Lady Healer,
maybe—and bring her back faster than I can get there?"

He was already shaking his head. "I won't leave you
again."

It was less romantic this time. "Rogue. I'm seriously afraid
I'm going to die. Or lose my hands forever." I gave myself
credit for saying this in a steady tone. I had grown up a child of
technology. Of all the strange, unsettling and downright
terrifying aspects of Faerie, the lack of actual medicine
bothered me a great deal. Magical healing was all well and
good—except when it landed you with life-debts, like mine
with Rogue.

I'd listed that for him once, as reason three of five that I did
not want to have his baby. Being cornered into agreeing to
give him my firstborn—and letting him sire it—had determined the course of my recent life. Giving birth in what
amounted to a Third World country just exacerbated a bad
situation.

I couldn't think about all of that at the moment. My current problem demanded attention or the whole giving-birth
problem would be well and truly moot. "I don't know what to
do," I confessed, hating to throw my fate any more in his lap—
literally and figuratively—than I already had. I'd meant it when
I said I didn't want to be dependent on him. Still. "I need your
help."

That changed something in him. In me. The shift
thrummed between us and he bowed his head, as if acknowledging a new agreement.

"Then you shall have it."

"What do I have to give in return?"

"We can decide later."

Having an open-ended bargain with a fae led to dire consequences—hence aforementioned firstborn child—but I couldn't muster the energy to insist on setting terms. Which showed how bad off I was.

"We will fly." He stood, uncoiling and bringing me with him. I almost protested that I could stand, but in truth my limbs felt weak and weary.

"Can you call the dragons then?"

"Don't be foolish—dragons can't be called. Besides they don't give rides."

"One gave us a ride when I asked." I sounded loopy but couldn't help myself.

He pinned me with a penetrating look. I'd surprised him, not easy and always delicious, even as terrible as I felt. "It seems you did many things while...we were apart."

"Believe me, I have stories to tell."

"I want to hear them all." He brushed my mouth with a tender kiss. So odd, this moment by moment exchange of caresses. I wasn't even entirely sure which bargains still stood between us. Though Rogue would know. He probably had a lobe of his brain dedicated to exactly that purpose. Another thing I'd have to set straight later, when I *could* think.

He carried me back to where the others were lunching in a clearing. Well—Starling and Athena were eating while Larch stood guard, scanning the skies. Darling Hercules came leaping through the yellowing grasses, projecting images of himself as a forest cat.

Starling stood, when she spotted us, "Lady Gwynn! Is everything all right? We—oh dear sweet Titania."

Her gaze fell to my hands and I realized I'd forgotten to replace the bandages in my feverish fog. I'd never seen someone turn green before, but she did, pressing her fingers to her mouth.

"I'm taking Lady Gwynn to a healer," Rogue informed her in a crisp tone. "Prepare her things."

I would have told him not to order her about like one of his magicked-up dummy servants, but she snapped to attention from long habit, bobbed a curtsy and scurried to do as he said. Better for her than worrying about me.

Athena stood on tiptoes to peer at my hands. "Those claws are wicked cool. Going to keep them?"

I choked a little. Tried to make it a laugh. "I'd rather not."

"You should." She flicked a wink at Rogue. "I bet none of his other women have that."

I loved her for being a smart-ass. And Starling for her steadfast loyalty, not wanting to leave my side. Yet I would be leaving them behind. "Rogue—we can't leave them here."

"We'll be fine, Lady Gwynn." Starling bustled up with a bag of my few supplies, soft brown eyes still wide with worry, the blond of her hair dulling with it. "Don't you give a thought to us. We'll see you at the Castle of the Dark Gods before long."

The name rattled me and not only because of the ominous overtones. I obviously didn't speak the fae language—sometimes I suspected each variety had their own dialect—and instead I telepathically understood the intent behind their words. Which was why they could all reference Titania, because they used euphemisms so as not to speak her name aloud.

The way this title translated in my head recalled what that innkeeper at Devils Tower had told me back in my world—that the Native American name meant place of the dark gods and it was the white settlers who figured that had to be the devil. Maybe the fever just had me confused.

"We're going to where again?"

"My castle," Rogue said in a dry tone.

Of course it was. "You never told me the name."

"You never asked."

"Oh yes, because you answer *all* of my questions."

"Hush, or I'll have Darling Hercules Goliath put you to sleep."

"You wouldn't dare. Besides, he's my Familiar and he, at least has to come along."

"Agreed, if only to help you with the pain."

"But the others—what if they're attacked again?" I fretted over it. Now I did want him to put me down. I needed to do something to see they were taken care of. But Rogue held me in an implacable grip, staring into the distance.

"Be still. They're nearly here."

Who was nearly here? But hoofbeats echoed over the meadow before I could form the question.

Out of the woods, a phalanx of black horses and armored riders appeared. At first I thought the soldiers wore helms, but as they drew closer it became clear that their heads *were* the helmets—uncannily reminiscent of Cylons. The horses moved in perfect synchrony, also automatons. I shivered at the sight, which became a full-out shudder racking my body. Just how high had my fever gotten?

Rogue studied my face, answering my unvoiced question. "Reinforcements. They will convey your companions to my castle in the best safety I can offer. Acceptable?"

I nodded. "Though they're creepy. Did you make them?"

"Yes. I anticipated you would not care for them." His mouth twisted in a self-deprecating smile. "See? I begin to know you."

Oh yes, he did. Possibly better than anyone ever had. How that could be when we weren't even the same species and came from such wildly different worlds, I didn't know.

"Because some connections go deeper than the limits of flesh," he murmured for my ears only. "And here comes our ride."

A whoosh of air made the grasses wave wildly and sent another chill through me. I ducked reflexively, then opened my astounded eyes to the extraordinary giant white bird with trailing wings now standing before us, regarding me with dove-gray eyes that sparkled with intelligence.

"Is that..." I trailed off in the face of the impossibility.

"A Liralen. She'll take us there."

The surreality of it all welled up. Perhaps I was hallucinating, trapped in a fever dream. "It can't be a Liralen. That was in a book. Not real."

"It's only the name you give it, my Gwynn. Nothing more."

Oh yes. If I concentrated, I knew the sounds that came out of his mouth were different. Not really a Liralen. Just to me. Which was enough.

"What is her price?" I asked. In the book, the Liralen's price had been very high—fearlessness—something I could not offer.

Especially now. Fear riddled me, maggots chewing holes and leaving me a fragile creation of lace that could shatter with careless handling.

"I will pay it." Rogue sounded grim. Could he afford it either?

"No, I don't want you to—"

"Let me do this for you." He glared down at me, demanding and maybe a little angry. Under it, that wild regret seethed. "I owe you this much, at least. You asked me to help you—something you've never done, I might point out—let me do it."

A little shocked, I agreed. Had I really never asked for his help before? Possibly not, because it always came with a price. And I never liked to ask for help from anyone. It just figured that it would take fear of my imminent death to bring me to it.

"I've lost track of what I owe you and what you owe me." I registered vaguely somewhere in my addled brain that I shouldn't have told him that.

"Your thoughts are quite porous at the moment. I would have known it anyway. Don't worry. Rest and let me take care of you."

The Liralen arched her wings and bent down. Rogue, with the same lithe strength, held me tight as he mounted her like a horse but under the vast expanse of her trailing wings. Darling Hercules Goliath leaped onto my lap, laying his soft and purring self over my hands, taking the pain away.

The great bird surged up into the bright autumn blue, making my stomach drop. We rose into the sky, the jeweled Technicolor landscape of Faerie spreading below us. Craning my neck, I took in as much as I could, plotting in my head the location of the Glass Mountains, glittering black and filling the horizon behind us. Beneath us, forest unrolled, tossing like a sea of gnarled branches that seemed to move of their own accord.

I wanted my grimoire, where I kept all my notes, to sketch the map of what I could see, since the fae had no concept of such things. But then, I couldn't write, could I? The thought filled me with black despair. This part of my old self that I'd clung to could also be lost. Athena had no idea what she'd asked me, thinking I'd want to keep the claws that destroyed my first and best tool, my hands.

Rogue slipped a comforting thought into my mind, like lacing his fingers with mine, and the simple gesture held me steady. I needed it, because this was one battle I would not lose. I might be pregnant with Rogue's baby, but I refused to be dependent on him.

I'd die first.

CHAPTER 3

IN WHICH I RETURN TO THE CASTLE OF THE DARK GODS

The landscape of Faerie seems barely more fixed than its denizens or the flow of time. Sometimes I think there are no maps because they would be obsolete in a day.

~Big Book of Fairyland, "Rules of Magic"

WE ARRIVED IN darkness.

Which just figured because I'd really wanted a good look at the Castle of the Dark Gods, my new home for...perhaps indefinitely. Not a pleasing thought as I had no good memories of the place. Last time I'd arrived and left unconscious—and in between the windows had all looked out on a formless shimmering gray mist. Not something I could live with.

There were good reasons I'd taken a job in sunny Wyoming and not, say, Seattle.

The Liralen landed on a drawbridge studded with blazing torches. The windows of the castle gleamed in the night. From the spill of light, the castle walls seemed to be black, glittering like mica. But from there it merged into the night and I couldn't make out any more detail than that.

"You will have many days to study my castle." Rogue sounded tired. I'd forgotten how recently he'd been so depleted he couldn't zap the flying monkeys. And now he'd been carrying me for hours. He always seemed so powerful and in control, I'd been inconsiderate of him.

"I can walk," I insisted. Though I wasn't sure I could. Weakness pulled at me, at my core strength. I felt drained in an ominous way, as if I could feel my life force ebbing.

"Not a chance," Rogue said, answering either my words or my thoughts, leaping down from the Liralen, carrying both me and Darling Hercules Goliath, who still lay across me, paws dangling. I couldn't feel my hands at all.

I told him to jump down—less weight for Rogue to bear—but he stubbornly refused.

"This won't take long." Rogue turned to face the Liralen, indescribably lovely with the graceful curve of her white neck and her eyes clear as the moon. His magic gathered, shaped into a bubble, gloss black spiked with deep blue lightning. It floated clear of him, and Darling Hercules tracked it with bright, interested eyes.

His arms holding me weakened as it detached with a sub-audible pop and I made a strangled cry of protest as the Liralen snatched it from the air, like a sweetmeat. Her glow intensified and she nodded her sleek head in acknowledgment. Then took off for the night sky, wings trailing like pennants.

A tremor ran through Rogue.

"What did you give her?" I demanded.

"Exactly what you thought."'

"I didn't want you to—"

"It wasn't your choice. I asked her for the favor, I paid the price. Believe me, it was worth it to me." Rogue strode with enviable long-legged speed across the drawbridge, which was manned at even intervals with more of the cyborg soldiers. It spanned a moat the size of a major river, judging by the length of time it took us to cross. The inky lines on the left side of Rogue's face seemed to coil like a living thing—a sign of his deep distress.

"My," I said, to lighten the moment, "what a large moat you have."

Clearly my insinuation came through. It was sometimes difficult to joke when we mainly understood each other through the telepathic translation. A killer on wordplay. But in this case, his eyes glittered and his mouth curved in a sensual smile. "All the better to please my lady."

We passed through some sort of archway, lined with a circular toothy sort of portcullis. More of the soldiers waited there, inhumanly still and malevolent. The inner courtyard loomed empty and full of shadows. Though something seemed to stir in the corners, something both animal and magical. The sense of sandpaper grated over my skin, the fever putting me more on edge.

Weakness seemed to pull at me, a lethal undertow.

People swirled around us, Rogue giving orders and various fae scurrying to comply. We climbed a winding staircase, one I hadn't been on during my previous visit. Windows studded the wall periodically, showing only dense night beyond. It seemed the moon should have been up by now. Even if it rose an hour later each night as it had in my world. Come to think of it, it seemed the moon had been full or nearly so for weeks. I should stop trying to make sense of it.

"Indeed," Rogue commented. "One would think dire illness would be enough to slow your restless mind for a while."

I wanted to retort but couldn't think of anything. Instead I rubbed my cheek against his chest, inhaling his scent, like Stargazer lilies and mace mixed.

We reached the top of the tower and stepped outside into the night sky. No, into a glass dome, so transparent it was nearly invisible. Above, the dense star fields of Faerie spun in silent splendor. The familiar constellations I'd seen all my life, arranged in their usual patterns, shone with the startling clarity and brilliant carousel colors of everything here.

Rogue carried me to a bed I recognized from the dreams he'd plagued me with early on in his relentless seduction. Massive with carved wood, the four-poster was draped in deeply colored velvets and mounded with pillows in shades of dark ruby and midnight emerald. He laid me on the downy mattress, and through the frame of the slats connecting the four posts, I looked up into the depths of the universe.

"This is your bedroom, I take it?" I asked, feeling dreamy. Darling Hercules Goliath licked my forearm and it occurred to me that he'd been feeding me more magical anesthesia, in anticipation of my upcoming surgery, no doubt.

"*Our* bedroom." Rogue brushed my hair back from my forehead. "Do you like it? I'd thought to bring you here for the first time under better circumstances."

"I do. I always wanted a room like this. I even drew a picture of it when I was a little girl."

"I know. I saw it in your mind once. That's why I built it."

Impossibly moved, I stared up into his intent midnight gaze. "Why didn't you tell me before?"

"Would it have made a difference?"

Probably not. I would have viewed it as another attempt to manipulate me, by making the prison as delightful as possible. "It makes a difference now." I only hoped I'd live long enough to enjoy it.

He smiled, wistful and concerned. "Lady Healer is on her way. You'll be fine."

"Just don't let her lay claim to the baby in payment." I tried to make it a joke—not funny—but he cupped my face in his hands, fierce and determined.

"Never."

"Lord Rogue," an imperious and familiar voice said from the doorway, "am I to work in the dark?"

His magic moved out and candles all around the room burst into flame. They drowned out the stars but illuminated the lovely furnishings—including a workbench much like the one I'd made for myself. As I watched, a maidservant bustled in and laid my grimoire on it with gentle reverence.

At least I could read it.

With a sigh I turned my head to face Lady Healer. She wore layers of green, her chestnut brown hair rippling down her back to the floor. Surprisingly, she curtseyed to me. "Lady Sorceress Gwynn," she said in a deferential tone, "how may I serve you?"

Apparently I'd come up in the world sufficiently that she might regret having once called me an undisciplined peasant wretch and a whore of a magical dilettante.

Not that I held a grudge or anything.

Oh, and guess what? I wasn't bound by silver anymore. Under the serene surface of her public mind, wariness and fear bubbled beneath. That would teach her to kick at someone when they were down. I might be injured and probably in danger of dying, but I could still do her damage if I wanted to.

Maybe it made me a small and vengeful person, but I liked knowing that.

"Her hands," Rogue informed her and stood, then paced over to the transparent dome and stared out, hands clasped behind his back.

Darling Hercules Goliath purred and made a cheerful *mrowing* sound at Healer as she sat carefully next to me. She rubbed his ears. "Hello, Darling."

"He's changed to Goliath," I told her. Darling had been her Familiar first, until he jumped ship to throw in his fortunes with me. "And Hercules most recently. I'm mostly calling him Darling Hercules Goliath—which is a mouthful."

Healer smiled with affection. "You always did want a battle name," she said to him.

"Unfortunately he keeps escalating."

"Good for him. Now let me see what we're dealing with here."

Obligingly he moved, stretching out along my side, purring and maintaining that anesthetic connection. I stared up at the glass dome while she examined my hands, asking me to bend my wrists and fingers.

"Well?" Rogue demanded, having returned to the bed to observe.

"You let it go long," she replied.

I laughed a little, remembering her saying that to him

before, and she gave me a slow nod of acknowledgment. Ah. Letting me know she wouldn't pretend not to recall on what terms we'd parted. Fair enough.

"You're wasting time." Rogue clenched his jaw. Not at all amused. He began pacing, the measured tread of his bootsteps on the stone floor making a comforting rhythm.

But she wasn't. Her magic had been flowing into me since she'd touched me. Sweet and green, like the cool undersides of leaves in summer. I hadn't known enough before to sense it— and then I'd been put out altogether.

"You're not worried about me losing control this time?" I asked her.

Her hazel eyes flicked up from her intent gaze on my injuries. "No. You've admirable control now." She started to say something more and stopped. She knew, then, what it cost me to get it. And had enough sense not to say more. "Your human physiology is interesting," she said instead. "Is your elevated body temperature meant to make your body inhospitable to the invading microbes?"

I really wished I knew what idea she articulated that my mind translated as "microbes." Fascinating that she had the concept. "Yes, actually. Though it's destructive if it goes on too long."

"So I sense." She nodded crisply. "The infection is cleansed from your body and your flesh knitted. Therefore I'm restoring a healthier temperature. Darling—ah, Goliath, that is—you may cease your efforts, so we can check that she's truly pain-free."

With an elaborate yawn, Darling Hercules Goliath stood, stretched and leaped off the bed, ambling over to gaze out the dome.

Like an airplane touching down, the fever tangibly dissipated and leveled out, leaving me clearheaded, feeling good and amazingly full of energy. Born of relief that the fix had been so relatively easy, no doubt. I raised my hands to see and must have made some kind of sound because Rogue stopped his pacing and appeared again at the bedside.

My hands were perfectly smooth and glowing with health—with three-inch feline claws extending beyond the second knuckle.

"You can't eliminate the claws?" Rogue framed it as a neutral question, but it was clear to me that he wasn't surprised. He'd expected this and hadn't wanted to say so.

Healer looked somewhat surprised, glancing back at me from him. "You don't want to keep them?"

"No." My voice broke a little. "But you can't fix them, can you?"

She took my hand again, examining it. Stalling, because the answer stood clearly in her mind for me to read. "I cannot," she admitted aloud, letting go. "This is an outgrowth of your magic. Much the same as—" she threw a questioning look to Rogue, "—your syndrome."

"The Sorceress is aware of it," Rogue replied in a clipped tone. He barely controlled the massive Black Dog that drew life from his magic, and disliked being reminded of it.

Lady Healer had warned me not to think of the Black Dog here, on that first visit, seeming afraid of it. Now I had my own version, some sort of pale feline spirit created by my magic, struggling to break free of my flesh. *A vine twisting in your soul,* Rogue had called it.

"Same situation," she continued. "That sort of transformation belongs to another realm. I can no more affect it than I could defeat either of you in a duel."

"Then what can I do?"

She gave me the look that doctors of all sorts developed when delivering news to irascible patients. "You can learn to live with it or you can retract them yourself."

"I don't know how."

"Can't you teach her?" she asked Rogue.

"Not this, no." His gaze rested on me, while his thoughts ran deep and private.

"Then you'll have to figure it out for yourself, Lady Sorceress." She dusted off her hands.

"Wait." I stopped her before she stood. "Can you tell me—I'm pregnant. How fares the embryo after all this?"

She tucked her hair behind her ears and smiled in truth. "I sensed that but wasn't sure if that was common knowledge or not." Nice that she observed the fae version of privacy laws. "May I?"

When I nodded, she placed her hands over my abdomen. Rogue drew near, watching intently. Healer's smile stayed serene. "The babe is well. Congratulations to you both. I assume there will be a wedding soon?" She frowned at Rogue. "She should at least be wearing a sign of your protection. You don't need me to tell you that."

He raised a supercilious eyebrow at her and she winced a little. "Lord Rogue," she added.

"I don't need protection," I grumbled. "Or, for that matter, a—"

"Yes, there will be a wedding," he confirmed, glaring at me

not to argue, "and her jewelry is here." He opened his hand, revealing my earrings on his palm. Shaped like inverted lilies, shading from lightest blue to indigo, they had been a gift from him. One not intended to come off. "Their loss was temporary."

Because I'd figured out how to remove the magical things—I don't much like having anything beyond my control—and then sent them to him in Titania's castle as a message.

"Excellent." Healer beamed at me, patting my belly. "Make sure he does right by you, Sorceress Gwynn. Even Lord Rogue cannot escape this particular leash." She stood. "I'll leave you to rest."

"We need to discuss payment."

"I'll take care of it." Rogue folded his arms, just to top off the continuing glare.

"Like hell," I snapped back.

They both tilted their heads slightly, the simile failing to translate.

"Allow me to rephrase. No."

"Are you refusing me, stubborn Gwynn?" Rogue asked softly, dangerously. Enough so to give me pause to sort through his phrasing. Clearly we needed to talk this through. I'd really thought the wedding nonsense was done with. The earrings declared me to be his concubine, which worked fine for me.

"I want to pay this debt myself," I answered, keeping my intent simple and clear.

"You have dragon eggs, I hear," Healer jumped in. "That would be a fair trade."

Behind her, Rogue shook his head slightly.

"My caravan has not yet arrived," I temporized, "and I really have no idea what state everything is in."

"Fine." She pouted a little. "We can negotiate when your servants arrive. Good evening to you both."

"Take Lord Darling with you," Rogue called over his shoulder, still staring at me with that intimidating look, "and inform everyone that we should not be disturbed. Indefinitely."

With a murmur of agreement, she left, the door clicking shut behind her.

CHAPTER 4

IN WHICH I OFFER TWO THINGS I NEVER THOUGHT I WOULD

The social mores of Faerie are not easily sorted. On the one hand, there's a level of licentiousness and openly sexual behavior that's widely accepted. On the other, a strict code of proper behavior and an almost Victorian sense of propriety.

~*Big Book of Fairyland*, "Social Structure"

IT TOOK A bit of finagling, but I managed to straighten my fingers enough to use my hands to lever myself up without slicing my palms to ribbons, and scooted over to the edge of the bed.

"What are you doing?" Rogue asked, still in that ominous tone.

"If we're going to have a big fight, I don't want to be lying in bed."

He blew out an exasperated breath and sat next to me, putting a hand on my shoulder to stay me. "We're not going to have a big fight. We only need to talk."

"Ah ah ah!" I wagged a finger at him, the effect rather

spoiled by the long, razor-sharp claw. "Anti-flirtation, remember? The 'death of romance,' you called it."

"We are no longer flirting," he ground out, looking ever more annoyed. I was pretty sure this counted as fighting, but decided not to point that out. "You carry our child. That part is over with, along with all of the associated, *limiting* agreements." Even though he was mad, his eyes gleamed with sensual intent, reminding me that nothing now stopped him from using every trick at his disposal to seduce me completely. Though he didn't really need to, the seed having been sown and all.

"So, all that remains is for you to seal the deal? A wedding and I belong to you forever, bought and paid for?"

"You always look at things in the worst possible light. We would belong to each other."

"But you would pay for everything."

"What is so terrible about that?" He seemed genuinely bewildered. "Healer serves me and I pay her accordingly already."

"I had to pay her before."

"You weren't mine then."

I decided repeating that I wasn't his now either would be a waste of breath. Instead I searched for the right way to explain. "Take this for example. When you gave me the magic chamber pot, I gave you something in exchange, so I wouldn't owe you anything."

"A kiss," he reminded me, tongue darting out to lick his lower lip. "An excellent one."

Don't get distracted. "So what happens if you, say, give me another magic chamber pot?" Far less expensive than healing, I felt sure.

He shrugged. "As my wife, you would owe me nothing."

"But I would. That's the rub. I'd feel like I owed you, for example, more kisses."

"Is that a problem?" His tone had gone icy. Dark emotions churned in him, coming closer to the surface.

"Rogue..." I started to scrub my scalp and had to stop myself. "We barely know each other and you want to commit us together for a lifetime?" *At least for mine, right?* Though we'd never discussed the implications of my mortal aging on our relationship. Something that came of not being sure you'd survive into the next week, most likely. "It seems beyond the pale to commit to being bound together by an irrevocable vow for all eternity. With the rules you people have on vows and bargains, you can't tell me there's a fae version of divorce. What if we grow to hate each other? Then we're trapped."

"I highly doubt that will happen."

"It happens all the time. People do that. And you have to admit that our relationship hasn't exactly been a smooth and trouble-free one."

He leaned in, the dare blazing in his eyes. "You wouldn't enjoy one that was. You love the challenge. The fencing and the sparks that fly."

I had to take it back. The man did know me pretty damn well. "But that's not what works for a marriage. I don't want to be married to you!"

A stricken look crossed his face. Impossibly, I'd wounded him. He stood and paced over to the glass dome, staring out into the night. I kicked myself mentally a few times and tried to think of what to say to make it up.

"Why did you come after me?" He asked it in a quiet voice. Carefully neutral again.

"What?"

"You heard me. Why did you risk your life, the lives of your precious companions and all of this independence you hold so close to your heart to accomplish the nearly impossible—wresting me from Titania's grip? Particularly when I told you not to."

Oh.

Why had I?

Rogue had literally disappeared in the middle of the night. No one but me believed him to be in jeopardy. With only dreams to go by—filled with his cautions and Titania's taunts that he belonged to her again—I'd insisted on chasing after Rogue. I'd risked everyone's lives to do it, to free him from the total mental enslavement she'd trapped him in.

It just hadn't been a question at the time. I'd had to do it.

"That was your out, cruel Gwynn. If you didn't want me, you could have walked away then and gone on with your life. I *told* you, over and over, not to look for me."

The pain in his voice cut through me. I struggled off the bed and went to him, the stone floor warm against my bare feet. He didn't turn, the elegant line of his profile remote and cold.

"Hey."

He didn't acknowledge me, so I had to snag his sleeve with a claw—which sliced the fabric. Oops. He glanced down at the tear and raised that eyebrow at me, haughty and removed as ever. Waiting for my answer.

"I couldn't *not* look for you, okay? These are two different things. I can care about you without wanting to be married to you."

"And do you?" he asked, watching my face. "Do you care for me, heartless Gwynn?"

The heart he claimed I lacked thudded hard in my chest, feeling bruised and swollen.

He unfolded his arms at last, and stroked my cheek. "Tell me."

I had to tilt my chin back to look up at him and considered wishing up some heels, so we could be closer to the same height. The words and feelings wound together inside me, fighting each other. "I know you can sense how I feel."

"I want to hear you say it."

"Just to torment me?" I had wanted it to be a joke, but my tone came out a little ragged.

"No." He passed his thumb over my lower lip, sending a thrill through me. "Because you like to hide behind your wit. You're careful of what you admit to out loud—as you should be, you've learned well—but this is important. No ducking behind omissions or clever wording. It's only you and me here. I'll hear you say it."

"You're one to talk," I retorted, but it lacked any sting.

His lips twitched on the left side, sliding into a smile. "You have always been an excellent pupil."

"Is this a way of trapping me into agreeing to marriage?"

That midnight gaze darkened, his thumb tugging my lower lip down while his fingers feathered over my jaw, as if he wanted to pull the words out of me.

"We will revisit that topic tomorrow, agreed?"

"Tomorrow being after dawn, yes," he specified.

At least I'd have a better shot of discussing the ramifications of such a step without the seductive influence of the candlelight, the nearby bed and...what was I thinking? Rogue would be present, which meant I'd be seduced regardless. Time to get it out there.

"Yes," I admitted, feeling as if I were standing with my toes hanging off the edge of the high dive. "I care about you."

The hand on my cheek slid around to the back of my neck and he wound his other arm around my waist, pulling me up against him, his lips a whisper from mine. "And do you love me?"

"Does it matter to you?" I answered, rattled enough to give the same response he gave me when I asked that question.

"I find that it does matter, yes. Do you?"

"I thought you weren't sure what it even meant."

"I'm learning. I've learned a great deal from you, passionate Gwynn. I did mean it when I said I loved you. This thing that throbs between us and makes your pleasure, your happiness, mine. It's new to me, but I'm learning to like it. I like that it made you come after me, and it feels like a wound to contemplate that perhaps you don't feel this same thing. Am I fool to have thought so?"

"No." I said it softly. "I didn't know you felt love is all."

"I didn't have a name for it. Call it love, if you will."

I'd told him I wasn't sure if it mattered. Hearing it then and now, I found it did. I even believed him, feeling the strength of it vibrating with a subsonic hum through his body into mine. Mesmerized by the look in his eye, I stepped off, fell, and let the water close over my head. "I'll call it love too."

His mouth took mine, fierce and triumphant. Breathless

from my risky confession, I returned the kiss, feeling starved for him. That thing he'd named, that throbbed between us, became a shared song of desire and need. I clung to him, willing in this moment to give up thinking about it all. I wanted to be with him.

But he pulled back, smiling when I protested.

He held out his hand and showed me the earrings. They glittered like jewels, inverted Stargazer lilies, limpid blue and luminous in the soft light. The man never gave up. "Will you wear them?" His voice held a level of warning and wariness. I'd worn them before, but mainly so he'd grant a stay on the marriage thing. This just put us back to where'd we'd been before Titania tried to change the game.

I nodded, knowing he needed this from me—and because I liked them, though I wouldn't tell him that—and he pressed them to my earlobes, the tendrils tickling and sending dark shivers through me as they attached.

"How did you get them off without me?" he asked, curious, since I should not have been able to undo his spell.

"A dragon's egg." The dragons—and all associated with them—nullified magic.

"Clever Gwynn."

"How did the horseshoe earring I gave you come off?"

He fingered his left ear where I'd affixed my one and only gift to him. "Titania."

Of course. Her power trumped mine. More powerful than a dragon?

"Do you have it still?" he asked, raising the eyebrow on the left side of his face, the black pattern snaking with the movement. He'd sent it to me, a message of his own. "I would have it back if so."

"I'd had it in the dress Titania poofed off me, back at her castle. It might be gone." That pained me, that I'd been so careless, but Rogue was already shaking his head.

"You made it. Only you can destroy it. Call it to you."

"How?"

"Hold the image in your mind and reach out to it. Imagine it landing in the palm of your hand. You can consider this your lesson for the day," he added archly, reminding me of our old bargain of exchanging daily lessons for kisses and him sleeping in my bed. My gaze went, as if of its own accord, to the big bed in the center of the room. It seemed we would be sharing it every night from now on. And more than kisses. The thought made me shiver.

"Problem?"

"No." I said it firmly, for both him and myself. One day at a time, right? I followed his instructions, mentally reaching for the golden horseshoe, which seemed to have a niche in my mind. As if anchored there. Interesting. I called and it appeared in my palm. Fabulous trick. And it explained much of what Rogue could produce on a moment's notice. Like, say, a creepy cyborg army.

Then, however, I was stuck.

I couldn't pick the damn thing up and place it on his ear. Eventually I might get good at using the claws like pincers, but I couldn't quite get a grip on it. Frustrated, I looked up to find Rogue patiently watching me.

"I'll hold it in place." He took it from me. "And you seal it there. Perhaps with a kiss," he added, inviting me with a wicked glint in his eyes.

Did he think I wouldn't? Carefully setting my palms on his shoulders, I stood on tiptoe, focusing the wish on my lips and bound the earring to his skin. He hissed at the sensation—I might have added more punch than I needed—and seized me by the hips, lifting me so I wrapped my legs around his narrow waist. I nipped at his earlobe, drawing it into my mouth and sucking on it, using my tongue to toy with the earring. Tasting his skin in lieu of burying my hands in his hair.

Rogue groaned and deposited me on the bed, coming down with me and pulling his ear from my mouth so he could kiss me, deep and full. "I believe we have unfinished business," he muttered between kisses.

"I should probably clean up," I protested.

"Do you think I care for such things?" He lightly bit the spot just under the corner of my jaw, pulling the skin into his mouth and making my head swim with need. "You taste delicious. Like yourself. Here you are in my bed, where I've dreamed for ages that you'd be. Don't make me wait a moment longer, cruel Gwynn."

The line of his cock pressed hot and urgent against my thigh and I was wet for him. More, I longed to have him inside me with a visceral and endless craving. "I don't want to wait."

His hands flexed on my hips, then moved behind me to lift my groin hard against his. "I want you naked," he demanded. "Wearing nothing but my earrings."

Overcome, I wanted it too. "Then do it."

Magic whipped out of him in a black-edged slice that left me nude, making me gasp. With sharp desire, not surprise. Rogue sat up, the candle flames flaring higher with the scorching desire in eyes, and moved so he could look at me in full. I flushed, brutally aware of his gaze and my vulnerability. I'd been naked in front of him once before, but I might have been a little drunk at the time. And then that night had turned out so badly.

"Don't think of that time." He ran a long-fingered hand down my flank to my thigh. "This is that night. It will replace it. Be what should have been. We are safe here."

"Okay," I whispered, easily losing my thoughts in the long caresses as he stroked me, tracing the curves of my body while I undulated under his touch. If I'd thought that this coupling would be fast and furious, the explosion following months—years?—of packing powder into our internal kegs, I was wrong. He used both hands, lavishing me with sensual strokes, following the swell of my breasts and circling my belly button.

"What is this?" he asked, bending his head to dip his tongue in the indentation, making me gasp and wriggle.

"My…navel," I got out. "It's leftover from growing in my mother's womb."

"Will our child have one?"

"I imagine so."

"Good." He glanced up at me, grinning playfully, a long lock of silky black hair falling across his deep blue eye. "I like it."

Then he followed my midline, licking and kissing as he went, so my belly fluttered. "Rogue…" I put my hands on his shoulders, urging him up. To no avail.

"Yes, beautiful Gwynn?"

"I can't wait."

"Yes, you can." He swept his tongue along the tender underside of my breast, sending electrical bolts all through my system. My thighs were slick and I scissored them together. "As you made me wait."

"So we'll be in bed for nearly a year?"

He laughed, warm breath huffing against my skin. "Not so long as that perhaps." He moved to the other breast, tasting that one also, in slow laps. Frantic, I clutched his head. He cursed and hot blood poured over my hand.

"Oh! Oh *shit!*" I yelled. A long lock of his inky black hair fell onto the bed beside me and Rogue had a hand clapped over his bleeding ear. "Rogue—I am so, *so* sorry!"

Absurdly, he laughed, sliding a glittering glance at me. How he could be so amused, I didn't understand. I hated the damn claws. Hated myself for being unable to control the things. Deep inside, cool and silver-white, the cat stirred. Stretched.

"Shh." Rogue palmed my breast with his free hand, a distracting caress. "Don't fret, delicious Gwynn. Look—already the blood is stopping. The ear will grow back, remember?"

The blood—crimson as mine—had ceased flowing so copiously and only trickled down his arm.

"I hate that I did that," I confessed. It felt as much a placing of myself into his power as telling him I might love him. *Not might. I said I did, heaven help me.*

"It is rather distracting," he agreed and kneeled up. Then vanished the blood along with his shirt. His bare chest gleamed golden, the black lines snaking and winding around his left side like a tattoo of thorns. "But I have a solution."

Across his palms, green ribbons appeared.

For a wild instant, I couldn't breathe. All those dreams. All the times he taunted and enticed me with the image of those forest-green silk sashes binding my wrists.

The moment had arrived.

So many emotions churned inside me, seeking a way out. If I'd been aroused already, the sight of those ribbons acted like a chemical catalyst, rocketing my internal reaction exponentially. I craved and loathed the thought of them. Of giving him physical power over me in that way. Ripping my riveted gaze from them, I looked into Rogue's face, hoping to find an anchor in this roaring sea.

He regarded me gravely. Serene, even. Despite the now-ragged ear and the shorn hair above it. But his eyes burned with searing flame, glittering with desire and the challenge.

"Did you always know it would come to this?" I managed to ask, my mouth a desert of apprehension and fascinated need.

"I wished for it," he answered. "Is that the same thing?"

"With you?" I let out a shaky laugh. "Probably."

"Give me your wrists, dangerous Gwynn," he urged me. "Let me bind you, even if just this once. You know you can remove them with a thought, if you need to."

"Do you promise me that?" I searched his face, reaching for the truth.

"Yes. These bindings, at least, are ones you can always shed."

Mesmerized, feeling that this might be another of those haunting dreams, I held out my clawed hands and crossed my wrists.

CHAPTER 5

IN WHICH [REDACTED]

꿎

*If knowledge is power in a technological world, then control
is power in a magical one.*
~*Big Book of Fairyland*, "Rules of Magic"

A STORM OF emotion surged through Rogue's body, so
strong it echoed through me and I nearly cried out with
it.

"Thank you, my Gwynn," he sighed.

With reverence, he wrapped the green silk around my
wrists, crossing it around and between. My heart thudded out
of control and my breath shuddered in and out of my body. I
couldn't look away, even when Rogue's dark head bent over,
his hair drifting across my naked skin, as he pressed a kiss on
the back of each hand. As if the binding amplified sensation,
the press of his mouth rolled through me. I moaned, a dark
and dissolved sound.

Taking the ends of the ribbons, he drew my hands over my
head, slowly but inexorably. Tipping my head back, I watched
as he tied them to a ring on the headboard. A ring he'd put

there just for me, I knew on some profound level. As one knows things in dreams.

Stretched and bound naked before him, my body bowed by the jewel-toned pillows, I gave up something. Some of my fear, perhaps. Or an anger. When Rogue framed my face with his hands and kissed me, his mouth hot on mine and the longing for me pouring out of his heart, I was undone.

He stopped teasing then, his hands dragging over my body in a ruthless possession I couldn't resist. It seemed as if he touched every part of me, tasted, nipped and kissed every millimeter of skin. I moved with him, while he played me with exquisite skill, as if we performed some bloodless dance of magic and art. He pressed and I bowed. He drew and I followed. For this and this only, he held all the power.

And I yielded it to him with a sense of glory.

Impossibly, the fire between us burned hotter than ever. Equally consuming us, it raged. Rogue muttered incoherent words against my flesh, as lost to it as I. He ravished me in truth, as he'd so often promised to do. I lost all sense of time, reveling in the ecstasy of giving up all my resistance.

I only regained focus when he finally parted my thighs and settled himself between them, pausing for a long and endless moment. I managed to lift my head to see him staring down at my open sex. He'd lost the last of his clothes and kneeled there naked, his cock, as long as the rest of him, jutting high. All over the left side of his body, from temple to ankle, the black thorned lines seemed to pulse. His gaze caught mine in a cobalt flare and he pushed my knees back.

His eyes on mine, he angled himself and pressed the head of his cock against my aching entrance. I held my breath, nearly frantic that it wouldn't happen, but he smiled, a slow wicked spread of satisfaction.

"Yes, my Gwynn?" he whispered, pushing in just enough to make me crazy.

"Oh please, yes." I thrummed, vibrating with the need. He'd promised long ago that he wouldn't take me unless I begged. And here I was. "Please, yes."

He speared into me.

I convulsed, back arching, crying out as I impossibly climaxed instantly. The blood pooled in my groin pounded back into my circulation, rocketing to my head and back again. My muscles gripped him and he thrust in and out of me, face close to mine, a rictus of agonized delight. He stared into me, seeming to see into the depths of my darkest heart. And drinking it in.

His lips brushed mine and I opened my mouth for him, letting him have that too. Giving him everything while my body absorbed the excruciating pleasure of his cock filling me, molten desire filling my veins again, an almost painful anticipation of the crest to come.

The tension rode him, his lean strength like steel cables against my softer flesh. The climax built in him, palpable, driving my own peak to greater heights. He slowed, stroking in and out of me with nearly languid skill. I almost screamed with the frustration, but he let go of his grip on my knees, holding my face again, making me look at him, pressing his thumb against my lower lip.

"Have me, my Gwynn," he demanded.

"I do," I answered, drawing his thumb into my mouth in a sucking caress and wrapping my legs around his hips. "Have me."

With a hoarse cry, he slammed into me, shattering us both, our voices and bodies winding together like the coiling lines on his body and mine.

ऽॐऽ

I MIGHT HAVE passed out briefly. No surprise there, given that the blood supply to my brain had been entirely co-opted for other purposes. I'd heard of *la petite mort*, the little death brought on by powerful orgasms, but had never experienced one.

Of course it had to be Rogue who brought me to it.

Still buried in me, he breathed out a laugh and lifted his head, nipping my chin. "And thus her mind starts up again, from blackness to sparkling life. The little death, indeed."

I opened my mouth to reply, but he flexed his hips, sliding his hardening cock through my overstimulated vulva and roughing against my clit. My eyes might have rolled back in my head as the renewed pleasure swamped me. Rogue's head dipped as he bent to take my nipple in his mouth, hands sliding down to cup my ass in a relentless grip, holding me still while he moved in me, breathing on the recently banked coals so I leaped into flame.

"Please don't tell me your inhuman abilities include being able to go all night." The thought scalded me on a number of levels.

"All right." He released my nipple to speak, but swirled his tongue around the peak. "I won't tell you that. But I do feel that there's been a certain amount of expectation built up—I wouldn't want to disappoint you."

"I don't think I can do this again." I barely had enough breath to speak.

He lifted his head and narrowed his eyes at me. "I think that's a lie."

"I mean," I managed, "I maybe can physiologically, but— oooh!" My words ended in a squeak when he bit my nipple. Not hard, but enough to electrify my nervous system, vaulting me up to the next level of arousal.

"No thinking," he instructed, kneeling up in the circle of my thighs, cock hard inside me. "I have an experiment to perform."

I groaned and dropped my head back, unable to think even if I'd wanted to. His long fingers stroked my open labia, which was slick and still engorged, unbearably sensitive after two powerful orgasms. I trembled as he pushed back the hood over my clit, studying it for a long moment. It seemed possible I could come eventually, just from the tension. His cock lying still inside me drove me into a near frenzy and I rocked my hips, trying to work up enough friction to break the impasse, twisting my wrists in the grip of the silk ribbons.

"Be still," he directed in that instructor's voice, "or I shall have to tie you down entirely."

I sobbed a little but did my best to hold still while he explored my responses, testing which touch most affected me. Holding my labia wide with one hand, he played with my exposed clit with the other, backing off when the touch was too intense, moving back in when I managed to still the frenzied shuddering of my body. When he found exactly the right rhythm and location, he continued, stroking my clitoris with intent determination, slowly driving me to the brink, his eyes glowing a demonic blue.

"Now what would my Gwynn say?" he mused. "My hypothesis is that you *can* do this again. Over and over. I theorize that even you will stop thinking. What say you?"

I glared at him, hovering on the edge of another climax, yet suspended there, exactly where he wanted me. "I say you can't have two hypotheses."

He laughed, low and sinister. "Can't I? I think I can have whatever I want."

With that he began to move inside me, slow, sliding strokes to match the tormenting caresses on my clit. I came apart, mentally, emotionally, unable to assemble the least coherent thought. My thigh muscles tightening, my heels pressing into Rogue's back, desperate. Panting like an animal and making wild keening noises.

Without warning, the orgasm took me over, screaming through me, an irresistible force that flung me into the burning kaleidoscope of the stars above and dropped me, bodiless and without form.

I came back to myself in the same position, Rogue still kneeling between my thighs, cock hard and throbbing inside my quivering vaginal walls. Thankfully, he'd left my clit alone while I recovered.

"I win the hypothesis game," he said with a deeply sensual smile. "Even now your mind is an enticing blur of pleasure." He thumbed my clit and I spasmed.

"Oh no." I gasped for air.

"Oh yes," he coaxed, pushing my knees over his shoulders and moving up, so he could kiss me, his tongue running along my swollen lips, his hair falling like a silken cape around us. "I've starved for you, delicious Gwynn, and now I am gorging. Again. Deep, like this."

He braced his hands on either side of my head, the position lifting my hips nearly vertical, burying his long cock deeper in me than I thought possible. I thrashed my head from side to side, unable to bear the intensity of the pressure.

"Yes." His eyes flared, as if lit from within. "Take all of me, my Gwynn. Now and forever."

It only took a few thrusts, the depth of the penetration almost agonizing in its intensity. I screamed when I came, while Rogue emptied himself inside me, his body rigid with the climax, his head thrown back, a picture of unholy delight.

ᘏ

THIS TIME—THANK ANY gods who will listen—he withdrew from my depleted body, falling onto his back beside me. Both exhausted and brilliantly alive and awake, I tested the magic and bade the ribbons to let go. Breathed a sigh of relief when they did and I lowered my bloodless arms.

Rogue rolled his head on the pillow and gave me a long, lambent look. "As promised," he whispered.

I gazed at him, wishing I could run my fingers over his skin. Far from sating my craving for him, actually having him—over and over—only sharpened the need. I turned on my side and he moved his arm, nudging me closer so I pillowed my head on his chest, my cheek resting on the midnight lines patterned there, inhaling his scent. With delicate care, I traced one with the tip of a claw, following its winding path, enjoying Rogue's shivering response.

"Will you prick me with your claws then, ferocious Gwynn?" His voice sounded slumberous, sated.

"What will I do if I can't get rid of them?" I said against his velvet skin.

He stroked my hair. "There is always a way. Besides, you were the one to show me the advantages of having the Dog. That magic will be exceedingly useful in the days to come."

"I wonder why that circumvents Titania's grip."

"What made you suggest it to me? Surely you had a reason to think it, knowing you."

I traced another line, that forked over his abdomen—like walking a meditation maze—and thought back to the moment when the inspiration had hit me to tell Rogue to shift into the Dog, which was more like setting it free from his flesh than anything, to shake Titania's grip on his mind. "Because the Dog can cross the Veil and Titania cannot. Therefore, the Dog possesses an ability that transcends her. Also the Dog isn't bound by vows and agreements—thus it logically follows that the Dog is beyond her reach."

"Only to your mind." He sounded admiring, which I secretly loved.

"Do you think my cat will be the same way?"

"It logically follows," he replied, making me laugh. "We can *experiment* some more."

My face flushed hot at the intimate reminder of how he'd played with me. Learning me. His cock rose too. Apparently ever ready. I ran a light claw toward it and his fingers circled my wrist like steel cable.

"Worried?" I teased him, instantly breathless from the

surge of desire the feel of him restraining my wrist sent through me.

"While it would grow back, I'd prefer not to lose another moment using it on you," he returned. "Speaking of which..." Before I knew it, he'd neatly flipped me on my back and settled between my thighs, pinning my wrists to the bed on either side of my head.

"I thought we were done." Then I gasped when he slid into me, smooth as silk and strong as iron.

"Never," he averred and moved, slow and sweet, dropping light kisses on my face, like a warm rain.

The pleasure ran through me with the same golden gentleness, filling and tantalizing, like devouring fresh-baked bread. This time, when I came, instead of crying out, I simply sighed out his name, saturated with the exquisite satiation.

Rogue placed his last kiss in the dimple below my lower lip, pressing his mouth there. Once more, he whispered, "Never."

Releasing my wrists, he relaxed over me, our bodies still entwined. I wanted to run my fingers down his back.

"We'll work on it today," he said, into my hair, clearly hearing my thought.

"Today? Is it already past midnight?"

"Yes. Dawn approaches."

I doused the candles, so the night sky bloomed all around us. "It looks dark to me still—how do you know?"

"Open your mind and I'll show you."

As if it wasn't already open to him, in every way, with him still buried inside me. I felt pliant and permeable to him. With languid ease, he took my mental hand and directed my senses to another plane. The life energies of all the fae around looked like fireflies. Rogue nudged me to see the web between them, filaments of light, some like cables, others bare spider-silk wisps.

The hive mind.

I'd always known it had to be there—judging by the way the fae all seemed to know the same things—but I hadn't known where to look for it. Pointing me in a slightly different direction, Rogue showed me how the fibers also extended to the trees, the earth—and the sun, stars and moon. All interconnected in a way that filled me with awe.

Rogue touched a filament to the sun, like plucking the string of a harp, and the knowledge filled my head too. Perhaps an hour from rising.

"You see?" Rogue's voice pulled me back from it.

"Yes." Extraordinary.

"Do you want to sleep?" he asked, levering up and brushing a lock of hair from my face.

"I should be exhausted, but I feel wide-awake. Not sure why."

He gave me that wicked smile of his. "I told you that lovemaking with me would be restorative."

"Yes, but I thought that was just another of your pickup lines."

"How cruelly my lady has judged me."

"You seem to have survived the blow well enough."

"You have no idea, my Gwynn." He sobered, then pushed off the mood. "What does my lady will then? Food? A bath?" He flexed his hips, stroking inside me. "Me?"

I pushed at his shoulder with the heel of my hand. "Remember I'm mortal. And a bath sounds amazing."

"I should have known." He shook his head, sighing dramatically.

"Let me up." I wriggled. "Now that a bath has been offered, I can't stand to be without another minute."

"Not if you keep moving in that distracting fashion," he replied in an arch tone, but he uncoiled in his loose-limbed way and strode naked across the room. Mesmerized by his grace and the enticing play of his ass as he walked, I watched him go, somewhat befuddled when he returned wearing a black robe and carrying a deep green garment.

"What's that?"

"My people call it a robe." He held it open for me, borrowing one of my snarky lines too. "Unless you'd prefer to parade around the castle naked, which would be your prerogative as its new mistress."

"As a mere houseguest, I'll go for the robe." I folded the curved side of the claws into my palms, which worked well enough to slide my arms through the sleeves. Rogue lifted my hair from under the collar, spreading it over my shoulders and leaning in to press a kiss just under my ear.

"That remains to be decided," he reminded me, in a silky tone that nevertheless carried all the warning I needed regarding his determination on the subject.

He came around in front of me, fastening the buttons and tying the sash. All very thoughtful of him—but this being unable to do things for myself would wear thin soon. The robe, however, draped over me, plush and thick, so perfectly fitted, it seemed to have been made for me. As it likely was. The collar stood high around my neck then dropped dramatically open to reveal the upper curves of my breasts. The buttons and sash snugged it around my waist, where it then fell into a luscious full skirt of velvet folds.

"You look ravishing, Gwynn."

"Thank you." I found myself not quite able to handle this level of romance and tender care from him. It eroded the last shattered remnants of my will. Call me perverse, but I felt on more solid ground with him when we were at odds. I couldn't help looking for the tricks and the loopholes.

"So suspicious." Rogue ran a finger down my cheek and under my chin, lifting it a bit. He didn't kiss me though. Instead searched my face for something. "Come with me. We'll go the back way."

"We're going somewhere?" Duh. He'd said "parade around the castle." Apparently phenomenal sex had the additional effect of addling my brain. Note to self.

He led me through another arched door, inset down below the wall of the dome, into a sort of vertical tube. We stepped into it, he pulled me close and told me to brace myself. The circular platform we stood on sank down, increasing speed in a controlled way. "Don't be alarmed. It's just an—"

"Elevator? You have a freaking magic elevator?"

He cocked his head at me, not quite hearing the word right. "Your world has this magic?"

If I could have patted him on the cheek, I would have. I settled for a condescending tone. "Honey, we have this *technology* and much more."

With a low growl, he squeezed my bottom and pressed me close. "You didn't have me."

This was true.

Before I could come up with a suitable answer—okay, I was a little distracted—the platform halted in a shadowy chamber with a set of stairs leading down. A shiver of recognition trilled across my skin, raising the tiny hairs. Tucking my arm through his, Rogue led me down into a torchlit bathing chamber.

The same one I'd dreamed of so many times.

CHAPTER 6
IN WHICH ROGUE GIVES ME A LIST

*For the fae, the concept of "true love" seems to be an almost
magical condition—more like a trophy or yet another
commodity to be traded upon. The way they speak of it seems
to have nothing to do with what I think of as love.*

~Big Book of Fairyland, "True Love"

T HE ROUNDED WARM stones of the torchlit chamber fit
against the arches of my bare feet in exactly the same
way as in my dreams. Though the room was fairly narrow, the
ceiling and far wall disappeared into utter lightlessness. So
much so that the depthless shadows created an illusion of
infinite distance. A few paces away, water edged still as glass
against the stones, transparent at the shallow layer, growing
black and opaque as ink in the depths. In the dreams, I'd
always had the feeling that it went on forever. The reality did
nothing to disrupt that impression. The room felt less like a
chamber than a gateway.

"Wait," I said, as Rogue unbuttoned my robe.

"Yes, my Gwynn?" His face held only polite inquiry, but a

glitter lingered in his gaze. Oh yeah, he knew I'd recognize it.

"Don't play coy, Rogue. You know I've dreamed of this place. More than once." And before I'd ever come to Faerie too. Sometimes the implications of the cross-consciousness, cross-worlds events made my mind reel.

"And you know that there is less boundary between dreams and reality than you'd like to think," he responded, dropping his gaze and resuming the unbuttoning.

"Why here? Was it always you and not just the Black Dog?"

For the Dog had been in the dreams too. Always watching. Leaving me feeling hunted.

Rogue slid the robe off my shoulders, letting it puddle at my feet, running his palms over my bare arms and settling them on my hips. "Not only me, my Gwynn. You also. You reached for me too."

Had I? I had been yearning for more, yes—but I hadn't known what. Just a formless longing, a rising dissatisfaction that suddenly burst and hurled me into an unlikely cascade of events that brought me to Faerie. "I didn't know you to reach for you."

He doffed his own robe and, fingers encircling my wrist, tugged me toward the water. It lapped, warm, enticing and soothing around my ankles. "Well, humans can be ignorant," he allowed.

"Careful, or I'll claw you again."

"Will you?" With inhuman speed, he captured my other wrist and held them both in a grip of steel behind my back, arching my naked body against his. "Perhaps I shall have to appease my angry lady." His clever mouth closed on one of the lily earrings and tugged, sending sparks into my system. He nudged it aside and found the pulse point beneath my ear, sucked lightly, then trailed down my throat.

I wriggled, which only caused my tightened nipples to brush against his leanly muscled chest. I kind of hated what it did to me, when he took me over like this. But not as much as I once had.

I might even grow to crave it. Which worried me greatly.

"Don't fret over such things." Rogue trailed the words over my flesh, then licked the hollow of my collarbone. His erect cock rose between us, pressing against me insistently. "I could never tame you, even if I wished to. Haven't you proven that already?"

"I can't believe you're ready to go at it yet again." I groaned when he arched my back more, his tongue finding my taut nipple and teasing it.

"I believe I can keep my lady satisfied, yes."

"That has never been a concern of mine."

"Good." He sounded all pleased, which really hadn't been my intent, and released me. "Now stop trying to seduce me. I want a bath."

Leaving me there, he waded in, then dove, his lean body sleek as a seal's cleaving the glassy black water, his long hair streaming behind him. So odd to be standing here, as naked as I'd been in those dreams, my body filled with the same arousal, watching this beautiful and alarmingly strange and intimately familiar man who seemed to be mine, for better or worse.

"Are you coming in, lovely Gwynn?" he called. "Or do you plan to stand there being decorative?"

"Ha-ha." But it gave me a flush of pleasure that he found

me beautiful too. At least, that he said he did.

I took my time, testing my footing and letting the sensation of the soft, hot water rise around me. So odd not to be able to see through it, though it felt like normal water. Some kind of optical effect, I suspected. When I got deep enough, I tilted my head back, to sluice the water through my hair. I remembered in time not to run my fingers through it, lest I slice mine off too. I could magically replace it, but *my* ear wouldn't grow back. It would be magical shampooing for me, too, for the duration. A pity as I would miss scrubbing my scalp.

"Allow me." Rogue swirled up, showing me a palm filled with dark blue liquid. I gave him my back and he worked it through my hair. The scent of Stargazer lilies surrounded me, sweet, spicy and now forever connected to him. Using his strong fingers, he massaged my scalp, exactly as I'd envisioned.

"Are you eavesdropping on my thoughts full-time now?" I asked, more than a little disconcerted by the idea. I hadn't been thinking all that loudly, I was pretty sure.

He laughed, placing a soft kiss on my shoulder. "Our intimacy has woven us closer together. It's a side effect. You can keep me out if you try." His soapy hands flowed down and over my breasts, leaning me back against him. "You just don't really want to," he murmured into my ear, running the tip of his tongue inside the shell of it.

I didn't, I realized. It felt good, this relaxing of walls, to sink into the sensation of being with him, without having to be wary of every word. He hummed in agreement, tugging on my earlobe with his teeth and running long fingers down my midline to dip between my legs.

I let my head fall back on his shoulder, floating while he supported me. A ping in part of my mind that hadn't been there before—my new connection to the mass mind of Faerie—told me the sun had risen. The suds swirled around us and, in a dreamlike haze, I watched the bubbles whirl away into the darkness.

How I could rouse again and again like this, I didn't know. His touch seemed magical—for all I knew, it was—digging deep in me and calling forth this unending passion. It rolled through me, gentle, even healing, waves of sensuality. With the one hand, he caressed my breast, kneading it and plucking at my nipple, while the other lightly stroked my clit, urging me toward yet another climax. All the while he spoke sweet, affectionate words against my skin, pressing them into place with small kisses.

The climax surged closer and I rolled my head on his shoulder to meet his mouth.

"Marry me, my Gwynn," he said, and kissed me before I could answer, his hands stilling on my body. "Say yes."

He'd leave me teetering there, hoping to sweep me through this one without argument. So I bit him on his full lower lip. "No."

Narrowing his eyes, he gave me a menacing stare. "No, you won't say yes, or no, you won't marry me?"

"Both." Feeling considerably less dreamy now, I struggled out of his grip and he let me go. To clear my head, I dunked it, shaking my hair out and freeing the last of the suds.

When I surfaced, I kept my head tipped back, so my hair would sleek back out of my face. I didn't realize Rogue had closed in until he caught me neatly by the waist, his face lined with grim determination.

I sighed. "Did you really think you could seduce me enough that I'd agree to anything in the throes of passion?"

"Hope springs eternal," he replied in a dry tone. "However, since that method failed, we'll just have to have it out."

"You plan to keep me trapped in this bathing chamber until I agree?"

His lips twitched in amusement and he lifted me a little, then let me sink again, clearly watching my breasts bob in the water. "That suggestion has its merits. Come, sit."

As if I had much choice. His grip on me unrelenting, he urged me over to a sort of carved-in seat invisible in the opaque water. I settled into it, as comfortable as in the classiest hot tub. Beside me, Rogue's thoughts darkened, as impossible to see through as the pool. Readying himself to battle with me then.

Best time to launch an unexpected offensive.

"I'm told you could have pretty much any female in all of Faerie." Probably outside it, too, if I was any indicator, and a good portion of the males too.

He paused, indeed taken by surprise. I awarded the first point to me.

"This isn't a contest," he said, with more than a little irritation.

Oops. I darkened my thoughts too.

"It doesn't matter who I *could* have." He'd modulated his tone now, smooth and silky. "It's you I want. I thought I'd made that abundantly clear."

"But you haven't made it clear why," I pointed out. My turn to be relentless. Above, the ceiling of the chamber vanished into shadow, far beyond where the torchlight reached. As if this place sat outside physical limits. Which seemed entirely possible.

"I told you—because you carry my child."

"Look." I took a deep breath, annoyed with myself that I felt a little hurt by that. *Get a grip, Gwynn.* "I know we come from different cultures, but to a woman from mine, that's just not a compelling reason. It's almost an insult."

He fell silent, contemplating that. "Because it implies I value the babe more than I want you."

"Pretty much, yes."

"But we already agreed that we love each other."

The image that came with his words made it seem as if we'd exchanged equivalent gifts. In some ways, I supposed that was accurate, if unromantic. "I can love you—" jeez, I stumbled over the words still, "—without marrying you. I can have this baby without being married to you too."

"But you don't understand the ramifications of that."

"Perhaps you could give me your reasons. Lay your cards on the table."

"I have neither cards nor a table."

Funny that one translated literally. "It refers to a human game. People hide the value of the tokens—the cards—from each other, in an attempt to bluff the other person into thinking they have more or less than they do. I'm asking you to show me what you're holding. What are your reasons for wanting this marriage, without the trickery?"

"I'm not as fond of lists as you are."

"Pity. I'm exceedingly fond of them. I want one from you. Consider it a courting gift."

He laughed at that, amused by me despite the frustration rolling off him. "Only you would ask for such a thing as a courting gift."

I grinned at him. "Why, thank you, dear."

Lifting his hand from the water, he stroked a fingertip down my cheek, an affectionate gesture that never failed to move me—something he undoubtedly knew. "If I give you this," he said, very softly, "I ask one thing in return."

Here it comes. "Tell me and I'll decide."

"Your silence. Don't tell anyone else—no matter how tempting it may be."

My heart stuttered a little. Was he finally trusting me with his secrets? "All right."

"Don't agree too easily. I know you, noble Gwynn, and you will be sorely tempted to share this information. You cannot."

Ooh. Maybe I shouldn't know. It would nearly kill me not to act on something if I found it important. Still, as I'd once told Starling, knowledge was power. *I thought power is power,* she'd replied. An observation that had stuck with me. "Yes. I will keep your list secret and will not share it with anyone—unless you give me permission."

His mouth quirked up on the left side, acknowledging how I'd circumscribed my promise "We cannot speak of it outside this room. Do you understand that?"

Oh, really? "You planned this, didn't you?" I accused him. "Once you knew I wouldn't simply agree, you engineered to have this discussion in this place, where you could give me the reasons you knew I'd ask for."

"You should know by now, clever Gwynn." He smiled and

some sorrow lurked behind it. "I plan everything."

I sighed for the truth of that. "Fine, fine. Just tell me already."

He lay back and looked into the endless ceiling. "Let's see. To give it numbers then, as you prefer—I believe I've learned how to do this. One, the first and most important reason is the one I've already given. You bear my child. Two follows on one—because you bear my child, I must do everything in my power to protect you and the babe. Three encompasses the first and second. To fully exercise all my power, I must bring you both within the circle of it. The child comes with you, thus having you means having you both. Fourth—I have two tools to make you mine, marriage or enslavement. You've made it abundantly clear that the latter is not an option." He said this last in a wry tone that spoke of his exasperation. "So I either go against your will or I convince you to marry me."

"Wait. You think you could enslave me against my will?"

He rolled his head on the stone and met my gaze with darkly grave eyes. "Yes. Always that has been an option for me."

My skin crawled at the ring of truth in his voice. I'd flung this accusation at him more than once, but I'd never really thought he *could*. He waited watching me process that. This then—this was a measure of the trust he offered, letting me know that he could have, still could, and had chosen not to.

"Can you enslave anyone?"

"With one notable exception, yes. Why—do you want me to teach you?"

"No." I wanted to rub my arms, though I wasn't physically chilled. I settled for breaking his gaze and staring up into the shadows, stretching my neck. "I don't want to be able to do that. I find it abhorrent that you can."

"You and I come from different perspectives on that."

"Yes, I know. Still."

"Gwynn." He wanted to touch me, but didn't. The gentle brush of his thoughts against mine told me that much. "I didn't do it to you. I wouldn't ever."

"Even if I refuse this marriage?"

He sighed. "Even so."

"All right. Let's set that aside. I assume there's more to your list?" I hoped there wasn't a lot more. Already I was having a bit of trouble following the flow of his Möbius strip logic. Fascinating insight into his alien intelligence, however.

"There are ten. Fifth," he continued, "if you are not under my direct protection, the child will be vulnerable the moment it's born. Fair play to anyone who wishes to enter the game, as you think of it."

"Cecily was married to Fafnir."

"Yes, but he delayed in sending for her, thinking to keep Titania's interest away. An expensive gamble that he lost."

For a while I'd hated the noble fae Lord Fafnir, thinking that he'd cut the fetus from his human consort's belly with a sword, leaving Cecily for dead. He had, as it turned out, but only as Titania's puppet. The look on his face when I told him the truth—because he'd demanded it of me, not because I wanted to—would stay with me forever. *I am not like the other fae you've met because I have nothing left to lose.* Looking into the eyes of an immortal at rock bottom was a sobering experience. Oddly, I'd come out of it with my hate transformed to deep sympathy. Not pity—he would hate that.

"He owes me a favor," I told Rogue, recalling that this was one of the many developments we had yet to catch up on following our long separation.

"How is that possible when I expressly told you to stay away from him?"

Oh. Right. "Well, in my defense, he came to me. Blackbird told me I couldn't afford to snub him and then he taught me to dance."

"Did he now? Which required you to engage in a conversation that ultimately led to him owing you a favor, which can only mean that you discussed what you knew about Cecily's demise."

"Pretty much, yes."

"At least the favor will be useful in the days ahead. We shall have to discuss it with him when he arrives for the wedding."

"I haven't agreed yet." I bit my tongue on that, kicking myself for adding that telling "yet."

"You will." Rogue's voice held a smile, which made me want to kick *him*.

"Besides, even if I do agree—which I haven't—the ceremony can be small and private."

"No, it can't. Because—and incidentally I've moved this up to the sixth reason—we need to make a show of solidarity. Everyone must see the culmination of the true love tale and know that we will stand together against Titania. This is a crucial strategy."

I narrowed my eyes at him—a wasted gesture since he had his eyes closed, his face in profile to me. "It's you who's been spreading those 'true love' rumors all this time."

"Any and all tools at my disposal, clever Gwynn."

"Do you even believe in true love?" It occurred to me that when he spoke of "true love," it flavored differently than when we'd agreed we loved each other.

"As opposed to false love?"

He had a point. Even I had no idea what people meant by it. I'd bet money that they didn't either.

"Okay, let me recap here. The essence of your argument is that to protect me and the kid—to keep us from becoming a kind of wild-card token in this bizarre game—you need me to be married to you."

"One essence, yes."

"Aha! But Blackbird and Fergus were married and she still had to give up Baby Brody to the Big Bitch. Marriage did nothing to protect them."

Rogue cracked an eye open, blue glittering through thick black lashes. "It protected them from everyone but Titania. She is in a category of her own."

"Isn't she always?" I muttered.

"If you're finished debating, I'll continue."

"I'm never finished debating."

"One of the many things I love about you."

That simple declaration hit me like an arrow to the heart. I buried my reaction as deep as I could, not wanting him to know how much it affected me. If he'd made his list six things he loved about me, I would have caved by number four. Who could have predicted I'd be this person? I'd always taken refuge in logic. Been the one to make jokes about love not registering on the oscilloscope. Now I'd become emotionally vulnerable in some profound change of character. Had it happened when my cruel teachers destroyed my will to teach me control?

Or was it Rogue?

Abruptly I realized that I *would* marry him. Because, on a fundamental level, I couldn't really refuse him anything. Not that I would ever let him know that.

But I didn't say so yet. I wanted to hear the rest of these supersecret reasons. He'd been quiet while I thought, waiting for the go-ahead, apparently.

"Okay, number seven. Hit me."

Fortunately that one translated just fine.

"This one you already know, as I mentioned it previously. Once we are married we can dispense with bargains and trades between us, which will felicitate the eighth reason—that we will also be able to share power more easily and fully. That combination may be the tipping point for effectively shielding the child and defeating Titania once and for all."

"A compelling reason." In a flash, his hands seized me, lifting me to straddle his lap. Dizzy with the surprise, my claws scraped with a nerve-jangling screech on the stone pool edge as I balanced myself.

"Are you saying yes?" The question came out as a demand, harsh with emotion. The force of it shook me, but I persevered.

"I want to hear the rest of the reasons," I whispered.

"Remember your promise to me." A caution and warning both. An omen of the juicy stuff. He'd hoped to avoid telling me, judging by the tension in his body. If I could have, I would have run my hands over his chest, to soothe him.

"I remember." I reinforced the promise with a caress of my mind. He twined a thought around it, as if holding my hand.

"For the ninth—" he dropped his voice, as if we could be overheard, "—with your human blood, you could be vulnerable to a *thing* that may happen. If you're married to me, that will protect you."

Each time he spoke the word, what I heard as "married" seemed to carry a more profound resonance, almost a sense of a magic spell. Which, given how everything else worked in Faerie, made sense. The ultimate vow. "What *thing?*"

"I've told you as much as I can. More than I should. More than I would have, outside this space."

Titania then. I turned it over in my head, while he watched me with that coiled tension, hands gripping my hips almost too tightly for comfort, as I absorbed the implications, growing more horrified by the moment. No wonder he'd worried about confiding this. Starling, Fergus, Walter—hell, all the humans in Faerie would be vulnerable. She could wipe them out. All except for me. I hated that, as Rogue had known I would. Then another thought occurred to me.

"What about the other side of the Veil? Could my world be affected, too?"

He lowered his gaze, not denying it.

CHAPTER 7

IN WHICH I AGREE TO SOMETHING I NEVER THOUGHT I WOULD

Oaths and agreements manifest much like spells and wishes—the weight of a far greater force binds them into reality.

~Big Book of Fairyland, "Rules of Magic"

M Y HEAD SPUN with the awfulness of it. "You can't let that happen!"

"I can hardly marry all of them, foolish Gwynn."

"Don't toy with me," I snapped, trying to lift myself off his lap, but he held me firm, even though I levered the heels of my hands on his shoulders. "I can't stand by when there's the possibility of annihilation of the human race. I won't allow it."

"All I care about right now is protecting you," he returned with ferocity.

"I'm one person and my children—even if I refused to marry you and had fully human ones, which I don't think they would be because the 'humans' in Faerie are still contaminated with magic—wouldn't be enough to carry on the race. Titania must be stopped!"

"Believe me, I've been trying." He gritted his teeth, looking pained.

I realized I'd dug the claws into his shoulders, and blood was running in bright rivers down his chest. "Oh God! I'm so sorry." I lifted out the claws and gripped the ledge again, pushing away from him in earnest. "I'm awful. Just let me—"

"No, Gwynn. I won't die and you are not going anywhere until we finish this conversation. Stop reacting and think."

Think? Usually he told me to stop thinking. His canny gaze focused on mine, a slight cock to his head. A clue in what he'd told me then. Something he couldn't say directly. I rewound the conversation in my mind, searching for something salient in what he'd said. *Believe me, I've been trying.*

"You've been trying to stop Titania?" I'd hoped, but hadn't been sure enough to count on it.

He just regarded me, lips pressed together. *Score.*

"That's what the baby thing is about," I mused. I needed my grimoire, all of my notes and theories on why Rogue wanted my firstborn child, what Titania did with them, why they had to be half-human, half-fae. It was all tied up with how I'd been drawn into Faerie in the first place and with change-lings and I didn't know what all. Then it crystallized.

"Oh. My. God." I breathed the words, very nearly a prayer, though I'd never been religious.

"That's why she's courting the Wild Hunt. They are her ticket through the Veil somehow." That realization severely irritated me because I'd been toying with the same idea, dammit. "And the Black Dog—no wonder she wanted you under her control. And the babies, she's using them as changelings, right? They're something like her secret agents on the other side, so she can, what? Conquer—"

He pulled me in for a kiss, stopping my words. "Even here it's best not to say too much aloud, my brilliant Gwynn."

I leaned my forehead against his. "I don't know what to make of this all."

"You don't have to solve every problem this moment. But do you understand now that if we have any hope of defeating her, then I must do everything I can to protect you?"

"Yes." I did see. It wasn't romantic, but the reasons were good ones. More, I believed he'd told me the truth. "But I feel like I'm marrying you for your health insurance or something."

His hands flexed on my waist, then slid up and down my back. "Make it clear for me. Are you saying you promise to marry me?"

I sat back a little. The rare times in my princess-obsessed youth that I'd nursed fantasies of this moment, I'd never imagined a proposal like this. Rogue, with his wild magic, feral sexuality and the black-thorned pattern ranging over his face and body, now running with rivulets of blood, would never fit anyone's definition of Prince Charming. Absurdly a line from Beyoncé's "Single Ladies (Put a Ring On It)" went through my head—a song I'd always considered irritating, if not downright anti-feminist. And yet some deep programming in me wanted to know where my diamond was.

"Do you laugh at me?" Rogue's voice came out edged, his eyes glittering into dangerous.

"No. Sorry." I rolled my eyes at myself. "A silly thought, leftover from apparently far too many Zales commercials."

"What does that mean?"

"It doesn't matter—really."

"Gwynn." He used that demanding tone that never failed to make me shiver. Speaking of anti-feminist. "Tell me."

"A dumb thing—in my world you'd give me a diamond ring when you asked. Which is hardly relevant because it's supposed to represent a financial sacrifice and you could just magic one up. Besides, it's antiquated and really kind of sexist because it stems from the need to display wealth to prove you can support a bride. Which is also not relevant in this situation, because—"

"Gwynn," he said again, interrupting my babbling, but gently this time. "Are you nervous?"

Oh shit, I was. My heart fluttered and I gazed into his so familiar but terribly alien face. What the hell was I getting myself into? And why did it seem to matter so much?

"Maybe," I admitted. "I mean, this is kind of huge. Like, the whole rest of my life huge."

"Did you have other plans?"

Once upon a time, I could have said yes. Before my life took a hard left turn into crazy.

"Wait." I grasped at the straw. "You still haven't told me the tenth reason."

"Yes, I have."

"No—the last one was the all-humans-must-die ninth one."

"Please don't say that outside this chamber."

"I won't. Only to you. You have to trust me."

"I do, my Gwynn." Rogue ran his hands up my back, coaxing me to lean into him, his mouth hovering just under mine. "The tenth reason is that I care for you, more than anything else. I love you—you taught me how to think and feel in a different way—and I want you with me always. You are the partner and lover I never knew to dream of—only enough to wish for. Tell me you'll be that."

I melted. See? He could have skipped right to number ten, suckering me in with the romance, after all. I probably should find out what all the rules were for being married before I committed, but...what the hell. We could always negotiate later.

"Then yes." I said the words I'd never seriously thought I would. "Yes, I will marry you, Lord Rogue."

I'd expected one of his fierce and possessive kisses, some of the victorious triumph he'd showed on other occasions when I finally capitulated to whatever he'd been maneuvering me into. Though—and maybe I was kidding myself—this didn't feel like a defeat. As if he knew it, too, he kissed me on the cheekbone, butterfly light, almost reverent. He kissed my other cheek, then the center of my forehead. It felt ritualistic and I trembled with each brush of his lips, deeply touched. Drawing back, he waited, solemn.

So I followed suit, kissing him first on the patterned side of his face, then the other, then the center of his forehead, the spot the Hindus called the third eye.

"It is agreed?" Rogue asked, more of the ritual.

"It is agreed," I echoed.

Something shifted between us, like a cord tightening, the strength of the vow like a magical binding that rippled through me. For a blazing instant, I felt it in him, too, as if I saw through his eyes, felt the slow turn of the Black Dog deep in his soul, the answering slice of the cat's gliding acknowledgment. If agreeing to this marriage unified us so profoundly, I wondered what the final ceremony would do.

Not that a ceremony of devotion had helped Fergus and Blackbird—in fact, quite the opposite. Memory holes had led to secrets that forced them apart.

"They are not sorcerers." Rogue spoke against my cheek, hearing my thought though. "It is different among us. Or so I've heard. Such matches are rarely made."

His lips whispered over my jaw, his hands winding in my hair to tug my head back, allowing him to trail kisses down my throat, sweetly thrilling. Something about the emotion of the moment made every kiss penetrate my skin. As if he'd managed to reach inside and touch the deepest, most vulnerable part of me.

"I want to be inside you, my forever Gwynn."

He lifted me, hands below my thighs, and lowered me onto his erect cock. Impossibly, he felt larger than ever, filling and stretching me. The pleasure reverberated, amplified between us. Holding my hips still, he pumped in and out of me, stoking me with sensation so keen it became a knife that might cut me open. It killed me that I couldn't touch him, because I wanted to, to sink claws and teeth and take more of him inside me.

He laughed, breathlessly with rising desire. "Then take me." Tipping back his head, he exposed his throat, laughing again when I fastened my mouth there, sinking my teeth into the muscle, releasing some of the powerful pressure in my groin. My platinum claws firmly on the stone ledge, I dug them in, too, holding on while Rogue worked me from the inside out.

Remarkably, he came before I did, with a wrenching spasm of his lean body, dissolving into incoherent cries of ecstasy that rippled through the skin in my mouth. I followed a moment after, releasing my teeth and throwing back my head with the uncontrollable arching of my spine.

Trusting Rogue to keep me from drowning altogether.

Trusting that, somehow, there would be a happy ending to all of this.

ᏇᏖᏖ

WHEN WE RETURNED to the bedchamber the great crystal dome was ablaze with sunlight. For the first time, I got a good look at Rogue's domain.

Fascinated—and maybe needing a little distance due to the emotional earthquake that still had my heart feeling raw and my thighs watery—I went to the curved wall, my claws clinking as I reflexively put up a hand to keep myself from falling through the transparent surface. Not surprisingly, our room occupied the tallest tower of many that rose out of a massive assembly of rambling wings, courtyards and barrier walls with wide walkways atop them, all formed of brilliant black stone that glittered in the midmorning light.

The moat that circled the vast complex shone a silver blue with an abalone sheen. Not as wide as the Mississippi, but huge to my Westerner's eye, it was formed of a natural loop in a river. A sense of premonition crept up my spine. Much like the geography around Devils Tower.

I'd fallen into Faerie from there, near that black, corrugated rock that rose from the circle of the Belle Fourche River.

From a distance, the conglomerate of Rogue's castle might look much the same as the tower. I'd known I'd come through somewhere nearby, but the intersection of the two worlds gave me a brief moment of dislocation, like an inadvertent double image. The overlap in look, feel and even name seemed portentous in a way I hadn't yet grasped.

I scanned the green hillsides in the distance, wondering if I would recognize the exact hill where I'd awakened—a futile search, of course, as they all looked much the same.

At Devils Tower, the much smaller river made a partial loop around the monument. In this landscape, someone had created a channel between the river loops to form the circular moat. Probably at the front of the castle, where a somewhat narrower section would allow the drawbridge to span it, were it down. But it was up and the iridescent spiney hump of an elephant-sized moat monster lazily patrolled the waters.

Along with the secured drawbridge, every wall and tower bristled with the Cylon-esque soldiers, like the ones Rogue sent to escort my friends. Everything I spied showed that Rogue was braced for attack.

"Do you expect her soon?" I asked him, without taking my eyes from the view, scanning the horizon for any indication of my crew. They would be days in arriving, however, if Rogue's estimate had been correct. Still I couldn't help worrying about them. Not that I'd given them much thought during the past twelve hours or so of sex-drenched mindlessness.

"Expect? No. But I would be a fool to be careless at this point." Rogue, who'd been standing back, giving me time to absorb it all, came up behind me and stroked a soothing hand down my hair. "Titania is unlikely to come at us with a direct physical attack. However, because she knows I know that, it pays to cover that avenue as well."

I nodded absently. To my left, the river streamed away from a great waterfall, which dropped over a sheer cliff in a single unblemished sheet. It looked as though it could have been engineered, like those falls from infinity pools—if humans could design one that fell a mile or more without breaking up or vaporizing. After circling the Castle of the Dark Gods, the river meandered off to my right, slow and lazy after circum-navigating the loop, winding through an endless meadow of indigo flowers.

I knew they would be blue stargazer lilies.

"Do you like what you see?" Rogue asked, much as he'd asked if I liked the room. It both gratified me, that he cared if I liked everything, and also worried me, as if the other shoe had yet to drop. Something I didn't think I should tell him.

"It's beautiful—but mostly satisfies my curiosity, since I couldn't see anything before. Everything out my windows was gray."

"It seemed wiser to conceal the location of my castle from you."

I looked over my shoulder at him, raising my eyebrows. "In case of what?"

His mouth quirked, but he didn't smile, just wound a lock of my hair around his finger. "In case I failed to exact an appropriate bargain from you and my enemies managed to turn you against me. Or should you have come after me yourself."

"What did you think I could possibly have done against you or this fortress?"

He gave me a cagey look, then wound my hair several more times around his finger, drawing me closer. "I didn't know, did I? You were an unknown quantity with enough power to yank yon river out of its banks."

"And now?"

"Now?" He tilted his head, studying me. "I suspect you could do most anything you set your mind to." His mouth brushed mine in a lazy kiss that, impossible as it seemed, roused my blood yet again. "So it's good to have you on my side. If," he qualified, "you remember to keep your wits about you. You still have a great deal to learn."

Okay, that dampened my enthusiasm. "Yeah, yeah, yeah. I assume that lessons will resume?"

"Yes." He let go of my hair, leaving it draped in a perfect ringlet over the breast of my robe, as if it had been wrapped around a curling iron. "Though we should plan the wedding first. Invitations will need to go out."

"Oh no—I'm totally letting Starling do the wedding planning. If she wants to," I amended, remembering some of her dissatisfaction at being assigned the less-adventuresome tasks. I wandered over to my grimoire, which was waiting on the workbench Rogue had made sure to have here for me. I wouldn't tell him that either, how much it meant that he paid attention to my habits and occupations. With a judiciously placed claw, I opened the cover, flipping the pages to the Rules of Bargaining section. So much to add about the marriage stuff and here I was, unable to grip a pen. Maybe I could write magically? A thought occurred to me.

"How are people invited, anyway?"

"Via Brownie, of course."

Of course. So, even with their amazing speed, it would take them days to reach everyone.

"Who all will we invite?"

"Everyone who matters. You can make a list."

"Ha-ha." Though he might not realize I already had a list of everyone I'd encountered, plus all the people I didn't know who'd sent me tribute to curry favor. At least, as far as Athena had gotten in memorizing them for me. "How soon do we have to do this wedding?"

"*Have* to?" Rogue came over and leaned against the bench, crossing his long legs at the ankle. "I *want* it as soon as possible. Don't you?" His voice had an edge, one I knew to tread carefully.

Now that the giddiness had started to wear off—especially with the evidence of all of the various rules I'd painstakingly observed and collected on other topics staring me in the face—my nerves were getting to me. I should have investigated before I agreed.

Too late.

"It's just that great, big weddings like the one you seem to have in mind take a lot of planning. That's the only reason I wondered."

"No, it's not the only reason, but you need not fear this, Gwynn."

"If you say so."

"I do."

"It seems really unwise to me to make a big spectacle when Ti—the Queen Bitch is determined to come after us. Wouldn't an event like a wedding, with all of our friends and allies gathered together, be a great time to attack? What if she shows up?"

"Of course she'll attend—she won't be able to resist the invitation."

My mouth literally fell open, the ten thousand things I wanted to say to that all jammed in my throat, crowding each other to come out. Finally I seized on one.

"You *cannot* be serious."

"I'm always serious."

Which was a lie. Though he looked deadly grave at the moment. I paced to the crystal wall and back, bursting with the need to do something about this horrible plan. I envisioned something like the christening in *Sleeping Beauty*, with Maleficent showing up in all her evil glory to curse the newborn Aurora. This was how it always worked in fairy tales—someone stupidly invited the nutbag relation, who then wreaked havoc on them all.

"You're going to all of *this* trouble—" I flung a hand in a wild, encompassing gesture at the fortified walls "—to then invite her in? That's insane."

"No more insane than not inviting her and risking even greater wrath."

"But she could scope things out. Learn all of your secret defenses and so forth."

He smiled at that. "She's been here before. Another visit could hardly matter."

That sunk in as though I'd swallowed a stone. Or taken a bullet to the heart. Suddenly, all those dreams or visions or whatever they were, rushed back to me. *You know that there is less of a boundary between dreams and reality than you'd like to think.* In those dreams I'd had while we were apart, when he'd been Titania's captive, I'd seen him as her lover. Both of them laughing at me.

Before that, she'd dropped hints about Rogue's abilities in bed.

Had it all been true?

I felt ridiculous, standing there in this fabulous crystal dome Rogue had made for me, wearing the robe he had given me, stupidly bound by a vow to be tied to him forever, my hands crippled beyond use. Had he played me? Maybe they both had. Despite my vigilance, regardless of all the efforts I'd made to stay sharp, be suspicious and beware of every damn bargain I'd made. I faced the yawning chasm of terror that I'd totally and completely miscalculated.

At the same time, I absolutely hated that I couldn't seem to simply enjoy the moment. I should be happy. Instead, fear and suspicion gnawed at me from the inside out.

Rogue straightened from his indolent posture, wariness changing the lines of his body as he surveyed me. "Gwynn?" he asked, his expression guarded. "What are you thinking?"

"Don't you already know?" I gritted out. "Don't you know every damn thing I think before I know it?"

"I don't, no," he replied in a cool tone. "As you well know, you are frequently as much of a mystery to me as I am to you. Tell me what you're thinking or let me see."

The cat in me didn't like that. She prowled up, irritated, reflecting my despair. Or did my emotions come from her? I couldn't tell and, at the moment, I didn't care.

"Is this all a lie?" My planned demand came out plaintive. "Is this all just the long con, to rope me in and put me under your control? Under her control?"

"Gwynn." Rogue said my name on a long sighed breath, carefully not colored with the sense of how he felt, which spoke volumes in and of itself. "How can I convince you? I don't know how to give you the truth in any other way."

"Tell me about *her*. The part you've been so meticulously avoiding."

CHAPTER 8

IT AIN'T JUST A RIVER IN EGYPT

*Though I'd known that I grounded much of my thinking in
scientific method and the reliability of empirical evidence, I
am discovering how difficult it is for me to believe in
something I can't quantify through an objective method. My
kingdom for one amniocentesis!*

~*Big Book of Fairyland*, "Private Notes"

ROGUE'S SHOULDERS, HIS whole body, sagged in weariness.
Damn me, but I felt bad for him, for what I drove him to.
I steeled myself against it. I might sound the jealous girlfriend,
but I needed this information. This tortured me, too, as I most
certainly would be happier not knowing. *Just because you're
paranoid doesn't mean they're not plotting against you.*

"What do you want to know?" He met my gaze, the blue
somehow young and without guile. In a flash, I recalled some
images I'd seen in his mind once. Him, as a boy, running on a
beach, black hair streaming, while raven's feathers filled the
air.

"Did you have sex with her?" I made myself ask. I didn't

like it about myself that I had to know, but I did need to, for myself or for him, I wasn't sure.

"What difference does it make?" He opened his eyes, blazingly dark. "You came after me anyway. You knew then. Don't tell me you didn't."

The stone in my stomach sat heavy, making me ill. I had known. But I hadn't wanted it to be true. "Because she forced you," I whispered, barely audible, but he heard me.

"Because I had no choice," he qualified. "That's part of what she won. If you want the truth, then don't dress it up as something else. Yes, I was her plaything and I had no reason to believe that would change. She wanted me and I..." Unusual for him, he fidgeted, picking up the rubber ducky that had lived on my workbench since I found it in my tribute stores. I kept it around as a reminder that some things did cross the Veil. Besides myself.

"What?" I prompted, when he'd dwelled on his dark thoughts for too long.

He pinched the ducky, the soft plastic rebounding under his long fingers. "You've been in a similar place," he said finally. "I might not have been bound in silver, but I was no less her slave. With no ability to resist, you just go from moment to moment, unable to hope for anything. It...altered me. I'm not sure I can explain more than that."

Aching for him, moved that he'd trusted me with so much—more of an insight than I'd ever had into his labyrinthine psyche—I pressed my lips together, afraid to say the wrong thing.

"Who gave you this thing?" he asked, a clear attempt to step away from the painful subject.

"I'm not sure. I'll have to ask Athena." When he raised questioning brows, I added, "She has a gift for knowing where objects come from. She's been compiling a *list* for me, of all the tributes given me and who sent them."

He smiled a little at my emphasis on "list," but his thoughts remained shuttered and his gaze opaque. "What else do you want to know?" He clearly meant Titania.

"We don't have to discuss it."

"Will you attempt to protect even me?"

"I only meant that—"

"No, Gwynn. Ask your questions. Better that than letting them fester between us, once again poisoning your heart against me. I'll hold you to your vow to marry me, regardless, but I still would rather not have you hate me, if I can avoid it. Ask."

I hated that it bothered me, but he was right. If I didn't ask, I'd always wonder. "What about those other times, when she visited, knowing this place so well?"

"Then too," he said, gaze steady on me. "Long ago."

"When?"

"Before we became the people we are today. Before she set her feet upon her current path."

It hovered on my tongue, the words like the ugly toads of fairy tale lore, to ask him if he'd loved her, but I refused to open my lips to it. He'd say that neither of them thought that way. Besides, I knew well how he felt about her now. No, what I wanted to know lay somewhere else. But I didn't know how to ask it, what phrasing to use.

"Just ask," he said, putting the ducky down and coming closer, though not touching me. Possibly staying out of reach.

"If I can answer, I will."

"Does she still have a hold on you?"

He cocked his head meaningfully. Duh. Stupid question. Of course she did or he'd be able to speak freely. *Certain restrictions have lessened,* he'd said to me after we'd broken him out of the Queen Bitch's castle, not that they were gone.

"Never mind." I waved a hand, the claws sliding against each other with a metallic chiming hiss. "Strike that question. Tell me this if you can. Can she take you away from me again?"

"Her powers are vast."

Meaning yes.

"More to the point," he said, "will you let her?"

"Her powers are vast," I snapped back and he inclined his head. Restless, full of both vague, formless worries and very pointed ones, I looked out at the meadow of iridescently indigo Stargazer lilies, imagining for a moment that their heady sweetness reached me, far in the tower above. Likely just the scent of my earrings, made in their image.

"What else, Gwynn? Your thoughts are very quiet."

"And here you're forever bitching about them being loud."

"I shall never complain again," he teased, though his voice sounded sad. I glanced back at him and away, unwilling to voice my deepest concerns.

Have I made a terrible mistake?

Will you use me and then be rid of me?

Will you betray me, in the end?

Not really the sort of questions one should ask one's fiancé, particularly right after your magically binding engagement. Although, I supposed these fears were as old as relationships.

And sometimes people discovered the answer was yes. They survived.

"I think these are questions I have to answer for myself," I finally said.

Rogue studied me, not satisfied. For once, however, he didn't push me. Instead, he waited me out. A new—and effective—strategy on his part.

"I feel very out of control of my life at the moment," I admitted. A big step for me, owning up to weakness with him. A deliberate effort on my part, to place trust in him. Call it hypothesis testing.

His lips twisted in a wry grimace and he closed the last bit of distance between us, pushing my hair back over my shoulders, smoothing it and looking into my eyes. "Welcome to my world," he offered and lowered his mouth, stopping just short of mine, waiting for me this time, instead of simply stealing the kiss.

With a sigh, I tipped back my head and met him the rest of the way, the touch of his lips, the passionate connection between us, restoring my sense of rightness. If only we stayed in bed all the time, the relationship could totally work.

"I'm willing if you are." He slid his tongue along the sensitive inside of my upper lip.

It was tempting, to give myself up to the storm again. But afterward, I'd still feel as out of control. "I think I need to take steps to regain some of my equilibrium." I reluctantly pulled back. "Something active. No more talking in circles."

"What would you like to do?"

"I want to work on getting my hands back."

His thoughts stilled, studiously smooth, but something of

concern flickered in his gaze. "Are you determined on that?"

"Yes." I flexed my fingers, the weight of the metallic claws dragging them into helpless lumps of flesh. "I can't live like this—not happily. And isn't this a good time? We're kind of resting and recuperating anyway."

He hesitated, only for a split second, but enough to be telling.

"What?" I asked. "No secrets."

"It might not be the best time, no." He chose his words. "You've reached a sort of balance with this spirit. Trying to take back the ground it's won might anger it."

"So let her be angry."

He smiled, almost despite himself, and tucked my hair behind my ear. "Even with all you've seen, you are so cavalier about matters that would terrify others."

"Ignorance is a beautiful thing sometimes. Why should I be afraid of pissing off my big kitty within?"

"Because, foolish Gwynn, you might not be strong enough to win."

Daunting thought. "Well, right now this does not feel like a workable détente to me. Are there things I can do to get stronger? Exercises or lessons or some such, to improve my odds?"

The questions seemed to take him aback. He considered. Then finally shook his head. "No, I don't think so. The learning is in the doing."

"Then there's no time like the present."

"Gwynn." Rogue moved away from me, raking his hands through his hair. "You haven't thought this through."

"How can I when I don't have all the information I need?

This is about my body, Rogue. I need my hands. I should be able to make these choices for myself. If learning through experience is the key, then let me try it."

"You don't know what you're asking."

"Then show me."

"Not here."

᛭ᛏᚻ

ROGUE TOOK ME to another wing of the castle—toward the back, I thought, trying to orient myself on the walk there. We descended via the stairs this time, then traveled wide hallways lit with torches, the large windows all shuttered against the invasion he'd assured me was unlikely to occur. Along the way, we passed all sorts of people, fae and human alike.

They bowed in greeting, murmuring various felicitations on the upcoming wedding. Of course everyone would know by now.

We ended up in an interior chamber that reminded me of the indoor riding arenas we'd used for lessons and exercise during Wyoming's harsh winters. Similar to the bathing chamber, stones lined the walls which curved into a domed ceiling. The mortar between these, however, gleamed silver in the sourceless light. The floor seemed to be packed dirt, reinforcing that riding-arena feel. A single door, barred behind us and also made of silver, led in and out.

"Silver boundaries and an earthen floor?" I voiced the observation as a question.

"Protects everyone else from magical errors," Rogue replied, raising an eyebrow at me, as if daring me to object. "And us from certain kinds of eavesdropping. Had events worked so that I'd been in charge of your training, it would have been here and you would not have had to be bound in silver at all times."

"Alas for that." I managed to sound flippant, proud of myself for it. If only events had worked that way, instead of the nightmare I'd endured.

"Indeed," he returned with feeling.

For the first time I considered how my torturous training had worked against Rogue. I'd been locked away, out of his reach, and when I emerged so embittered it had taken all this time for him to woo me into a bit of trust. *Once again poisoning your heart against me.* Had it worked out otherwise, I might have studied here with him, fallen hard for my devastatingly sexy professor, and our child might already have been born.

Sobering thought. One I didn't care to entertain, for several reasons.

"Why not a silver floor?"

He gathered his hair at the nape of his neck, tying it back with a leather thong, doing it manually instead of by magic. "You asked me once how I drew from resources outside myself."

"The ground—really?"

"Mother Earth is the font of all our life, magical and otherwise."

"You say that like it's a real person."

"The earth is not real to you?"

"Sure it exists—but the ground is just a composite layer crust over a layered lava sea and probably a metal core. The earth is a planet circling a star, not a person."

"In *your* world, perhaps that's so."

"I don't see how these fundamentals could be that different. If I can live here, then Faerie has to share some physical characteristics with the same universe. Clearly the basic laws of physics still operate—gravity, cohesion of molecules, atomic structure—so it follows that the fabric of the overall world is the same."

"Then I shall introduce you to Mother Earth sometime and you can argue with her about it."

"Are you teasing me?"

"Believe me, charming Gwynn, I have far more diverting ways of teasing you." He grinned at my blush. "However, you elected to spend our time this way. Do you wish to debate further, which we could do in the comfort of our bedchamber, I might point out, or will you pursue this reckless course of action?"

"I'll take door number two, thanks." Determined, yes, but apparently also easily tempted. Didn't hurt that I preferred Rogue seductive over quietly wounded. I took a moment to settle my wayward thoughts. You'd think I was twenty again and full of randy hormones.

"The magic will do that," Rogue replied to my thought. "Already we foment that in each other, as I'd hoped."

I nearly made a dirty joke about "fomenting," but restrained myself. "Okay, then, teach me how to control the cat."

He gave me a stern look and folded his hands behind his back, all set to lecture me. I smiled to myself, loving his professorial bent too. "The first thing you must remember, my forgetful student, is that you cannot *control* the cat. Though it grows out of you, it is not part of you. You can no more direct its growth and actions than you will be able to with the child, once it's parted from your body."

"Can we just leave the theoretical embryo out of the conversational equation for the time being?"

His gaze drifted to my belly, where I fancied I detected an answering flutter. Raising his gaze to mine, he stared into me. Annoyed? "Not discussing the babe won't make it disappear."

"I don't want that." Not that it wouldn't be a resolution to innumerable problems that plagued me. "I need... Let's focus on one thing at a time, okay?"

"It's all of one thing." Rogue frowned a little but dropped the subject. "So lose the idea of control. There is no defeating it. Think in terms of coexistence. A push and pull."

"Is that what you do?"

"Unless sorely pressed by circumstances, yes." He said this in that dry tone, implicitly reminding me of my role in some of those events. "I find that it helps to allow the Dog its time to run. That satisfies it and keeps it from growing too...hungry."

My skin crawled a little at the word. Not precisely what he'd meant, I knew. At least, the term he'd used conveyed a sense of voracious need.

"So this is why I get the impression the Dog sometimes...escapes you." I picked my way around the phrasing, not wanting to insult him.

He simply raised a supercilious eyebrow at me. "More than sometimes, until the beach, thanks to you."

That night returned to me in vivid, horrific images. I'd thought the Dog had killed him, ripping itself out of Rogue's body, leaving only tattered flesh behind. He'd lost control because I'd betrayed him. I'd thought he was dead. Indeed, it seemed he might not have been able to return to himself on his own. He might be immortal, but more and more I understood that the fae were mutable. Somehow, I'd managed to stabilize the magic and bring him back. I still didn't really understand what I'd done, except that it had sprung from some deep instinct.

"I'm not certain either," Rogue admitted, to my surprise. "You bring an unprecedented element to the magic, powerful Gwynn. You gave part of yourself over to me, something that I lacked. I'm hoping that you'll be able to bring the same...ability to bear in dealing with your own beast."

The cat, white-cold, stirred in answer, my fingers stretching as she extended her metaphorical claws into my real ones. A deeply unsettling feeling.

"She likes having them." Rogue was still looking into me, with a peculiar unfocused gaze. "You'll be hard-pressed to convince her to give them up. Perhaps you should consider letting her keep them, as a bribe."

"A bribe?"

He looked at *me* now. "To satisfy her enough so that she won't push for more than you can give."

My throat tightened as I recalled what he'd said, when the feline spirit first manifested, that she'd take flesh from mine— something my mortal body certainly could not withstand.

"You said you would help with that."

"I said I would try. And I know you asked me not to say this, but I must point it out since you seem to be in denial of this truth—the stakes are higher. Should our efforts fail, the child will likely die."

And, not incidentally, me along with it. "Dang—and then you'd have to go find some other human from my world to knock up. Just think of the inconvenience."

"Do you mock me, cruel Gwynn?" he asked, voice deadly quiet.

He was right, I didn't want to think about the reality of this baby inside me. I would have to come to terms with it at some point, but it pissed me off that this was a factor in my life now. This pregnancy I had never agreed to or wanted. Maybe I didn't even totally believe in the baby's existence. It would be nice to see an ultrasound or something. I had no way of knowing how far along it was. Though I'd tried to keep track of days in my grimoire, it still worried me that time moved differently here.

Besides it wasn't as if I had any sort of experience along these lines. Completely out of my depth with no medical resources to guide me. Who could blame me for being in denial?

Still.

"You're right. That was mean and uncalled for. I take it back." Kind of. "It just continues to eat at me that I'm only important to you as some kind of vessel for your progeny."

"I think that sometimes you say these things to me so that I'll reassure you that they are not true."

I cringed, hating that he'd called me out on my insecurity. Also, it seemed I could never explain my very mixed feelings about this pregnancy. *I'm not thrilled about giving birth in what amounts to a Third World country.* How much he understood of that, I didn't know. But what still remained a theoretical construct to me seemed to carry considerably more import for him. His next words confirmed it.

"I didn't tell you this before, because of the way you fret that the child is more important to me than you are, but the babe you carry is my one and only opportunity." His eyes burned like the heart of the flame on a Bunsen burner. "So, my tenderer feelings for you aside, I also have a stake in this battle of yours."

CHAPTER 9

In Which I Fight an Epic Battle...Against Myself

Sometimes I wonder if the commonality of references to forces like "Mother Earth" reflects a parallel between my world and Faerie, or if that's simply my own frame of reference contaminating my observations.

~*Big Book of Fairyland*, "General Observations"

"So, if that's where you stand on the matter, why are we even here?" I gestured at the practice arena, feeling more than a little heartsick about it all. "I'll just loll about and gestate."

His jaw flexed, and it perversely pleased me that I'd annoyed him. "We are here because I already agreed that it's your choice. I would likely want the same thing."

"But I'm risking the embryo's viability." Took some getting used to the idea. "You're right. I didn't want to think about that."

"And, not incidentally, your own life."

Now that part had become quite familiar. "Let me ask you

this." I weighed my options. "Okay, if I give this up, let the cat keep the claws until at least the baby is born, what kind of guarantee does that give us? Will it be enough to satisfy her—particularly if I'm having to work magic, given what lies ahead of us?" One thing I did know—the more I worked magic, the more the cat stirred. I could probably graph it on a nice exponential log scale.

Rogue contemplated my questions. "You do have a rather ruthless method of breaking down options."

"I take it that's a no."

"Beyond the fact that there are no guarantees?" He shook his head, bothered. "I must admit that you are right. The détente, as you called it, is unlikely to last long—particularly if you draw heavily on magic, as you'll undoubtedly be required to do. This is a downside to you being a sorceress that I failed to consider."

"Hey, even you can't plan for every damn thing."

"If you only knew. Shall we explore your other options then?"

"I can't wait."

He began pacing. "The principle to understand is that the cat is a separate entity from you. Though her roots twine in your soul, the seed that gave her life came from elsewhere."

"Like some kind of elemental spirit." I tried out the concept on him, to see if it would click or not.

"If you will."

Okay, good. "So, when I work magic, I create a sort of fertile soil that allows her to grow and draw strength." A closer parallel to the embryo than I liked. *Don't think about that now.* "But why does Falcon have one? He works no magic."

Falcon—call him General—had been in charge of my life for too long. I'd enjoyed pushing him into the involuntary reaction that made him a falcon in truth. Small joys.

"Yes, he does—you're simply not aware of it."

"Really? What is it?"

He stopped his pacing and glanced over his shoulder at me, the tail of his long hair sliding like ink over his shoulder. "You won't like it."

I snorted, wanting to fold my arms but settling for sliding the razor edge of one index-finger claw against the curved back of the other. It made a satisfying hiss. I seemed to be improving with my dexterity. Small comfort. "Color me shocked."

"He mentioned it to you—his services to those such as Lady Healer. He has a gift for giving pain."

"The opposite of Darling's anesthetic abilities."

"Close to that."

"Not terribly useful, as magical gifts go."

"No, but then he's never been imaginative with its application either. Instead he squanders it on sexual play with those who crave such things." Rogue raised a brow at me. Significantly.

I nearly choked. "You think that *I* would have…" I couldn't complete the sentence, the image revolted me so thoroughly.

"Falcon did imply as much." He lifted one shoulder. "And it's not as if I didn't find you seeking pleasure with that human man."

"That was…" a mistake. A diversion. A desperate attempt to rediscover my own agency. And the betrayal that had nearly cost him his body, if not his life. And I'd failed to finish yet another sentence.

"You asked me about Titania." He pointed that out with relentless calm. Ouch.

"Then no. I didn't even really want him. And I did not dally with Falcon. You're the only one I've ever wan—" Shit. I should *not* have confessed that. And three time's a charm.

Rogue pounced, literally, on me in a moment and lifted my chin so I had to look into his face. "The only you've ever... what?"

My face grew hot. Along with the rest of me. "Really wanted. Like this."

"Like how?" He feathered a kiss across my mouth, as if tasting what I might say.

Desperately. Unceasingly. Beyond will and reason. Easier to show than say it, I opened my mind to him again, only then becoming aware of how tightly I'd shut it on that set of feelings. No wonder he'd been uncertain.

His mouth turned hard, demanding and as voracious as the spirit animals he'd described. My own hunger billowed explosively to his spark. In a moment, the kiss was over, leaving me blinking in confusion.

"I feel the same," he said. Then grinned. "Your technique of needling for extra reassurance is an excellent one."

I groaned, dropping my forehead on his chest. "I've created a monster."

"No," he replied, with easy charm that belied the anger that swirled from inside him, "that happened long before you met me." Before I could respond to that, he continued, setting me back on my feet and stepping back. "Turn your eye inward, toward your animal like you did for yourself when I asked that question. What does she want? How does she want it?"

Ignoring for the moment the sneaking suspicion that this whole conversation had been a teaching ploy, I did as he said, searching her heart as I'd searched my own, asking for her feelings.

Unlike the reasonably quiet inner chambers of my mind, hers ran wild and hot, a quicksilver slide of seeking desires. Sharp teeth wanted bloody meat. Razor claws needed to rend and tear. Sinews to slide and stretch. Muscles to run.

"She wants out," I whispered, profoundly rattled by the power of the cat spirit's need. "Nothing else matters."

"But she can't be out." Rogue's voice was firm. "She cannot last long without your life to draw from. If she comes out now, you'll die, which means her death also. Make her understand that."

"She doesn't care. It would be worth it."

"She's wrong. She doesn't know. Tell her what she can have if only she waits, has patience."

"What? What can I have?" The voice purred inside me, speaking with my tongue. Disconcerted by it, I almost lost the focus on her, but a brush of Rogue's thoughts directed me back. *Keep the thread.* I clung to the anchor with gratitude.

"You could have centuries," he offered. "Power beyond dreaming."

"Flesh?"

"Flesh to wear and to rend and to eat. But, if you spring upon the prey too soon, it will escape you. Patience rewards the wily hunter."

"Patience," the cat hissed from deep inside me. "The hunter knows patience."

"Yes. Take back your claws. Keep them until the time."

She balked at that, resisting. My fingers burned with her annoyance. The claws anchored her to the world, let her taste and feel it.

"You can bring them out again, from time to time," I told her. "We'll run."

"And hunt?"

"Yes. To reward your patience."

She growled a bit, considering. "Take them then. For now."

I tried, wishing the claws gone. Wishing them transformed to air. The magic dissipated, as if it found nothing to attach to. "I don't know how."

A nearly fatal mistake to admit that.

The growl became a purr of amusement. She nudged at the inside of my skin, then pushed with more vigor, making my ribs creak with strain. "Perhaps you offer me nothing. Why should I not seize what I can? You have no power. You are weak and worthless."

"That's not true. I am more powerful than you."

"Prove it." She issued the challenge in the hissing silence of my heart. With a liquid lunge, she hurled herself against my rib cage, threatening to burst free as I'd once seen the Dog erupt from the shreds of Rogue's broken body.

"Gwynn!" Rogue's shout echoed, a useless warning from an unbridgeable distance, for I was already wrestling with her. The anchoring rope of his thoughts slid away from my grasp. It was all I could do to fight the cat down with all of my strength. She had me by the throat and I dug my claws, the ones she'd foolishly lost to me in her greed, into her soft belly.

For this, too, Rogue had handed me the power, stoking the

desire in me. But I needed more. All those lean, despairing days while I had searched for him, the final conflict with Titania, my brush with death—they all left me without reserves. I'd begun refilling the well, but watching the power drain away, I knew it wouldn't be enough.

I should have waited.

Waiting would not have helped.

She, too, drew from me and would grow stronger as I did.

It would not have saved me to wait. Perhaps nothing could.

Eager, feeling me weaken with the onset of despair, the cat closed her jaws on me. Just as the Black Dog had in my first few hours in Faerie. I found myself on my back, claws digging into the packed earth of the arena, my body pressed flat. The internal rack of her determination stretched me, my muscles and sinews threatening to tear asunder.

The learning is in the doing, Rogue had said, but what could I possibly do?

I hurled wishes at her, but they slid off, mercury on glass. My energy drained away with each attempt and I made myself stop.

With a delighted purr, she flexed, and I screamed with the pain. Worse, the extent of my dreadful miscalculation eroded me further. I'd been so determined, so stubborn and now... Now I'd lost not only my own life, but our unborn child's also. I couldn't let that happen.

I needed another source of energy, now.

I have resources outside myself.

Mother Earth is the font of all our life, magical and otherwise.

With nothing left to lose, I reached down into the earth,

seeking that font. At first I flailed, finding only what I expected—dirt, the crust over magma beneath. There had to be more. Rogue had said as much. He would never lie to me about something that important. I refocused, looking wider, without expectation.

The magma layers roiled, not like the dull diagrams in the textbooks, but vivacious and bubbling. The blood of the earth, hot and stoked with unimaginable potential.

Deep in the center and beating like a living heart lived not a metallic core, but a vivid, eternal and infinite fountain of fiery life.

I approached feeling as I once had standing before a dragon. It burned with a similar heat, both wholly magic and impervious to it. The same sense of worshipful awe infused me. My heart beat in time with it—a rhythm that somehow synchronized with both my own 2/4 atrial/ventricular pattern and the 3/4 that belonged to Rogue.

No, not that belonged to Rogue this time, but to the fetal heartbeat within me.

My fae child resolved into being for me at that moment.

Vividly real. Precious and perfect.

The earth's core welcomed me, mother to daughter to granddaughter, and I drank from it, filling myself and layering my fleshly body with her enduring strength.

I turned to the cat, which still tried to savage me, desperate to separate from the soil it had grown in.

Don't try to control it.

My thought or Rogue's? Mother Earth's? For this was her daughter too.

Mentally, I stroked the feline, showing it love and care. I

had no desire to trap her. Together we would find a way. In good faith, I shared Mother Earth's energy with her, feeding her.

She didn't exactly give in, but she subsided, drinking in what I offered and, replete for the first time in her conscious existence, relaxed.

As compromises went, it was a good one.

ℰττ

I OPENED MY eyes.

Rogue sat nearby, long arms wrapped around his bent knees, chin resting on the backs of his hands, watching me with midnight eyes that revealed little of what was going on in his head. A fleeting impression made me think he'd been waiting a long time.

I sat up, aches in every fiber of my being, somewhat dismayed to see the curved platinum claws still extending from my fingertips. But the magic surged through me, the steady pulse of the heart of the earth.

Not to control, but to coexist. Rogue had suggested that from the start, but apparently I'd had to learn it for myself.

With a pointed thought, instead of getting rid of the claws, I retracted them. An important distinction, the pulling of them back inside me, from whence I could extend them again.

Or I could, the cat murmured, sleepily and from a great distance.

Yes, I replied. *If I agree.* Then I flexed my fingers, delighted to have this key characteristic of my humanity back. At least on the surface.

"Well done." Rogue uncoiled into a more relaxed position. "Though it was a near thing."

"She nearly escaped me."

"Yes. I saw."

"But you didn't interfere."

"As I've tried to persuade you many times, my Gwynn, some things are beyond even me. Though your confidence in me is gratifying.

"That's why you wanted to do this in here," I said, the light dawning. "If she had broken free, the silver here would have contained her.

"Hopefully, yes. It should come as no surprise to me that your animal is more powerful—and in an unusual way—than any I have seen. It would not have done to have her loose in the castle or the countryside."

"If silver could contain her here, then wouldn't silver have kept her inside me, also?"

Rogue's eyes gleamed in the sourceless light. "Of course."

"Then why—"

He shook his head at me, the abrupt movement stopping me. "Do you think I forget my promises to you so easily? I swore never to bind you in silver again. Even to save your life or our child's life, I would not violate my oath to you, my Gwynn."

Oh. From the resonance of his words, I knew he meant more than the typical consequences for oathbreaking, becoming vulnerable to Titania's psychotic whims. That was plenty bad enough. No, he meant something else here. Something intimately between us. I was an idiot. "If I'd realized before, I could have made peace with it. Maybe it would be different, if I'd made the choice."

As he studied me, his lips twitched, in a not-smile. The black lines on his face seemed to unfurl then tighten again. His animal crawling near the skin. The Dog, pressing to escape. My own skin itched at the left temple and down my cheek, knowing how it felt.

"I've seen inside your head," he said. "I know what that did to you. Know something of it myself. Some prisons are worth self-destruction to escape."

"Thank you." I said it quietly, but with firm intent, knowing full well what such an expression of gratitude could mean.

He inclined his head, accepting it.

"You might have told me, though, about finding the earth," I added, with some asperity, to lighten his grave mood.

"I couldn't, no. First—" he raised a brow to stop my argument in its tracks, "—some teachings cannot be spoken or shown. You might consider them a sort of final exam. If a student cannot find the connection on their own, they will never be able to use it. Second, you were *thinking* too much. Sometimes teaching means shoving a student in the right direction and hoping she trips over it instead of her own wagging tongue."

"Ha-ha." Something occurred to me. "Who taught you?"

"Why do you ask?" he returned smoothly. Too smoothly.

"Son. Of. A. Bitch." I strung out the words, watching his face for the slightest twitch, chasing the fleeting thought through his mind. "It was *her*, wasn't it?"

Rogue gazed back, a world of memory passing behind his eyes. My turn to wait him out. With a mental sigh, he let me see. The boy running on the beach. Raven's feathers flying through the air, dense, denser until they blackened the skies. Crying out, the boy stumbled and Titania, all lissome loveliness and sugarcoated poison, smiled down at him. Swathed in impossibly long silver hair, fine as tinseled spiderwebs, she picked him up and took him by the hand, her delicate, multijointed fingers weaving with his, making him hers.

How I hated that bitch.

I looked around the arena with new appreciation. "This was her castle." That, too, showed in his memories. "At least, one part of it."

"It's mine now." He said it with implacable firmness, making me wonder how he'd managed to drive her out. A surge of pride filled me, for his indomitable strength of will. And deep sympathy for what he must have suffered, belonging to her then and again so recently. It made me love him all the more.

Something I hadn't been very good about showing him. So many fears and suspicions holding me back. I really needed to get over it.

I crawled the few feet over to him, the dirt soft on my declawed fingers, the skin there sensitive as new flesh, and pushed him onto his back. He gave way, curious, not quite certain of my intentions. Straddling his narrow hips, I perched on his flat abdomen, running my hands over his shirt, then parting it down the center. With the gleeful delight of a kid on Christmas morning, I pushed the material aside and bared his skin.

"As *you* are mine now," I told him. Titania would have a serious fight on her hands if she tried to take him away from me ever again.

"Is that so?" he asked, with something of a pleased look.

"Yes. Don't argue. I'm tired of you playing hard to get."

He laughed and lay back, letting me explore him as I hadn't been able to this past—had it only been a day? Surely it had been longer. At some point I'd likely need to sleep. For the time being, however, I felt wildly replete with life energy.

And I wanted him.

"No one will disturb us here, will they?"

He shook his head, slowly. "The door answers only to me. And, now, you."

"Good." I tugged at his sleeve and Rogue laughed again, a breathy sound, full of rising desire.

"It would be easier to magically dispense with it, sweet Gwynn."

"Shut up." I wrinkled my nose at him. "I'm enjoying doing this for myself."

Obligingly, perhaps a bit bemused, he levered up so I could pull the shirt off entirely. While he was upright, I freed his hair from the leather thong and brought the silky mass of it around to drape over his shoulder on the unpatterned side of his body, before I made him lie back again. Arranging the glossy locks into a long, trailing fan over his lean chest, I indulged myself in its texture, compared to the brushed satin feel of his skin.

Freed of the claws, I savored the winding of the thorned lines covering the left side of his body, how the black-patterned skin felt no different than the golden-hued rest of him, Following the path up, over his collarbone, throat and jaw, I finished at the cut-glass edge of his lip, where that vine ended in an infinitesimally fine point. Turning his head ever so slightly, Rogue pressed a kiss to my fingertip, his dark blue gaze finding mine and burning.

He lifted a hand and touched my left temple, tracing over my cheekbone to the corner of my mouth, with the same grave tenderness. Like him, I showed my internal animal on the surface of my skin. It had started as a branching line on my temple, silver-white. By the lingering glide of Rogue's finger, it had grown larger and more complex.

Soon it would engulf my body, too, leaving me unrecognizable.

"I will always know you, my Gwynn. Never fear that."

He pressed his other hand between my shoulder blades, urging me close enough for his lips to reach mine in a long, soul-searching kiss, then slid down to my thigh, pulling up my skirt.

I wriggled away. "No. Be still or shall tie *your* hands."

"Promises, promises." He smiled, wickedly, but stretched his arms obediently over his head, letting me have my way with him.

I'd done this once before, but I'd been tipsy, if not outright drunk. This time I wanted to learn him as he'd learned me, testing which kind of touch excited him most. His heart thumped and his unblemished belly fluttered as I kissed my way down it.

Finding the way to open his pants, I started to peel them off, pausing when I encountered the dagger at his hip, the silver blade searing me. I knew this knife—he'd held it to my throat once before—and it hadn't burned me then. A sign that the magic was infusing my tissues, transforming me as surely as a bombardment of gamma rays. Withdrawing the knife from its sheath, I looked up his body to find Rogue returning my gaze calmly.

"You didn't tell me you brought this."

"I didn't want to frighten you unnecessarily."

"Not this time."

He smiled ever so slightly. "You pay much better attention than you did then."

"Amazing how that works," I said drily, then cast the knife aside so it skidded through the dirt. "You're a ruthless bastard, you know."

"But you're not angry?"

"Nope." I grinned at him and freed his cock, grasping the solid length of his shaft in my hands. "After all, I'd do the same for you."

"Why doesn't that—" He broke off with a strangled sound when I cupped his balls and took him into my mouth.

After that, neither of us had much more to say.

PART 11

MASSAGING THE DATA

CHAPTER 10

IN WHICH I AM REUNITED WITH MY WACKY SIDEKICKS

&7₹

Like any society, Faerie has its social pariahs.

~Big Book of Fairyland, "Flora and Fauna"

STARLING, ATHENA, LARCH, along with my erstwhile supply caravan and entourage had arrived at the far edge of the moat by the time we emerged from the practice arena.

Though I was, naturally, relieved and delighted to have them safe, I tried not to feel like the honeymoon was over.

Rogue settled his hand on the back of my neck under the fall of my hair, rubbing lightly while we waited for the enormous drawbridge—it had to be the length of a football field—to lower its ponderous weight across the water. Teams of human men, brawny muscles flexing, shouted in unison as they worked the chains through the great wheels.

"Why a manual system?" I asked Rogue. "You're forever championing how much easier magic makes everything. And that thing has to weigh tons." Probably a lot more than that, but there were reasons I hadn't gone into engineering.

He stroked the hollow formed by the cavity below my occipital bone, one of my most erotically charged hidden points, as he'd discovered and loved to exploit. "What one sorcerer can affect magically, another can also. Try your magic against it."

I tested it in a nondamaging way. Wouldn't want to compromise castle security, after all. It did not turn bright pink with blue zigzags as I'd planned. Too bad, because I'd really wanted to see Rogue's face at that one. Alas. "Interesting. And stop that."

He stroked that point again and smiled down at me with warm desire. "Only to remind you that the *honeymoon,* as you so quaintly picture it, will never be over."

That got me and I shivered a little, but with heat.

"We don't have to wait for them." Rogue leaned in and brushed my left temple with a kiss. "Let me leave them a message that we'll join them for dinner tonight. Or breakfast tomorrow."

I peered at the bright light showing through the arched portal, not able to see the height of the sun. "How long from now is dinner? I'm suddenly starving."

"You know how to find out. And I'm not surprised, it's been days since you've eaten. Even magic cannot sustain your mortal flesh indefinitely."

"I hate how you say that like it's some fatal flaw." I groused about that instead of commenting on the passage of time. I'd been afraid of that very thing. Later I would check the mass-mind calendar and see if I could measure just how long it had been. While I was in there and at my leisure, I would do some exploring too. And take notes. "No," I answered his initial proposition, "I want to greet them."

"And welcome them to your new home," Rogue said, with implacable firmness.

"Yes, yes—lady of the castle, blah, blah, blah."

"As such, you might dress appropriately then."

I rolled my eyes but obliged, turning the very dusty gown I'd worn to the practice arena into a shimmering black velvet dress that matched Rogue's outfit.

He glanced at me with some surprise that I'd willingly donned his colors. "Thank you."

"Hey, I can play nice."

"Who knew?"

"Ha-ha."

By then the group had nearly made it to us. The creepy Cylon guards peeled off as they advanced, stationing themselves at regular intervals along the way. I supposed they had the virtue of perfect discipline, much as they raised my short hairs. Starling in the forefront clearly simmered with so much impatience that she easily kept up with Athena and Larch, though they were all on foot.

"Why are the horses staying behind?" It didn't make sense. "Do you stable them elsewhere?"

"In a sense. Once the people have entered, I will change the entrance the drawbridge leads to, so that the livestock and wagons go to the correct part of the castle."

"Including the human soldiers," I noted, seeing them still standing on the far bank.

"Don't start, stubborn Gwynn."

It was an old argument between us—though I felt a bit of nostalgic fondness that he and I even had old arguments—that

I disagreed with his total disregard for the human folk who lived in Faerie. They weren't exactly like the sort of people I'd left at home, but neither were they *livestock*.

"These guys are in the main part of the castle." I indicated the men resting by the drawbridge chains, preparing to pull it up again. "Shouldn't we banish them below-stairs or some such?"

"We'll discuss it later then." He gave the nape of my neck one last sweet caress before stepping aside as Starling ran the last few steps and barreled into me, seizing me in a fierce embrace.

"Gwynn!" Starling nearly shouted in my ear. "You didn't die!"

I couldn't help it, I laughed, though my sore ribs creaked under her grip. "No, I didn't. I'm just fine."

She laughed too, and pulled back, wiping away a couple of tears. "I know I'm silly, but I—we—were *so* worried about you, and look at you!" Her gaze fastened on the left side of my face, her expression not horrified but certainly shocked. She quickly looked away from it. "What did you do to your hair?"

I put a hand to my hair, feeling the wild snarls. A telling sign that I'd been totally absorbed in Rogue. I cast him an irritated look. "Why didn't you mention it?"

He shrugged. "I thought you'd adopted a new style."

I sighed to myself. So alien and yet still so *male*. The scene out the arched door had changed to a lovely view of the river, with the moat monster serenely gliding by.

"Happy to see you, Sorceress Gwynn—" Athena gave me a cheeky smile, "—no matter the hairstyle. Too bad about the claws though."

"Don't you worry—I have them close to hand." I winked at her and she grinned in appreciation at the joke.

"My Lady Sorceress." Larch bowed with his usual gravity.

"Welcome to the Castle of the Dark Gods," I said to them, trying to sound gracious and comfortable with it. Rogue settled a hand in the small of my back. "Lord Rogue and I bid you, um, welcome."

Athena snickered and I glared at her. Clearly I needed to practice this.

"I add my *welcome* to Lady Gwynn's," Rogue inserted with considerably more suave charm. "I'll have servants show you to your rooms, so you may rest and freshen yourselves before you meet us for the welcome feast."

I managed not to roll my eyes at the phrase "welcome feast." Rogue knew—hell, they all knew—how much I hated the endless fairy feasts. In the background, the men renewed their chant. The view had changed back to the drawbridge and they were hauling it up again. Had the rest of my soldiers made it over? I glanced up at Rogue and he nodded, answering before I could ask.

"Meet you?" Starling's happy mien crumbled at the edges. "Am I not still your maidservant? You've cast me aside then. All right, I imagine the maidservants at the Castle of the Dark Gods are ever so much more *special* and—"

"Would you stop?" I interrupted her tirade. "I don't have a new maidservant, okay?"

"Well, that explains the hair," she muttered.

"I've been busy." Mostly having a lot of sex, but also dealing with stubborn elemental spirits too. And healing. "But you can come fix me up for dinner if it makes you happy. Lord

Rogue only thought you might want to relax a little."

Rogue's hand drifted down my lower back to just brush the top curve of my bottom, a reminder that he'd had something else in mind.

Darling Hercules trotted up just then, waving his tail in hellos, and informing me that the mouse population of the castle had rebounded in his long absence, but that he was working on it.

Goliath, he reminded me.

"We're not in battle," I told him. "We all agree that, since Goliath is your battle name, it should be reserved for that very special occasion." I widened my eyes at the others, who hastily nodded in agreement. Except for Rogue, who looked coolly amused.

Darling Hercules considered and, to my surprise, agreed. Then asked about supper. With a resounding boom, the drawbridge connected with the castle, sealing us in once again.

"So, my Lady Gwynn," Rogue said, taking my hand, turning it over and pressing a burning kiss to my palm, "since you will be busy being appropriately groomed by Lady Starling and I have business to take care of, I shall take your leave until the feast."

I narrowed my eyes at him. "What business? Don't tell me the minions aren't sufficiently oppressed."

"Nothing interesting," he replied breezily. "Besides, I'm sure you'll want to start *your* minions on planning the wedding."

Starling squealed like some tropical monkey and clapped her hands together. "A royal wedding! At last. I *told* you true love would triumph in the end."

I ignored her, concentrating on scowling at Rogue for throwing me to the wolves. He grinned, completely unrepentant, then tugged my hand and pulled me in for a kiss that turned considerably steamier than appropriate in front of friends.

Just as I resolved to push him away, he broke the kiss, giving me a very smug look, and strolled away. "I'll return in time to escort you to the feast, my lady," he called over his shoulder.

Starling sighed on a long croon of delight. "He is positively dreamy."

"He's positively an asshole, is more like it." I gazed after him, proud of myself for summoning the correct sour tone but unable to keep from admiring his very fine form. With a bit of a wrench, it hit me that we hadn't been apart in days—or however long. And here I missed him already. Whoa. I seriously needed to take a step back.

"My Lady Sorceress?" Larch spoke up. "Do you wish me to stay or go?"

"Go?" I echoed blankly.

"The Castle of Dark Gods houses many pages. You may not have need of me, in your new household." His blueberry face looked stolid as always, giving no clue to his preferences.

"Well, do you *want* to go home? Or back to Falcon's camp? It's really up to you."

"If you no longer wish to employ me as your page, I would as soon not stay, as I would have to find a new place in the hierarchy here."

"He means it would suck, Gwynn," Athena put in, pulling out her dagger and spinning it in a complex pattern so it wove between her fingers, like coin artists would do back home. She'd been practicing. "He'd probably get stuck scrubbing pots or something. You owe him better than that."

Larch purpled and glowered at her. "The most powerful Sorceress Gwynn owes neither you nor me anything, you upstart fairy. You're lucky they even let you—"

"Kids." I held up my hands in a referee's gesture. At least it wasn't Starling and Athena bickering this time. "You all saved my life more than once and you're also my friends. Of course I owe you. I haven't seen any sign of Rogue having a personal page, so why don't you continue as mine—I mean, ours. Would that work?"

Larch puffed with pride, something that made his fireplug body look a bit more like a plump blueberry. "I shall serve you faithfully and well, my Lady Gwynn! With your permission, I shall familiarize myself with the staff."

"You don't need my permission, Larch. Have at it."

He trotted off wearing an imperious air that made him seem taller somehow.

"You realize you probably just completely overturned the entire chain of command in this place, right?" Athena looked more amused by this possibility than anything.

"That's Lady Gwynn's right. After all, Lord Rogue made it clear that she carries equal authority. She may do as she sees fit. And, with her new station, you should call her Lady Gwynn all the time now." Starling finished the reprimand with a little sniff.

He did? I supposed he had. He'd been saying as much to me, though I hadn't quite assimilated the import of that. "No, you should both call me Gwynn or I'll have to kick you.

Besides, we're not married yet."

"How about that royal wedding, huh?" Athena needled me, her lovely lavender eyes sharp with sarcastic humor. "Gonna have a big fancy dress with a crippling train?"

"No," I said.

"Yes," Starling said more loudly, at the same moment, then sent me a firm look.

Athena burst out laughing and pointed her dagger at me. "You are so in for it, Gwynn. Can I be the flower girl?"

"Absolutely. If I can dress you in cotton-candy-pink ruffles."

She snorted at that, very much the same sound of derision I made when amused. "You'll note that *I* did not ask if I could stay, because I plan to stick around. Plus I've never seen the famous Castle of the Dark Gods. Darling Hercules, care to give me the tour?"

The cat, with a fondness for the fairy girl he showed few others, waved his tail and they wandered off.

"She's gotten an enormous attitude," Starling complained. "You really need to take her in hand."

"Athena is fine." In truth, I felt more than a little guilt for the spell I'd worked on her. She was like the small-town girl who'd gone off for an Ivy League education and now had no one to talk to at home. I couldn't imagine where she'd go, if she didn't stay with us. Besides, I liked her. "She's just figuring out who she is. Come on, I'll show you our bedchamber." At least, I thought I could find it again.

Maybe I should have gone on the tour with Athena and Darling Hercules.

"That's not appropriate. It's her place to be told who she is—and yours to tell her."

I looked sidelong at Starling. "Are you just cranky from the journey or is something else eating you?"

She tipped up her pert nose. "It's part of my job to be aware of your social status and manage your staff accordingly."

"First of all, I don't have a staff, and second, Athena wouldn't be part of it anyway."

"Are you sure this is the correct direction?"

I frowned at the great winding staircase. It looked just like the one on the opposite side of the elephant-sized hall. And like the one at the shadowed end. All no doubt led to different towers. The whole complex was like a giant puzzle-box. "Well...I'm not sure," I confessed. "I haven't been wandering around all that much."

"No?" She drew out the word with impish delight, seeming much more her familiar playful self. "What *have* you been doing, hmmm?"

"None of your business," I muttered, more than a little chagrined.

"Here, you." Starling snapped her fingers, startling me and grabbing the attention of a passing purple sprite. "Show us to the Lady Gwynn's chambers and be quick about it."

The sprite bowed, literally scraping its bulbous head on the stone floor, then scampered toward a fourth staircase entirely.

"One of your staff," Starling said, with a little simper.

"Gee, it's so nice to have you back, Starling."

"I know." She giggled at herself. "It's lovely to see that you need me. Tell me I get to plan the wedding."

What had seemed like a fine idea when I flippantly suggested it to Rogue kind of scared me now.

"No trains."

"You *have* to have one. It's expected. You wouldn't want to bring shame on Lord Rogue, would you?"

"No, no—heaven forbid I should do that."

"Exactly," she replied, apparently oblivious to my sarcasm. "People will already be expecting the worst. You leave everything to me and it will be a brilliant affair. It will be the richest, fanciest, most glamorous wedding Faerie has ever seen! This is an awful lot of stairs. Don't tell me your chambers are at the very top."

"Of the tallest tower," I couldn't resist capping the question. "You don't seem to be lacking for breath, however."

"Ha-ha. You deserve better than this, Gwynn. Really. It's not done. Prisoners are kept at the tops of the tallest towers, not—oh great Titania!?"

We'd emerged into the crystal dome, ablaze with the lowering sun, so ripples of gold fire and rosy pink shimmered through the transparent walls. Down below, a pair of moat monsters played, their scales glittering as they arced up out of the river and splashed down again. A vase of virulently blue Stargazer lilies sat on my workbench, along with a pitcher of wine and a tray of cheese and bread. The man never missed a beat. I gazed at the wine with longing, realizing that I shouldn't be drinking it. Though I had been, not thinking I could be pregnant before recently. Recalling the fetal alcohol syndrome studies, I knew a glass or so a day would be well below the titres. I'd just have to limit it. Alas.

"What in the world is this?" Starling spun in a slow circle and breathed the question in a tone of reverent awe.

"This, my friend—" I grabbed a chunk of cheese and poured us both wine, half a glass for me. "—is true love."

CHAPTER 11

THE PATTERN, THE BATH AND THE WARDROBE

I've noted before that the facial patterns on some fae seem to be a barometer of the animal within. Further observations indicate the phenomenon goes deeper than that. Rather than a symptom or side effect, the pattern might be the disease itself.

~Big Book of Fairyland, "The Black Dog/White Cat"

OKAY, MAYBE A little overly dramatic, but one good thing about Faerie was that I could get away with the occasional grandiose statement.

Besides, no one had ever gone to this much trouble to see me happy. Rogue deserved at least that much credit. Starling surveyed the room more critically. "I see. Well, it's certainly unusual—we can play up that angle for the glamour. And it's very *you*, isn't it?"

Yes. It really was.

"I don't see a tub. Where have you been bathing?"

I swallowed an overly large bite of cheese—it felt like I'd

never be full again—and contemplated how to answer that. Probably the bathing chamber was secret, what with the hidden magic elevator and "Don't speak it outside these walls" thing. Also we needed a mirror, particularly if I was going to supervise whatever diabolical hairstyle Starling had planned for me.

"Oh! I see, through here," Starling called out, saving me the trouble. She'd found another recessed door and I dutifully followed her down a flight of stairs. The bathing and dressing chamber filled the entire floor beneath the bedchamber, with floor-to-ceiling windows all around. Nice that I wouldn't miss the spectacular sunset underway. A large mirrored central pillar boasted an elaborate vanity table on one side and a walk-in closet on the other.

Starling had already disappeared inside the closet, making all sorts of happy sounds. "This, at least, is as it should be," her muffled voice pronounced.

"Good God." I halted in my tracks. It looked like the interior of a high-end boutique. Racks of clothes in every color imaginable lined the walls, and several black-velvet benches perched in strategic locations, in case I wanted to sit and contemplate my wardrobe. "Isn't part of the point of being able to magic things up that we don't need to have all kinds of stuff lying about?"

"No," Starling answered in prim disapproval. "You have rank to uphold. It's expected."

That word again. "I've never been all that comfortable with people having expectations of me."

"Then get used to it," she advised. "General Falcon has nothing on some of these society dames, believe me. They'll spot one of your magicked-up gowns in a second and gossip about it no end. There are reasons I've tried to get you to be more careful of your real clothes."

"They might not be able to." I regretted leaving the cheese tray upstairs. "I bet I could spell a gown to be indistinguishable from any of these."

"Sure and you could. If you actually paid attention to them and made the effort. But you don't care enough."

She had a point. And smiled when I didn't argue it.

"All right then, I'll call to have the tub filled and—"

"I'll do it." I stopped her. "My magic may be too blue-collar for high society, but I can do hot water." More, I didn't care to encounter those weird drudgelike creatures who had performed manual labor such as carrying buckets of water on my last visit. More of Rogue's mind-control, enslavement techniques that gave me the heebie-jeebies.

"Which gown do you—"

"You choose." I started to get the wine and cheese, then remembered my new trick and summoned them to a little table next to the tub. Made of a pearly substance reminiscent of the deep interior of a conch shell, the tub looked big enough for two. A man for detail, my Rogue. Speaking of details—"But nothing too froufrou!" I called to Starling, then smiled to myself at her irritated reply.

I had missed her and definitely needed her for the apparent minefield to come.

Judging by the dirt that washed off my skin and knotted hair, I'd done more than a bit of rolling around on the arena floor. Also, I'd been apparently absorbed enough in the question of Titania's previous visits and on dealing with the hampering claws that I'd never combed out my hair after Rogue washed it for me. Something Starling went on about at some length as she did the washing this time—which I let her do because it made her so happy.

All this time I'd avoided looking in the mirror, frankly afraid of what I'd see. The time had come for it, however, and I sat in the vanity chair as instructed. Starling dove into detangling my locks with such great enthusiasm that I bore the painful tugging and didn't add any magical unsnarling assistance. Plus the distraction helped me avoid looking too closely at my face.

Finally she finished and I looked, seeing my eyes go wide in my paling face.

The pattern had grown exponentially. What had been a small tendril of silver at my temple now spiraled with metallic brilliance around my left eye, over my forehead and cheekbone, then down to my mouth, jaw and trailed off into fine points on my throat. Spiking out from the lines, which were unmistakably more sinuous and feline than the ones on Rogue's body, like thorns on a climbing rose vine, were finely honed claws.

The similarity to the blood-poisoning streaks didn't escape me. A contamination of another sort, the cat spirit's magic infecting me, affecting the composition of my skin and very likely more. Only this toxicity wouldn't kill me when it reached my heart.

I hoped.

Interesting—and perhaps salient—that the corruption originated at my temple, like a brain tumor that eventually revealed its presence through changes in the surrounding bone and surface tissues. Something to consider. Would I have time to make notes on this before the feast?

Following on that thought came the realization that I'd be able to handle this too. Inside, I remained myself, with my same thoughts. The external didn't matter. The cat chuckled, somewhere in the vicinity of my heart, and I ignored her.

By way of settling myself and fixing up for the party, I "did" my makeup, magically adding the colors and shadings I would have used in my old life. Might as well make an effort to look nice tonight. Though it warmed me that Rogue hadn't apparently cared about my rat's nest snarls and smudged appearance. It certainly hadn't dampened his ardor any, which spoke well of him and argued well for our long-term chances, since I was unlikely to improve on that front.

The clawed vines around my left eye gave me a bit of trouble. I couldn't change the color of that skin, which didn't really surprise me. More troubling, when I wished up eye shadow and a brush—mostly for experiment's sake—I couldn't cover over the pattern either. The powder fell away, much as water parts and beads off on an oily surface.

No hiding who you are.

Starling, with her innate talent for knowing what I most needed, had left me alone for this confrontation with my new face. Now she bustled back in with the dress she'd chosen.

"All right then?" Her tentative smile told me she'd understood far more of how I was feeling than I thought. Come to think of it, she hadn't said as much while I bathed as she usually did. Tremendous restraint on her part.

So I resolved to play nice and put on the dress she liked— even though it reminded me of Scarlett O'Hara's mourning ball gown, with easily twice the flounces and entirely covered in glittering black jewels. The thing had to weigh fifteen pounds. All in the skirt because the long, glove-tight sleeves ended at my upper arms, leaving my shoulders—and, more notably, most of my cleavage—totally bare. To exacerbate the situation, the bodice fit more like a corset, complete with laces up the back, which worked to raise my breasts into alarming mounds.

Sue me if I tried to tug up the neckline a little. Though that was a misnomer—more like nipple line.

Starling smacked my hand away. "Stop that. And no magical additions, either."

"It's a little much for an evening home with friends, isn't it?"

"This is the welcome feast. Weren't you listening?"

"Apparently not closely enough. Aren't we just welcoming you guys?"

She sighed, shaking her head so her golden hair swept her shoulders with its paintbrush-thick ends, and tightened the bodice laces more. "No, Gwynn. This is to welcome *you*. As the new Lady of the Castle of the Dark Gods. Everyone who can manage to be here will be, to look you over, if nothing else. And to make sure to wrangle an invitation to the wedding—which, as I've mentioned, will be the event to attend. They'll be looking to curry favor with you too."

I groaned, summoned my glass of wine and took a hearty—no, a tiny—sip. "Kill me now."

"Sit." She gave me a little shove back to the vanity chair, then took up various implements of destruction to put my hair up in some elaborate, formal do.

"Yes, yes." I glowered at her in the mirror. "Sit. Stay. Roll over. Get married."

"You didn't look unhappy about it when Lord Rogue kissed you in the hallway. In fact, you absolutely glowed."

"Well," I conceded, hating that I actually blushed, "I like that part quite a lot."

"Do tell."

"Absolutely not."

"Oh, come on, Gwynn." Starling pouted, but her brown eyes sparkled. "Just tell me if he's amazing in bed."

"No."

"Let this old spinster live vicariously through you."

"I don't want to discuss this and you're hardly a spinster."

"I only want to know if the stories are true."

"What stories?" I bit on her bait without thinking.

"Ha!" She pointed a jeweled hairpin at my reflection. "Now she wants to discuss it."

"That was a cheap trick and I've changed my mind. Don't tell me. You know what they say—comparisons are invidious."

"Who says that?"

"Very wise people."

She sniffed at that and fell silent for a few moments. "Have you heard from Walter?" she asked, in a much too casual tone.

"No one is going to hear from that idiot in a very long time."

"Don't call him that."

I studied her face in the mirror and mentally reviewed some of her interactions with Walt. Another human immigrant, but far more contemporary to me, though he'd been in Faerie much longer—yet another time-flow conundrum—

Walter was also able to work magic. He'd also tried to kill me in a duel. I'd happily won but had been unhappily tasked with sentencing him.

When he insisted on getting the kind of training I'd received...well, I hadn't wanted to but I had finally agreed. I'd been a little freaked out about seeing my torturers again—and by Walter's suicidal impulse to be trained by them—so I hadn't really paid much attention to Starling as an "and Walter" scenario. But they had been talking up a storm on the way to Marquise and Scourge's domicile of pain and humiliation.

"You're not sweet on that little shit, are you?"

She thumped my shoulder with the hairbrush.

"Ow!"

"Oh, that didn't hurt," she snapped back. "And that was mean. Don't call him excrement."

"Walter is in terrible physical condition, smells bad, lacks all social skills and doesn't even have very much intelligence. Plus he's a humbug and will be lucky to come out of that training with his sanity, if he makes it out at all. He's not for you."

Starling put her fists on her hips. "You're not usually cruel. What is your problem?"

"That's not cruel—or mean. I just don't want you getting starry-eyed and pining away for this guy who looks much more enticing for being physically and emotionally unavailable."

She finished my hair in silence, hurt wafting off her. Maybe I had been harsh. What I'd said was the truth, but had I really needed to vocalize all that? There might be more balancing with this cat spirit than I'd considered. Her predator's perspective left little room for delicacy and consideration.

"I'm sorry," I offered, as she completed the final touches. "Walt hoped that the training would make him a better person as well as a more effective wizard—he said as much to me. Maybe he'll emerge as a guy good enough for you."

She didn't respond immediately—and didn't meet my gaze in the mirror, either. Then she wiped her nose with the back of her hand and I felt worse.

"Look," I added, "if you want me to, I'll use the crystal scepter to spy on what's going on over there, see how he's doing."

Now she looked up. "Really? You would do that?"

"Yes, I will." I said it firmly, to make the promise to myself not to back out of it. Never mind that it was a good excuse to get my hands on the scepter again. I felt much better now and I kind of itched to experiment with it.

"That means a lot to me. But I know how you feel about that place and...revisiting anything that happened there. Don't look. It won't change anything anyway. Besides, I doubt he's interested in someone like me."

The self-deprecation in her voice just about killed me. "That's ridiculous, Starling." I stood and took her hands. "This is exactly what concerns me. You are lovely and smart, so talented in so many ways, plus you're a plain wonderful, caring person. This thing where you worry that no guy will ever want you is destructive. Don't settle. Hold out for the best."

"Like you did." She sniffled a little, eyes filled with tears.

"Believe me. I was all set to settle before I got whisked into Faerie. It's easy to do. Much easier than holding out. You have to wait for the right one to come along. Sometimes it takes a while."

"What do I do in the meantime?" She nearly wailed it, as she pulled her hands away and started some rabid tidying up.

"You have the wedding to plan, right? And everyone is counting on it being the event of the century, so it really gives you a chance to shine." I couldn't believe myself, but there it was. "And after that, well, this is a huge castle complex—it will need organizing and looking after. I can't do it, for sure." And then it all would go out the window if Titania attacked, but I wasn't going to bring that up right then.

"Th—that's Mother's job, as your seneschal." Starling hiccupped.

"Aha! But Blackbird isn't *here*, is she?"

It would be interesting to find out if they had discovered anything more about Brody's fate. Of course, my new theory that the babies, if they survived Titania's vicious testing process, were now changelings in my old world altered the situation.

I wouldn't say anything on that yet, since I had no supporting evidence. How could I possibly test that hypothesis? Would the scepter see through the Veil? Something else to test out tomorrow.

"Mother *did* say, when she first sent me to you, that I might rise to that role someday. Seneschal of the greatest castle in the land." Starling peeked at me through her bangs and I pretended to scowl at her.

"She totally set me up for this, didn't she?"

Starling sighed. "She does plan ahead—very efficient that way."

Yes. I recalled very well how efficiently she'd managed me.

The noble Fae could give Japanese corporations a run for their money with long-term strategizing. "Okay, the job is yours, so far as I'm concerned."

With a happy squeal, Starling hugged me, clinging like a barnacle.

Hopefully Rogue wouldn't object. But this was what he got for handing me authority. Probably better for him to learn right away what kind of wife I'd be. I cringed at my own thought. "Wife" sounded so…staid. And here I'd been running around barefoot and pregnant too.

"Okay." I patted her on the back. "You need time to get ready for the feast, also, right?"

"Oh, gracious!" She let me go and pivoted to take in her reflection. "And I look a fright. I'll go find my rooms straight away."

"You could stay here. I'll magic you a fresh bath and you can borrow one of my ten thousand dresses."

She was already shaking her head. "Not done, Gwynn. And don't you dare make a similar offer to Athena because the little twit won't know better and then we'll all look bad."

"Yes, ma'am."

She wrinkled her nose at me. "You look lovely, if I do say so. I'll see you at the feast."

She raced off and, alone at last, I carried my cheese tray back upstairs, resolutely leaving the wine behind and happily settling myself at the workbench. Full night had fallen outside the dome, but all the towers and walls were ablaze with tall torches at regular intervals, too bright for me to see the stars.

Opening my *Big Book of Fairyland*, I flipped to the section I'd titled "The Black Dog" and modified it to say "The Black

Dog/White Cat." Then I set to writing down as many of my observations as I could, from the way the claws had torn out of me during the fight with Titania to the struggle in the practice arena and how my facial pattern appeared.

I wished up a standing cosmetic mirror, so I could look in it and attempt to draw the pattern at this moment in time. Being able to chart its growth might be important. Stymied, as always, by how to apply a date the entry, I decided finally to call it Day 0. Then I created new pages at the back of the book and began sketching a timeline, with Day 0 about a third of the way down the page.

I added salient details to remember this day by—leaving the practice arena, the gang's arrival and the Welcome Feast. Adding a few hash marks to be filled in when I figured out exactly how many days it had been, I put a *Day 3?* for my arrival at Rogue's castle. It would have to do.

Going back to the original section, I sketched the facial pattern as it had been the last time I remembered looking. When had that been? Back at Walter's castle maybe. I should have kept a better record of it. But there hadn't been that much to it—a curl on my temple, a suggestion of branches, a hint of a curved claw at the high point of my cheekbone.

"There she is." Rogue's hands caressed my bare shoulders, soothing my little start of surprise. "My scientist in her natural habitat."

I turned my head to look up at him. "You listen to my thoughts more than is healthy."

"But I find you fascinating, my studious Gwynn." He leaned down and kissed me, a sweet kiss that rapidly deepened. The desire for him seemed to burn constantly, easily stoked into full flame with the slightest breath from his tantalizing mouth. Humming with pleasure, he dropped a hand to cup my breast and I arched into it. "You look as lovely in this dress as I'd imagined." He pulled back to eye my prodigious cleavage.

"Let's just hope I don't fall out of it during the feast."

"That would be entertainment indeed." Caressing my nipple, he leaned in again to brush my patterned temple with a kiss. "However, I prefer to keep such sights all to myself."

I reached up and wound a lock of his silky hair around my fingers. "Then let's stay here. Skip the feast."

He laughed and, neatly untangling himself from my grip, stepped out of reach. Also in black, but matte where mine sparkled, trim compared to my flouncy self, he looked amazing in the same way male celebrities in Armani tuxes outshone any couture dress on the red carpet. "I would be flattered by my lady's great desire for me, if I didn't know you'd prefer anything to a feast."

"Maybe not *anything*," I grumbled, standing up and straightening the dress. I would have magicked the neckline higher, if Starling hadn't made me promise not to, damn her foresight. "Fine. Let's go."

"First I have a gift for you. Two gifts, actually."

CHAPTER 12

IN WHICH I RECEIVE SOMETHING (MOSTLY) UNEXPECTED

Interesting how Rogue treats my values and idle whims with the same gravity as any covenant. I suppose in Faerie, nothing is truly without deeper meaning.

~Big Book of Fairyland, "Rules of Magic"

I OPENED MY mouth to protest—or negotiate—then remembered that no longer applied between us. However, I felt enough on the short side of the gift-giving at this point that I wasn't thrilled to accept more. I still couldn't quite drop the bargaining habit I'd so painstakingly acquired.

Gifts in Faerie always came with a price.

"Okay," I said, trying to keep my tone neutral.

Amused, probably by my obvious reticence, Rogue nevertheless didn't comment. "The first gift I've had planned for some time, as you'll see." He held up his hands and a necklace appeared, hanging delicately between them. Made of inverted Stargazer lilies in shades from deepest indigo at the centers to the barest pale blue of midsummer sky, glowing like living flesh, they matched the flowers dangling from my ears.

Though Starling had piled the front part of my hair on top of my head, the rest trailed down my back in elaborate ringlets, so I turned my back and held it out of the way while Rogue draped the fabulous creation around my throat. The largest of the grouping hung at the lowest point, like a pendant, exactly at the valley between my breasts.

I looked in the mirror on my workbench. It was beyond exquisite and the woman looking back at me seemed more like some elfin princess than anyone I recognized. *Let it go, Gwynn.*

"Thank you." I faced him again, feeling self-conscious for some reason. "It's very beautiful."

He seemed pleased, but oddly uncomfortable also. Unusual for him. Made me wonder what all lay in store for the night ahead. I would have brought up that he hadn't fully filled me in on the importance of this feast, but that was typical of him and one of those things I'd likely have to learn to live with, so I made an effort to set that irritation aside.

We all had our flaws.

Rogue came closer and toyed with the lowest hanging lily, examining it closely, his thoughts elusive. Fidgeting.

"And the second gift?" I prompted, terribly curious about what could have the eternally unflappable Rogue acting what I would call nervous on any other person. Of course, the man lacked nerves—or they were made of tensile steel—so that couldn't be it.

He met my gaze then, his eyes as vivid as the lilies. "I find myself at a loss, it's true, my Gwynn. I want to do this correctly and I feel strongly this should occur before we meet our guests, but I'm uncertain as to the correct protocol. I don't want to make a critical error."

That made *me* nervous and I sealed up my reaction as deeply as I could. What the hell did he have up his sleeve? Just when we were learning to grow easier with one another, he wanted to give me a gift that could be a critical error. I laced my fingers together so I wouldn't reach for my throat.

Please, not a collar. With a pitch of stomach-sinking apprehension, I feared he planned to coerce me into exactly that. I'd refuse. We could stay here all night and fight about it, miss the feast and insult our guests, but I would not let him bend me on this one.

"Ah," he reflected in an even quieter tone, "and now you've gone silent. No reassurance from my lady that I could do no such thing."

I made myself look him in the eye and not lose myself in how deeply I wanted to tell him that very thing. The words in my mouth like dusty moths, instead I said, "I wish—in the abstract way—that I could promise that. But it wouldn't be true."

He sighed. "And you would not be who you are if it were. Very well. I shall have to take my chances and hope for forgiveness should I blunder, since blind trust is out of the question." He let go the necklace and opened his hand. "My forever Gwynn—"

"Maybe you should wait," I blurted out, really not ready to fight with him.

Narrowing his eyes, he studied me, then shook his head, an abrupt shake that reminded me of a dog shedding water. "No. Tonight we present ourselves as a betrothed couple and you said you required this. I will not let *that*, at least, jeopardize our agreement."

That I required? What had...? I stared in shock at the diamond ring on his palm.

Of all the ridiculous things. He'd taken that stupid remark about engagement rings seriously—but of course he had—and, worse, I started crying. Just a few tears, but they flowed faster than I could wipe them and pretend they hadn't happened.

Rogue's face fell. "Is it wrong?"

"No." The one word was all I could get out before I had to swallow down the excess emotion. The diamond was like nothing I'd ever seen—cut in a perfect sphere with minute facets, brilliantly refracting the light. No human of my world cut have cut a gem like this. "I'm an idiot. This is perfect. But you really didn't have to."

"You should agree to this marriage in the tradition of your people too."

"It's kind of a dumb tradition, really." To my surprise, though, it did mean something to me. My mother would have gone crazy over this and she would never know, which only made more tears fall.

"Is the weeping part of it?"

I laughed, watery, and pressed the heels of my hands into the corners of my eyes. "Apparently. Okay, let me get a grip here." At least magical makeup didn't run when you cried. "All right, I'm ready."

"What do I do?" Rogue's eyebrow winged up. At least he wasn't nervous anymore, which helped immensely.

Feeling a bit silly, I held out my left hand and pointed to my ring finger. "You just slide it on this finger."

"I did not magic this up, since you said it shouldn't be

made that way, so it might not fit. Is it against the rules to adjust the size that way?"

"That is well within the rules," I replied, working hard not to laugh.

His magic whispered out, a tiny touch of black and blue, eddying around the ring as he slipped it on my finger. "Now what?" he asked, still holding my hand.

"That's it."

"No promises to go with it?"

"You already asked and I agreed, so that part's done." He looked unconvinced so I added, "The ring symbolizes the vow. It comes from an older tradition, where you make a vow and then never remove the ring until it's complete."

"So be it then," Rogue affirmed and a bit of magic shimmered around us, cementing it into place. With a slight smile, he bent over my hand to kiss the ring, holding my gaze all the while.

"Rogue," I breathed his name, groping for more words to express what this gesture meant to me and settled for something he'd once said to me. "You undo me."

His eyes went to my cleavage, then roamed over the rest of me. "I would love to undo you from that dress, but we would be late to greet our guests."

"*Traditionally*, my people would celebrate this moment with sex and champagne. Maybe chocolate-dipped strawberries too." I raised my eyebrows at him, going for a convincing expression, but he only laughed.

"You are a terrible liar, my gorgeous Gwynn. When you mean to hide how you feel and what you want most, it's clear as day in your mind. The feast will not last all night."

"Why should this one be any different?" I groused.

"Because this is our home and we decide."

I did like the sound of that.

ℰᵗₑ

UNLIKE THE FIRST reception and banquet I'd attended at the Castle of the Dark Gods—again on Rogue's arm, but this time with considerably more awareness of what was going on, not to mention feeling like I looked pretty fabulous—we did not circulate and mingle before sitting down. Probably why they'd all referred to it as a "reception" plus banquet before and "feast" this time.

Rogue seated me on his right at a carved wooden table on a raised platform that overlooked the football-field of a banquet room. Tall swathes of filmy color draped from the ceiling, banners without emblems, softening the stone walls. A group of assorted fae played instruments, adding a merry tune to the proceedings, though fortunately without the hypnotic crooning song they sometimes added.

I perched on the edge of the massive wood chair, which was heavier than I could move on my own, with arms that met the edge of the table if I wanted to reach my plate. Furniture built for noble fae with their long limbs and unearthly strength, not for on-the-short-side human women.

I glanced at Rogue and mentally tested the composition of the chair. Handmade and by some human man whose face I could nearly make out in my mind. Not magic. Rogue returned my look with an inquiring lift of his brows. Smiling sweetly, I changed the chair into something lighter, a bit higher, with a ledge for my feet to rest on, instead of dangling like a child's.

He inclined his head in wordless agreement, altered his chair to match in general appearance and picked up my left hand, kissing the skin just above the ring.

Who said we weren't getting better at communicating?

The guests began to file in, entering through the great doors—easily two stories in a human building—directly opposite and mincing down a long black runner, to bow and curtsy before us. To begin, most seemed to be the statuesque and willowy noble fae—all the best people—but the other castle denizens soon mingled in. Various sprites and pixies skipped through and paid homage in their ways. The petite fairies I thought of as dragonfly girls danced down the black carpet in their wispy gowns and adorable curls, filling the air with musical giggles. Some types of fae I didn't recall having seen before and I tried to keep track, so as to add them to the *Flora and Fauna* section of my grimoire.

A page of Larch's Brownie ilk stood by the doors, announcing them, but the names, most of which I heard as designations or descriptions anyway, washed into a blur after a while. If I'd been thinking, I would have had Athena nearby to record them all with her eidetic memory, so I could transcribe them into my list later. Letting my eyes travel over the room and the tables that filled as more guests paid their respects, I spotted Athena standing beside, of all things, a potted palm, Darling Hercules at her side. She saw me looking and gave me a jaunty thumbs-up.

Perfect. Then I frowned at her dress—a rainbow-hued gossamer dream that I knew she wouldn't have willingly worn in a million years, but typical for a dragonfly girl outfit. She fingered the material, made a gagging gesture and shrugged.

It was a bit of a reach for me, across the great hall and with milling, chattering people between, but I concentrated and changed the dress to a deep amethyst velvet sheath that would complement her eyes. With a broad grin, Athena put her hands together in a *Namaste* position and bowed.

Uncanny the things she'd picked up from my head.

"You spoil that one," Rogue spoke in my ear and handed me a shimmering crystal glass filled with ruby-red wine.

"Is that a problem?" I asked in all honesty, surveying his expression. He looked a bit exasperated, but not angry. I tasted the wine, braced for the Kool-Aid sweet stuff the fae tended to serve, pleasantly surprised by the smoky warmth of it. Too bad I couldn't drink much of it.

"Not yet. But the other servants will notice and there will be trouble. Also, in your inattention, you snubbed Lord and Lady Ladybug."

I couldn't help it, I giggled. "Really? I mean, oh no."

He took my hand, thumb passing over the diamond. "Truly. Perhaps it's for the best that you were only distracted and not laughing in their faces."

Another couple, covered in matching outfits of salmon-pink feathers, came up and bowed. I practiced looking regal, going for a Grace Kelly style of poise, managing to hold it until they finished saying their inane social things that always translated as utter nonsense or outright lies to me—a huge reason I abhorred these sorts of social occasions—and wandered off to be seated.

"Better?"

"A noble effort." Rogue sounded not at all convincing.

"Hey, you knew I was socially challenged when you roped me into this gig."

"True. I'm not marrying you for your hostessing skills."

"Nice. Be honest—am I screwing this up? Starling said tonight is important."

"You're doing fine. Just pay attention when they address you, nod, smile. And control your temper on this next one," he added, squeezing my hand.

Uh-oh. I followed his gaze only to see one of my top five least favorite people in Faerie. A notable achievement, as I had a lot of folks on that list. Lady Incandescence—though I liked to call her Nasty Tinker Bell, due to her irascible personality and arrogant attitude, and for nearly pouring soup over my head when I was an invalid—pranced down the black runner, totally naked but for her porno-blond hair and a pair of transparent heels with black ribbons that crisscrossed her long legs to finish in a petite bow at her crotch. The first time I saw her I'd thought she could be Rogue's fraternal twin. Over time I'd become better at distinguishing the fae features and now saw she looked nothing like him, other than being the same species.

"Who does she think she is," I muttered under my breath to Rogue, "the Queen Bitch herself?"

"I feel certain her ambitions reach at least that high, though they may overreach her abilities."

Rogue raised his voice as she drew near and thanked her for welcoming his fiancée, using a formal tone clearly meant to be a reminder to me. Fine.

"Lord Rogue." She slipped a finger into the black bow on

her mons, tugging at it suggestively. "You haven't *visited* me since your return. I've been so lonely. I thought surely you'd tire of slumming it."

"It hadn't crossed my mind to do so." He sounded gratifyingly uninterested. "You've met my fiancée, the Sorceress Gwynn."

"Lady Incandescence." I tried to emulate Rogue's tone, totally mollified that he'd referred to me by my abilities, rather than arm candy status. "What a surprise to see you tonight."

She giggled ostentatiously. Oh yeah, definitely a Titania wannabe. Exactly what we did not need.

"A surprise?" she cooed. "Not so. After all, I live here."

I supposed I knew that. Not so wonderful to have it thrown in my face, but that was why she'd said it.

"So many people live here!" I exclaimed, using my mother's brightest social voice. "It's a wonder anyone can remember you're here at all."

Her fake smile froze. "I remember you though. It seems only yesterday I had to spoon-feed you soup."

Such a sweetheart. "Funny, isn't it? And now here I am—equal to Lord Rogue's authority in this castle."

That pissed her off, her pretty gilt eyes flying to Rogue for confirmation. I held my head high, really hoping I'd understood Starling correctly and hadn't misspoken.

Rogue picked up my left hand and kissed the diamond ring. "As my lady deserves and will exercise as she sees fit."

Nasty Tinker Bell's gaze fastened on the stone and her pupils visibly dilated. I caught a burst of emotion from her—with stunned anger predominant. She stalked off, her tiny ass clenched.

"Please tell me she can't do magic."

"She can't do magic, which is why I reminded her that you can. However, she does have powerful friends. Don't antagonize her needlessly."

"She antagonized me first."

"Even then."

"But I can antagonize her needfully, right?"

He glanced at me, amused. "Should I worry about you becoming a tyrant?"

"Probably," I agreed cheerfully. "Always was one of my stretch goals. Should I worry about every other female needling me about having shared your bed in the past?"

His lips twitched. "No. I doubt it can be more than every third one. I may be immortal, but I'm not that old."

"Ha-ha."

We greeted several more guests and I studied the diamond in my ring under the guise of toying with my wineglass, which I'd filled with water. Sigh. What had bothered Nasty Tinker Bell about it so much?

Though we sat alone at the end of the table, with no one flanking us, the rapid arrival of more guests awaiting introduction kept me from broaching the question I should have asked in the first place—where *had* the diamond come from, if he hadn't magicked it up? A good lesson there. Never get so overwhelmed by the sparklies that you neglect to ask for provenance.

Or for the price tag.

The arriving guests slowed to a trickle and I thought we might finally get to eat. Probably a good thing there was no fae equivalent of the bread basket or I'd likely have decimated it by now. On top of snarfing what amounted to a round of Brie while I got dressed. I spotted Starling by the door the servers had emerged from last time, flushed with her new status as seneschal, being imperious to a fae woman I didn't know. That boded well for dinner coming soon.

Putting her in charge had been a good idea. Starling wouldn't let me starve. I turned to Rogue to mention my staffing additions, when a whirlwind of pink, green and yellow burst through the archway. Lord Puck, surrounded by dancing dragonfly girls, each wearing a dress in a different pastel, executed a complicated whirling dance step down the carpet. Draped in flowing scarves in all the colors of his companions, he resembled nothing so much as an exploded carnival cotton-candy machine.

He ended up before us with a flourish and a tickle of unseen bells, bowing grandly, long strawberry ringlets bouncing. "Lady Gwynn!" he exclaimed, as if totally surprised to find me there. "At last we meet again. And to think they claimed you'd been eaten by dragons."

"Not this time." I had to laugh at his antics. "I confess I'm surprised to see you here also. Didn't you say you were obliged to stay with General Falcon on the front lines?"

"But the war is ever so *boring* without you there." He made an exaggerated moue of disappointment. "Besides, we heard that this is the place to be for all the latest developments in battle fashion." Puck slid his mismatched gaze over to Rogue, the green-and-blue eyes sharp with interest.

"I believe you shall not be disappointed," Rogue replied.

"Excellent!" Puck did a spontaneous jig that included jazz hands, bizarrely enough. "I do so detest disappointment.

So…disappointing. I'm glad we all decided to come here instead."

"All?" I echoed and looked over to Rogue to see if he knew what Puck meant. If Rogue had been the type to roll his eyes, he would have.

"All the pigs one might wish to have rain from the sky!" Puck agreed, obviously expecting me to be delighted. "Consider it a wedding gift, fair sorceress Gwynn. A girl can never have too many pink piggies."

With that he danced away, his entourage following.

"I have *no* idea what that was about, do you?" I asked Rogue, but his face had gone eerily remote, his profile sharp with displeasure. Not with Puck, I thought. Using his method, I laid my hand on his, raising my brows in silent question. He looked at me, eyes sparking with irritation, the black lines shimmering with incipient movement. Pointedly he looked to the archway at entrance to the hall and General Fafnir stepped into view.

Stern as an old soldier, but resplendent in silver-gray that matched his close-cropped hair, he cut an imposing figure. His gaze sought me immediately and he strode down the runner, his face showing as close to an expression of pleasure as I'd ever seen on him.

"Lord Rogue," he acknowledged with a dip of his chin, ever polite, then he swept me a deep bow. "And Lady Sorceress Gwynn. You look beyond ravishing, an oasis of beauty in the endless desert. I understand felicitations on your upcoming nuptials are in order."

Rogue turned his hand and laced his fingers with mine. A bit too tightly to be a gesture of affection.

"Indeed, General Fafnir," I answered, keeping my attention on him. What was Rogue's problem with the man? "I did not expect to see you this evening. Surely you don't dwell within the castle, as I've discovered so many do."

I hadn't really meant to slip in that barb, but Rogue didn't have much room to be annoyed at my connection with Fafnir with the likes of Nasty Tinker Bell prancing about. At least mine had clothes on. Every third female indeed.

The pattern of gray on Fafnir's face—the right side for him—shifted as he inclined his head. More abstract than some, the dappling reminded me of blurry snowflakes or oddly articulated scales. "As soon as I heard the *good news*, I could hardly stay away."

This seemed directed at Rogue, who did not respond, and the odd emphasis on "good news" struck me as referring not just to the wedding, but specifically to my pregnancy, which I had denied the last time we met. In all honesty, but still.

"Apparently no one expected me, so I used unorthodox measures to enter the castle. Locked up tight as a drum, Rogue—well done—though you might check the chinks here and there."

"I intend to remedy that immediately." Rogue's voice held an echo of a growl.

"Wise." Fafnir smiled at me, a bit stiff with it, as if he was out of practice. "We shall talk more later, Lady Gwynn. I have a story you'll appreciate. I understand there will be dancing. Perhaps we shall share a dance together as we enjoyed so much last time."

He bowed out and sat somewhere on the other side of the hall. Servers streamed in with platters of food, having clearly waited for this final audience to end.

Beside me Rogue seethed. The black anger rose high enough under his skin that I didn't try to tug my hand away, lest I set off his transformation into the Dog. I wasn't entirely sure what the exchange with Fafnir had all been about.

"If you don't want him here," I said, "make him leave. I won't argue."

"We cannot afford to alienate anyone at this time."

"Then why—" I started, but he cut me off.

"Later."

"Do I have to wait until then to get my hand back?"

Rogue turned a look on me that, had it truly been heated chromium, would have melted my face off my skull. "Why," he asked, steel-edged as his sword, "what do you plan to do with it?"

CHAPTER 13

IN WHICH I MEET A DOPPELGÄNGER OR FIVE

*More and more, I perceive how the physical laws of the
universe are common between my old world and Faerie, but
are perverted by magic in the latter realm. Or, to be fair, are
made mundane in the former.*

~*Big Book of Fairyland*, "Rules of Magic"

I STUDIED HIM. Not intimidated, because I knew he wouldn't hurt me, but uncertain how to handle this side of him. Not that he was Mr. Even-Tempered, but this felt different. Jealousy?

"Did I do something wrong?" I inquired, keeping the question as cool and reasonable as possible.

"Did you have to dance with him?" he snapped back.

Really? "No. I could have caused a diplomatic incident instead. You know how I love that. It was a real toss-up."

"You've never hesitated to say no to me."

"Does this mean we are discussing this now?"

"So it would seem."

If he only knew how difficult it had always been for me to refuse him, even back when I'd been much better at it than I was these days. "Rogue." I threaded my tone with as much of the deep feeling my heart held, wondering if it would translate to him as "dear Rogue," or "my Rogue," the way my name did on his lips. "You know how much I hated him from Mistress Nancy's tale and, at that point, I didn't know otherwise. It made my skin crawl to be in the same room. I never wanted to dance with him. In fact, the whole time all I could think was that it should have been you." *But you weren't there.*

I didn't say the last out loud and I didn't have to. We both knew that truth and Rogue no doubt caught my flash of emotion on that, since it broke through so unexpectedly that I had no opportunity to hide it. Probably I was still worked up from the whole ring thing—not to mention everything else— but how I'd felt when Rogue had apparently abandoned me, the things I'd faced alone while dreaming of him laughing at me from Titania's silken arms, it smacked me between the eyes just then.

Rogue released my hand and stroked his down my back, sending some of his energy into me. "Your point is well-taken. Neither of us can change the past. Eat. You're hungry and worn-out. If I could have avoided the timing on this feast, I would have. Even with the magic you've ingested lately, you'll find that the babe drains you faster."

I'd noticed that, on the journey to Titania's castle in the Glass Mountains, though I hadn't thought I could be pregnant and so I had put it down to the lack of Rogue's stimulating presence. "Why would something physiological like that affect my magical energy?"

"Sex involves your body, too, doesn't it? And that has an effect."

That was oh so true.

"I would love to eat, as soon as someone feeds me."

Rogue indicated the platter of pastries, fruit and other sweets that had appeared in front of me as if by magic—except that I knew someone must have set it there. Meat courses would come later, so I tried not to gorge on the empty calories and save room for some protein. The fae had missed the concept of silverware so I tore apart something like an almond croissant with my fingers and scanned the army of human servants swarming the room now. None of those uncanny drudge guys in sight. What had become of them?

"I eliminated them," Rogue replied to my thought.

"You did? When?"

"Early on, when I began preparations for you to return with me. I knew you didn't like them."

I hadn't—and it touched me that he'd been so considerate, yet again—but I also worried what "eliminated" meant. "So, you…sent them away?"

He slid a look at me from the corner of his eye. "I convert-ed them into more of the Black Guard, which you also don't like, but you at least have no need to interact with."

"It's not that I don't like them—I worry about intelligent beings having no agency of their own. Even if they are Cylons. Besides, you shouldn't fuck with technology. That shit never turns out the way you expect it to."

He clearly didn't think I was funny, but at least he seemed less pissed. "If you'd like to speak to one, I believe I can demonstrate that they are neither intelligent nor beings. At least," he amended, "not in the way you think of that idea."

Hmm.

"I appreciate it," I said, "if I haven't told you already or enough. All the work you've done to see me happy here. All the things you're still doing." With my thumbnail, I rubbed the band of the diamond ring, so the gem moved in glittering glory. None of Rogue's magic clung to it. But something else did. Another flavor of magic I didn't recognize.

"There is very little I wouldn't do to please you, my suspicious Gwynn. Please try to remember that the next time you fret over my motivations."

I decided not to ponder the vast gasp between "very little" and "nothing." I knew full well he chose his words as carefully as always, leaving room for the ever-present option that he might not have any choice in acting against my happiness.

"Where did the diamond come from?"

The falter in his demeanor would not have been visible to the casual observer, but I sensed it in the tremor of his muscles, the bare hitch before he replied.

"I didn't magic it up, as you put it."

"So you told me."

He glared at me, full of offended pride. "I swear to it. You laid the parameters for the quest and I—"

"Just slow down and back up there, Prince Charming. I did not lay out a quest—certainly not intentionally—so relax. I can recognize your work as easily as you identify mine, so I know you didn't make it. Also I believe you went to some kind of extraordinary lengths to get it, even though I can't imagine where you found the time."

"So why are you asking?"

"Because of the way people look at it." *And because I told you it should be a sacrifice to obtain and I'm worrying what it was.*

His thoughts had gone as quiet as mine and I ate, anticipating that he'd either refuse to answer or would duck the specifics in some way.

"From the dwarves," he said finally and very quietly, like an admission of guilt.

I tipped my head and studied him, looking for clues. "I guess I don't know the import of that. What did you exchange?"

"That much I cannot say."

Had sworn not to then. Not that I could have pressed. Already my long-passed Grandmother had started up a lecture in my mind about how tacky it was to try to find out the value of a gift.

"You went while I was with Starling?"

He flicked a glance at me. "You think I would have left you alone in the practice arena?"

No, I hadn't thought so. Still, I liked knowing for sure. "Just seemed like not much time."

"It didn't take long." He sounded amused and I wondered why. "And, as I told you before, I wanted you to have it before this event."

"Why did the welcome feast have to be tonight?" I asked, dipping a slice of sweet bread into bowls of butter and honey. It tasted like wildflowers made liquid. Heaven. But nutritious? Hmm.

"It didn't."

"You said if you could have avoided the timing, you would have."

"Ah. That."

"Yes." I waited. Might have poked him with my fork, if I'd had one. *"That."*

"Your...involvement with the heart of the earth sent certain ripples through sorcerous society, engendering attention that was best brought into the open as soon as possible." He kept his voice pitched very low. This seating arrangement worked quite well, however. With no one beside us to easily overhear, and the rest of the hall ringing with exuberant conversation and music, it made private dialogue much easier. "No doubt that's also why Lord Puck is already here and General Falcon is on the way with the rest of his army."

Oh, interesting. "So, there are other sorcerers here?" I didn't recall any from the introductions—from when I *had* been paying attention.

"Not in person. They will have sent secret representatives."

"Spies?" That kind of tickled me.

Rogue cocked his head, no doubt confused by the onslaught of fictional images behind the word, then nodded slightly. "Close enough."

"What do we do now?"

"You will eat and relax. I will concentrate on the situation."

"I thought we were supposed to be a team."

"Don't be concerned there. I fully intend to use every one of your many abilities to the utmost." He gave me a salacious smile when I blushed at the image behind *his* words. "Follow along, if you like. Let me know what you notice."

Rogue's gaze ran over the crowd in idle curiosity, seeming to revel in being the generous host. I'd seen him play this role before and it had confused me, how little he seemed to care.

This time, though, the electricity of his cautious attention sounded loud in my ears, like a radio tuned between stations. Falling silent, which provided the additional benefit of allowing me to eat at the most rapid rate possible, I piggybacked on his thoughts, following along as he dipped in to read different minds, sampling their conversations and the deeper motivations beneath them.

"Go back to the last one," I murmured. "The woman talking about my dress."

He slid me a dubious glance and I smiled, close-lipped, my mouth full of some kind of delicious gravied vegetables. Then tipped my head in the woman's general direction.

His mind, so incisive and powerful in his confidence, arrowed straight back to the fae woman I'd pictured. Riding it felt like being on a horse at full gallop, exhilarating and impressive. He'd passed by the woman quickly and I absolutely understood why. She still hadn't finished talking about my gown and speculating how many silk nymphs had died while weaving, sewing and affixing the tiny beads.

I really hoped none of that was true. I also made a mental note to add "silk nymphs" to my species list. Where I would put Rogue's nonintelligent nonbeings bore some contemplation.

Showing a level of trust in my assessment that warmed me, Rogue stuck with the woman despite the inanity of her monologue. There. What I'd glimpsed before. Rogue caught it now, too—the black, ropy signature of Titania's mind control. Many of the fae probably had some taint of it, if examined closely, but this one coiled around a different part of her mind, around the part that knew who she was. A spy secret even from herself.

"What was her name again?" I asked Rogue casually. "You know me—I just can't keep all these strange names straight."

"Sweetheart, you recall Lady Nimbus."

"Oh, of course!" A pretty decently coded message there, given that he'd never called me "sweetheart" in all our acquaintance.

Of course, we couldn't discuss much more than that. By mutual accord, Rogue continued dipping through thoughts while I kept an "ear" on the garrulous spy. The more I listened to her, the more I thought that even she didn't know who she actually was. What did the spy novels call that—something like a sleeper? Seemed as though there had been movies like that, with some American kid growing up thinking he was all normal and then the trigger clicked in and he was suddenly a Russian spy. Always seemed unlikely to me, knowing how the brain worked, though the fiction had been entertaining.

With the addition of Titania's potent magic, anything seemed possible.

Bored beyond belief by the woman's chatter—she had to have spent thirty minutes on my shoes, which I'd barely noticed beyond them being black, sparkly and low-heeled enough for dancing—I almost missed it when she turned her attention to the diamond ring.

She was, it finally penetrated, cataloging every detail about my appearance. From counting the lilies on my necklace to the cascading curls of my hairdo. Embroidering the narrative with social details that made her conversation sound like a celebrity-watcher, she nevertheless had minutely described how I looked at this moment. Who for? Someone listening from afar in some way?

I could think of only one reason someone would want to know so much about how I appeared at this exact moment.

To create a doppelgänger.

Leaving me to watch our one known spy, Rogue had diverted his attention elsewhere, though he looked as much indolent lord of leisure as ever. I put my hand on his and he shook his head infinitesimally, his thoughts clearly across the room.

Dropping my hand to his thigh under the table, I squeezed harder, impatient to get his attention. Though, as long as we sat side by side, what could happen? It wasn't as though someone could drag me away and replace me with some puppet of myself without him noticing. Still, he needed to know my suspicions ASAP.

Just then, a little ping trilled along that new sense, where the mass mind freshly brushed my awareness. The assembly fell silent, the musicians ending the tune as if on a preplanned flourish. Enviable timing on their part—terrible on mine.

Rogue stood and drew me up with him, his fingers brushing over the diamond on my hand like a talisman.

He spoke words of welcome and general hospitality that sounded like *blah blah blah* to me. A nonsense political speech. Everyone smiled at me, particularly the brainless lady, her bright bird's eyes fastened on me with unwavering attention. Unsettled, I clung to Rogue's hand, as if that might stop a kidnapper from grabbing me.

Then everyone stood and cheered, startling me. Rogue gave me a warning look, which made me think that I wasn't behaving appropriately, so I forced a smile.

"To the dancing!" Rogue proclaimed.

If I'd hoped to lag back, whisper my concerns in his ear—no such freaking luck. Servants pulled apart the table in front of us and we stepped from the raised platform and down some steps, leading the way to the ballroom through a narrow aisle of congratulatory faces that made my head swim.

"I have to talk to you." I hissed the whisper at Rogue.

He patted my hand on his arm and stepped into the ballroom. "Later," he said. "Not now. Not here."

"But I—"

"Have a care, my Gwynn. I do not say this lightly." With a gracious demeanor that belied his curt tone, he led me to the center of the ballroom. Apparently we would lead off the dancing. From where we stood, the mosaic tile floor radiated in a spiral, like the start of the yellow brick road, only crimson. It spun all the way to the walls, also circular and entirely paneled with mirrors. I'd never been in this room, having been drugged and carried off for torture before the dancing started last time. Not that I was bitter.

Okay, I was bitter and I really needed to let go of that stuff.

"Thank Titania," Rogue commented in a dry tone.

So he was happy enough to listen in on that thought? Excellent. I pictured the spy and—

"Stop." He wrapped his arm around my waist and gripped my right hand in his, levering me up enough that I stood on tiptoes, my heart skipping in alarm at the warning in his eyes. "Dance only."

The music flared into life and Rogue swept me into a whirling waltz that took all my attention to keep up with. Not that I had any choice. No surprise, but Rogue led with irresistible certainty, making following a foregone conclusion. Probably he would have picked me up and carried me along if I resisted.

The headiness of it took me over, allaying my fears for a small space of time. He held me so tight that no one could separate us. The 3/4 waltz rhythm synced with his heartbeat and that of the life inside me, soothing me further. Rogue's flare of anger subsided into intense regard, his blazing blue eyes intent on my face, ignoring all else as we danced in widening circles.

We were tracing the path of the spiral, I realized. Like following a meditation path, only via the flowing dance Rogue was waltzing us through. As we neared the mirrored walls, I glimpsed our reflection in the gaps between the assembled guests.

With a bolt of renewed alarm, I saw myself multiplied tens, if not hundreds, of times. It seemed a terrible omen.

We finished the dance and, in what should have been a heart-wrenchingly romantic gesture, had I not been worried out of my mind, Rogue dipped me over his arm and kissed me thoroughly, to the delighted applause of the assembly. I clung to his neck, tempted to spring a claw, just to get his damn attention.

"Don't do it," he said against my mouth. "One or two more dances and we can politely retire. Then you can share what concerns you so much."

"Don't let me out of your sight," I urged him.

"Never," he promised and brought me upright. "Besides, you are safe inside the castle. If that weren't the case, I would never have left you alone this afternoon. There's a reason we have it locked up and with a full guard on alert."

Except for sleeper spies and people like Fafnir. What shape had he taken, to creep through the chinks? The guests surged around us, congratulating and making polite noises, then taking to the dance floor themselves.

"Lord Rogue. Lady Sorceress." Fafnir appeared at my elbow, as if I'd called his name, bowing with his characteristic gravity. "Seeing you dance together did my old heart good. I greatly hope, Rogue, that you forgive my dancing with your lady during your *absence.*" He put a light flourish on the final word, making it clear he knew as well as we did where Rogue had been.

"I understand there's nothing to forgive," Rogue replied, absently, as if far more interested in the dancers, his frivolous mask in place. "What is one dance?" He waved a hand. "Nothing."

"I believe we danced several, but true nevertheless. Compared to having your lady for life." Fafnir's gaze rested on me and I had to clear my face of the reflexive wince at him needling Rogue. He might have been seeing long-dead Cecily, the way his gaze grew melancholy. "In that case, Lady Sorceress, will you pity me and dance with me once more?"

"Oh, I couldn—"

Rogue squeezed my hand—I really began to miss my claws, and somewhere deep inside me the cat purr-growled in agreement—reminding me that the whole diplomatic-incident thing still applied. "Go and enjoy yourself, my lady." Rogue laid my hand in Fafnir's, smiling at the man with clear challenge. "I shall keep a close eye on you from here."

As Fafnir pulled me into the crowd of dancers, into the

center of the spinning reflections, the fractured images of my hundred selves kaleidoscoped through my mind.

Asking Rogue to watch for me had been a dire mistake.

CHAPTER 14

IN WHICH I UNCOVER A CABAL

Dragons are not only nonmagical, but they—and their eggs—seem to emit a magic-deadening field of influence. How far this field extends from the living dragon seems to be variable. Perhaps even within conscious control?

~*Big Book of Fairyland,* "Flora and Fauna"

I TRIED TO keep Rogue's position fixed in my head, but the ballroom doors, also mirrored, had been closed, leaving me bereft of that landmark. The crimson spiral should have given me a clue, but it broadened with each loop, finishing in a wide border that circumnavigated the ballroom, making all angles look the same.

"Are you quite all right, Sorceress?" Fafnir inquired.

"Actually, I feel a bit faint." I seized on the excuse. "Perhaps I should return to Lord Rogue."

"No, no—you must sit immediately. I well recall how weakening your condition can be." Full of solicitude, he found me a chair near the mirrored wall and coaxed me to sit. I craned my neck, searching for Rogue. Fafnir made a signal and a dragonfly girl brought me a glass of something so strongly alcoholic, I nearly gagged on the fumes.

"Try that," Fafnir urged. "You'll find it most invigorating."

"Oh, I can't. It's bad for the unborn child. Would you bring me some water?" I asked the girl. She bounced off happily and Fafnir sat beside me. "I'm terrible company, General Fafnir. I'll rest a moment and then find Lord Rogue. Please go enjoy yourself. Find another partner."

"I'd much rather sit and talk to you, Sorceress. Remember how I mentioned I have a story to tell you?"

"Perhaps another time?" I started to stand and he put a restraining hand on my arm, hinting of that terrible strength all fae possessed, his eyes flat as a snake's, the pattern on his face glittering. Scales, not snowflakes. Abruptly I knew what his animal must be, that could slither so handily through a break in the stones. "Should I be insulted, Sorceress? I thought we had something of a friendship."

Where was Rogue?

Chasing after my doppelgänger, no doubt. He wasn't far, I felt that much through the cords between us. If only I dared reach for him in thought.

I sent a question to Darling Hercules, who should be nearby, aiding the dancing with his anesthetic skills. He answered with a distracted *Hmm?* I asked him to send Athena to me. If anyone overheard that, it should seem innocuous enough.

"We are friends," I assured Fafnir. *We cannot afford to alienate anyone at this time.* "I am just overcome by the press and all the excitement. Do tell me your story."

I resigned myself to it. Even if Rogue did watch a copy of me instead of my actual self, what harm could it cause as long as I stayed safe? Rogue knew my internal self as well as, if not better than, my external appearance, so he couldn't be fooled for long. The greatest danger would be if someone wanted to grab me and use an imitation to distract Rogue. But I wasn't without weapons of my own. I readied several defensive wishes, accepted the glass of water from the dragonfly girl who reappeared, and forced myself to relax.

"You knew I meant to visit the Inn of Seven Moons and pay my respects to Cecily's resting place."

"Right." I believed he had loved Cecily. I hoped, for her sake, that he had. "How did that go?"

"I took into account your cautions that the proprietor would be frightened to see me, so I went in disguise. Mistress Nancy is unusually sharp for a human."

"Yes, she is." I smiled in fond memory of the Cockney-accented innkeeper from the 1800s who'd also ended up in Faerie. Not a sorceress, she boasted other gifts that allowed her to prosper far better than our native human counterparts here.

"She quickly recognized me anyway, though I did not recall her at all—something she also seemed to intuit. Right away she asked if you'd sent me."

Smart cookie, indeed. Nancy would have known that Fafnir would have no reason to come back on his own. She thought he'd murdered Cecily and left without a backward glance.

"I told her yes and she sends her regards. She also asked me to tell you two things. If there's to be a wedding she'd love to assist."

"Ah—I appreciate the message."

"I asked her to show me Cecily's grave and for the story

she'd told you. She wasn't surprised, saying you wouldn't have sent me if I hadn't been bespelled at the time. Apparently the fact that I did not recognize her played a part in her confidence."

"I'm glad you were able to at least pay your respects to the grave."

"Yes, and retrieve the body. She's rather decomposed—mortality is so disconcerting, I don't know how you manage it—but I can work with what's left."

The food I'd stuffed myself with rose in the back of my throat and I took a moment to swallow it down and make it stay there. I so did not want to ask. But I had to.

"Does Mistress Nancy know you took Cecily's corpse?" I eased my way into the treacherous waters.

"Oh, Titania, no! I think she'd be revolted, with her human sensibilities. I returned later and removed Cecily in secret. The grave will appear undisturbed."

"And what do you plan to do..." I trailed off, my own sensibilities jangling.

"I'm hoping for your assistance there. You have a unique combination of skills, Sorceress Gwynn, with both your powerful magic and understanding of mortal flesh."

"I see." I couldn't think of anything else to say. Athena, with impeccable timing, walked up right then.

"Can I fetch anything for you, Lady Gwynn?" she asked, the soul of discretion.

"Would you find Lord Rogue and let him know I'm taking a break from dancing and where I am?"

Her blue-fringed eyes wide and full of polite obedience, she nodded, then spun her dagger between her fingers. "A pleasure to see you again, General Fafnir. I'll be back straight away."

Multiple messages delivered. Better.

"I'm surprised Rogue lets you keep that one. She's most insolent."

"Lord Rogue doesn't decide for me."

"Doesn't he?" Fafnir's expression took on an acquisitive gleam. "I'd hoped that might be true, given how badly he's treated you and only offering you marriage after the fact. You know he was off fucking Titania, yes? Very bad form, even if they've been lovers for centuries. I would treat you far better, Sorceress." He took my hand. "Come away with me. I will cherish and protect you. We can work together. Let this be my favor to you—I'll spirit you away this very night."

"But…" My thoughts struggled to latch on to something that made sense, though I possessed the presence of mind to snatch my hand away. "I promised to marry Lord Rogue. I can't be foresworn."

"Did you agree to a date? I understand the wedding is not yet firmly set."

I pressed my lips on the reply, unwilling to give him any further fuel.

"Aha!" Fafnir pounced on the opening regardless. "Rogue has always been overconfident with females. It will not bother me if you remain engaged to him. Indeed, it will provide a useful leash for us to control him."

I laughed at that, right in Fafnir's face. Absurd to think anyone could control Rogue.

Fafnir's visage clouded with angry insult, but I was beyond caring at this point. Surely he counted as alienated already. "You laugh at me, Sorceress, but we've carefully planned for this, for much longer that you can know. Rogue may think I've lost the game, but there's more than one way to play."

We? This must tie into my talkative spy and the other sorcerers Rogue had thought to tease out with this party. Looked like he'd done a fine job of it. I needed to play along, if I wanted to find out more.

"I don't mean to laugh." I twisted the diamond ring, trying to sound contrite and fearful. "It's just that he's so powerful. How could I possibly escape him?"

Fafnir radiated all kinds of smug. "We have taken care of it. Come with me and you'll be safely hidden before he knows you're gone."

I frowned, going for befuddled. "But he keeps close tabs on me, why wouldn't he miss me immediately?"

Fafnir leaned in, lips cold as they brushed my ear. I had to steel myself not to recoil. "I am part of a powerful cabal. As we speak, several simulacrums of you are leading Rogue on a merry chase. I have transport on the roof. Come with me now."

Dammit. This explained why Athena hadn't returned, if she was chasing Rogue while he followed "me." He should have let me warn him. Still, I didn't think the danger was all that great. I'd simply refuse to go.

"Who are they?" I whispered back. When suspicion creased his brow, I hastily added, "Your cabal, how can I trust they're powerful enough to protect me if I don't know?" I suspected this might be the first time in my life I'd had occasion to use the word *cabal*.

"Believe me, Sorceress, they are. And all with a vested interest in the child you carry. There's one more thing. Recall that I said Mistress Nancy sent you two messages?"

Ooh. I'd bet money I didn't want to hear this.

"She also asked me to point out that, despite my wish not to, I was forced to turn over my and Cecily's baby. Take heed of that lesson, for Rogue, despite whatever pretty love tokens he gives you—" and here his gaze caressed the lily necklace, "—has long been Titania's creature. She turned him before and she can do it again. Neither you nor the child is safe with him. Look into my mind and you'll see the truth of it."

Unbidden an image came to mind, the old painting of the serpent tempting Eve in the Garden of Eden. The snake hadn't lied to her, had just broken the shell of her innocent ignorance. I had no doubt Fafnir believed every word he said. But knowledge could be used many ways. Though Fafnir's cautions echoed fears I already nursed, I would take my chances with Rogue.

"I'll think about it," I tempered, going for fearful indecision.

"There's no time. It must be tonight. It must be now." Fafnir's hand snaked out, but I dodged it and stood.

"Then I have to say no. I couldn't possibly make such an important decision on such short notice."

Fafnir put a hand in the pocket of his sober gray tunic. "I'm sorry to hear that."

I queued up a wish, ready to fire it off, and sent a call for Darling Hercules. Just in case I needed backup. Something pricked the back of my neck and Fafnir smiled at me gently, almost paternal, as the wish fizzled and died. Even as I wove on my feet, I tried for another wish, but couldn't quite connect to it.

Totally fucking ambushed.

I was an idiot.

Strong arms wrapped around me from behind. I wanted to struggle as my unknown assailant lifted me, but I could no more make that happen than anything else. Whatever they'd given me somehow prevented me from exerting my will on my muscles or my magic.

Enslavement.

Inside my head, I shrieked for Darling, for Rogue, for anyone who could hear. But the plates of my skull were as impervious as they'd been back in my fully human life.

"Don't worry," Fafnir reassured me. "You no longer appear to be you. My associates have created a complex illusion that settled on you as we spoke. We anticipated that you might be too cowed to take your chance for freedom."

He followed along as my abductor carried me out of the ballroom. "Too much to drink!" Fafnir told a gawker with surprising cheer. They carried me up a staircase, not the one that led to my bedchambers.

"This is for your own good," Fafnir continued, giving me an affectionate smile. "I won't let what happened to Cecily happen to you. You believe Rogue loves you, but we are incapable of love. He has simply discovered what you wish to hear and uses it to manipulate you. Truly, he's exceptionally good at it. I'm told you even glimpsed him playing lover to Titania after you were safely carrying his child and yet you forgave him. He's brainwashed you. After some time away from his dreadful influence, your mind will clear and you'll thank me for this."

The stairway narrowed into smaller spirals and we

emerged abruptly into the crisp night air. Fafnir waved a hand at the sky and turned to face me. "Our ride is coming, and once we have you safe, the spell that binds your will can be lifted. I regret it came to this. You'll only have to wear silver a short while. Once we're sure of you, it will be removed. I promise."

The cat inside me snarled, feeding on my sudden rage. Those words had been enough to trip me over the edge. Inside I laughed as the cat moved, unhampered by whatever they'd given me. If I could have spoken, I would have said it.

You won't like me when I'm angry.

The platinum claws sliced out of my hands and the cat took possession of the body I couldn't control. We whirled on my captor, slicing off his head with inhuman strength and speed. With a detached sense of horror and shock, I watched the decapitated body of what surely had to be an ogre topple over the edge of the tower. How the hell had they disguised that thing from us? Surely *it* hadn't slithered through a chink.

The cat, uninterested in such observations, had already spun back and was stalking Fafnir, who seemed frozen in terror.

"Sorceress Gwynn?" He ventured, then screamed when the cat sliced through his midsection and laid open his face with the other paw.

Fafnir scrambled to escape, but the small area of the turret left little room. What had become of Rogue's Black Guard on this particular tower? The cat pursued, relentless, shredding Fafnir faster than he could heal. The man had been totally melted before, by Mistress Nancy's account. The immortality of the noble fae seemed to allow them to magically recover from anything so I didn't fear that we'd kill him.

Not that he didn't deserve it.

Great wings beat through the night sky and a shadow covered the moon momentarily. Now that I knew to, I recognized that slight deadening of my magical senses that meant dragon. Detecting the absence of input was much like first learning to find the blind spot in my retina, where the optic nerve passed through—once you knew where to look, it became obvious, and also easy to pinpoint again.

A good lesson, too, in being aware of your own blind spots.

The cat ignored the dragon in favor of toying with her prey. With the caring appreciation I'd learned from the heart of the earth, I began hauling her back, suggesting we get off the tower before the dragon snatched us. She didn't like it, but reluctantly honored our new agreement, slowing her attack, remaining present enough to keep my body upright. A whoosh of air chilled me, not just from the loss of body heat, but also the draw on my magic as the dragon passed right over me. I wished I had enough control to crouch low, to avoid being snagged by the man-high talons. That wish did me no more good than the others had.

Instead, though, the dragon dropped, wheeled and hovered, one luminous eye like the lantern in a lighthouse level with my head. It surveyed me, hot breath flowing out and warming the air considerably. It shouldn't be able to hover in place like that, lazily sweeping its tremendous membranous wings in slow arcs. Hummingbirds managed the feat through speed and a characteristic circular motion that created a vortex like helicopters use. The dragon's wing movement should have depended on forward motion to keep aloft, much like a fixed-wing airplane. That the dragon didn't drop from the sky meant magic.

But how did an anti-magical creature use magic?

Fafnir's throat healed enough for him to begin sobbing and making frightened noises. Maybe I'd been distracted by the dragon's ability to hover, but I wasn't afraid. The cat, perhaps, with her predator's complete lack of fear. Or something else.

Now you lay claim to both of those things.

Fafnir had said that earlier, though surely this was the "ride" he'd mentioned. Yet, the dragon hovered, appearing to patiently await my instructions.

Fafnir's cries faded into a hiss and he shifted, a large gray snake—a constrictor, by the look of it—formed from his body. It had happened this way to Falcon, too, when I'd injured him. Almost like a protective instinct. Less explosively powerful than my or Rogue's spirits. Still unable to move, I helplessly watched him slither away.

Ah, well. Not like I could have turned him over to the cops or anything.

The dragon tilted its great head, examining me. Then it glided closer, the breath scorching. I braced myself—mentally, because I could do nothing more—and it stretched its neck, delicately touching my chest with its snout.

The spell fell away, along with my lily earrings, and the dragon backed off with what could only be a smile on its odd, reptilian mouth. I stretched, retracting the claws and reveling in the sheer joy of owning my body again, including the magic, which roared up in a wave as the dragon backed off in urgent need of direction. With nothing in mind to wish for, now that the crisis seemed to be over, and the dragon apparently going nowhere, I reached around in the stones of the tower I stood on. Partly threaded through with Rogue's blue-black brand of magic and also older, other varieties. A definite whiff of Titania, but different than how she came across these days. Her younger, possibly less corrupt self.

Finding a grip in the interweaving, I wished the circular turret larger. *Much* larger, into a platform big enough to hold a dragon at repose, and the tower itself strong enough to hold it.

With what looked like a pleased expression, the dragon landed, neatly furled its wings and lay on its belly, taloned front feet and head dangling over the edge, looking down at the courtyard below with great interest. Like a knife to the heart the image reminded me of how my cat, Isabel, had loved to do that.

One day I would stop missing her so much.

And feeling so guilty that I'd abandoned her, however unwillingly.

Noises rose up from below, shouting and various cries. I ventured toward the edge—not too close, because I'd left off any kind of barrier, thinking the dragon wouldn't like it—to peer down. Humans, fae and Black Guard alike teemed and scurried, the military sorts forming regimented groupings and the fae, well, looping about unhelpfully.

"Day late and a dollar short, guys," I said out loud and headed for the stairway to go tell everyone I'd rescued my own damn self. It kind of pissed me off, after Rogue's grand and persuasive talk about protecting me. Our first public event and he gets suckered in by one of the oldest tricks in the book and nearly lets me get kidnapped.

Not nearly. I *had* been abducted. Never mind that I'd escaped the worst consequences—Rogue had not stopped it.

Just as I reached the stairs, the devil himself launched out at top speed, long black hair tossing in the crosswinds, platinum sword at the ready, a viciously feral look on his face that transformed to searing relief at the sight of me. Okay, he'd been seriously worried, which made me feel a damn sight better.

Also the crushing embrace and kiss filled with all sorts of emotions edged in desperation went a long way too.

CHAPTER 15

IN WHICH I ACQUIRE A NEW PET

*The shift to, or, more precisely, release of an animal form,
while largely involuntary for all, seems be less wrenching for
some fae. I can't draw a direct conclusion, but I'm toying
with the notion that there is a correlation between difficulty
of shift and power of the animal form involved.*

~Big Book of Fairyland, "The Black Dog/White Cat"

O KAY, ROGUE MIGHT not have rescued me, but I clung to
him as any damsel in distress might, beginning to shake
with the adrenergic reaction. Having him arrive, even
belatedly, helped to steady me again. Bonus points for being on
top of a tower.

I buried my face in his chest, my fingers wound around a
lock of his hair and I breathed him in. Stargazers, sandalwood
and mace. The scent of security and home. Rogue held me
close, pressing more kisses to the side of my face. Then pulled
back upon finding my bare earlobe.

"What happened to your earrings?" he demanded.

Not really the first thing I'd expected him to say to me.

"Duh," came Athena's voice from behind him. She stopped cleaning her nails with the point of the dagger long enough to use it to point with. "Did you miss yon dragon?"

Apparently Rogue had been focused enough on me—also making me feel much better—not to have paid attention to the dragon that was now watching us with amber-fired interest.

"Yes, the earrings are here somewhere." I scooped them off the ground and pressed them back to my lobes, their magical tendrils weaving back into my skin like another kind of kiss. "I hope you don't mind that I modified your tower. The dragon seems to be happy though."

"Indeed she does." Rogue had an odd expression on his face. "You mentioned before that one gave you a ride. Were you planning on going somewhere?"

The pissed-off feeling returned in force. I planted my hands on my hips. "Oh sure! While Fafnir and his fucking 'cabal' had you chasing after my doppelgänger—which I tried to warn you about—I thought it would be fun to be magically immobilized by him and kidnapped via dragon back."

"Fafnir." Rogue ground out the name and ignored the rest of what I said. "He will answer for this. Where is he?"

I threw up my hands. "Who the hell knows? After I sliced him up, he turned into his snake self and slithered off. He's no doubt holed up somewhere. Or has escaped. I would have stopped him, but there was that whole magical immobilization thing I mentioned. I'm fine now, by the way."

"Are you?" Rogue looked me up and down, amusement at me transmuting his anger into desire. "You seem to be concerned that I don't care enough, my valiant Gwynn. Maybe I should check you for injuries you may not know about." He vanished the sword and pulled me into his arms again, running his hands over my body and seizing my lips in a fervent kiss. Surprisingly, my own smorgasbord of disrupted emotions seemed happy to convert into answering lust. I returned the kiss with interest.

And ignored the little voice that noted how we returned to sex to reconnect. I needed whatever connection I could get.

Athena cleared her throat ostentatiously. "I'm gonna get the search going for snake-boy."

Rogue paused long enough to say, "Do that. The Black Guard will assist you," before resuming the torrid kiss."

"Yes, sir. You two join us when you're ready. Or don't," she added with a snicker. "It might be best for all of us if you two go to your room and stay there."

I couldn't reply as Rogue had my mouth occupied, so I settled for flipping her the middle finger. She laughed. Translation complete.

Then I lost track of time for a bit, my own adrenaline-fueled desire blazing up to meet Rogue's as I drowned in his touch. One would think we'd been apart for ages.

Only when his hand moved up my thigh, under the voluminous skirts, did I regain some sense and protest. Incoherently, as we'd never stopped kissing, just gasped for breath as we adjusted angles and devoured each other again. His long fingers brushed my swollen, wet labia and it shocked me enough to wrench my mouth away and push my hands against him. Rogue opened his eyes, lambent and full of hunger.

"We have an observer." I jerked my head in the dragon's direction. Judging by the floodlit amber glow around us, it was watching us still.

Rogue flicked a dismissive gaze at it. "I doubt she cares." And nibbled on my neck, making my head swim.

"*I* care."

"Why?" he asked, clearly stalling me and not interested in the answer. I'd pressed my thighs tight together and his fingers brushed the seam of them, teasing me. "I care, too—that's what I'm proving to you."

"No," I laughed, feeling myself melt. "Besides we can't have make-up sex until we've finished fighting."

"What are we fighting about?"

"First of all, I can't believe you thought that other...*person* was me."

He shrugged, rubbing me against him. "There were several and I knew none of them was you. I only followed after to discover who was behind it."

"Leaving me to fend for myself."

"I didn't expect that you would run off with Fafnir." Anger crept back into his voice and he nipped me.

"I didn't! He abducted me." And I really hated that it had been so stupidly easy.

"I didn't know that then, did I?" he pointed out with calm logic. "Besides I knew you could take care of yourself, which you did, my resourceful and powerful Gwynn."

I sighed, partly from arousal and mostly from the mix of pleasure at his faith in me and chagrin that I kind of wanted him to have worried about me more. Dumb atavistic feeling there. I was full of them lately. Pregnancy hormones? I'd heard stories like that. "How did you know she wasn't me?" I insisted. Okay, fishing maybe.

"Because, my delicious Gwynn, she did not smell like you." He ran the tip of his tongue along my throat.

"Smell? *This* is how you know me?"

"Yes." He bit the cord of neck muscle under my ear and inhaled. "It's something sorcerers without animals frequently forget."

"Fafnir has an animal—a snake."

"Doesn't count. They can't smell."

Not exactly accurate. Their tongues had chemoreceptors that functioned in a similar way. I lost the thought, however—no doubt exactly as he intended—as he kissed his way down to my generously displayed bosom and, nudging the bottom lily aside, dipped his tongue in the crevice between my breasts, making me shiver with heat. "More, your scent here is unique to this spot. I believe I could identify each part of you in total darkness."

"I certainly hope you weren't sniffing *her* in that spot—or any other."

"What if I did?" He sounded sly and tugged on the dress, freeing my nipple and taking it into his mouth. I clutched his hair, trying to keep my balance. "Would you punish me for it?"

"Not in the way you're picturing, for you'd enjoy it far too much," I replied in as tart a tone as I could manage, given the tantalizing things he did with his agile tongue. "And stop that. I am not putting on a show for the dragon." *Any more of a show,* I mentally amended.

I could swear I heard a jewellike tinkle of amusement.

Rogue frowned over my shoulder at the dragon. "I believe your friend is indeed observing us."

"Told you."

"Perhaps she'll give us a ride to our own tower then. We can have the champagne celebration you wanted. And I can spend more time enjoying you in this dress." Though he allowed the scandalously low neckline to cover what it could again, his fingers continued to trace the curves of my bosom. I had to concentrate on what he'd said.

"Dragons are not taxis, Rogue. And how do you know it's a her?"

"She clearly is and, look, she's standing up."

I twisted enough to take a look and, sure enough, the dragon opened her wings, amber eyes gleaming, and held up a taloned foot as if we might climb aboard. Still, I hesitated. "I don't know. It doesn't seem right."

"If we go back through the castle, people will expect us to rejoin the party."

"Dragon ride it is."

Rogue laughed and swooped me up to carry me over to the dragon.

"I can walk," I protested.

"Hush. I'm rescuing you from the tower. Don't ruin it."

"Is there even a way to get in the dome from the outside?"

"There is now." With his usual agile grace, Rogue stepped into the dragon's palm and sat. The talons closed around us in a glittering cage, making me fervently hope we'd read her intentions correctly. But she leaped off the tower and easily surged across the torchlit complex to the tallest tower, topped by the glowing globe that was ours. A rigid net of flat rungs bisected the tower, a few levels below our room, connected by an encircling ring, for all the world like the kind on humming-bird feeders.

The dragon landed on the ring on her hind feet as if she'd done it a thousand times, the substrate flexing under her weight, but it held. She laid her forefoot on the rung in front of us and opened the talons, allowing us to walk free toward a new doorway that opened onto a landing in the stairway.

Neat work for that fast.

I didn't mind that Rogue carried me on the flat but narrow rung so I didn't have to look down. Looking at the dragon over his shoulder, I sent a mental thank-you, surprised when she bobbed her head. She took off and Rogue set me down just inside the doorway. I watched her wing away while he looked up at the illuminated curve of the globe above.

"This should be far enough down that they won't be able to sit here and peek in," he commented.

"They?"

"Where there is one dragon, there will be more." He laced his fingers with mine. "And this one seems inclined to stay."

I had expected her to keep going, but she landed on the other platform again, dangling her clawed feet over the edge, perfectly content to all appearances.

Letting out a long breath composed of wonder and more than a bit of feeling overwhelmed bit it all, I squeezed Rogue's hand. "Guess I'd better order some apples."

⟡

WE NEVER GOT to the champagne, as Rogue bent his considerable focus and nimble fingers to getting me out of the dress he liked so much, and then into bed. I gave myself over to his relentless seduction—easier and oh so rewarding. He made love to me with all the starvation of the first time and I drank it up. In the morning, I would think about the progression of this relationship and the worrisome things Fafnir had said.

The sex, too, provided the exact catharsis I needed to purge the fear and tension from my blood. After the final, wrenching climax Rogue wrung from me, I fell deeply and peacefully asleep.

I awoke once, to a jewel-hued song that echoed through the crystal globe, making it hum in harmony. In bed alone, I sat up to see the sun's rays pinking the horizon. Rogue moved through the shadows to sit beside me, smoothing my sleep-tousled hair. "Your dragon, greeting the dawn. Go back to sleep."

"Just what we need," I grumbled, "a dinosaur-sized rooster."

Going back to sleep wasn't a question, however. I crashed again as if drugged and awoke hours later to the sun high and bright in the sky. As happened more often than not, Rogue was nowhere about. He had been nearby when the dragon woke me at dawn, though he hadn't been asleep in bed. Maybe he didn't sleep and that was why he was rarely there in the mornings. Couldn't be all that compelling, hanging out while someone slept.

Blinking up at the poetically clear expanse of perfect blue above, I took a few moments to scroll back over recent events. Having this vividly intense sexual relationship had proved to be as distracting as I'd anticipated. Made it difficult to keep one's thoughts on track.

My mental to-do list had become overwhelming:

1. *Feed dragon.*

2. *Find out about this cabal.*

3. *Deal with pregnancy.*

4. *Deal with possibility probability that Rogue remains under Titania's influence.*

5. *Plan strategy for Titania's surely imminent attack.*

6. *Check in on Walter for Starling (retrieve scepter from Athena)*

7. *Explore mass-mind web and perfect skills / add to timeline*

8. *Add notes to grimoire on recent events.*

9. *Plan wedding.*

Really I needed to write this down, as the priorities were all out of order. It almost made me miss the days when *Stay alive* topped the list, for the way it put everything else into perspective. Not that it shouldn't still be on there. Maybe I'd just gotten back to the point where that was implied and not something to keep at the forefront of my mind. It really irked me to have planning a stupid wedding on the list at all. Maybe I'd take it off and put it on Starling's list.

And none of this would get addressed if I lolled in bed all day.

I wandered naked down to the bathing room and used the magic chamber pot. No need for indoor plumbing with those handy things, which vanished anything put inside to parts unknown. My hair still had pins in it and stuck out in wild curls, so I brushed it out, leaving Starling's hair-torture implements in a neat pile. Rogue must have told her to let me sleep or she would have turned up by now. Or she was too far from this room to have her alarm-sense of when I was up and about. Likely both.

Either way, I liked having the quiet and the opportunity to do for myself. I borrowed back a few of the pins, coiled up my hair and took a quick bath, to get the sex-smell off. Toweling dry, I glimpsed myself naked in the full-length mirrors for the first time in what seemed like ages. Did my belly look rounder? I turned sideways and ran my palm over it. I'd never been so skinny that I had a flat abdomen—or, Cosmo-save-me, the daunting concave variety—but I looked more slender than I had since my teens.

The Grueling Journey through the Glass Mountains with Little Food Culminating in Blood Poisoning Diet. It would never catch on.

Despite the slimmer me, my belly rounded out significantly. Plus it felt firm, the hardness of uterine muscle instead of adipose tissue. I had no idea, however, what that indicated for how far along I might be. While some women in my department back at the university had been pregnant at various times, I'd never much hung around for the blow-by-blow conversations on the physical details of the experience. Those seemed to devolve rapidly into horror stories. Mainly I knew some women "showed" sooner than others. Not a big help.

And, though I knew a lot about physiology, particularly fetal and embryonic development as it applies to neural systems, that information all revolved around the internal processes, not how it felt on the outside. Starling possessed even less knowledge. Blackbird, though she'd given birth, according to Starling, didn't know human bodies.

Mistress Nancy did though. And had sent me her regards.

I've done a bit of midwifing in my day. She'd said that during our conversation at the Inn of Seven Moons.

Of course, that had been right before she mentioned how she hadn't been able to save Cecily or her baby from their gruesome fates.

I shouldn't juxtapose those things, however. Asking her to help me wouldn't necessarily recreate the same scenario—that was subscribing to false causation, which led to superstitious thinking. Never mind the seeds of doubt Fafnir had planted, that Rogue could no more resist Titania's hooks than Fafnir had.

Regardless of anything else, I was no Cecily.

I strongly suspected Rogue had planned it that way.

After locating a robe, I went upstairs, took my grimoire to a sort of wide armchair, which had a view of the waterfall, and curled up in it to make my list and notes on all that had occurred. Before I had worked for long, Rogue strode into the room, wearing a long cloak and carrying a basket.

"Good morning, lovely Gwynn." He dropped a kiss on the top of my head, the scent of fresh air wafting over me, and set the basket in my lap.

"What's this?" I surveyed the fruit. "Breakfast?" Or lunch, judging by the slant of the sun.

"You said last night that you wanted apples." He unclasped the cloak and tossed it aside, then fingered the coil I'd forgotten I'd put my hair in. "You have your hair up?"

"To keep it dry. I took a bath."

"May I take it down then?"

"Sure." I said it casually, but it moved me somewhere deep inside that he wanted to. This daily intimacy and attention still took getting used to. With gentle pulls, he removed the pins, unwound the twist and spread my hair over my shoulders. Then he sat on the floor, gazing out at the view and leaning his shining head against my knee.

"Fafnir has been captured and the doppelgängers dealt with." He offered that information much as he'd set the basket of apples in my lap. Buttering me up or making up?

I shivered, though, at the thought of multiple mes running around the castle complex, still dressed in last night's seductive gown. An eternal walk of shame. Good that he'd taken care of getting rid of them. "Who were they, anyway?"

"Some of Fafnir's cohorts. They've been returned to their proper forms. And Fafnir has been neutralized. He won't bother you again." He sounded too satisfied with that. Hopefully that wasn't as grim as it sounded.

"So, he's captured, you say?" All these things I didn't think about upon awakening for my list. Where are my doppelgängers? Did anyone capture the bad guy? No, I took a bath and fretted about the pregnancy.

"Yes. Your Athena found him and he's biding his time in silver until we've decided what to do with him."

I flinched a little at the mention and Rogue untucked my bare foot from my robe, brought it over his shoulder and kissed the hollow next to my ankle, right below where my silver cuff had once contained me. The touch soothed me.

"As for the other things that just flew through your mind, I took care of them, thus you didn't need to. We can share such responsibilities."

I threaded my fingers through his silky hair, as always unable to resist touching him. A surge of affection filled me. In many ways it didn't matter what doubts I harbored or that a psychologist would likely hand me a list of the ways in which my relationship with Rogue fit the term *dysfunctional,* I loved him, fully and completely.

I felt right in my skin when we were together in a way that I didn't when we were apart. It was an odd sensation, because it wasn't as if I felt wrong without him—I just felt more right with him. A rightness I'd never before experienced in my life. That meant I had to do my best to make this work. *Love as an active verb,* as I'd once told Starling.

Not that difficult when he gave me the least thing I mentioned wanting. He'd brought me a basket of apples.

"This was very thoughtful of you—all of it. And thank you for the apples." I took one and bit into it. Perfectly crisp and sweet.

"I didn't magic these up either. I picked them for you."

"You didn't have to do that."

"You think magic is easy for me and means nothing."

"That's not true." I ran my fingertips over the curls of his ear auricle, the way he liked. "Not everything has to be a grand gesture. I greatly appreciate the thought, but I don't think I'm that high maintenance." Not like Titania was, most likely. Probably where all of this was coming from. More baggage. More reasons not to be that way.

"Then why did you mention apples, specifically?"

I puffed out a sigh for my carelessness. Note to self on accidentally assigning quests for Rogue. "Sorry—I meant the poisonous apples like at Castle Brightness. It turns out the dragons eat them."

He fell quiet, contemplating, moving his head slightly

under my caress, the way a dog showed it was enjoying being petted. "Perhaps it's time you told me more of your adventures while I was...away. And why you're so bothered this morning."

I shouldn't be surprised that he read my emotions so easily. Though this whole thing of him being interested in how I felt seemed like a new phase for us. Go figure.

So, I opened my grimoire to the timeline I'd started, referencing what I'd already added and making notes as I talked. One thing about telling a long story to an immortal, especially a tale punctuated with pauses, was they have near-infinite patience. Rogue barely stirred, listening without comment, until I got to the part about visiting dragons in Walter's castle.

"You have to be the only being in all of Faerie," he said, "to have given a dragon's egg *back* to a dragon."

"It smelled the egg in my pocket and wanted it." *She* wanted it, I mentally amended, since I was reasonably sure this was the same dragon. Not like it was easy to tell them apart, however. "Why wouldn't I have given it to her?"

"They're valuable."

"So I understand, but I imagine they're even more valuable to the dragons themselves."

Rogue laughed and rubbed his cheek on my velvet-covered knee. "It's just no wonder they like you so much. I've really never heard of such a thing before."

"Walter said they're drawn to our human flavor of magic."

"That could be. They certainly don't mix well with mine."

Rogue sounded rueful and I recalled my theory that the nullifying presence of dragons in Walter's domain had weakened his abilities. And the distilled dragon's blood elixir

I'd concocted had affected Titania with devastating force.

"Does it affect you negatively—having the dragon here?"

"Why?" Rogue tipped back his head to look up at me, his voice full of amused irony. "Would you run her off for my sake?"

Okay, the image of me fighting the dragon for him was a bit absurd. "Or at least *ask* her to go, yes."

He smiled and rested his head on my knee again. "Thank you, my gracious Gwynn. So far, I and the rest of the castle denizens seem to be fine. Your dragon is keeping to herself, and the people seem to be generally excited about the notoriety."

"Oh. I suppose her presence is a bit attention-grabbing."

"At this point, the more attention, the better."

I supposed that was true. Titania liked to take advantage of ignorance, working in the deep shadows of memory loss, mystery and secrecy. Rogue seemed to be going for the fae equivalent of living our lives on the front page, with the major newspapers knowing everything, so that if something should happen, at least our disappearance should raise questions.

No one had missed Cecily. Outside of Nancy and Fafnir, I'd never heard any mention of her. And he hadn't even known where she was buried until I told him—something I now regretted.

"Shit! I just realized that I should have used my favor to stop Fafnir from abducting me! Why the hell didn't I think of that?"

"You managed to extricate yourself without using up the favor."

"True. Plus he already thought he was saving me so it

might have been difficult to word."

Rogue went still at that. He had an inhuman turn to it, as if he turned his body off, making it momentarily lifeless. Yet, within that stillness, his mind spun, a whirling mosaic of thoughts, images and emotions.

"Saving you from what?" he asked, finally.

"I'm sure you know. Do you want me to say it out loud?"

"Yes, I want to hear what he said. Choose your words carefully, but you have more...freedom to say what you wish without consequence."

"He said that what happened to him, having his mind turned so that he killed Cecily and gave the infant to the Queen Bitch, could also happen to you. He offered to protect me from you."

After a time, Rogue moved again, beginning with a long breath that sighed out, cold and lonely. "You should know this. He could be right."

PART III

HUMAN TRIALS

CHAPTER 16

IN WHICH I USE A LOT OF FEELING WORDS

In Faerie, the shortest distance between two points is almost never a straight line.

~Big Book of Fairyland, "General Observations"

"I KNOW," I replied, feeling remarkably Zen about it for the moment. And touched, that he trusted me enough to admit that. Once, the thought would have scared me shitless and I would have done all in my power to get away. Look at us, and how far we'd come.

Rogue let his head fall back, gaze brilliant blue through his thick black lashes. "You knew, were already in fear of this possibility and yet you did not take the escape Fafnir offered?"

I tucked the grimoire by my feet and leaned over him, brushing my fingers over the pattern on his face that always fascinated me so. "I've known since Nancy told me the story. Even before that, I figured something along those lines could occur. That's part of why I fought you so hard, for so long."

He considered my words, face grave and somehow vulnerable. "And now?"

I lifted my shoulders and let them fall. "Now I'm done fighting you, my Rogue. You asked me to trust in you, to be your partner forever and I agreed—that's not something I take lightly. We're in this together. I don't believe anymore that you'd willingly hurt me or the child, so we fight the possibly that you could be forced to the same way we'd defend ourselves against any other attack." As I said the words, I realized they answered my questions too.

"I should have known you'd be as stubborn at my side as you were when I was trying to get you there."

"Yes, you should have." I bent over him, kissing the sueded silk softness of the skin just below the temple, then down over his high cheekbone, taking my time getting to his mouth, which waited for me, hot and greedy.

My hair fell around us and he wound his fingers in it, holding me there. Lazy desire unfurled in me, in him, spiraling between us, sweet, hot and heavy. The depth and growth of my feelings for him alarmed me on one level—as if by admitting them I'd somehow provided the catalyst for the chemical reaction between us to rage past all theoretical boundaries. Frighteningly out of control.

To my surprise, he broke the kiss. "Finish your tale and tell me what has you in such turmoil."

A bit disappointed, I sat back and took up the grimoire again, wondering how I'd messed that up. Not that I'd ever counted seduction in my skill set.

Rogue gazed out the window. "You forget, my lovely Gwynn, how many of your thoughts I hear. I know you worry that I distract you with sex, that I use it as a way of avoiding difficult conversations. Isn't this true?"

Nothing like being called out on your thoughts. This was worse than going to counseling together. Talk about total honesty.

"It's true." I coughed a little, to cover the laugh that wanted to well out at the image of Rogue exploring his feelings on some faux-leather couch. "Though it feels very strange to be having this discussion with you. At least we don't have to argue about whose family is worse and where we should spend the holidays."

"And answers such as that are your technique for deflecting me, isn't it?"

Damn. Caught me out there too. I looked out at the serene vista, our gazes parallel. "Okay, jokes aside. Yes, I worry that we don't communicate well—a sentence that still sounds absurd to me, given that I'm saying it to an alien being while I'm looking out at a landscape full of impossibilities. But, even without the *geas,* or whatever it is that keeps you from being able to tell me everything, this whole deal like last night, when I'm not supposed to tell you about something important…it seems fraught to me. I still don't understand all the rules—I don't even know if you sleep at night. I've promised to marry you someday and we still know so little about each other."

"Someday will be sooner than you think, perhaps."

"Because of what Fafnir said?"

"One of the reasons, yes. He has a point. Until we're married, you are fair game to be 'protected' by another. We might have him in custody, but this cabal he spoke of will simply try yet again. You are a valuable prize."

"I don't like being a prize."

"You didn't like the abduction attempt either."

Fair enough.

"Tell me why you fretted about the babe."

He was relentless and I didn't really want to talk about it. "Let's stick to the agenda—when you say 'sooner than I think' for the wedding, when would that be?"

"The winter solstice would be the most auspicious timing."

"That's soon?" And here I'd been braced for "next week" or "tomorrow." I flipped to my timeline and frowned at it, wishing yet again I'd thought of making one sooner and had kept better track. "The night we rescued you from QB's castle was All Hallow's Eve, which would be October 31 in my world. Solstice, depending on the year, would be around December 21, give or take. So that would more than a full moon cycle away."

Rogue cocked his head, assimilating the various images. "What you call the moon cycle makes no sense. The moon is the moon. It does not change."

Fascinating, really, and as had recently occurred to me. "It never appears as a crescent or a half? As if part of it is in shadow?"

"No," he said in a reflective tone, giving it due consideration. "What could cast a shadow on the moon?"

I snorted to myself. Oh, only a planet, which we didn't seem to be on. "Okay, we've got a reasonable rotation of day and night that we agree on—how many nights from now?"

"Ah—three."

Keeping my lips close together, I blew out a long, steadying breath through the small opening, concentrating on keeping it even and smooth. I'd suspected this about time. It shouldn't rock me, to know that what should have been seven weeks had passed in something like one for me, even allowing for lost time when I'd battled the cat. If I figured it had been the equivalent of early September when I'd conceived, then I might be four months along. Utterly terrifying to contemplate.

"Tell me, Gwynn." Rogue spoke softly, tracing my toes with apparent fascination. "I only get pieces of this worry about the babe before you tuck it away again."

"I don't know if I can explain it, even to myself."

"Try."

I supposed I owed him that. "Let me start with a story. In my world there are these things called movies—images and sound that tell a tale. I watched this one about animals in another part of the world from where I lived, called elephants. Do you have those?"

He shook his head slightly but stayed silent, forcing me to go on.

"Elephants are what biologists call sentient—they're capable of recognizing themselves in a mirror, for example. They're smart and can form emotional attachments, even paint pictures. I'd seen them in captive situations, but this showed them wild. A group of them, a herd, traveled through desert, seeking water. It took them a very long time and some died along the way. There were baby elephants too." My voice thickened and I sucked it back, trying to maintain. "Then there was this dust storm and—they couldn't see where they were going, but they made it out. Except for this one baby elephant that got confused. All turned around. And when the dust storm cleared, it was still walking, but in the wrong direction. Back into the desert."

I wiped an escaping tear away, glad Rogue was facing away from me. He stroked my foot. "And it died?"

"I don't even know. Maybe the people filming it—recording the pictures—rescued it. But the thing is, the image of that baby elephant trotting off hopefully into the desert, thinking it would find its mother...it gives me an almost physical pain to contemplate it. And that's an animal, totally unconnected to me, irrelevant to my life, and its death would be part of nature. As a biologist, I know and understand these things. But—" I broke off, not really willing to take the next step.

"But this babe you carry will be relevant and connected and not an animal. You see the child as this baby elephant—torn from you, lost and dying."

I nodded, though he couldn't see, not trusting my voice. All those women had been right. The pregnancy hormones were a killer. Rogue waited me out.

"So, the other part is that, were I in my own world, I'd have a lot of metrics to track the baby's development. I'd have pictures and various tests. I would be able to take vitamins and predict when it would be born. Here, I have none of that."

"The babe will grow on its own, yes? Without you having this knowledge?"

"Yes." My laugh sounded watery. "But, see, this is who I am. I'm the person who's always used knowledge to understand and control my world. Maybe I'm the one wandering in the dust storm. How can I save my child when I'm in danger myself? A danger as huge and as far beyond me as a force of nature."

Rogue pressed a kiss to the top of my foot, then to the

instep, sending a warm current up to my heart. "Because you have me. I will clear the dust storm and bring you water. If you get lost, I will find you. If Fafnir had succeeded, which he didn't, because your powers are far greater than any of his or his foolish cabal's, then I would have found you. Haven't I always found you before, when you tried to hide from me?"

"This is an excellent point." Ironic, even.

He turned on his hip, kissing my ankle and tracing a line up my calf muscle with his mouth. I had to shift to accommodate the stretch, which opened my legs.

"Trust me in this, my Gwynn, together we can win. Perhaps I frighten you with my cautions, but I would never have gambled all I have if I didn't believe we could triumph."

"You don't know any more about birthing a baby than I do."

"Lady Healer will assist."

"She doesn't know humans." Besides, I didn't trust her.

"Then we'll find someone who does." His mouth found the sensitive skin on the back of my knee and I hummed at the sweet sensation.

"Mistress Nancy. I want to see if she'll come help me."

"Done. Whatever that canny woman decides to charge." He lifted my knee higher, his desire meeting mine with renewed strength as I melted under his lips and tongue. Pushing my thighs wider apart, he kissed his way up the tender skin there.

"Is this you not distracting me with sex?"

"This is me, drying your tears and rewarding you for telling me what was in your heart. Besides, it seems we've discussed everything on your agenda." He turned fully now, hands sliding up inside my robe to cup my bottom and coax me to the edge of the chair. Giving me a wicked smile, he opened my robe, gazed down at my naked, already wet sex and licked his lips. "Consider me seduced. Let me please you, my Gwynn. Unless you're saying no."

Like I could manage to, when he looked at me that way. "Please me then," I whispered.

His hands flexed hard on my hips, the barest of warnings. I lost my breath when his avid mouth seized me, and I didn't regain it again for a long time thereafter.

꿈

MY BODY NEARLY limp with relaxation, but my mind and nerves buzzing with energy, I felt at least more in equilibrium and ready to deal. Purged of both emotional and physical tension, I dressed in the least over-the-top gown I could dig out of my closet, resisting the urge to modify it, and brushed out my hair again.

Rogue remained where I left him, looking out over the countryside with his hands clasped at the small of his back, that sense of shimmering impatience coalescing around him, as if the sexual release lifted it only briefly. He turned to survey me, taking in my mental and emotional state also.

"Back to your agenda, then?" he asked.

"Yes. Dragons to feed, weddings to plan—a woman's work is never done."

"Then winter solstice is agreeable to you?"

I ignored the pang of trepidation and shrugged. "Might as well. I already said yes. Delaying won't change anything."

"And might make our situation worse."

"There is that," I agreed. I wound my fingers together. So odd how I could feel totally at home with Rogue one moment and tentative the next. "So...I'm going to do some planning. Get my act together on several fronts. What are you up to this afternoon?" *Catch up on email? Maybe some pickup basketball and a beer with the guys?*

"I thought I'd interrogate Fafnir, see what else I can find out about this purported cabal of his, and fetch Mistress Nancy to attend you."

"You mean, you'll ask her."

Rogue frowned at me. "I already promised that you'll have her assistance. Would you have me leave room to fail you in that?"

I sighed. "It wasn't a promise. I absolve you of it. Take me with you and I will ask her. I'd rather do that anyway."

He'd started shaking his head before I finished talking. "It's not safe for you to leave the castle until we're married. And don't get that look on your face like you get when you start talking about how I want to lock you up. You know full well how tempting you are—for Fafnir's ilk and others like them. It's only for a few days."

"Fine." I tried to make it sound calm and not irritated.

"Is it fine?" Rogue's thoughts brushed mine. "Or will you be frustrated by it and brood with your mind hidden?"

"Welcome to marriage with a human woman. How about if we agree I get to stew about it a little bit, but I'll make an effort to be gracious overall and look forward to increased freedom in the future—will that suffice?"

He smiled, very slightly. "I would also 'stew' in your position. We are not so different in that way."

"And in others?" I had to ask.

"I do not sleep, no, not unless injured."

I nodded, letting myself assimilate that, though I'd suspected as much. "How about food? You've eaten with me, but do you need to?"

"No." Rogue looked somber. "Does that bother you?"

"Some." I rolled my shoulders, loosening them. "So you just pretended to, for my sake?"

"Not to deceive you, no. I enjoy it, but as with many fae, my true sustenance comes from magic. Eating, however, is a ritual of trust. So is sharing a bed. In many ways, I'd say it means more to me to do those things with you because I choose to, rather than it being necessary."

"An interesting point."

He cocked his head slightly, listening, thoughts touching mine like a kiss. "And the part you're not saying?"

Gah. I stretched my fingers, enjoying the freedom of movement, my restored humanity. "So, there's this thing. In my culture, people tell stories of human women impregnated with alien babies. Monster babies." *Changelings.*

"As I've done to you."

"Well, we did it to each other, but yes—it feels strange, not knowing who—" *or what,* "—the child will be."

"Something we cannot know until it is born."

"I know. You asked."

"I did. And you have another question."

Fine. "Do you ever think about it, Rogue? We are different species. Have you thought through that I'm human and mortal? That I'll become an old woman and eventually die."

He came to me and, lacing our fingers together so we stood palm to palm, looked into my eyes. The connection between us throbbed like a heartbeat, a commingling of my one-two rhythm with his waltz beat, each a counterpoint to the other.

"None of that matters. A moment with you or an eternity—neither is more valuable than the other. Should everything end now, I would call myself blessed."

My heart rolled over. "You do know how to say the right things."

"Besides," he added, glancing at my belly with a wicked glint in his eye, "the way you think this word 'species' means being able to interbreed. And we've certainly done that."

And wasn't that just the cherry-topper?

It puzzled me still, the ways our physiologies intersected and how they diverged. It shouldn't be possible for us to interbreed. Nor for a fae woman like Blackbird, who was not mammalian-born, to give birth to a half-human child in a fully mammalian style. For a while I'd joked to myself that the fae all fruited on the vine, except even fruit had navels. In a rational world, higher organisms could not reproduce in a way other than the way in which they themselves were conceived. Lower organisms, however, could "choose" to reproduce either by recombining genes with another individual or by essentially cloning themselves. Parthenogenesis. Though theoretically possible in humans, it had never been documented—beyond those seeking to rationalize virgin birth stories.

Still, there seemed to be enough similarities among particularly the lower-tier fae to suggest parthenogenesis. That could be just my foreigner's eye, leading me to believe they all looked the same. Funny that I'd been ruminating on the development of the embryo or fetus within me. One aspect of fetal development I did understand was that ontogeny recapitulated phylogeny. In other words, a human child went from a single cell and developed into an increasingly complex organism by following the same path as evolution, from amoeba to fish to monkey to human, in essence.

Could it be that this shift in reproduction among the immortal noble fae represented a sort of evolutionary leap? It would be working at an extraordinarily accelerated rate, a saltational evolution producing the very essence of the "hopeful monsters" the thesis predicted. I pressed my palm to the round ball of my belly. A changeling child as the hopeful monster.

Rogue's eyes, shades darker than the brilliant sky framing him, but no less bright, glittered as he listened in on my thoughts without commenting.

"I want to ask you a question you maybe can't answer," I said, stepping away and opening my grimoire to the new section in Rules of Magic: Changelings.

"No, I did not grow on a tree like an apple."

"I'm totally writing that down."

"Of course you are."

I laughed. This was better. "Can you tell me how you did grow? I've seen images of you as a juvenile—not your adult self—were you an infant? Do you have a mother?" A daunting thought, a fae noble mother-in-law who would no doubt deeply disapprove of me as a match. All I needed.

Rogue didn't reply. An answer right there. How else could I ask the question?

He strolled idly over to the basket of apples he'd brought me and selected one, holding it up for inspection. "After the wedding, I'll take you on an excursion. A celebration of your freedom. Would you like that?"

Wiser to his ways at last, I nodded. He planned to show me then. Fascinating. Too bad we couldn't go right away. Rogue chuckled, set the apple on my workbench and picked up my left hand, stroking the diamond, intent gaze full of warning. "First things first, however."

"I know. I know." Though it didn't *feel* like the correct order of priority to me. Still, to please him, I turned to my notes page and wrote:

1. *Discuss wedding with Starling.*

Though he couldn't read it, I pointed to it and raised my eyebrows significantly. "There. Wedding is first. Happy?"

Rogue rewarded me with a kiss. "With you? Always. Do you wish to be present while I interrogate Fafnir?"

The image behind his intention chilled my blood. Though it hardly compared to what I'd done to the guy with my claws. Still. "No, that's okay. But, um, there's something you might ask him about."

Rogue's face hardened into sharp lines as I relayed what Fafnir had said about stealing Cecily's corpse. "He's a worse fool than I thought. I'll discuss his plans with him. Among other things."

"Is he trying to…resurrect her somehow?"

"If only." Rogue gave me one more kiss, an absent one, his thoughts deeply shrouded. "I suspect something much worse. But I shall be sure to tell you what I find out."

And, with those tantalizing words, he left.

CHAPTER 17

IN WHICH I PERFORM A CUNNING ARRAY OF STUNTS

ϵ

Much as I like thinking, sometimes it's better just to act already.

~*Big Book of Fairyland,* "Personal Notes"

O KAY, OKAY—I REVISED the list as soon as he left. But only to satisfy my own sense of order. I'd never been particularly inclined toward obsessive/compulsive disorder; however, as control in one area of my life slipped, I felt justified in getting persnickety about others.

Besides, I'd forgotten to ask how to summon Starling and I couldn't exactly get going on el numero uno until I did. That moved things around right there. Feeling better, I surveyed my new list, now organized by short-term and long-term goals.

Okay, maybe I had a titch of OCD.

Short-Term

1. *Explore mass-mind web*

   a. *call Athena to bring scepter & dragon eggs*

    b. call Starling to discuss wedding

2. *Plan wedding (or delegate to Starling)*

3. *Check in on Walter for Starling*

4. *Feed dragon*

5. *Add notes to grimoire on recent events. Perfect mass-mind calendar skills/add to timeline*

Long-Term

1. *Find out about this cabal—discuss w/Rogue*

2. *Conception field trip*

3. *Deal with possibility/probability that Rogue remains under Titania's influence*

4. *Plan strategy for Titania's surely imminent attack*

My last two long-term goals loomed at the bottom of the list, daunting in their size and unpredictability. But I left them there. Conversely, I resolutely removed "Deal with pregnancy" from the list as my nod to inevitability. Besides, I had no doubt Rogue would deliver Miss Nancy—by hook or by crook, as the saying went, which brought up amusing images, though hopefully he wouldn't actually employ any of them—and thus I'd done all I could. The baby would, as Rogue pointed out with flawless logic, arrive on its own. Not so much the wedding.

First things first, indeed.

Tired of sitting, I paced as I mentally looked for the mass-mind web. Without Rogue's guiding touch, I fumbled around a fair amount, finding instead various startled minds careening around the castle on their errands. Clumsy me. To my surprise, however, my mental reach extended much farther than I'd have predicted, based on past experience. In fact, as I paced toward the center of the dome, minds even more distant popped up on my mental radar.

The crystal dome—why hadn't I realized before?—acted to amplify my abilities, much as the scepter did. Rogue hadn't mentioned this, which likely meant he'd meant for me to discover it on my own. I could see why. Our very bedroom gave us an edge on the competition.

Hopefully it wouldn't exact a similar price. Somehow I didn't think it would, but that would be a thing to watch for.

Standing in the exact center of the room, I focused my virtual gaze out from the minds themselves to the delicate strands running in and out of them. Connected, yes, like a web, a fiber leading from each to the next. The threads also spiraled out, attaching to the earth, the trees, even the castle walls. That big null spot must be the dragon. Curiously, similar blank lines emanated from her, too, ending abruptly, as if encountering other unseeable walls. A network of dragons? Hmm.

It was a mistake, however, to see Rogue's mental metaphor of a spiderweb in geographical terms, however. While physical proximity mattered to some extent, power of the mind involved factored in more. Rogue, for example, stood out to me like a tower of blue-black flame, the connections between us flowing like tributaries to a great river that flowed in both directions. He noticed my passing with a fond thought.

Titania, too, blazed through the network as a supernova of magical power, scintillating, in constant motion. Through the icy aura, however, black holes drilled down, much as sunspots on the moving surface of a star. Her wounds, no doubt. So, this was how Rogue had known her level of recovery. I stayed far back from her.

Especially because, all around her, the web seemed to fold and double back. It put me in mind of graphics I'd seen depicting the way wormholes and other singularities bent the fabric of space. The sheer number and variety of interconnections overwhelmed me. It frightened and nauseated me to attempt to get my brain around the phenomenon.

Rogue—all the fae—would have developed within this framework, understanding how to move within it reflexively, as a human child learns to put babbling sounds into words. No—as a human child learns to walk upright would be a better analogy. For me, this felt like moving in a new form of gravity, one where my muscles worked all wrong.

What I needed to do was reframe it to a more workable metaphor for my mind. Imagining the mass mind more like folders and subfolders on a computer, I wrestled the unwieldy concepts into an order I understood. I breathed easier, having tucked Titania's blaze into an essentially locked folder. No sharing properties. Ha!

After that, it became easier to find and sort the people I wanted to access regularly. It seemed rude to knock directly on people's minds, but in lieu of going out and searching—and possibly getting lost again—I fixed on Larch as someone who might not mind. I'd located him easily, his solid blue feel familiar to me, and tried the telepathic equivalent of ringing the doorbell.

He answered immediately and without rancor, promising to send a page—as I asked, since I figured Larch's promotion meant he wouldn't fetch for me anymore—to ask Starling and

Athena to come visit me. I could have asked them directly, but I seriously didn't want to get in the habit of summoning my minions to me from the remote loft of my tower.

Way too Snow Queen.

Starling arrived first, which didn't surprise me. Athena likely had to retrieve the scepter from wherever she'd stowed it. She might even be sitting in on Fafnir's interrogation, unflinchingly interested as she was.

Looking me over, Starling nodded in satisfaction, and I felt as if I'd passed a pop quiz. "Will I do?" I asked her in a dry tone.

"Yes, actually. Though the dragon is a bit outré," she replied in a saucy tone. "You might have warned me. Your seneschal needs to know these things."

"The next time I'm abducted and unexpectedly acquire a gigantic house pet in the process, I'll be sure to send you a memo."

"That would be very thoughtful of you. See that you do."

"Someone is feeling feisty this morning."

"Afternoon, that is, Lady Gwynn." She winked at me, her hair shining in the sunlight. "And yes—I *like* having a staff. I've already started amassing the pages to send invitations. Winter solstice for the ceremony then?"

"I don't know why anyone bothers asking me." I frowned at her.

"Form only. I know how you dote on protocol."

"Okay, so, two questions—if this amazing event is three days away, how can the pages possibly invite everyone in time for them to travel here? Why don't we just announce via the mass mind?"

"Everyone *knows*, of course. The invitation by page is

more a formality." She went on from there, explaining who should be invited and in what order.

Starling would be one of my hopeful monsters, should my theory bear out. Though a second child and not firstborn, she looked very nearly human. A tall, long-limbed and graceful woman, yes, but not so much that you'd think twice about it. Her peaches-and-cream skin glowed with perfect vitality that whispered of magic, though it would be put down to youthful health in my world. Her glossy brown eyes sat a bit wider apart in her face, over human-flat cheekbones, with a scattering of freckles grown darker in our journeys. Melanin response, just as in human physiology.

"Lady Gwynn." Her tone caught my attention. "Are you even listening to me?"

I rewound her explanation in my head. "Yes. You'll send out page-borne invitations immediately, ranked in order of recipient's importance, starting with the Queen Bitch, the last person I want at my wedding. The silk nymphs will arrive tomorrow to begin work on the gown. Rogue and I need to decide on a location for the actual ceremony—though I got the distinct impression from him that it would be here, but I'll ask. You will consult with Mistress Nancy when she arrives about catering. Athena has volunteered to corral the dragonfly girls to gather flowers. Yes, the Stargazers from the meadow would be fine and most appropriate—I'll check with Rogue that it's okay to cut them. You'll handle the rest of the decorations."

Starling narrowed her eyes at me. "I don't know how you do that."

I gave her a cheeky grin. "It's a gift."

She snorted and opened her mouth to say something else,

but Athena arrived, carrying Walt's scepter, Darling Hercules at her side. She set a velvet bag on the workbench. "Your dragon eggs. I brought them all." Then she whistled, tipping back her head to take in the expanse of sky. "Nice digs. Lord Rogue is a class act."

"He is that."

Darling slipped an image in my head of him in eye-blinding armor, performing the ceremony. *"I don't think so,"* I replied and he flicked his tail in annoyance. The presence of the scepter in the room sizzled with a subsonic hum.

Though Darling had brought up a good point. "So, who will marry us?"

Athena and Starling cocked their heads in that quizzical way, while Darling Hercules leaped up on my workbench and batted the rubber ducky off with the cat equivalent of a smirk. I moved the grimoire out of his reach.

"You marry each other," Starling finally said, nice and slow for the idiot girl.

"No, no." Hell, it confused things in good old American English too. "In my world, people get married according to a religion. So a priest or representative of that god or goddess performs the ceremony for them." Or the judge did it for the government. Pretty much the same thing, in the end. Snarky me.

"Are you saying you want Titania to perform the ceremony?" Athena raised her powder-blue eyebrows in astonished arches.

"God, no!"

"It's your special day." Starling glared at Athena. "You should have what you want."

"No. I don't want it to be like that." Watch me turn into Bridezilla. Given Faerie magic, I'd morph into Godzilla in a froufrou gown. "When Blackbird and Fergus got married, how did that work?"

A little line appeared on Starling's brow. "I don't know. I'll ask when they arrive."

"They're coming?"

"Of course, Gwynn!" Starling nearly stamped her foot. "They wouldn't miss the wedding of the millennium. I've been trying to tell you—everyone who is anyone will be there."

"Clearly excluding the everyones who aren't anyone," Athena observed. *My little fae Che Guevara.*

"I agree, everyone should be invited. *After*," I specified, seeing Starling's aghast expression, "the bigwigs receive their invitations." *Rogue would not be at all pleased to have humans at the wedding, but if the bride is one, I say the others get to come too.* "Now—how is it possible that Blackbird is coming? Are you saying Fergus found her and is retrieving her from sailing the sea?"

She lifted one shoulder. Let it fall. "I don't know. Fafnir mentioned at the feast that they're on their way."

All so convoluted. I'd check in on them too. It began to feel as if the Castle of the Dark Gods had a big homing signal on it, with all of my personal pigeons flocking home to roost.

Starling gathered her skirts. "I'm off then. I have work to do." She stared pointedly at Athena, who grinned cheerfully and didn't move.

"Oh! Before you go, Starling—can we arrange for magic apples to feed the dragon?" *Look at me, Queen of Delegating.*

"Already requested." Starling gave me a smug look.

"You are amazing," I told her. "How much do I love you?"

"Not nearly enough." She sniffed, but she bustled off with a happy bounce in her stride.

"I'll hang for a few." Athena said, when I looked at her in question, maintaining her grip on the scepter, giving me an implacable look.

"You don't trust me alone with the scepter?"

"Nope." She popped her lips over the word, making me realize she'd said it in English. So much of me had leaked into her. "I'll wait while you use it and then put it away again."

I itched enough to get my hands on the thing again that I respected Athena's caution. The scepter definitely possessed some sort of addictive quality. My recent discovery of the dome's properties might mean I could use that as a tool instead, but for now I intended to fulfill my promise to Starling. That she'd left without arguing further, her glance flicking to the scepter and away, indicated she hadn't forgotten, but had simply been good about not nagging me.

Gravely, Athena handed me the scepter, standing by like a weight-lifting spotter while I settled cross-legged into my chair, laying the awkward object across my lap. A heavy crystal sphere on one end of a fairly long staff, the scepter didn't balance well. It looked great for brandishing, however, as Walter had done frequently before I took the damn thing away from him.

Darling leaped onto the other arm of the chair, my flanking sentry.

"I'm not going to go psycho with one peek," I said, trying not to be irritable. The scepter sang softly in my hands, the staff smooth, solid, fitting my hands perfectly. The crystal globe swirled with light, beckoning me to touch.

"Then it will be no trouble for you to hand it over again." Now that Athena had given me the scepter, she'd pulled out her dagger, spinning it artfully. The slightly menacing aspect, complemented by her spiked hair and that sharp, restless mind, got my attention. Not that Athena wasn't always serious—sometimes dismayingly so, despite her flower of a face and lavender eyes—but she clearly meant business.

"I won't use it if you think it's that bad." I definitely wouldn't mention the dome's properties. Rogue wouldn't have built it for me if he thought it could be damaging. Right?

"It's a good experiment," came her nonanswer. "Let's see how you do, since you're...better."

Better than what? But I knew exactly what, even before Darling Hercules gave me an image of my haggard self, riding through the Glass Mountains, a starving husk with despair written all over her. Surely I hadn't looked that awful. Athena and the cat simply gazed back at me, lavender and green eyes sharing common sympathy—and determination. I'd never mentioned the dreams to them, of Rogue in Titania's bed, of them laughing at my efforts to find him. It hadn't been all about using the wizard's staff.

"Fine. Poke me if I get weird. But don't get blood on the carpet."

Even Athena didn't laugh at that one. Some humor was simply lost on the fae.

I put my hands on the crystal globe. And, oh yes, it satisfied some deep craving, like a shot of whiskey after a four-hour department meeting. As if I'd strapped on a mental jetpack, my thoughts took off with fabulous speed and power. Belatedly it occurred to me that the scepter and the dome would amplify each other.

It felt so amazing that I couldn't find it in me to care. Better than riding on the Liralen.

Barely did I think of Walter than I was there, hovering somewhere right behind his forehead. Wrenching and sordidly disorienting. I should have braced myself for the return to the scene of my horrific sorcery training. One day it wouldn't bother me so much. I hoped. For the time being, however, the scene I happened into made me reel. I'd left Walter with my erstwhile trainers, Marquise and Scourge, knowing full well their predilection for sadistic kink as a tool for teaching self-discipline.

I'd tried my best to warn Walter and, sure enough, they were working him over. Being in his head while they did it sent a flood of revulsion through me.

Marquise's eerily beautiful face gazed up, contorted with pleasure, words of endearment falling from her lips, her Christmas-ornament eyes glittering. The erotic joy of fucking her filled Walt's mind with delirium, urged higher by the agonizing pain from Scourge's whip falling on him from behind.

I nearly vomited. Would have, had I not been out of my own body.

I yanked myself away, the point-of-view refocusing like a camera panning back to a wider angle. The scene still played out—still deeply disturbing to my scarred self—but blessedly less immediate. Walt was determinedly working to please Marquise as Scourge whipped him—and as he magically altered a nearby cube from white to black, to a sphere, to a pyramid, instantly and perfectly at each of Scourge's shouted commands.

Lessons in exacting magic under the most distracting conditions. Well did I remember those trials.

And how grateful was I that Rogue had taken the steps he did to spare me actual rape by those two. Steps that had ultimately placed him in Titania's grip, and in her bed.

Marquise smiled, a delighted expression that had nothing to do with Walt's steady efforts. *Hello, precious pet,* she mentally crooned at me. *Felicitations on your nuptials. We all three shall attend.* She blew me a kiss, her tinkling laugh following when I zoomed myself back, their castle spinning into a dot below me.

Okay, I panicked a little. Arguably, I had what I came for. Though I obviously wouldn't tell Starling all of it. Interesting that they intended to bring Walter.

The rushing power of the scepter cushioned the rawness of exposing myself to that past trauma, so I rode it longer. Why not visit all of my old friends? I thought of Blackbird and, indeed, found her already back on land, riding behind Fergus on his battle stallion, racing dramatically across the countryside. Her black hair streamed behind her like a pennant of silk and she looked dreamily happy, leaning her cheek against her husband's back. Fergus must have been still in princess-rescuing mode because he looked like a handsome avenging prince.

I checked in on Falcon's army. No longer encamped by the sea engaging in entertaining but pointless naval battles, the entire force was marching instead, traveling at magically amplified speeds. As the general, Falcon rode at the forefront, stern in mirror-bright armor.

I pulled back my view again, trying to get a feel for the landscape. Apparently it didn't work that way, however. I might be able to "see" physical people and places, but only with a specific focus. I couldn't seem to just soar about and take things in. I needed people and I'd pretty much used up everyone I knew, except Mistress Nancy who might be already here and, well, Titania.

She might be tucked away in my secured mental file folder, but she still blazed on the edge of my consciousness. It was tempting to drift closer, to sniff around a bit. Getting better at my control, I coasted closer, careful to stay back far enough that she couldn't detect my presence as Marquise had. Her palace seemed very quiet, with none of the activity I'd seen in other vision visits. She had to be there, however, if my mind's eye drew me to that place.

I tried seeing on the mass-mind level, instead. As if I'd flipped the lens on a microscope from bright field to phase-contrast, a new level of detail jumped out. The black, oily rope strands she used to connect to the people she manipulated radiated out from her palace in a complex, horrifying web.

She was in there, all right, spinning her nasty plans.

Worse, amid the many cords that connected me to Rogue, which seemed iridescent with golden light in my mental metaphor, fine black threads snaked through, seeking me. Reaching from her to Rogue to me.

Worming their way to our unborn child.

I couldn't allow it. Working my mind through the cords, I pushed outward, using my own light and power—shimmering platinum and green—through the fibers, filling them and using that pressure to force oily black away.

Preoccupied with the effort, I didn't realize how much

closer to Titania's palace and presence I'd drifted. When I did notice, and tried to pull back again, I couldn't. As if caught in a tractor beam from the Death Star, I gained speed toward her instead.

Pulling on more power, I fought the drag. To no avail.

I reached for the cat to assist, but she didn't seem to be present. Not active in this dimension? I dug for that connection to Mother Earth. Nothing, nothing, nothing.

My virtual self hurtled into Titania's palace of unearthly beauty and unimaginable cruelty. Deeper, through twisting tunnels, I helplessly tumbled. Until I stopped, abruptly, in an inner cavern—perhaps deep inside the mountain, the walls like blacked-out plate glass windows—everything looped and shrouded with billows of cobwebs.

All around, fae of both higher and lower forms were co-cooned, wrapped in the web, some screaming, some weeping, some ominously shriveled and still, while Titania reclined in the center. She wore the same face, no longer half-melted from my dragon-blood grenade, but the rest of her looked more like a spider than a woman. In addition to her multijointed fingers, she sported two extra limbs, her arms and legs the same length as those, and all tapped into her various cocooned prey.

Sucking sustenance from them as she healed.

Her lovely face didn't move, just as a plastic doll couldn't change its expression, but she nevertheless smiled to see me. *The troublesome sorceress pays me a visit? How obliging of her. You'll be exactly what I need. Come here, tasty lamb.*

Unable to resist, I did as she commanded, even as I shrieked inside. Surely it couldn't end like this. Flailing, I pulled on the connection to Rogue.

Pulled with all my might and will.

CHAPTER 18
IN WHICH I ENCOUNTER A SETBACK

Every rule was made to be broken.
~*Big Book of Fairyland*, "Rules of Magic"

AN ABRUPT YANK.

My head spun, giving me vertigo as if I'd dropped without warning down the last high hill of the Mister Twister roller coaster and I was eight years old again, screaming my guts out in raw, plunging terror.

"Gwynn!" Rogue's voice rang through my terror, strong, steady and full of irresistible command. "Attend me immediately."

I opened my eyes to find him bare inches away, eyes midnight dark, his ferociously strong grip biting into my arms with bruising force. No, my eyes had been already open—I just looked through them again, the physical vision less brilliantly acute than the virtual seeing. Energy from both the cat and Mother Earth poured in and my heart started beating with an alarming thump.

"Gwynn," he repeated. Cranking to life again, my brain

delivered the information that he'd been saying it for a while.

"I'm here," I said. "I'm back. And ouch, you can let go before you break my arms."

Instead of relieved joy, he glared at me with enough fury to make my heart skip a beat. But he relaxed his grip. Still not letting go of me, however.

Behind him, in my peripheral vision, Athena held the scepter, her purple eyes deep bruises in her ghostly white face. Darling Hercules stood on her shoulders, back arched Halloween-cat-style. As I spoke, he lowered his spine, but still fixed me with an angry stare.

The silence stretched on, nobody moving. My hands throbbed as if burned and I really wanted to look at them. Rogue seemed to have a hold on my gaze, however, and I couldn't look away.

"I'm *okay*. Let me go."

"What in the name of Titania did you think you were doing?" Rogue asked in a menacingly low tone that nevertheless echoed back from the dome with deep reverberations. "I swear I should chain you to the bed, if only to keep you out of trouble."

"Don't ever say that, even in jest." My own temper, raw from all I'd seen, flared in response.

"I'm not joking, foolish Gwynn. I'd rather you hate me than be lost to her as you nearly were."

"You'd rather destroy my spirit than see me dead?"

"Yes." He stared back, unapologetic. "And you wouldn't be dead. Just wishing for it. And that wish, my dear Gwynn, is one wish that would never, ever come true."

The image of those cocooned people came back to me and

the gorge rose in my throat. "I'm going to be sick."

Finally he released me, but with a fury that still simmered palpably. He stepped away and I fought to control the nausea.

"Give me that toy," he commanded Athena and, mutely, she handed it over. Rogue looked as if he wanted to break it over his knee. He raked me with a cold look of contempt. "I've brought your midwife. Have her see that you didn't endanger the babe with your wantonly reckless behavior. And get those cursed dragon eggs out of here—they stink." Without another word, he strode out, taking the scepter with him.

"Goddamn it." I fumed. Where did he get off acting like I'd disobeyed or something? Particularly when he did not get to give me orders, no matter what our relationship status was, and besides, he'd never told me not to use the scepter that way. *Wantonly reckless behavior.*

"I'm so sorry, Gwynn." Athena absently petted Darling Hercules, who slinked out from under her hand and trotted over to jump onto my lap, purring and sniffing my hands. They looked normal, but still sizzled where they'd been in contact with the crystal globe. "You looked dead. I panicked and summoned Lord Rogue. I should have known you had it under control."

"Is that how it looked?" I rubbed Darling's ears and scooted him off my lap so I could stand, stretching against the stiffness and wincing at the catch in the small of my back. "It's good you called him. I needed help." Which didn't help my pride to admit, but I'd own up to it.

"Are you going to be sick still?"

"No—that passed." But I was such a morass of other emotions, including roiling anger at Rogue's behavior and obvious displeasure with me, that I couldn't sort it out.

Athena nodded, fingers tugging at her dagger but not drawing it. Starling would have demanded to know what happened. I appreciated that Athena didn't ask. "I'll take you to Mistress Nancy then."

"She can't come here?"

"No. Lord Rogue says no humans in this tower—this wing of the castle, actually."

"Does he now?" More of his autocratic decisions. I nearly told Athena to overrule that order, for the sheer joy of countermanding His Royal Highness. But that might just get Athena and Nancy in trouble.

No, this was about him and me. He did not get to run my life, no matter how much he tried. I wanted to find him and tear him a new one. To add to my internal confusion, I also wanted to apologize and convince him not to be mad at me. Which was ridiculous, since I was mad enough at him that I didn't want to even lay eyes on him. I hated the way he'd looked at me—and felt simultaneously outraged over it.

What a freaking mess.

This was where love got you. At that moment, I wanted nothing more than to walk away and never speak to him ever again.

Not very mature of me. So, in lieu of confronting him further, if I even could, I followed Athena to visit Mistress Nancy. We wended our way down the tower steps, Darling Hercules leaping down them like an antelope clearing barbwire fences, with easy grace and an abundance of energy, then across several great halls and to another wing. I couldn't call it grungy, but this side of the massive complex definitely paled in grandeur to the rest. We passed kitchens clearly intended for the human denizens and I blanched at the unclean conditions. Starling would have to add that to her list, and if Lord Rogue objected, he could go fuck himself.

Mistress Nancy had been installed in a decent-sized and sunny suite of rooms, with a set of glass doors that opened into a private courtyard. Okay, not exactly a slum. She was out there showing a redheaded boy some kind of sandbox. I'd forgotten about her son when I'd asked for her. What was his name? Billy.

Nancy straightened when she saw me, smiling in genuine welcome. "Lady Sorceress—you're a sight for sore eyes. I'd worried after ye." Her broad Cockney accent sounded so familiar and welcome that I impulsively took the few steps to hug her. Surprised, she patted my back. "'Ere now, lovey. Don't you fret. Mistress Nancy will take care of you and the wee bairn."

I blinked back tears and hiccuped a little. Then let her go and scrubbed at my face, embarrassed. I seemed to be weeping all over everyone lately. Not a good image for the powerful sorceress and Lady of the Castle of Dark Gods. If Rogue even still wanted me. Oh wait, of course he did. He just wanted me more obedient, curse him.

He'd talked a good game there for a while, but the megalomaniac never lurked all that far from the surface. Never mind that he had good cause to be upset, seeing as how I'd nearly succumbed to Titania's clutches, killing my body and the baby along with it. But he didn't have to be such an ass about it.

I really could not live with someone who talked to me that

way.

"Billy, you stay out here and play in the magic sandbox while I give the Lady Sorceress a look-see. She's your liege, so you should bow and show your best manners."

"Oh, no, he doesn't have to do—" I broke off at her sharp look.

"Oh, yes, he does. Best to learn his place now than step over the line foolishly later."

I saw her point and did my best to accept the little boy's timorous scraping. Once released, he scampered with good spirits back to the sandbox. It looked to be filled with a shimmering material composed of rainbow particles—a sort of cross between Silly Putty and glitter. At his touch, the stuff swirled and built itself into a tower, which he shaped, adding on ledges and windows.

"It's a lovely gift to have waiting for him." Nancy gazed at the boy fondly. "You're most thoughtful to provide it."

"I didn't," I replied, noting that she'd been careful not to thank me. Most likely it had been Rogue's thoughtfulness, but I wasn't about to hand him any credit at the moment. Nancy had a canny and careful mind, which was why she'd survived so well in Faerie without magic. Though, judging by the rest of us immigrants, the magic should be affecting her in some way. Perhaps she possessed a gift that emerged under specific circumstances, like Fergus had.

She made Athena and Darling Hercules wait outside also, which they seemed happy enough to do, though Darling immediately swatted the magic sand castle to Billy's scolding complaints. Nancy settled me on the bed and gave me a surprisingly thorough and professional examination. I shouldn't have been taken aback, but it felt like so long since anyone familiar with human medicine had touched me, that it seemed almost foreign now. I also had very little idea how much expertise a midwife of her era would have. I'd somehow expected her to wave magic hands over me and pronounce the baby fine, not give me the full gynecological prodding.

Though I supposed that was why I'd hired her.

"Ro—Lord Rogue asked you to come nicely, didn't he? He didn't bully or demand?"

Her head popped up over my skirt-clad knees and she winked at me. "He's not so much for asking nicely, but I did drive a most excellent bargain, if I do say so myself. 'Specially since I woulda come anyway, seeing as how it's you, dearie."

"Thank you." I stared up at the ceiling, trying not to flinch. For the baby, I reminded myself. Had my body really died while I was out of it for so long? A horrible, foolish risk to have taken. But I hadn't known, had I? Mistress Nancy withdrew her hand but flipped my skirts up higher, laying her cheek against my round belly. It *felt* like the baby still lived. I could have looked for that living cord but even the thought of opening my mind into that phase world at the moment made me queasy.

"Is—"

"Hush now," she directed.

I lay still, wondering if she could truly hear anything. It seemed not possible and I waited for permission to speak, at which point I would offer to wish up a stethoscope.

"All's fine." She pronounced, drawing my skirts down, though she didn't look happy. "I'd say you're about five months along in human time. You'll start showing more and more. Have you had the sicks much?"

"Not really."

"Lucky you. Still, you're a bit roughed-up-like in your nethers. Perhaps tell Lord Rogue to take it a bit easier on you."

My face went totally hot and I knew I must be scarlet with the blush. "Ah. I, um, I didn't think it would..." I floundered.

"Hurt the babe? No, Lady Sorceress, it won't. Spare the gymnastics, but the child is well cushioned. I'm thinking more of you." She dropped her voice to a whisper. "Did he force you into this, Gwynn? Because I'll help you away if you ask it."

More people wanting to rescue me. And awful if she thought he'd been raping me.

"No. No—not at all. I, um, I love him, see and I agreed to the wedding. It's fine." It sounded weak to me, especially in the face of her doubt and my not particularly feeling the love at the moment. It flashed in my head that poor, doomed Cecily had said the same things.

Though I couldn't hear Nancy's thoughts as I could most people's, her expression said it all.

"Really. I have things under control." Ha to that!

"All right then, dearie." She patted my knee, indulging me, not believing. "Up with you then. I'm going to see that you get food from the human kitchens. The fae food isn't all that good for a growing bairn."

Ugh. And Nancy likely had no better idea of food hygiene than the rest of them. All the more reason to set Starling on the task. I could wish my own food clean, but I'd be happier to purge the source, for everyone's benefit.

Athena elected to stay playing with Billy. I guessed him to be about eight or nine and she looked remarkably about the same age, with her girlish size. Except for the punked blue hair and cynical expression, she could pass for his playmate. They'd made considerable progress on the castle and were debating how to create a waterfall and moat like the real ones. She seemed happy in a carefree way I'd never known her to be. I also knew that, with her awakened consciousness, she ached for family relationships. It might be good for her to hang with Nancy and Billy.

Somebody should be happy around here.

Darling Hercules went with me, cheerfully agreeing to show me the way to the dragon's tower. Part of my problem stemmed from the castle complex not following what would be a standard building design to me. Titania's palace and Castle Brightness had been this way also—I'd just had people leading the way in those places. Or dragging me about, more often. Castle of the Dark Gods had been obviously modified and added on to over vast expanses of time, making it almost more like a small walled city. More than that, the insectile quality of the fae perspective showed through in its design. Spirals instead of rectangles, spherical and ovoid rooms, smaller chambers leading into larger ones in long chains. There were no central hallways, but rather a concatenation of passages, no doubt exacerbated by the magically moving entrance gate. What I'd thought of as the main hallway when the gang arrived had been only one of many.

No wonder I'd gotten lost.

If I was going to live here any length of time—and it was a mark of my black mood that it seemed unlikely and even unthinkable at this point—then I'd need a system of markers. Hell, I'd make signs for me and the kid and hang them on the walls.

The image of me, years in the future, walking these halls with a boy like Billy or a girl of Athena's size, reading the signs to find our way, took me aback. Likely my half-breed child would exceed my abilities and would need no such markers. It would be me on my own, forever not truly belonging to this place. Without real family—just fae connections.

The thought depressed me utterly.

The dragon looked pleased to see me, puffing out a sparking breath in the chill air and nodding her chin at a basket of the apples. How Starling had gotten them so fast, I didn't know, but I appreciated it. Darling Hercules and I stayed out of range of her magic dampening field, which she seemed to considerately keep close.

I took the velvet bag of eggs out of my pocket and opened it, setting the remaining four in front of her. As I'd planned to do all along. But no, Rogue had to be a jerk about them. He'd been good about the dragon the night before, and that morning. Probably he'd just said something out of his general pissy mood. Not that it excused him.

It was worth it though, to see her amber lantern eyes gleam with delight. With a gentle claw—which seemed unnecessary to me since the things were hard as gemstones— she gathered them close. Then she plucked an apple from the basket and held it out to me.

"No, thank you," I said, as politely as I could. "They're poisonous to me."

With a dip of her chin, she insisted, and I stretched out my hands, again with that sense of reverence I'd felt when I first encountered one—probably her—in Walter's castle. In the late afternoon light, she glittered as if covered with jewels herself.

Immense and full of tangible power, she filled me with awe. As if some racial memory from a cavewoman ancestor whispered to me of dinosaurs walking the earth.

Not at all logical, but there it was.

She dropped the apple neatly into my cupped hands and dipped her chin again, indicating it. I examined it, though I'd seen them before and this could be one I'd plucked myself during the harvest at Castle Brightness. But no—the apple had changed, seeming to be made of purest gold. The basket still held regular apples, shining deep red. Well, as regular as poisonous fruit that fed the magic-free dragons could be. So, she'd changed it. Transmutation into gold.

She winked at me then, slow and deliberate. Some kind of message for me.

Not for the first time, I missed that we couldn't seem to speak directly. All those years of my life *not* hearing mind-to-mind communications and now I felt crippled by its lack.

"Are you warm enough?" I asked her, more rhetorically than anything else. Though the sun shone bright, the wind possessed a cutting edge. Enough that I wished up a cloak— not the one Rogue gave me—and a gust caught at it, making it snap like a pennant. "We could move you to an inside room, like you had at Walter's."

I caught a rustle of amusement before she set her great head protectively over the eggs and closed her eyes. Guess that was a no.

And a clear dismissal.

Pocketing my golden apple—wasn't one part of the story with Aphrodite, Helen of Troy and Paris?—I walked with Darling Hercules back inside. He suggested some mouse hunting, which I declined, to his disappointment. If I followed my list, I should go back to my tower room and make notes. I seethed with too much restlessness for that and my black mood made me unambitious, to boot. Blame my stubborn nature, but mostly I wanted to leave the castle. To go anywhere else, now that I couldn't. I felt stifled, cooped up. Yes, I'd promised to try to be gracious, but that was before Rogue smacked me down like a disobedient toddler. An insidious voice whispered that I had indeed traded away my freedom, as I'd dreaded all along.

I loved Rogue. No escaping that fact. But it didn't change reality.

After all, the feeling of being in love was all endorphins and, like a junkie coming down from a high, without that drugging influence, I saw my current situation in a cold and sober light. No wonder Nancy and Fafnir thought I'd been coerced. Seduced counted. It only felt more pleasant while it happened.

I didn't know what to think and I really hated being in that place.

Worse, I had no one to talk to. No one who didn't have some stake in the outcome, who could give me unbiased, objective feedback. Darling Hercules sent me an image of a handsome young man, his former self, possibly, listening intently.

"Thank you, but you're not good for advice. I mean that in the nicest way."

Not sure where I wanted to go, except far, far away, I plopped down on the tower steps, unable to motivate myself to go any farther, and Darling perched beside me in glum agreement. The tower had no windows, which made it comfortingly dark. It served as a place to hide, at least for a while. I could have sat outside with the dragon, but the wind was blowing too cold and she didn't want me there anyway. Mostly I wanted to drink too much wine and drown my sorrows—to an alarming degree, given that I couldn't do *that* either.

After a time, footsteps came up the circling stairs, the scent of Rogue's blue-black magic preceding him. He appeared around the bend, expression carefully blank.

"I don't think I want to talk to you right now," I said, before he got too close.

"So you'll sit in a dark tower instead?"

"I couldn't think of anything else to do."

"Not like you."

"That's me—full of surprises."

"I won't apologize for being angry with you." He'd stopped a few steps below me, one foot higher than the other.

"Makes for a short conversation, anyway."

He said nothing to that.

"Fine. I'll go first. Unlike you, I *am* sorry for what happened. It was a mistake, but I didn't know. The baby is fine. I won't do it again."

"I know you won't, because I'll keep that cursed scepter out of your reach. Had I any idea what you'd laid hold of, I'd never have let you use it."

"*Let* me? I'm sorry—I think you've mistaken me for a fuck-toy after all."

"Don't start with that again. You were wrong and you said so."

He just didn't get it. Worse, it seemed more and more likely that he never would. A lifetime of this battle lay ahead of me. I sighed. "Darling Hercules—would you excuse us?"

With an affectionate thought and sweep of his tail, he trotted down the stairs, swiping a paw at Rogue as he passed.

"Come now, stubborn Gwynn." Rogue made an effort to sound coaxing, but I'd had enough of being coaxed and seduced. "It was a misunderstanding. Let's go somewhere more comfortable. Have you eaten? Mistress Nancy said that—"

"I think we shouldn't get married."

That stopped him. "You already promised. Will you break that vow?"

"I wouldn't be breaking it. I promised that I would marry you, but not when."

"You agreed to winter solstice. Only hours ago."

"Yes, but you said that agreements between you and me like that no longer held the same binding force of a bargain." Loopholes had saved me before.

"Gwynn—" He started up the next step.

"No. Stay there. I don't want you touching me. I—I'm very unhappy with you." Though the words were mild, my voice shook with the force of the emotion behind it. "There's a saying among my people that doing the same thing over and over and expecting a different result is the definition of insanity."

"Meaning?" he inquired in a stiff, formal tone.

"Meaning that we keep coming to agreements and then you revert to type, every time. You pretend that we're equal partners and then you go autocratic and treat me like an idiot that you need to manage."

"What you did was idiotic," he insisted.

"You think I don't know that? I'm grateful you dragged me back, that you saved my miserable life, yet again."

"I didn't." He bit out the words. "I couldn't. Where you'd gone, how you'd done it—I couldn't reach you. I thought I'd lost you forever." His desperate terror glinted like a flash of a raven's wing, tossed in the ocean and submerged again.

"Then how?"

"You grabbed *me* and pulled yourself back, through the connection to Titania, so far as I can tell. You couldn't come straight to me, so you went through her. It shouldn't have been possible."

No wonder I felt sick, coated with her mental slime. "It scared me too. She's nearly healed. I saw her. And, in that place, I saw her ties going into you and from you into me, working their way to the baby. She can get to us through you. It's not healthy for us to be connected to you."

"What are you saying?"

"I'm saying I want out. I can't do this. I can't be your wife. Live in this place. Let's do whatever ritual we need to do to cut the ties. I'll hide somewhere, have the baby and we can work out some kind of joint custody."

"And go into the desert alone?"

"So unfair of you to use that."

"I'm not using it." With a heavy sigh, he set his back against the curved wall and slid down to sit a few steps below me. "I can't apologize for being angry, but I regret that it upset you. It came from a place of fear. I'm not accustomed to feeling that way."

"That doesn't excuse anything and it doesn't change my

mind."

"Sometimes we are going to disagree. Even fight with each other, stubborn Gwynn."

"That's not it." I didn't think it was. "I think marrying you would be a mistake."

There. I said it. The words echoed cold and heavy between us.

"Be that as it may, the cords cannot be cut. You're welcome to try, as you no doubt will since there appears to be nothing you won't attempt, but you will not succeed."

"Till death do us part then. Meaning mine."

"Not even that."

Ominous. "What it that supposed to mean?"

"I found out what Fafnir's plan is—just now, so don't be angry I didn't tell you sooner. It appears Cecily's spirit remains tied to him. He believes their child might still be alive."

A changeling in my world? "Then he does want to reanimate her corpse."

"He hoped to study you and your connections to our child, then use her flesh to...find them."

The implications of that rippled through me. Like the Catholic version of the soul, confined in purgatory. This did make me feel better.

"So, you're saying there's no going back for me. I'm trapped. For eternity if I am to believe that kind of claptrap."

"If you care to see it that way, then yes. From the beginning you've been tied to me, and with the passing of time, those cords have strengthened. All that's changed is your awareness of them. I've done my best to make it palatable for you, but like it or not, here we are, each bound to the other."

"I don't like it."

He laughed, a bitter sound. "Don't you see? It goes both ways. If she had you, she had me. And vice versa. We're stuck with each other, my spirited Gwynn. And you will marry me in three days' time. Virtually all of Faerie has been invited, which means you made that agreement with each and every one of them and thus so did I. You've asked for honesty, for me to explain things. There you are. You don't have to be happy about marrying me, but you will do it. For your own damn good, if nothing else."

"I hate it when you treat me like you know better than I do."

"On some things I do."

He was, of course, right about that. Not that it sat any better with me.

He stood and started down the steps again. Paused. "If you won't do it for your own good, consider doing it for mine. That might not be enough, but at least give it some thought."

"You just want to win."

"Yes," he answered without ceasing his descent. "For us all."

CHAPTER 19

IN WHICH I STAR IN THE CENTER RING OF THE THREE-RING CIRCUS

๕๙๕

Never invite the evil queen to your wedding.
~Big Book of Fairyland, "Personal Observations"

W E DIDN'T SEE much of each other over the next couple of days.

Good for regaining perspective, for clearing my head of the fog of sex and seductive emotion. Also lonely. Which only served to both add to my doldrums and also piss me off more. Mostly I was mad at myself, but it was easier to push that onto Rogue and his high-handed ways.

If you won't do it for your own good, consider doing it for mine.

Like I owed him something. Pompous autocratic control freak.

I really wanted to talk out my concerns and it made me feel crazy that he was the only one I wanted to talk to.

Starling kept me busy with inane activities and meaningless decisions. I didn't care what color my dress should be, so she badgered me until I told her anything but white. As to where the ceremony would take place, I referred her to Rogue, stopping just short of telling her I didn't give a shit. None of it mattered a whit to me, except that I had gotten myself well and truly stuck. All the preparations took on such a surreal cast that I found it hard to take any of it seriously. I visited the dragon several times, fantasizing about riding off on her back to some remote location where I might hide and never be found.

Only the prospect of breaking my agreement with all of Faerie—and the specter of Titania's spidery self draining me dry while I never quite died of it—kept me from running. And maybe a dollop of guilt.

Otherwise, I would have, I told myself. But I was fresh out of loopholes.

On the rare occasions I did see Rogue, he treated me with polite and wary distance. He neither ate with me nor shared our bed. I suspected he mainly kept out of my way. Self-preservation, perhaps, though he seemed dangerously on edge also. I began to feel like one of those maidens in historical romances, forced into a marriage of convenience with the brooding and perhaps deranged gothic hero.

Only it didn't suit me to play the role of naive virgin.

More and more people began arriving, Starling breathlessly informing me of each and every one. Mostly I didn't care about that either, except the ones who verified the long-distance seeing as accurate. Fortunately, Lord Rogue didn't require me to greet them, probably not willing to test my temper that far. I wouldn't have been able to face any of them, particularly not Marquise and Scourge with Walter as their hapless slave. Starling mentioned that she'd seen them, her tone carefully neutral, and said nothing more when I didn't comment.

I'd already given her an edited version of what I'd found out and that was all I cared to say on the topic.

I couldn't discuss what weighed most heavily on my mind, and everything else seemed too frivolous to bear. Everyone tiptoed around me and my foul mood, which suited me well enough.

Everyone, that is, except Puck.

The night before the wedding—to my relief, there seemed to be no fae version of the bachelorette party or, if there was, Athena and Starling knew better than to suggest it—he waltzed into my tower with no announcement, wearing an outfit seemingly constructed of turquoise cabbage roses. "Lady Gwynn," he sang out, "I have a pig to pick with you."

I looked up from my grimoire, where I'd been trying to work out how the fae phyla and species might branch from one another, to distract myself from feeling like a pitiful prisoner. "I think you mean a bone to pick."

"What fun would that be?" He did a shuffle step and jingle bells hidden deep in the cabbage roses chimed. "Which, neither are you."

"Fun?" I stood and stretched. I should walk more, but without anywhere to go but inside the castle, which just put me more on edge with all its unsettling twists and turns, I'd kept to my room. I hadn't cared to run into Rogue or someone like Nasty Tinker Bell either. "I think I'm facing enough serious issues that I don't need to be trying to make merry."

"Nonsense. That's when the most merrymaking modalities must may be."

He'd spoken to me in English, as he sometimes did. Nevertheless. "You realize that made no sense."

"Does anything?" He shrugged elaborately.

"Good point."

He flopped onto the bed, crossed hands under his head and stared up at the sky. "Tell me, doctor, all of your problems."

"I think you have our positions reversed."

"Ah, yes—then I shall tell you. You're being foolishly mortal. There. You can pay me in wine."

"For lousy advice? I don't think so."

"Is this better? Love looks not with the eyes, but with the mind."

"Seems I've heard that one before," I replied in a dry tone.

"And yet you seem to think your eyes have been blinded by fairy dust."

"It's not beyond the realm of possibility, right?"

"But not within probability."

"Meaning?"

He hopped up and tapped me on the nose. His nails were painted pink. "Meaning, you're a smart girl. Trust your mind, not your eyes."

"That's just it—I don't know if I can trust my own mind."

"You always have before. Yes? Yes? Yes?" With each question, he executed a box step, adding the jazz hands that made me laugh despite everything.

"Yes," I finally agreed.

He snagged my ever-present carafe of wine and drank it down. "Much better!" And Puck left as abruptly as he'd arrived.

Use my mind, huh? Hardly seemed like useful advice, but I sat back down and set myself to composing a list of pros and cons on whether to marry Rogue. He might imply I had no choice, but if I really didn't want to marry him, I'd find a way out.

I didn't care what anyone said—there's always a choice.

Pros
Security from cabal
Protection from QB's final solution
Companionship
Excellent sex
Understands me and my flaws
Protect child
Save humanity?

Cons
No divorce
Might be a trap
Giving up personal agency/happiness
Different species
Rogue can annoy the hell out of me

When I looked at the list, the possibility of protecting the child and hopefully saving all of humankind from Titania outweighed the rest. Especially since the cons mostly consisted of variations on my uncertainty and lack of future happiness. And it didn't escape my notice that the pro list was longer.

As Rogue had so coldly pointed out, I didn't have to be happy about it. And, as Puck had noted, however obliquely— being happy would be up to me, regardless.

I'd been in this place before, at a dead end, trapped. Then

I'd had the opportunity—however impulsive and badly handled—to walk off and I had. A decision that ultimately had led me to this place. As tempting as it might be to run away from this, I would not.

The decision firm in my mind that I'd wed Rogue at the moment of solstice the next day, I retired to bed alone and gazed up at the impossible firmament of Faerie. So starkly beautiful. The skies of Earth doubled over and intensified.

I tumbled into tangled, hallucinogenic dreams—the first like them I'd had since rescuing Rogue. In them I wore silver chains and I'd been trapped in a cell. No, inside an egg. Though I pounded to break through the leathery substance, it only flexed under my fists. I dug my nails in, the platinum claws springing from my fingers, and I sliced at it. The shell seamlessly resealed. Then I couldn't slash anymore, the chains held me back. The air grew thick, lacking oxygen and I choked on it.

It wasn't an egg after all. No, it was a cocoon and I was wrapped up in it, with Titania embracing me, inserting her proboscis. To feed. Or to lay eggs, like a wasp.

I screamed.

"Gwynn. Wake up." For the second time I came back to myself with Rogue's gaze filling my vision. He had my wrists pinned to the bed, his face bleeding a little from a trio of scratches. With an effort of will, I retracted the claws and he released my wrists. "You cried out in your sleep," he offered, as if in defense.

"Sorry. I'm surprised you heard me."

"I always hear you, my Gwynn."

"I'm sorry for that too."

"Don't be. There's enough room for regret between us without adding that on."

True enough. An awkward pause fell between us. I didn't know what to say except that I wanted to apologize and I didn't know what for. Then the moment was over and Rogue stood, moonlight glinting white off his loose hair.

"Go back to sleep, Gwynn. I'll keep watch over you."

"You don't have to."

"Are you saying you don't want me to?"

"No. I'm just sure you must have better things to do."

He sat down again. Seemed like he might touch my cheek, but stopped himself. "Nothing is more important than you are."

"Except for your Grand Plan, whatever it may be."

"*You* are the plan. There is nothing else. If I behave in ways you don't like, it's because of that. This is the only type I revert to."

Even in my blackest moments, it always amused me, his eidetic memory, how he recalled my least remark. Somehow, in the dark with my mind befuddled with the nightmare, I couldn't muster the same self-righteous anger I clung to in the light of day. I could make a list of his personality flaws, yes—and then make at least an equal column of my own.

"I'm sorry you dread marrying me so much," he said. "If I could change your heart on that I would."

"That would be against the rules."

"I need no reminding of that." Exasperation filled his voice and I nearly smiled to hear it. At least I drove him as crazy as he made me. A better person wouldn't be pleased about that, but I wasn't a better person. I was only myself.

"I'm just afraid," I whispered.

"Of me?"

"Yes."

"Am I so terrible?" He sounded...something. Wounded. Weary.

"You could be. How do I know you won't be my destruction?"

"This is why we must wed. Once we do, you'll understand. Your fate will become mine."

"And vice versa."

"Yes."

"That takes a huge amount of trust. What if I'm wrong?"

"Are you never mistaken?"

"I wish."

"Good." Though I couldn't see his face, I heard the smile. "Then your wish will come true. Sleep now."

Amazingly I did, falling into a deep, untroubled slumber, the sight of his black silhouette at the window obscurely comforting.

༅

IN THE MORNING, Starling woke me with a cheerful warning that I needed to hustle to be ready in time. The light seemed dim. I gazed up at the sky, to find it white. No—full of snow. Shrugging into my robe, I went to the edge of the dome and found the moat billowing steam in the frosty air. Dragons— dozens of them—wheeled circles in the sky, dive-bombing snowflakes and each other in a playful dance. The meadow of Stargazers, the blossoms standing out like sapphire jewels against the shimmering snow, provided the only other color in the landscape. Even the castle itself had been frosted with ice.

I couldn't decide if it was a good omen or a bad one, so I let it go and went to take the bath Starling ordered me into.

She worked on my hair with the help of two maidservants, creating an impossible tower of it. Their presence spared me having to converse with her, though she occasionally leveled me with an assessing look. In the background, her worry over Fergus and Blackbird crackled like a radio between stations. I had nothing more to offer her than she did me. So, almost as if by mutual accord, we behaved as if getting my look just right mattered more than anything else.

By the time they'd finished, I looked like a dark-haired Marie Antoinette. The image was helped along by a corset worthy of that era, sapphire blue and silver whirls decorating it, the tight lacing lifting my bosom. Thankfully Nancy intervened and made them leave the lower part loose, to give my belly room.

It seemed to have grown every time I looked at it and I wondered if the dream hadn't come from the child, anxious to escape the confines of my body.

Starling gave me leave to do my own makeup, but watched closely, directing the process. Blacker, thicker lashes. Redder, glossier lips. Whiter, smoother skin. I drew the line at changing my eye color to blue to match the dress, even though she pouted.

The platinum-silver pattern on the left side of my face also could not be changed.

They dressed me in lace drawers—would Marie have called them pantalets?—and then dozens of silk petticoats and underskirts. The silk nymphs had done their work well, creating shimmeringly translucent leaves of skirts in all shades of blue and silver. They layered over each other, creating a vision of depth, of azure summer skies and ghostly moonlight at once.

At least it wasn't white.

The final overdress looked like brocade but whispered light as air. A deeper blue than the rest, it seemed to float as I moved. A long train of broad sapphire and silver ribbons trailed behind me. I donned the blue lily necklace to match the earrings, which I'd never removed. I'd kept the diamond ring too. All a sign that I'd never truly thought I'd get out of this.

Maybe that I hadn't really wanted to, despite my fears.

I'd thought about it, though, in my fantasies of escape. The dragon's field would release the earrings and I'd leave it all in a little pile on the tower for Rogue to find. Just as I'd left my belongings behind at Devils Tower, in the mirror to this castle.

Darling Hercules, resplendent in a sapphire-jeweled collar someone had fashioned for him, led the way down the winding tower stairs. The others had to hang well back so as not to tread on my train. Served Starling right. I went slowly in the high-heeled blue leather boots, tooled in whorls of silver that matched the ones on my face.

Where the stairs widened at the bottom, opening into the great hall, Rogue waited for me. Resplendent in matching blue and silver—of course—he looked gravely serious. He'd braided his hair, so it hung down his back, woven with ribbons that matched mine and studded with jeweled stargazer lilies. The horseshoe stud I'd made for him glinted in his ear. His eyes, both deeper blue and more glittering, fastened on me. I caught a whisper of relief from him, before he shut the doors on his mind.

"Afraid I wouldn't show?" I asked, quietly, so no one else could hear. Amusing at least myself.

With a slight lift of the left side of his mouth, he inclined his head slightly, acknowledging the point. He lifted my left hand and placed a kiss on the diamond. "You look beautiful, my ravishing Gwynn. Thank you for that. And for not running, yes."

That startled me. I'd been careful to keep those thoughts very quiet, after all.

"Did you think I can't see that much, even without hearing your thoughts?"

"I may have wanted to, but I didn't. I'm here and I'm going through with it."

He seemed about to say something more but didn't. Instead, he dropped my hand and offered me his arm. "Shall we, then?"

My hand shook a little as I slipped it through his elbow and turned to face everyone. The hall dripped with the Stargazer lilies, blue and silver ribbons, and rafts of candles, the room redolent of the sweet blossoms and the hot vanilla scents of wax. Athena and the dragonfly girls had outdone themselves. People filled the hall. Falcon glowered at me, while Lady Healer on his arm smiled serenely, lovely in a formal grass-green gown. Fafnir appeared to be escorting Nasty Tinker Bell, the silver collar around his throat as obvious as his frown. Puck waved fingers at me, a handsome elfin-looking man gazing at him adoringly. Marquise and Scourge, she dressed in glistening black and he in spotless white, leaned their heads together, fond expressions on their faces.

Beyond these, ranks of fae and humans had gathered. Brownies, dragonfly girls, soldiers, fae nobles I recognized from various occasions. All staring at us with rapt interest.

"Breathe, my skittish Gwynn," Rogue muttered. "It's a wedding, not a human sacrifice."

"Easy for you to say. You're not the human," I answered. But his taunt had snapped me out of it and I felt more myself. I scanned the ranks again. No sight of Titania.

"Is *she* here?" I asked.

"No. Not yet."

"Maybe she won't come."

"Wish upon a star, my powerful Gwynn. If anyone can make it true, you can." He led me down the aisle formed by the assembly. They bowed as we passed, then fell in behind us, as if we led a parade.

"Flattery will get you everywhere." It must have been the nerves, because I'd voiced the quip before I'd thought about how the flipness wouldn't translate, only the intent.

"That bodes well for my chances then. Have I told you how beautiful you look? How intelligent and brilliantly magical?"

I snorted out a tiny laugh. He drove me crazy, but I'd missed him these past days. If nothing else, he did understand me. And forgave me for my foibles. I should find it in myself to do the same for him. Rogue's thoughts brushed over mine, like a caress down my spine.

"I missed you, too, lovely Gwynn," he whispered.

"Thank you for being there last night—for waking me."

"I promised I wouldn't leave you alone again."

"I dreamed that she—"

"I know. Don't say it. That's why we're doing this. To prevent that. For us both."

We stepped outside the castle, onto the drawbridge, which had also been draped in cloth of silver and blue. Snowflakes fell huge and thick, some spheres, others feathery. I tipped my head back and they swirled down in thick waves, so I felt I might be inside a snow globe. The little gold plate would read Royal Wedding in Faerie. A funny image, if I didn't feel so afraid.

"Is it wise for us to be outside?"

"Inside or out, it doesn't matter. She will interfere or not as it suits her. I've done all I can to distract her with the pomp and circumstance."

"Distract her from what?"

"Shh. You will see. Trust me."

I couldn't decide how I felt about that. It went without saying that pretty much anything Titania wanted to happen did not bode well for me. But I put it aside, as I'd resolved to, and walked with Rogue across the drawbridge. As we reached the midpoint, a moat monster rose on each side and sent spouts of water arching overhead, a dazzling display, as the streams sparkled with ice crystals and curled with steam.

I laughed then, in truth. And it felt so much better than the dread of the past few days. "You've got to be kidding."

Rogue slanted me a smile. "Larch's idea, I believe."

They'd all gone to so much trouble to make everything amazing. We walked on a continuing ribbon of silk, that remarkably remained free of snow, to a pool at the base of the waterfall. Instead of thundering into impact, the skyscraper-tall sheet of glassy water sliced into the aqua pool like a blade, soundlessly perfect.

We stepped up to the snowy bank and Rogue moved to step into the water. I hesitated and he untucked my hand from his elbow and laced his long fingers with mine. "Trust me," he repeated, in a sterner tone. Demanding it of me.

It went unspoken that I'd failed to. That I'd come this far and there would be no turning back, regardless. Feeling as if I might be stepping off a cliff, I went with him, our booted feet touching the surface simultaneously. The water rippled out at the contact, then firmed, buoyant but solid.

Extraordinary.

We walked out to the center, our guests fanning out in a wide circle on the banks. Starling and Athena stood with Darling Hercules at the forefront. Larch stood just behind Athena, and a man I vaguely recognized flanked Starling. Walter? I must not have paid enough attention to him in the vision, because he looked like a different man than the one I had dumped on Marquise and Scourge's doorstep.

Rogue stopped and faced me, taking my hands in his. My ribbon train floated on the water, the otherwise invisible current pulling it into a lazy spiral around us. The guests were far enough away that I thought they wouldn't be able to hear the vows, or whatever.

"Who is marrying us?" I asked after a long pause.

"We are marrying each other."

I laughed a little at that echo, then realized he meant it. "Really? I did ask around and that's not how it's usually done."

"No. Usually someone of greater rank seals the marriage. But, think on it, my Gwynn. There is no one in Faerie who outstrips our united power. Thus we'll marry each other."

"Not even…" I trailed off, unwilling to name her, even in oblique reference, given his particularly strenuous warnings.

"As you so ably demonstrated the other day, not even her."

Wow. "So, how do we do this?"

"No one recalls sorcerers of equal power marrying before."

"Did you say equal power?"

Inclining his head slightly, he looked wry. "Yes. Thus I'm making this up as I go along."

I couldn't help but smile. "The ever so powerful control-freak Lord Rogue is winging it? You sound like me."

"There are merits to your techniques."

"To my wantonly reckless behavior?"

He didn't take the bait. So much more disciplined than I with such things. "Even so. Are you ready to marry me?"

Okay, I could do this. "Why not?"

"I need a real answer, my Gwynn. This won't work unless you can mean it with all your heart." His words, his face intense. "You have to be absolutely willing."

"You didn't mention that before."

"It seemed wiser not to give you time to think about it."

To talk myself out of it, he meant.

"Always maneuvering, stacking the deck."

"Yes. You know me well. Once you said you loved me anyway."

Dammit. I took a deep breath, realizing I was clutching his hands hard enough to make a human's numb.

The moment of truth.

"Yes, my Rogue, I'm ready to marry you."

"Open your mind to me."

With only a little fear, which I ruthlessly kicked down, I did. Found his already open to me, like a warm embrace. It helped immensely and I clung to that as well.

"Make the wish. I shall do the same." He stopped himself from saying more, though I clearly read the caution in his thoughts. *Be specific. Be precise. And truly want it.*

Wishes never did work right, unless you truly wanted them to come true.

"Take the time you need and show me when you're ready."

Did every bride do this? Did they all stand at that moment of saying "I do" and gaze down at the chasm of years? So many people regretted that vow, wished to take it back and never could. The devastation of divorce only made it worse and I faced far more dire consequences.

I tried to ignore those thoughts and muster the energy for the wish, but couldn't find the wanting. I needed the desire to make the fuel, to set the spark. Apparently I lacked the heroic gene, because marrying Rogue to save humanity turned out not to be enough for me. Instead, I tapped into my emotions around our unborn child, giving her a face, using her as the reason.

But no.

All this time, Rogue held my hands, watching me, listening to my thoughts. Knowing I couldn't make it happen. Because I didn't want it enough.

He acknowledged that with a bare nod and a sigh. "I understand," he said. "We'll find another way."

"I'm sorry," I whispered.

He smiled, a self-deprecating twist of his mouth. "I blame

myself." And chasing behind that thought came an image of the boy, alone on a beach, as thousands of dead birds rained around him. His fault. No wonder I couldn't love him.

But I did.

Despite logic and reason and all the lists in the world, I did.

I gazed up at his unearthly beautiful face, caged behind the pattern of spirit lines. Silver frost gilded his inky hair, his blue-black magic like a nimbus of light around him, so alien, and saw only the man inside. *Him.* Not with the eyes, but with the mind. Though we occupied different kinds of bodies, came from different worlds, we were the same on some fundamental level.

Like to like.

I'd looked for him even when I hadn't known what to look for.

If you won't do it for your own good, consider doing it for mine.

If it was a mistake, so be it, but at that moment, nothing existed but the way I felt about him. I added to it, a measure of shining hope for what our future could be, what we could build together. He borrowed that feeling from me and fed it with his own desire, that I would care for him, let him care for me, and we would be one mind, one voice. A force that could not be put asunder.

He knew it before I did—as always—and, at the moment I formed my wish for us, he set the blazing spark of his intention to it.

At that precise instant, just as we set intention to desire, we kissed.

Minds, mouths, wills.

We joined them together.

Made them one.

It detonated around us, our combined wish a shock wave that set the water beneath our feet boiling in reaction. The waterfall curled up on itself, then unwound with crashing force, sending up a chime of songbirds without number.

The wedding guests cheered in thunderous approval.

Echoed by Titania's shriek of rage.

CHAPTER 20

SEND IN THE CLOWNS

Magic, like individual creativity, is shaped by the person who wields it—and is limited only by their imagination.
~*Big Book of Fairyland*, "Rules of Magic"

THE INHUMAN SOUND of Queen Bitch's fury reverberated through the air and across my nerves like aluminum tapping a mercury filling.

Rogue kept hold of me though, mouth hot on mine. *Steady.*

His thought in my head, unvoiced. Barely discernible from my own.

Yes.

It seemed wrong to keep kissing under the circumstances, but the days away from his touch had left me hungry for him, as if he supplied some vital vitamin I withered without. The sound faded away, though it lingered in the bones of my skull, my heart pounding to the sonic boom of utter rage.

Rogue broke the kiss then and smiled at me. A rare smile of pure and utter delight, unreserved, almost innocently joyful.

"It worked."

"The marrying each other spell?"

"Yes. The first step in her destruction."

"That's why she's so angry."

"And afraid. Never mistake but that she's afraid now."

"Why didn't she try to stop this?"

"Because, powerful Gwynn, she didn't know it was possible."

"But you did."

"I hoped. You showed me the way."

I did? "I don't remem—"

A roar went up from the dragons circling above, a clear warning. *Better get everyone inside.*

I wasn't sure if it was my thought or his—and ultimately it didn't matter, though this would take serious getting used to—and as one we turned, crossed the water and told our guests to run for their lives. Most of them already were. The scorching compression of Titania's imminent arrival thickened the atmosphere, vaporizing the snowflakes before they fell.

Everyone knew what her advent meant and none wanted to face it.

"So much for the receiving line," I muttered, feeling Rogue's grimly amused response.

The first of the guests poured across the drawbridge, seeking the castle's sheltering walls.

We stayed back, by mutual accord, to draw Titania's ire away. Oddly, though I should have been afraid, I wasn't. Maybe I'd gained some of Rogue's insouciance, born of invulnerable immortality, but I felt only the keen edge of readiness.

Bring it, bitch.

Darling Hercules stayed with us, parking himself at my ankle. *Goliath,* he demanded, so I gave it to him, pulling on the magic—mine, but with blue-black shadows—and made him as big as the dragons coming to land around us. They dropped from the sky, fast as lightning, landing with puffs of snow that made them seem light as dandelion fluff. For a moment, I reflexively cringed, but they turned their great scaly backs to us, forming a defensive perimeter.

I fretted that, by enclosing us in their circle, they'd create a magic-null field inside, crippling us. But Goliath retained the great size I'd gifted him and his sentient intelligence. The lead dragon, my dragon, if I wasn't mistaken, glanced back at me with what could only be a smirk. Oh yeah, they could totally direct it.

The ground shivered and Titania appeared, outside the circle of dragons. She looked as she had before I melted her face—exquisitely lovely in an inhuman way. Like the faces of angels too terrible to look upon. For once not naked, she wore a cloak of fire, oranges and reds teeming in it, swathing her body, hair like silver tinsel trailing down it and dragging through the snow. Leaving it melted in her wake.

"Am I late for the wedding?" she asked. Her voice rarely seemed to be an actual sound. Instead, like the sonic boom, it crept inside my head, insistent. In my dream I'd seen her as a parasitic wasp, the kind that immobilizes prey and lays her eggs in it, to feed on the haplessly fresh victim when they hatched.

The image dissolved, replaced by Rogue's unmistakable presence. Buffering me.

"I'm afraid you missed the ceremony, my queen," Rogue spoke with courtesy, but without the obsequious bowing he'd shown before. Power had shifted. She observed it, seeming ready to pop with fury. "You are, of course, welcome to join in the reception, feast and celebration."

I hated that but knew he had to say it.

"You—you—" She stuttered into silence, overcome by daunting rage. Her image similarly lost cohesion for a moment, her face blurring, as if momentarily depixilated. Not really present then? *No. But just as dangerous.*

"You *worm*," Titania managed. "You think to outwit me? I made you, Rogue. You are mine, made in my own image and you cannot escape me!" She finished on an ultrasonic shriek that sent agony through Rogue's sensitive ears and made mine ring.

"We shall see." He showed none of the pain he felt. A master of the poker face.

"You have chosen your ally poorly." She turned her attention on me. "So mortal. So sweetly vulnerable. What will you do when I wrest her from you, make her and her precious cargo mine?"

Rogue didn't reply, because I did.

"You couldn't do it before." I shrugged, dismissing her. "You'd simply fail again."

Her face contorted, the melt showing through. Resolving and then blurring again. Not completely healed.

"Will I? Yes, Rogue," she said, pointedly ignoring me. "We shall see. In the meantime, I brought you a wedding gift." She dropped the cloak, revealing her voluptuously naked, feature-less flesh. As it hit the ground, the cloak broke apart into tens—

or hundreds—of thousands of spidery creatures, seemingly made of pure fire.

Titania laughed and waved her fingers in a little wiggle. "Bye now." She vanished in stages, her chiming giggle lingering in the air after her image was gone.

In her wake, the scorching heat of her power rolled over the ring of dragons and down, a fireball of raging insanity. Without time for thought, Rogue and I deflected it, but it hit the invisible wall of the dragons' null field and shattered into myriads more of the fire-spiders. Glowing, multilegged flames, they swarmed over us, burning and biting until we destroyed them.

Those outside the circle of dragons found themselves snuffed as they tried to cross between. But plenty fell inside, anchoring into Goliath's fur and setting him ablaze. The Rogue part of me doused him with water from the pool, leaving him unscathed but furiously drenched.

Another fist of power hit, knocking us to our knees as the ground destabilized.

"Told you we shouldn't have done this outside," I had to say.

"You wanted to work that marriage spell inside and shatter the castle?" Rogue snapped back.

Together we held off that wave until it dissipated.

"Point taken."

"I knew you'd see the light."

Hard on his words, a flare went up from the castle, a precise shaft of black and white that tasted of Marquise and Scourge. In the distance, people were screaming. The promised army advanced from the opposite direction, crawling over the snowy hills like a ravening horde of locusts, obliterating the pristine whiteness with menace. From the seething ranks, missiles catapulted at the towers, some striking the glittering stone with shattering force, others dissipating before contact. More hit than didn't.

Rogue narrowed his eyes, seeing farther than I could. "However, we can't let her keep us from getting back. She appears to have changed her target."

"Poof yourself there—they need you."

He barely glanced at me, a dangerous flintiness in his gaze. "I'm not leaving you."

"Let's go then."

The dragons moved with us, blessedly keeping their defensive perimeter. More spiders swarmed, crystalline, black as oil, with impossible numbers of legs. They poofed into freezing fog or, worse, blood mist, as they struck the null field. We had to be careful to keep to the center, the edges like Novocain on my hyped-up senses, not easy as we lobbed back or busted the missiles that hurtled toward us too. The magical ones were easier to neutralize.

Some, however, were physical. One, a silver torpedo, breached our defenses and slammed into one of the dragons. Null magic didn't protect it from the impact. The missile shattered the beast's great wing, tearing the leathery membrane that stretched between tarsal bones like a bat's. The multihued jeweled scales glittered in the sunlight, ironically lovely as its yellow blood fountained and the beast trumpeted in the pain.

We forged on, however, and the dragon kept up, dragging its broken wing. Feeling the urgency, we all picked up the pace. Goliath, behind us, lagged too long and abruptly returned to his usual size. Fortunately it wasn't enough of a hit to addle his brain, but he wasn't happy.

I began to tire, feeling the drain of continuous magic use, especially after that monumental wedding spell. I reached for Mother Earth and Rogue stayed my mental hand. *Let me.*

As if he'd slipped inside me in the most intimate physical way, his magic flowed in, stroking my senses with a wash of his essence. This was far more than when he'd fed me energy on Felicity's back.

Far more.

We made it to the drawbridge where the creepy cyborg army was fighting off more spiders that were trying to swarm it, to penetrate the castle. Though they drowned in the moat, the monsters happily surfacing to gobble them down, they kept coming, walking on the backs of dead ones. The gate inside spun, so that any of the spiders that entered the doorway were flung away again, pinballs ricocheting from the center flywheel. More missiles, blasts of pure power—Titania had scaled up in the Faerie arms race—rained down on the castle, sometimes deflected, sometimes not. A tower fell and we winced. Hopefully everyone had been smart enough to hunker down.

The dragons peeled away at the drawbridge, the foremost ones taking wing to perch on the towers, breathing fire that blasted the magical missiles from existence. They couldn't step on the drawbridge, I realized—or I pulled the information from Rogue's brain—without breaking it. The downside of a mundane bridge. We would be on our own to cross.

Can't plan for everything.

"Is she inside?"

"No—sending her minions. If she entered, she'd be a guest. If we can get across the bridge and through the doors, we're safe."

"Sign me up."

"Fast or slow?" Rogue inquired, eyes glittering with battle fury as he eyed the expanse.

Slow would let us fight along the way, but extended our exposure.

I enlarged Darling Hercules into Goliath again, giving him lightweight and encompassing battle armor to keep the spiders off, and he preened as I tightened my grip on Rogue's hand. He manifested the platinum sword in the other.

"Fast." Before I finished uttering the word, we took off running down the drawbridge, booted feet pounding, Goliath leading the way. Rogue's stride outstretched mine, of course, but he couldn't carry me this time, using his sword and magic together to keep the creatures off us. I concentrated on keeping up and poofing any creatures that tried to attack Goliath.

Having the time of his life, he swatted the spiders and Cylons alike off the drawbridge with his great paws, clearing the path. *Mice! Mice! Mice!* He chanted the manic creed in my mind. I skidded on a patch of ice and Rogue yanked me up, bolstering me until I found my pace again. Locks of my hair came undone, tumbling from the artful array, and a yank on my trailing ribbons, quickly released, told me something had nearly gotten me from behind.

We poured on the speed. Never had a bride and groom pelted back up the aisle as we did.

With my newly acquired way of knowing Rogue's thoughts as they occurred, I understood that passing the gate would be the trick, then bringing up the drawbridge. He had to stop the spin long enough for us to enter, which would allow the spiders inside as well. Goliath, at my direction, spun to defend us and Rogue, to my shock, handed me his sword. Nearly as long as I was tall, the thing almost knocked me over, but then a spider came over the side of the bridge and, with skills never taught me, I swung the sword at it, slicing it cleanly in two.

A starburst bomb went off over my head, raining down more tiny spiders. I created a parasol to hold them off as Rogue worked what appeared to be a magical lock. "Where is she getting all this power?" I yelled over the roar of the spinning gate.

"You know."

I did know. All those fae trapped and cocooned in her lair, feeding her. We'd put a stop to that. Even Rogue agreed. Or couldn't disagree, with my sense of compassion bleeding through him. The gate abruptly silenced, Rogue snaked a long arm around my waist and yanked me through.

Goliath resisted my urging to come inside and spun around to continue to defend the drawbridge. He showed me the image of Titania trying to blast him with power back in her palace, to no effect. His immunity to her gave him a great advantage, so I didn't argue.

My gut wrenched as Rogue spun the castle like a roulette wheel. I lost my grip on the sword and would have fallen if he hadn't held me upright. I wished the spiders away from us both, but not before they took some nasty bites from my skin.

Rogue gripped me hard, energy zinging between us—adrenaline rush for me, wild magic for him. Or maybe the same for both of us. Like to like.

With something close to desperate hunger, he dug his fingers into my hair. Cupping my skull in his hand, he lifted me flush against him, his mouth covering mine in an echoing kiss. Feeling his need like my own, I wrapped my hands around the braid at the nape of his neck, crushing the little lilies. Briefly, he tore his lips away and laughed.

"Did you see what we did?"

He laughed again and resumed kissing me before I could answer. Though the question needed no reply. We'd managed to win that battle—without trickery, might against might. And without great damage.

Outside, however, the attacks continued to thunder. Perhaps damage had yet to be assessed.

"We'd better go find everyone," I said, though Rogue had already retrieved the sword, taken me by the hand and started down the hall before I finished the sentence. This would get old.

"The effect should fade, except for when we're actively using the bond," Rogue answered out loud, the thought behind it echoing in my head like a bad cell phone connection.

"I thought no one had done this before."

"They haven't—I'm extrapolating from empirical data."

I began to know how Dr. Frankenstein felt—except that in this case the monster had gone and made a scientist.

"Very funny," Rogue commented.

"I thought so."

We turned down yet another hallway, this one ribbed like

the inside of a centipede in a most unsettling way, from which we burst into the hall filled with flowers and candles. We should keep it that way forever, so I could find the stairs to our rooms.

"I hope you know what you're doing, Rogue." General Falcon, yellow eyes glaring like flashlights, strode up, his face set in even harsher lines than usual. "You've gone and made traitors of us all."

Despite the wedding decorations, the scene reminded me of the one from *Gone with the Wind*, with the wounded laid out all up and down the hallway. "Oh, God," I gasped. "Oh no."

Rogue steadied me, absorbing my shock and guilt. Then he turned and addressed Falcon, leaving me to assess the damages. Even as I walked away, I felt his mental caress stay with me. The peace of our mutual accord, of which of us would handle which crisis, shored me up as much as his strong hands had. I'd thought this marriage would be like an anchor, the heaviest of chains around my neck—instead it gave me a foundation.

Which I sorely needed.

Fae of all types lay bleeding, poisoned edges of spider bites eating into their flesh. Mistress Nancy moved among them, performing a gruesome sort of triage, having some of Larch's healthy Brownie fellows move the less worse off to another hall.

"Where is Lady Healer?"

"I don't know that one, dearie. Healing would be a blessing, though, if ye can arrange it."

Giving up on protocol, I reached through the web for Athena. She responded alertly, showing up at my elbow in moments, blood on her hands.

"Fetch Lady Healer, would you? And find Starling—we need her organizational skills."

"Gwynn—"

"You summoned me, my lady?" Healer glided up, irritation oozing out of her at my inadvertent summons. Too loud, as always.

"Yes. Okay, Athena—just go find Starling, would you?"

She hesitated briefly, then took off.

"Lady Healer, this is Mistress Nancy. She's organizing the wounded by severity of their injuries. If you would—"

"Excuse me?" she interrupted, then waved a languid hand at the array of suffering. "They should be put in order of rank. I don't work on the lower fae. Or humans."

"Oh, is it beneath you?"

She missed my sarcasm entirely. "Yes."

"You worked on me."

"Nonmagical humans," she clarified. "I'm sure you understand."

"What I *understand* is that you now work for me as much as for Lord Rogue. I'm telling you to treat according to Nancy's order. If you choose to leave this employment, I'll see you're put out of the castle immediately. There are some nice playmates for you outside."

She whitened. "You wouldn't."

"Try me."

I must have looked mean with it because she physically flinched. "Agreed. I will treat according to that Nancy's order." She picked up her glamorous skirts and went to do my bidding.

It's good to be queen.

Or, whatever my rank was.

In the back of my mind, Rogue was still arguing with Falcon and some of the other nobles. Just as glad not to be part of that, I snagged a page and asked him to lead me to Larch. The Brownie was ably directing a crew of his fellows—or minions, I couldn't be sure—in sealing up a breach in the hallway leading to the fallen tower.

Several Brownies were manning buckets, dousing the fire spiders that streamed in. I asked Rogue to send me someone who could do magic and Fafnir appeared in moments, a sardonic twist to his hatchet face.

"It appears I'm useful after all," he said. "Enough to get me out of silver for a while."

"You and I can talk later. Meanwhile, stay here and get rid of these spiders."

He licked his lips. "With pleasure." And he dissolved into his snake form, licking up great swaths of the swarming things with zeal. Wasn't what I'd had in mind, but it would work.

"And don't eat any of the Brownies," I told him. "Or anyone else, for that matter."

As Larch had told me this was the only breach in the castle defenses, I returned to the hospital hall. Still no Starling in sight. Now I began to worry, pacing up and down the rows. I caught sight of Athena's distinctively spiked blue hair, a human man kneeling beside her so their heads were even.

Walter?

Oh shit.

I ran, the voluminous dress that Starling had worked so hard to provide me with thankfully light as air. Athena gave me a pinched look, Starling on the floor next to her, bleeding from hundreds of blackening bites. "She ordered me not to tell you," Athena burst out before I could say anything.

I knelt down, too, brushing Starling's shining blond hair—the color she'd wanted so badly—away from her face. Her skin felt chill and clammy, her breathing shallow.

"She stayed back, on the drawbridge, making sure everyone got in," Athena said. "Said it was her responsibility and you'd expect it of her. I told her she was being stupid, but she wouldn't listen."

"You're being stupid," Starling muttered and half-opened glazed eyes. "Oh Gwynn, no! You'll get blood on your dress."

I shook my head at her, half exasperated, half terrified. "Get Lady Healer."

"I tried. She said Starling's not highest priority according to your orders and she can't break her vow. There's dozens worse off."

Dammit. It would be wrong to make an exception for Starling, right? Bad leadership precedent. Maybe I didn't care about that.

"I can help her," Walter offered. Then ducked his head when I looked at him. "Hey, Gwynnie. Happy wedding, huh?"

"You've learned to heal?"

"Who knew? All those doctor shows maybe. Turns out it's one of my best skills."

"How's your control?"

He both looked ill and proud—an odd combination I was one of the few who'd recognize and understand. "Perfect," he said in a near whisper. "You know."

"I do." And, following impulse, I gripped his hand.

He looked surprised, then squeezed back. "Some club, huh?"

"I don't even want to see the T-shirts. Do it. Starling needs you."

Walt cocked his head and tapped the silver collar. "You'll have to get the key."

I stood, scanning for Marquise and Scourge. Last I'd heard, they were at the gate, lasering any spiders that made it through. Heavens knew where in the castle the gate would be located right now. Mastering my discomfort, I touched Marquise's mind. She responded with a mental kiss, a filthy suggestion—and offered me the silver key. With a precise wish that had her smiling like a proud tutor, I manifested a lead box for her to put it in, then pulled the whole thing to me and unlocked Walter's collar, touching it as little as I could get away with.

Walter looked much better than he had the last time I saw him. Of course it wouldn't have taken much. But he'd lost the greasy chubbiness and certainly smelled better. Most of all, his former whining snarkiness had been replaced by a certain amount of steady character. With the silver removed, his personal magic welled up, full of browns and golds, distinctly human-flavored and earthy. Grounded. He'd never be a handsome man, but the discipline had given him a surprisingly attractive manliness.

"Decent power," I commented.

He had his hands on Starling's shoulders, looking into her. I tried to see what he did, but I slid into that mind-web world instead. Not somewhere I wanted to be with Titania waving her psychotic antennae outside. Odd that healing wasn't one of my things, given my training in physiology. Sometimes I thought I knew too much and my brain got in the way.

"You were right," Walter replied absently. "A few days away from the dragons and off the silver-tainted cocoa, and I stopped feeling so damn weak and crazy." His eyes flashed up at me. "The staff too. It works on you."

"I know." I didn't need reminding of *that*.

Starling whimpered and concern creased Walter's brow. "Hush, fairy-fly. You'll be okay."

The blackened edges of the bites bubbled, poison edging out, oily black. "This stuff is slippery though. Hard to get a hold of."

"I might be able to help." I'd encountered Titania's trademark goo before, though mainly in memories. The physical stuff looked the same though. "Mind if I look in?"

He snorted. "My head is an open playground these days. I have no secrets left. Come on in. Watch the land mines."

Knowing what he meant—I certainly had plenty of PTSD tucked away from my own training with Marquise and Scourge, though it bothered me less and less these days—I eased in, careful to stay in his surface thoughts, following the bright lens of his concentration on Starling.

I caught my breath. Even gravely ill and covered with the unsightly wounds, she appeared radiantly lovely in his eyes. Almost not quite the same young woman I knew. But to him, she seemed almost like a goddess. Not the nasty kind, either. Somewhat abashed to witness the depth of his feelings, I pulled some clinical distance between me and that part of him.

The poison did slip away from his healing grasp, tunneling deeper into Starling and also sending out waving tendrils, reminiscent of parasitic worms, seeking to spread their spores.

Reaching for me and the child I carried.

CHAPTER 21

IN WHICH I LET GO

*It's tempting to classify the various fae as more or less
advanced based on intelligence. However, I fear I'm applying
anthropomorphic standards.*

~Big Book of Fairyland, "Flora and Fauna"

THIS WAS GETTING old.

Though I had to give Titania credit for single-minded persistence. Knowing full well I must have some of the poison in me, from my few bites, and that nothing less than a full quarantine could protect us from the rest, I set the knowledge aside. Rogue might be willing to burn everyone bitten on a pyre of incinerating magic, but I wasn't.

In the back of my head, he let me know we weren't done deciding that.

But neither did he interfere. Part of my mind registered his activities too. He'd been the one who knew where Marquise and Scourge were located. Now he'd retired from the hall to argue with Falcon and the other nobles about our predicament. They were worried that he'd made them all traitors in

Titania's eyes and weren't listening to the possibility of shedding themselves of her yoke—most of them aghast that Rogue even spoke the words aloud.

As if she hadn't figured that part out already.

I paid little attention. In our moment-by-moment division of labor, Rogue could handle the political shit. Never had been my forte and he excelled at it. At the thought, I felt the light touch of his hand on my cheek, an amused blush of pleasure, as if I'd inadvertently given him a great compliment.

There would be no living with him.

Focusing on the task at hand, I guided Walter's mental touch as Rogue had done so often for me, showing him how, instead of wrestling with the oily stuff, to dissolve and weaken it. We got better at it, working more quickly, finally flushing the last of it from Starling's body.

By the time I withdrew, she looked much better to my not-crazy-in-love eyes. Her breathing came more easily, her skin warmer and she'd slipped into a real sleep. Walter worked painstakingly to heal each of her wounds, though I could see her own half-breed magic had taken over.

Finally I stopped him. "She'll be okay now. There are other people who could use your help." I glanced at Athena, who'd stood by all this time, something that might surprise Starling. "Could you see that she's taken to her rooms? Walt, you can go with her, but maybe after she's settled, you could—"

"No, Gwynnie." He gave me his impudent grin, a shadow of his former cocky self. "I have a lot of karma to make up. I'll stay here."

I sent him to help Lady Healer, and to show her what we'd learned about dealing with the poison—hopefully she'd pay attention—then surveyed the hall. It looked less ghastly than when we first arrived, with the lightly wounded weeded out and taken off to recover in other parts of the castle and the most severely wounded, or killed, similarly carried off. Still, the gorgeous wedding decorations provided a strange backdrop to the aftermath of our impromptu battle. The Stargazer lilies, with the satin glow of living flesh, in all shades of blue, gleaming in the candlelight, their sweet scent overpowering the smell of pain and death.

Happy wedding, indeed.

"Lady Gwynn."

I turned to find Officer Liam saluting me. The human officer usually in charge of General Falcon's cannon fodder looked a bit haggard, blood-streaked and with varied bites. I hadn't glimpsed him since that day they all arrived, at the other end of the drawbridge. For once, though, his thoughts toward me weren't full of salacious attitude. I'd found that attractive once—enough to flirt with and kiss. Or, I'd been running so hard from Rogue that the man in my path had seemed to be pulling me toward him.

"How fares the human population, Officer Liam?"

He smiled, just a little. "Better than the fae, it seems. The bites are nasty, but the poison seems to hit the magic-bearers worse. You appear to be fine."

I gave him an arch look. "The blessing of being human in truth."

His gazed strayed to the left side of my face, where the silver lines no doubt gleamed in the soft light, though the cat had been mostly quiet through it all. He nearly made a remark—which, I heard in his head, of course—but decided against it. Rogue growled in the background. Then let me know he needed me. *Better move this along.*

"What can I do for you, Officer?"

"Begging your pardon, Lady Gwynn, but with the feast being held off and the seneschal wounded, people haven't eaten for the full day and it's well into night now. Some of the wee ones are growing quite hungry."

Oh, dummy me.

When had I last eaten? Sometime the night before, though I didn't feel it. The part of me that drew on magic took care of that, but it couldn't be good for the baby. I'd become some sort of magical chimera, like Rogue's spinning gate, switching from one to the next.

Liam smirked, reading my dismay as clearly as I heard his distaste for my progression from purely human. Athena—bless her unerring timing—showed up then.

"Starling is sleeping. What else can I do?"

I put a hand on her shoulder with utter gratitude. "Could you go light a fire under whoever's second or third in charge of the food around here? Nancy's needed here, but surely someone else can handle getting everyone fed."

"Sure thing, Gwynnie." She stuck out her tongue and made crazy eyes when I glared at her. "Ol' Walt's a piece of work, but he sure cleaned up okay." She skimmed Liam with a look and shook her head. "Can't say the same of everyone."

I smothered a laugh and started to go.

"One more thing, Lady Gwynn." Liam put a hand out to touch my arm, but dropped it before he made contact. "I know we have had our disagreements and you have reason to dislike me."

"Water under the bridge, Officer Liam. We both made mistakes." I emphasized the last word. Talking to him felt like having to endure a conversation with any of a number of guys I'd gone out with once in college. Those one-off dates that ended in kisses and fizzled expectations.

"True enough." He had the grace to look abashed. "However, I still hold you in high regard. And I'm concerned for you."

I really couldn't take anyone else warning me about my association with Rogue. "I'm afraid that ship has sailed."

"No, not that." He grinned, some of his sunny nature showing through and he shook his head. "I knew you were out of my league even then. But you can't blame a guy for taking a chance, right?"

Rogue could, but I figured a little payback wouldn't hurt him. He stopped grumbling in my head at the reminder.

"No," Liam continued. "I notice you don't have your weapons about you. You should. Despite your many...gifts, you remain a mortal woman, yes? Sometimes the fight comes down to who doesn't bleed to death. I'd hate to think I failed you in not reminding you of that."

"Good point. Thank you, Liam."

He bowed, grave now. "Keeping you alive may be the saving of us all, in the end."

Bemused, I watched him go, then went to find Rogue.

I followed my instincts to the current location of the front gate, which felt easier than it had before. Probably Rogue's long familiarity with the castle leaking into my own memories. Certainly the place seemed less uncanny and spine-tingling than it had only a few days ago.

When I found him, he was standing with Marquise and Scourge, surveying the great maw. I hesitated, but screwed down my courage and made myself walk up to them. He wrapped a long arm around my waist and drew me against his side, both comforting me and situating himself firmly as a buffer between us.

"Titania's forces are nearly to the moat and long-distance sight shows more on the way," Rogue informed me. "We need to get the drawbridge up."

A team of human men stood by, ready to work the great wheels. I probably needed someone to send them food too. Athena cheerfully acknowledged the thought before I realized I'd projected it. Rogue, answering a question for Scourge about the drawbridge's nonmagical properties, gave no evidence that I'd been too loud. Apparently I was getting better at this.

"To get the bridge up, we need to stop the spin. Stopping the spin lets the spiders in. Besides, it's draining you to keep that up at this speed." When Rogue raised his eyebrow at me, I smiled. "Goes both ways, cowboy—I can feel it."

"We can douse or vanish the spiders at a certain range," Scourge put in, black teeth gleaming against ebony skin, "but they replenish too fast for us to keep them out long enough to raise the gate."

"Goliath is doing a positively heroic job of guarding the gate, but we can't raise the drawbridge with his enormous self standing on it." Marquise both spoke and projected the words at Darling and he mentally preened. Now there was a sucker for flattery.

"What do you want me to do?" I asked Rogue, ignoring the other two. I could stomach being in the same room, pretty much. Friendly chat was beyond me.

He looked down at me and pulled me a bit closer against him, wiping a smudge of something from my cheek. I probably looked like a wreck. The advantage of magical makeup, though—it never smeared or faded.

"I thought you might have an idea," he said. "You're the inventive one."

"She always was, you know." Marquise crooned.

Scourge nodded. "So creative. Smart for a human. And responsive. Why, I remember—"

Rogue gave him a scalding look that I felt but couldn't see. Stopped Scourge in his tracks, for which I was hugely grateful.

"If you're up to it," Rogue said to me, once again searching my face, no doubt feeling my weariness too. He certainly had a point—neither of us could keep this up indefinitely.

"Yes. It needs doing. We need to get Goliath inside and the drawbridge up. The dragons will be fine outside. What about the Cylons?"

"Will you worry about even them?" Rogue teased with a half smile.

"Yes. Get used to it."

"They cannot be harmed."

"And the moat monsters?"

"You can't protect everyone, soft-hearted Gwynn."

"Then it's not sympathy, but political. I've been hearing the discussions. You're promising everyone protection. That means everyone we possibly can. Leave anyone out—even a moat monster—and it could come back to bite you. I mean that both literally and figuratively."

A look of almost comical exasperation crossed his face.

"Where exactly do you propose to put them?"

"It's a big freaking place. You and I can make a lake to put them in—in the practice arena maybe. Can we poof them there?"

Marquise made a tsking sound. "Not a living creature, pet. Honestly, sometimes you say the funniest things."

I rolled my eyes, which Rogue caught and laughed at. No doubt pleased to see someone else on the receiving end of it. "Do they have legs? Can they survive outside the water for a short length of time?"

"The point of a moat monster, as you call them," Rogue explained in a tone of great patience, though he was clearly amused, "is for them to defend the castle by swimming around in the moat. Bringing them inside the castle renders that point somewhat moot, don't you think?"

Fine. Focus on the main problem. A slew of dragonfly girls showed up then, distributing what looked like meat sandwiches to the winch team, who gobbled them up with gusto. Rogue gave me a questioning look.

"People need to eat," I explained sweetly, as if I'd been on top of this all along.

"Indeed." He snapped his fingers at one of the girls—a pretty buttercup-yellow one—who bounced over and gave him one of the sandwiches. He handed it to me. "You too. Eat while you think."

I would have argued with him about ordering me about, except the scent of the meat made my stomach growl. Voraciously hungry, I gobbled it down, along with the second one Rogue grabbed for me. By the time I was done, I had an idea.

"Okay, this is actually an easy workaround. You don't want to have a magical door in place because the mundane works so much better as a seal against magic attacks. But it can work for a temporary solution. You'll stop the spin, Marquise and Scourge will nuke all the spiders they can reach, Darling Goliath will come in, I'll create a magic door, put it in place to hold the seal while the guys there pull up the drawbridge. Once it's closed, I'll poof the magic door. Slam dunk."

I loved a simple plan. I know I've said so before, but I really did.

Of course, it wasn't nearly so simple in the execution. On the first try, Marquise and Scourge nearly fried Goliath, the black-laced white spear of their magic setting his fur on fire before I doused it. Which meant a wave of spiders poured into the opening because I didn't make the magic seal in time.

Rogue set the spin going while we adjusted tactics, the inertia of setting it into motion dragging at his energy. Marquise and Scourge argued with me and called me sentimental and crazy, but finally agreed to aim around my Familiar.

On the second try, Rogue fumbled the spin—something I never thought I'd see—and a sign that he was tiring more than he showed. We stopped well past the drawbridge, facing Titania's encroaching troops, who hurled a flaming missile of globular green fire straight for the doorway. Marquise and Scourge flung their readied spell at it instead, while Rogue wrenched us into motion again.

"Are you okay?" I asked him quietly, and he nodded but rested a hand on me. I fed him all the magic I could spare while keeping a healthy portion to execute my share of the spell. The black-and-white twins indulged in a long, probably incestuous kiss to bump up their own magic.

"Let's hope three's a charm," Rogue said. "Ready everyone?"

We settled ourselves, cooling and focusing. Gathering our meager reserves. To make sure my timing would be perfect, I listened in on Rogue as he executed the complex spell to stop the spinning relocation of the gate. I might bring an inventive approach to magic, but he worked the medium like a maestro. Yes, it turned me on. That was the kind of gal I was—won over better by passionate expertise than by all the flowers in the world.

He knew it, too, sliding me a hot blue glance. For once, I didn't mind. We needed all the power we could dredge up.

Rogue's spell clicked into place with finesse, stopping the spin on a dime right at the drawbridge. And none too soon. Titania's forces had reached the other end and ran toward us, brandishing spears, flaming torches and tortuous devices I didn't care to contemplate. Marquise and Scourge smoothly nuked the spiders with a blanket of magic that slid under and around Darling Goliath—who then leaped through the doorway, sending me an annoyed thought when I caught the tip of his tail as I slammed a magic force field into place.

The men sprang into action, chanting furiously as they drew up the drawbridge, flaming spiders and fae tumbling off the rising plank like passengers tumbling into the sea from a sinking Titanic. The moat monsters churned the water in their frenzy, gobbling up the unfortunate fae. They likely had no more choice in this battle than we did. Just hapless puppets to Titania's will. It made me sick and sorry to witness it—I should have thought to make the force field opaque. But holding it there was sapping enough of my magic, especially when the catapults nailed it with a few more flaming missiles. I couldn't split off attention to alter it.

Rogue, recovering from the drain, wrapped his arms around my waist and drew me against him, now supplementing my magic with his.

At last the ponderous drawbridge sighed into place and the men cheered, anchoring the great pins that held it in place. I dropped the force field with relief, leaning back against Rogue, grateful for the sudden peace of sealing the army outside.

It was past midnight. Faerie never slept, of course, since so few of its denizens did, but the castle grew quiet. No more missiles. Titania had either exhausted herself or was devoting her considerable deviousness to surrounding us and planning her next move. Everyone in the Castle of the Dark Gods, safely fed and sheltered, had retired to nurse their wounds or those of others.

Everyone was accounted for—at least those who rated names and notice—except for Blackbird and Fergus, who had yet to arrive. And Lady Incandescence, aka Nasty Tinker Bell, who'd gone mysteriously missing.

Fancy that.

I headed in the direction of our tower, but Rogue took my elbow, guiding me down a different hallway. "Dammit—I was sure I had this figured out now."

"We're not going to our tower. Yet."

"We're not?"

I flipped through in my mind what I'd missed. Then I flipped through *his* mind.

"Dancing?" I shook my head, confused. "We spend the day fighting an enraged queen of the fairies and you want to finish it with dancing?" Actually, put that way, it sounded reasonably logical.

We'd reached the ballroom across from the feast hall and Rogue opened the doors. Beautifully decorated also, it waited for wedding guests to fill it. The mirrors ringing the room reflected warm candlelight and rafts of blue lilies. Ribbons tumbled over every surface and glittering indigo sand was scattered across the dance floor like glitter. Or fairy dust.

"Yes." Rogue guided me to the center of the floor. "We also spent today marrying each other and it's traditional, for both our kind, I believe, to seal the wedding with a dance."

Well, and consummation.

"We will do that, too," he promised, with a lascivious thought that seared through me. "Besides, the last time we danced, you were too preoccupied to enjoy it."

"Can you blame me?"

"No. But I want to dance with you when you're thinking only of me. Of us." He took my hand and swept a formal bow, pressing a kiss to my skin. "Will my lady favor me with a dance?"

Apparently I was a romantic fool at heart, because I could only nod. Music swelled up from nowhere, a waltz to match his heartbeat, and Rogue drew me into his arms, holding my gaze rapt. We swept around the floor, the glittering dust swirling up to our passing, making its own elaborate dance in the air. It would have been a phenomenal sight with hundreds of guests dancing, but it seemed perfect in that moment that it was only the two of us.

Everything seemed to come back down to that, Rogue and I, in our eternal waltz.

We moved as one, a glorious feeling, entwined so closely that he barely led. Instead of the formal distance usually required, he held me close against him, one arm pressing against my lower back, the other holding my hand tucked up against his chest.

His scent wove in with the flowers, a masculine spice that echoed their redolent sensuality. I lost myself in his depthless eyes and, when he bent to kiss me, our steps never faltered. We whirled around the room, a work of art and magic.

Even without Darling's anesthetic assistance, I could have danced all night.

Eventually, I realized we'd stopped dancing and simply stood in the middle of the floor, locked in a breathless kiss. I'd wound my hands tightly around the back of his neck and stood on tiptoe, even in the high-heeled boots, stretching myself against him to indulge in more of his amazing, seductive mouth.

With a long breath, I pulled back, surprised at the level of my hunger for more of him.

Rogue smiled, smoky, delicious. "That was much better. I like it when you're focused on me."

"Don't get used to it," I retorted, but I lacked conviction. At the moment it seemed impossible I'd ever think of anything else.

"Oh, but I plan to, my seductive Gwynn." With that he swept me up and carried me out of the ballroom with long ground-eating strides. "Your feet are sore," he noted, before I'd opened my mouth to argue.

As soon as he said so, I felt it. Funny how it worked, that I only noticed the pangs of mortal flesh at particular times and otherwise cruised on magical energy. Almost like being on methamphetamines or something. Hopefully I wouldn't eventually pay for those highs with a major physical crash.

Rogue nuzzled the spot under my ear, then took the lobe in his teeth and nipped it—a tingle that made my nipples tighten.

"You're thinking again," he murmured. "You know the sort of measures I'll have to take to put a stop to that."

"You're not going to do it here in the hallway."

"Is that a dare?" He sucked my earlobe into his hot mouth and I moaned a little.

"No. And you should look where you're going."

"Believe me, luscious Gwynn, I know exactly where I'm going." The double entendre reverberated through me, especially with the images running through his mind. His urgency fed into mine, stoking my building arousal.

We reached the stairs to the tower and Rogue took them three or four at a time, leaping up them with athletic grace. For once I didn't mind not having to climb them myself. Instead I indulged with kissing his throat, savoring the salt tang of his skin and the tantalizing thrum of his response to me.

This amplified feeling each other was crazy good.

"And we've barely started." He flung the door open with a thought and set me down in the center of the room.

It, too, had been transformed and I blinked back a prickle of tears at all Starling had accomplished for me. She must have sent some of her staff after we left for the ceremony. The bed had become a bower of silk, flowers and romance. Bunches of the Stargazers were tied to the bedposts, trailing blue and silver ribbons. Petals in every shade of blue floated over the floor, the sheets, sometimes lifting with a breath of air and fluttering down again.

Rogue knelt at my feet. "Why are you—?" I started to ask, getting my answer when he slid his hands under my skirt and began unbuckling the straps on the boots. Oh.

Outside the dome, snowflakes swirled again. A reverse snow globe.

I hoped the dragons weren't cold.

Rogue sighed at my thought, and at the same moment an amber lantern eye popped up, peering in the glass at us, no doubt from the perch ring below. I smothered a laugh and gestured at her to go back down before Rogue spotted her.

He eased the boot off my foot. "If I hadn't heard that laugh, or sensed your surprise, I'd know that it was there from the light those eyes cast. Tell them if they peek I'll skin them all and use their hides for rugs."

"I don't think they listen to me." But I tried sending the message anyway, the sound of it swallowed by their nullness, like dropping a rock into a bottomless well. "Besides, I thought you didn't care if they watched."

"*I* don't." He grinned up at me with sly wickedness, drawing off the second boot and sliding hot hands over my calf up to the edge of the silly lace bloomers and down again to rub the arch of my foot. "But I don't want you feeling inhibited. By anything at all."

Oh my.

His caress felt like molten gold on my skin, buzzing with tiny sparks, champagne bubbles of sensual electricity. I drew in an unsteady breath and set my hand on his shoulder for balance. He looked up at me, eyes burning with that sapphire flame so uniquely his. "Do you remember this?" he whispered.

Yes. Oh yes. Back when Rogue first turned up to woo me, he'd put his hand between my legs and driven me to orgasm with that simple vibrating touch. "It was a long time ago."

"Does it feel that way to you?"

"Ages ago and yesterday."

"Exactly."

He removed his hands and reached over my skirts to unlace the ribbons that held the overdress on, then pushed it off my shoulders. I stood there in the corset and all those layers of leaflike silk, translucent and rustling. He tugged at one and it came away.

"Starling will skin *my* hide if you ruin this dress."

He smiled, slightly, but his face burned with intensity. "It's meant to come off this way. I want you to stand still while I strip you naked, bit by bit. Will you let me?"

Scalded by the heat of his words, by the blaze of demanding desire that licked through him, I could only nod. He circled me, removing the dress leaf by leaf, baring my limbs, then my breasts, kissing my skin as it appeared. I tasted myself through him, saw myself as he saw me. And I slowly melted into a trembling mess, barely able to stand. When I swayed, he backed me up against the bedpost and, with a long look that dared me to object, tied my wrists with the ribbons high above my head.

Transported, I let him. The way he relished having me helpless before him, increasingly vulnerable, ratcheted into my own mind, amplifying my need. They became two faces of the same feeling, both the had and the having, power reflecting from dark to light and back again.

He unlaced the corset and pulled away the silk beneath, lavishing my breasts, rib cage and belly with more kisses, that golden buzzing touch penetrating my skin and making my blood simmer. The bunched lilies over my head exuded their scent, so I felt I might be under a soft rain of sensation. Rogue slid the pantalets down my legs with exquisite care and made his way back up my body, leaving none of my skin unkissed, uncaressed.

All the while, he wrapped me in utter attention and emotional focus, somehow strumming my heartstrings as well, sharing his delight in me. Every sound I made, the smallest of my reactions to his touch, aroused him more, which he then shared back with me, increasing my responses.

In an erotic delirium, I let him turn me to face the bedpost, gasping when something silken brushed my skin. Not his hands, but both soft and lightly prickling. It left a sizzling trail in its wake. The warm burn of cinnamon, the evaporative cool of alcohol, the scent of lilies.

I looked through his eyes—it was a lily. He'd taken a blossom and stroked my skin with it, tracing my curves. It left a shimmering trail of pollen behind, painting me in all shades of glittering blues that tingled, invading my blood and making me drunk with it.

"You know I'd do nothing to harm our child," Rogue replied before I completely formed the concern, his voice rough with passion. "And I want to drive you wild, make you desperate for me."

This wasn't wild enough? "I am desperate for you." Surely

he had to know. My breasts ached with arousal and my thighs moved slickly as I scissored them together.

"I'm not quite convinced." He coaxed my ankles apart and I moaned, following his anticipation.

"Oh Rogue, I don't—" I threw my head back, the words clenching in my throat as he drew the blossom between my thighs, dragging the petals against my swollen labia, the pollen mixing with my fluids and setting me on fire.

CHAPTER 22

IN WHICH I GO FOR A SWIM

The theoretical physicists say that time is what keeps everything from occurring at once. Under the influence of magic, time in Faerie still performs this function, but in apparent fits, starts and billows.

~Big Book of Fairyland, "Rules of Magic"

I DID GO wild.

My focus narrowed to Rogue and the diabolical things he did to me with his hands, mouth and that flower. I hadn't known what desperate was until he'd driven me to the edge over and over, while I pleaded with him and made all sorts of wild promises.

Especially when he turned me to face him and started over on the front of my body.

I let myself go in a way I never could have while hanging on to my suspicions and fears. He knew it, too, drinking in my utter surrender and giving me back his.

In this way, our wedding night did become a consummation. The paired wish we'd used to cement our connection sang between us with increasing power, and we layered it with shared passion, mutual need and love.

Maybe even true love.

Because this felt unlike anything I'd imagined. A kind of emotional and mental harmony that seemed impossible to achieve. By the time he untied my wrists and draped me over the bed, hissing in fierce pleasure as his skin absorbed the blue pollen from mine, I seemed to be as much in his head as my own.

His cock ached as much as my sex and the sensation of my hot, slick channel clamping around it, combined with the drenching pleasure of him entering my body, shattered me. As we'd danced, we moved together, giving and taking, possessed and possessing, fusing ourselves into one body.

He drew out the moment, keeping me from coming as he kept himself, until we both were so taxed, so desperate, for one another, that there was no holding back.

We climaxed at the same instant, tumbling together from the heights, entirely tangled, consumed, each dissolved into the other.

꽃

I CAME BACK to myself disoriented. Taking a moment, I blinked up at the arch of the dome and the snowflakes falling to briefly stick in crystalline complexity and then melt away. The candles had gone out and Rogue was still draped over me, like a blanket of man, his face buried in my hair, breathing deep and even. I stroked a hand down his long back and he stirred, lifting his head to look at me, lighting one candle so he could do so.

"Did you fall asleep?" I asked, meaning to tease.

But puzzlement entered his gaze. "I may have. I'm not sure."

"That was extraordinary. We'd have to expect unusual results."

"Would we, my Gwynn?" His mouth quirked in that smile and I felt the laugh behind it. He flexed his hips, moving in me. "Are you inviting me to experiment?"

"Yes," I answered, meaning it. "Though maybe not tonight."

"Yes," he echoed. "Not tonight. We have an errand to run in the morning."

"An errand?"

"I haven't forgotten I promised to take you on a trip."

"Aren't we under siege now?"

A look of mischief crossed his face. "That will make it even more fun."

I had to laugh at his idea of fun—but I also couldn't wait to see what he had to show me. This time tomorrow, I'd have the answer to how Rogue—and all the fae perhaps—were conceived and born.

When I awoke to bright sunshine, Rogue was still with me. He was lying on his back and holding me cuddled against him with one arm, thoughts lazily dreaming. Feeling me waken, he pressed a kiss to my forehead.

"Beauty awakes."

I laughed. "Hardly." We were both smeared in blue and I could only imagine how my elaborate hairstyle looked now. Plus I had to pee, quite desperately. So much for romance. Yet, I hated to end the moment. "Did you stay with me all night?"

"Yes." He kissed my forehead again. "It's restful. And I didn't want to be away from you just yet."

"That's...lovely." I didn't want to be away from him either. It might take time, getting used to the ways we'd commingled.

"But you want to clean up," he observed. "Go ready your bath and I'll join you. No doubt Mistress Nancy has your special human food waiting."

"You make it sound like Purina People Chow or something." But, relieved, I gave him a quick kiss and dashed naked for the bathing room and my new best friend, the magic chamber pot. I did look like the creature from the black lagoon, with my hair in astonishing disarray, but somehow still mostly still piled on my head—glittering with the pollen. Marie Antoinette yesterday, Marge Simpson today.

And they said marriage didn't change anything.

I also looked amazingly—even radiantly—happy. Rogue's regard remained wrapped around my heart, a warm blanket of love I carried with me. Where I'd felt alone before, marooned on an alien planet, I now had a deep and permanent connection.

For better or worse, I would always have that.

An unlooked-for gift.

I managed to wrestle my hair down and brush it out by the time Rogue joined me, setting a breakfast tray on the vanity. He stood behind me, surveying my reflection in the mirror, splaying a hand over the hard round of my belly. I almost superstitiously expected him not to appear—though I knew him to be as physically present as anyone.

"Growing bigger every day," I remarked.

"Yes." He pressed a kiss to my left temple, saying nothing more. Really, we'd already said it all.

"Turn around," I told him and he obliged me. I unbraided his hair, setting aside the ribbons and miniature lilies that remained magically uncrushed. He smiled at my determination to do tasks like this physically, but waited patiently while I finger-combed the silky length of it, the kinks from the braid making it glint in the light.

When I finished, he pointed me at the tray. "Eat. I don't want Mistress Nancy upbraiding me again. She was most put out that you only ate the sandwich yesterday." He went to soak in the bathtub to wait for me.

"You talked to her? Did she say how Starling is?"

Rogue ostentatiously pressed his lips together and pointed at the tray.

"Yeah, yeah, yeah," I muttered, though I didn't need much prompting to devour what looked like a full Scottish breakfast, complete with fish, sausages, browned potatoes and onions, English muffins with lemon curd, oatmeal and three glasses of juice and two of milk. Surveying the empty platter, I groaned at how much I'd eaten.

"I shall become as big as one of the dragons, only shorter."

"That shall be entertaining," Rogue replied, holding my hand to steady me as I stepped in the tub. "Starling is recovering. You'll no doubt want to visit her before we go."

"Definitely. Any sign of Blackbird and Fergus? Or Nasty Tinker Bell?"

He frowned, ever so slightly, pulled me to lie back against him and began soaping me. "None of any of them. Perhaps Starling mistook the message and Blackbird and Fergus are still on the Endless Sea—out of range."

"No—I saw them, riding this way." At his mute surprise, I showed him the image in my mind. "When I used the scepter, before you had your tantrum."

"Hmm." He diplomatically did not say anything to that. "And *Lady Incandescence*," he emphasized her title, "is likely hiding."

"From us?"

"From you," he corrected.

"Am I after her for something?"

"That remains to be seen, doesn't it?"

Hmm. "I looked out the windows and I don't see a besieging army."

"They seem to be hanging back. She's playing some game with us."

"That goes without saying."

"Indeed. Now dunk your head, so I can wash your hair. You don't want to be leaving a trail of fairy dust where we're going."

I giggled, then double-checked the image in his head. Fairy dust, indeed.

۶¯

STARLING HAD A lovely set of rooms in the next tower over. Nothing as spectacular as mine, but spacious and elegant. She was propped up in bed, looking wan but much better. Walter was keeping her company.

"Gwynn!" Starling burst out when she saw me, then started to get out of bed when she spotted Rogue behind me. "Lord

Rogue, forgive me, I'm—"

"Under orders to stay in bed," Rogue replied in a smooth tone that nevertheless contained stern command. She shivered and obeyed. I sympathized with that reaction.

She turned sad eyes to me. "Oh, Lady Gwynn—your beautiful wedding—ruined. I take full responsibility."

"Really?" I raised my eyebrows and sat on the side of the bed, a spot Walt vacated for me with a little nod. "You mean, you had a master plan to defeat the Queen Bitch and you failed to use it? I am annoyed with you then."

She laughed a little. "Well, when you put it that way..."

"Exactly. Could you guys give us a little privacy?"

"Oh sure!" Walt jumped, stricken, and took off without another word. I'd have to be careful what I said around him.

Rogue smoothed a hand over my still-drying hair and picked up my hand to kiss it. "Don't be long, my ravishing Gwynn. I'll wait for you outside the door."

"No eavesdropping, either," I warned and he flashed me a devastatingly wicked grin.

"You look radiant, Gwynn," Starling said after Rogue left the room. "I hoped you would be happier, once all was said and done."

"Yes, well, I wanted you to know I'm sorry I was such a bitch these last few days."

"The course to true love never did run smooth," she replied. Shakespeare? Surely not. Must be my own brain supplying that. All Puck's fault.

"However we got here, things are good. Aside from being under siege and all that."

"And Mother and Father going missing." She looked sad

and fearful.

I supposed it had been unreasonable to think she wouldn't have noticed they'd never arrived. "That too. But I'll look for them."

"Not with that scepter, you won't," she replied tartly. "Athena told me what happened, since you didn't see fit to."

I sighed. "You two can't get along except to snitch on me."

Starling beamed. "It's one thing we agree on—that you need looking after and we're the ones to do it."

"Lucky me." I tried to make it sarcastic, but really I was touched that they cared so much. "So…Walter? Escorting you to the wedding, staying by your side, night and day?"

"Oh, pish!" She said it airily, but her fierce blush gave her away. "He arrived just moments before you did. I think he's quite changed for the better, don't you?" She looked at me searchingly, brown eyes hopeful, seeking my approval. I'd really screwed that up before.

I patted her hand, still a little cool to the touch. "I think he's come a long way. And I'm glad he's keeping you company while you rest."

"I should be looking after the castle and all the guests," she fretted.

"Delegate, darling. My best advice. I'm off for a bit—I just wanted to check on you. I'll send Walt back in."

"Where are you going?" She knit her brow in suspicion.

"Not far. I'll be back soon." At least I thought so. And look at me, sounding as evasive as Rogue ever was.

Walter waited in the sitting room, staring out the window. In a loose brown shirt and pants, he looked both nondescript but also far better than he had in the stained and disheveled wizard's robes he'd worn when I first met him. No silver that I could see.

"Still off your leash?" I asked.

He turned and gave me a wry smile. "So far, yes. I feel both freed and terrified."

"Yeah." I searched for more words than that, but ended up not needing them. Our shared understanding of those experiences filled in the gaps. He didn't seem nearly as broken as I'd felt, but then maybe it didn't show on the outside. And maybe he'd been better at bending than I had been. He'd certainly been more willing.

"If I can do anything…" he trailed off, sounding uncertain. "At any rate, I know it's not the thing to say in these parts, but I owe you, Gwynn. I know it. I'd like to make amends."

"Healing Starling and the others you helped went a long way. Keeping doing that and we're fine. Don't fuck up, okay?"

He grinned. "It's kind of nice to hear that in English again."

"I know what you mean."

"Um," he started. Then stopped. "So, Starling…"

"Is her own person," I filled in. "She's a big girl."

"I could maybe find her folks, if I had the scepter again," he ventured.

No.

Of course Rogue was eavesdropping.

"I'll see what I can do," I told Walt, mentally sticking my tongue out at Rogue. "Meanwhile, keep your nose clean."

"Yeah. Um, Gwynnie…" He fidgeted. Glanced toward the window and back to me.

I raised my eyebrows, reminding myself to be gentle with him.

"I know that you…saw some stuff, when you looked in on me—nice of you, by the way. And I figure, well, Starling knows what you went through, to some extent, but…" He trailed off again, swallowing down the rest of the words.

"I'm not going to gossip about the details, if that's what you're asking." The very thought made me vaguely headachy. "It's private shit. It stays that way as far as I'm concerned."

His relief colored the air. "You don't know how much I appreciate that."

"Yes, I do." I managed a cheeky smile. "And now you really owe me."

As promised, Rogue waited for me in the hallway, leaning against the wall in an indolent pose that didn't fool me for a second.

"I know you didn't destroy the scepter," I said, by way of greeting. "So don't bother to pretend you did."

"Were you spying on me then?" He took my hand and started walking, sounding amused by the idea that I might have.

"I didn't have to. I can feel the thing, in the back of my mind."

"I'm not well pleased to hear that, my precious Gwynn. It has an unnatural hold on you."

"I agree. That's why I'm mentioning it. Spirit of teamwork, honesty, all that."

He made a snorting sound, but didn't comment further.

"Maybe, if you don't trust me with it, Walt could have it again. It's a powerful tool," I continued.

"Oh yes. I'd love to hand a dangerous magical weapon I don't understand to a human wizard who tried to kill you.

Brilliant idea."

"Did you just admit that there's something you don't understand?"

"Many things," he replied in a dry tone. "Including you, my delightful lady."

"After all that swimming around in my head? Seems like I'd have no secrets left."

"You'd be surprised."

"What surprises me is that we're going back to our rooms. Aren't we going on the field trip?"

"Yes. You'll see."

I'd been privately betting on some form of astral travel, but once in the rooms, he guided me to the magic elevator. The bathing chamber? Sure enough, down we went to the warm, humid rooms, with the black pool of water that seemed to go on forever.

"We could have bathed here." I mentally sighed for my hair, which would need to be combed and let dry again. Maybe I should start taking the magical shortcuts on that.

Rogue gave me a mysterious smile and took my hands. "Do you trust me?"

Jeez. Every day was going to be an exercise in that. "More walking on water?"

He narrowed his eyes at me in playful menace and didn't reply.

"Yes, I trust you."

"Hold still."

His magic traveled over me, a miasma that flowed over my skin, then sank inside my body, enveloping me in a cloud of black with blue lightning flashes. The sensation reminded me of the sparking buzz of his hands when he chose to touch me that way, and my desire roused to it. But the buzzing faded as it went deeper. I could have resisted it, but through dint of will, I let it infiltrate through me, Rogue's appreciation for my trust brushing through me with a surge of tenderness.

He tugged me toward the water and I went, not objecting that we both remained fully dressed. We stepped in, the water rising to envelop us as we advanced, but not wetly. It felt almost more like a slightly thicker, warm cushion of air. It closed over my head and I panicked, just a little, as the stuff flowed in my nose.

Then I breathed through it. Miraculous. The water buoyed me up and we swam through it now, breathing it in as a fish might. I grinned at Rogue in pure delight and he smiled back, looking as he had running on that beach as a boy.

We swam onward, never hitting any wall. Exactly as I'd imagined—or somehow intuited—the pool had no far barrier. Gradually, the clear black lightened to deep ocean-blue, then to lighter marine colors. The water became shallower, the floor below a bed of white sand with remarkable shapes that could be the Faerie version of coral.

Fish appeared, large and small, all of them bizarre to my eye—some tumbling in tangles of iridescent tentacles, others nearly transparent, except for the shimmer of inherent magic. One creature, reminiscent of a shark but covered in unearthly violet feathers, swished past, baring scarlet teeth at me.

I expected we'd eventually surface onto some shore and go from there. Instead, Rogue led me to a great reef, with tunnels here and there. We passed through a narrow underwater channel, a magical barrier briefly prickling my skin, and then we emerged into an enclosure made by curved walls. Above the surface, the cavern arched into shadow. Beneath, it shimmered with rose light, like the inside of a heart. Or a womb. The walls glittered with refracted light, possibly crystalline.

But no, as we drifted closer, it became clearer that the crystals were bubbles. Thousands of bubbles, great and small, clinging to the walls, immersed in the blood-warm water.

Not bubbles. Egg sacs.

Moving as close as I dared to one, I peered at it. I half expected Rogue to stop or caution me, but he simply followed behind, interested in my acute curiosity. A thick translucent shell anchored deeply in the wall encased some sort of clear amniotic fluid, and a small shape floated within, its heartbeat flickering at hummingbird speed. Close to fully developed, the inhabitant of this one very much resembled a fairy of Athena's ilk.

The fae didn't fruit on the vine, they hatched from eggs.

Though it wasn't my field, I'd seen this sort of thing before, at an aquarium I visited for a reception at a professional conference. One of the exhibits had the collagen-shelled shark eggs attached to the viewing window, so visitors could see the developing occupant. These looked much the same.

But instead of staying an amphibious or aquatic creature, the fae that hatched from these eggs ended up on land.

I'd thought it before—ontogeny recapitulates phylogeny. Somehow the developmental cycle of the fae carried them along in a greater arc than the creatures of my world experienced. In my paradigm, a creature born to a particular species would recapitulate phylogeny to a certain point. A fish then might start as a single cell and grow more complex until it fit the definition of *Osteichthyes* and hatched. Likewise a human fetus started as a single cell, grew more complex, for a time resembled a fish, but matched *Homo erectus*, more or less, by birth.

If the theory I was rapidly assembling was correct, the fae continued to develop well after hatching. And possibly throughout their life spans.

It wasn't unprecedented for a species to continue to change after birth. A human infant required an extensive juvenile period before becoming a sexually mature individual. Many of the more complex mammals did.

Somehow, in Faerie—and true to type—the fae, especially the immortal variety, continued to evolve into different species even after reaching maturity. Or was *that* the key? Perhaps younger fae nobles were essentially juveniles for hundreds of years or longer, and only later matured into being capable of mammalian-style reproduction. After all, the reproductive organs of a fish were not so different from a mammal's—a few developmental tweaks could get you there, with the proper stimulating agent.

Magic definitely could serve that purpose.

Rogue paced me, a steady presence in the back of my mind, as I studied the groupings of the egg clusters, able to identify some species of fae, while others remained a mystery. I itched to draw them, to take notes. More, I longed for the textbooks that would provide me with the references I needed. Not that they would have *this* in them, but how long had it been since I read D'Arcy Thompson's *On Growth and Form?* Grad school, easily.

Principles were principles. If gravity applied here, so did basic laws of biology and form. If Rogue and I were similar enough physiologically that we could interbreed, then the rules I understood had to apply. The answer to all of it lay here. I just knew it.

Including one to my newest question: *Who was laying all the damn eggs?*

CHAPTER 23
IN WHICH I QUESTION MY ANSWERS

❧

Evolutionary change, in my understanding, occurs slowly over many generational iterations. In Faerie, however, with the profound influence of magic on the flow of time, evolution can be so accelerated, and organisms so long-lived, that evolution can occur within a single individual.

~Big Book of Fairyland, "Flora and Fauna"

NOT TITANIA.

I was pretty sure of that. Ninety-five percent. It didn't make logical sense. No, she wasn't the mother, but the mad scientist. My monstrous reflection, running her brand of human trials on her own people, cross-breeding the sexually mature fae nobles with human to, what end? World domination, no doubt, but through what method?

Also, where were the juveniles? I'd seen Rogue in his memories as a boy, but no others. Starling, too, had images of being a young girl, growing up at Castle Brightness. But then she'd been born human-style to Blackbird. Who had taken care of the young Rogue?

The next cavern held part of the answer to that.

Only a few eggs in this one, larger and set on the ground like stalagmites. More encrustation on these and larger forms inside. Child-sized. It gave me the chills, in that horror-movie way. I even found myself casting a nervous eye at the deeper shadows, half expecting the alien queen to emerge.

The floor of this room, also that same warm rose color, gave me more of a clue. With more gaps between egg sacs, the surface showed itself to be not rocky, but fleshy, pulsing with the beat of fluids. The cavern wasn't simply reminiscent of a womb—it *was* one. Spontaneous generation? I'd likely have to observe over time to determine that.

Rogue took my hand and let me know we had to leave.

I didn't want to, but I had a great deal to contemplate as it was, so I let him pull me along. He did so slowly, at least, allowing me the opportunity to take in as much as I could as we drifted by.

And there. Serendipitously, a grouping of pastel eggs hatched.

Like minnows, the hatchlings poured out, swirling in a cloud and heading for the surface. I swam closer. A rush of sheer delight filled me. Few joys rivaled having a theory supported by experimental results. The hatchlings resembled tiny dragonfly girls, with bulging bellies. Following them to the surface, I saw them pop above the still surface, taking in their first breaths.

Careful not to interfere, I observed from below. Also because Rogue stopped me from putting my own head above water with a stern warning. Probably I couldn't breathe air *and* water at the same time. Alas.

The dragonfly girl hatchlings drifted in a group toward a rocky outcropping. I imagined some sort of beach and crevasses, perhaps tidal pools for them to continue their next life cycle. From fish to amphibious to land-dweller. Though safe enough in this hatching cavern, like the enclosed nursery bays in my own oceans, they'd no doubt face danger once they emerged. Thus the large numbers of eggs and hatchlings. Without parental care, they depended on numbers for some individuals to survive to maturity.

It explained so much about the fae culture. The careless disregard for life. That the lower forms of fae were simply another tier of the animal kingdom in Faerie. Only the noble fae fit the same top-of-the-food chain position as humans did in my world. *Barely intelligent fruit,* Blackbird had once carelessly dismissed the fairy girls like Athena.

I mulled it all over as Rogue swam us out of the cavern. The fish thronging the outside, past the magical barrier, took on a sinister aspect. They were waiting to feed on the newly hatched that wandered out. Or who grew big enough to take their chances and seek the greater world. Probably the swollen bellies of the dragonfly girl hatchlings were part of the egg sac—nurturing them for a time as they grew.

But they'd have to leave the safety of the nursery cave eventually.

It made me sick and despondent to imagine those feeding frenzies, like the gulls swooping on the hapless sea turtle hatchlings as they made their long, desperate way down the glaringly empty beach to the water. Comfort brushed through my mind, much like the sensation of Rogue smoothing his hand over my hair, along with a sense of the baby elephant, heading into the desert.

My thing, apparently.

And he was, right, I couldn't save them all.

I could however, do those things that *were* in my power.

The water grew dark again, that peculiar ink-black that was simultaneously as clear as glass. We popped up into the bathing chamber, the light of the familiar torches. I took in a breath. And couldn't.

My lungs weighed heavy, full of water and I panicked, turning blindly to Rogue. He lifted me, carrying me to the stones. I collapsed there, still unable to draw breath, unable to cough out the water as I knew I should. My ribs and sternum ached and terror filled me with the certain knowledge that, even should I wish the water away, my lungs would collapse.

Rogue needed to help me. I showed him and he picked me up, bending me over one strong arm by the waist and thumping my back, so the water poured out. I managed a gasping breath and coughed, more water coming out of me, more than seemed possible.

Finally, I could draw a deep breath again, the air burning the tissues of my lungs, as I lay on my side. Rogue sat beside me, rueful.

"Well, that was a terrible idea," he said.

I shook my head. "You couldn't know. I left my own amphibious phase behind a lot longer ago, physiologically speaking, than you did."

He cocked his head studying me, helping me to sit when I struggled to do so. "Sometimes I think that, if I just listen harder, I'll understand the way you see things."

"But you never quite do? Welcome to my world."

His lips curved in a smile, but he looked somber. "Did you find what you sought?"

"Quite a bit of it. Most important, I have new questions."

"And…this pleases you?"

"Yes!" I laughed at his perplexed expression and knelt up to push the wet hair back from his forehead. "You see, half the battle is knowing what question to ask. Vague questions bring vague results."

He narrowed his gaze, sifting through my surface thoughts like fingers running through my hair. "What now?"

"I want to look in your mind—for something specific. May I?"

"Of course. What's mine is yours, my lady."

A bit shaken by it, I realized he meant that literally. As much as I'd worried about being in his power, I'd neglected to fret over the sheer responsibility of his being in mine.

"Imagine that—you forgetting to fret about something."

"Ha-ha." But I grimaced in acknowledgment. Altering the position of my fingers, I touched them lightly to his temples. I probably didn't need to do it this way anymore, as closely as our minds interfaced, but he'd first taught me this way.

I felt more than saw his smile over the shared memory. How hostile and uncertain I'd been, standing between his knees while he coaxed me to look into his mind, to discover his true intentions.

Forever ago and yesterday.

He stilled as I went deeper, searching for that pivotal memory I'd caught that first time and several times since. Ah, there. Himself as a boy, running on the beach, feathers raining through the air. I knew where this went.

I wanted to see immediately before.

Patiently I retraced, stretching the edge of the memory bubble to before that intensely emotional event that etched this moment so strongly in his memory. It wasn't easy. The memory wanted to play forward, to rush down the tracks to the center of its gravity, to the birds dying and Titania taking his hand.

Rogue had grown tense under my hands, so I edged onto his lap, wrapping my legs around his waist, kissing him with gentle affection. He thawed, hands lifting to settle on my hips to support my back. It ached, I realized, from the swimming and the wrenching coughs. He kneaded the sore muscles and I dropped into his mind again, a sensation much like falling asleep while he held me.

The memory scrolled on, playing that same reel. I edged it back again, coaxing. Running on the beach. The sand sharp against his tender bare feet, danger breathing just behind. The world so beautiful, so new. Glorious and terrifying. Massaging it back further, I found it.

The boy, swimming. Limbs stroking through aquamarine water. A few others around him. Screams as the sharks attacked. Terrified, the boy swam harder, faster. Seeing the beach and striking out for it.

Dragging himself out of the water and through the rocks onto the sandy shore. Climbing onto it and looking around. Amazement. Curiosity. Safety.

And then the ravens.

Enormous, with clawed talons and sharp beaks. They dove on him, raking wounds down his body, seeking to carry him off. So much huger than he. He ran. Ran for his life. The land felt wrong and hard on his weak limbs but something else filled him, radiant energy running in his veins.

All of a sudden, he wasn't so powerless. With vindictive rage, he lashed out, sending the magic—the coils of feral blue-edged black I knew so well, but raw and undisciplined—and vaporized the birds. With a thought he killed them all. All birds. Everywhere. The bubble pop of their nonexistence reverberating through Faerie, feathers swirling through the sky.

He ran from that, too, a sick sense of horror settling through him.

And Titania appeared.

So beautiful in his eyes. Strong, lovely, shimmering with pink-gold magic. Far from being upset about the birds, she laughed and took him by the hand. "Oh, my powerful sorcerer boy," she crooned, "come with me. We shall do great things together. I will protect you and care for you. Forever."

Rogue regarded me with his standard grave intensity. He'd learned not to care. Not immediately, but over the years and decades. As the magic infused his body, as he grew, matured and became eventually unkillable. That destroying the birds had been simply a careless demonstration of power. A young sorcerer, newly hatched, arriving in Faerie. Survival of the fittest in the extreme.

And one of my first acts of magic had been to bring the birds back.

"At least temporarily," Rogue commented, following the thought. "I quickly sent them back to your world, before Titania noticed. Still—an odd coincidence, yes."

"When magic is involved, mere coincidence seems improbable." Especially with Rogue and me, with the many uncanny ways our fates intertwined. Once I would have declared the concept of fate superstitious nonsense. These days…well, not so much.

"There is that," he conceded.

"You know," I said, cupping his cheek, "you were only a child. Very young mentally. Striking back at the birds that would have killed you was a natural impulse."

He turned his head to press a kiss to my palm. "I know that now. My fortune was simply that I had more power than I knew how to use properly. You would understand that."

I did. And though Marquise and Scourge had been my teachers, my lot paled by comparison to what Titania had put him through. The glimpses I'd caught were enough to steer me away from those memories. As I'd told Walter, some things were too private to share. Still, I hated that he'd been recaptured by her for my sake. That she'd hurt him again.

"You needn't worry about me as you are," he continued. "Though your concern is far more gratifying than when you are full of suspicion, I don't…experience things in the same way you do. Those memories don't haunt me or cause me pain. Not like yours do to you."

Ah yes, this song and dance. He'd tried to persuade me from the beginning that he didn't have real feelings. That none of them did. I didn't buy it anymore.

They experienced emotions, all right. Every last one of them. Just with the same distortion as all of Faerie—inside out, more brilliant, asymmetrical. The world I knew, mutated.

By magic.

PART IV

PEER REVIEW

CHAPTER 24

IN WHICH WE DO MUCH STRATEGIZING

*I have long suspected that the war is nothing more than a
game to pass the time.*

~*Big Book of Fairyland*, "Falcon's War"

H IS OBLIGATION TO me satisfied, Rogue called a war
council meeting.

Normally this should have pleased General Falcon and his
commanders, who had demonstrated they loved nothing
better. This time, however, not only was Rogue in charge, but
their erstwhile enemy also sat at the table. General Fafnir,
grizzled and dour as ever, arrived with an entourage of nobles I
recalled from either the welcoming ceremony or the wedding
itself. They ranged down one side of the table, Falcon and his
staff, including Lord Puck and Lady Healer, down the other.

Glowering at each other.

Rogue and I sat at the head of the table in side-by-side
chairs, which pleased me. Starling, Larch and Athena—who I'd
insisted on having present, despite their nonnoble status—sat

behind us, which I tried not to be irritated about. Marquise, Scourge, looking amused by it all, and Walter, back in his silver collar and clearly chagrined by it, sat a ways down, on "our" side.

Darling Hercules sat on the table next to me, still preening from his gallant defense of the castle.

"Is this all the noble fae?" I asked Rogue, as the others bickered among themselves.

He cast an eye over the group of maybe fifty. "Excepting Titania, her loyal following, Incandescence, Blackbird and a few who keep out of society altogether, yes."

Very small pool, even if I figured on an equal number hanging with—or cocooned by—Titania. Not nearly enough to form a heterogeneous population for breeding. Of course, that followed the evolution of immortality, right? That piece must come later, however, since clearly many didn't survive their hatching and emergence onto land. Only those with magic and strength—or luck—survived that transition.

Once past that and without death, the population had to maintain itself in other ways, which meant zero to no reproduction.

Except for Titania's mad gambit.

"I wish to register my continued complaint against our noble host," Falcon cut through the initial chatter. "None of us can afford to be in contention with our noble and lovely goddess. This is Rogue's problem. I say we leave him to deal with it."

"Agreed." Fafnir flicked a glance at us and away. "Ever have we been on our own. Victory is not possible. Thus we should return to our individual pursuits."

Falcon slammed a hand on the table. "Exactly my point. And you two—" he pointed thick yellow nails at Rogue and me, "—still owe me assistance in my battles."

"And I wish to reclaim *my* sorcerer, as is right and just," Fafnir proclaimed, sweeping a hand at Walter, who looked ill at the notion but manfully ignored his erstwhile general. "Now that Lady Gwynn has trained him for me, he'll be even more valuable in the contest."

"He cannot beat the combined forces of my two," Falcon sneered.

"Ah, but my wizard calls the dragons his and, once the scepter is returned to him, then—"

"The scepter shall not be returned," Rogue declared without force but with implacable will.

"And the dragons are mine," I added.

Falcon preened at Fafnir's crushed expression.

"Also, as you should well recall, Falcon—" Rogue steepled his fingers, "—we agreed that I would perform all magics, not the Lady Sorceress Gwynn. Now that we have combined our magic, such a separation is no longer possible. Thus the terms are moot and the bargain void."

Falcon's turn to gnash his teeth in frustration while I turned an admiring smile on Rogue. He played a deep game indeed, if he'd planned for this that long ago. His face revealed nothing, but I knew on a profound level, he was pleased to have surprised me.

"Then our war comes to nothing," Fafnir said, looking bleak.

"What exactly were the two factions fighting over?" I asked. "It's never been clear to me."

"Victory," Fafnir grated out.

"To triumph!" Falcon pounded his fist on the table.

They glared at one another.

"It's what we *do*, Lady Gwynn," Puck said with a giggling lilt, nodding at me so the jingle bells in his ears chimed sweetly, "in lieu of other battles."

That showed a surprising amount of rational thinking—especially coming from Puck. His playful mien no longer distracted me. Of all of them, he'd always given me the wisest advice. Much like his mythical counterpart, the bringer of mischief, the wise fool who capered through and saw the most clearly. I smiled at him, grateful that he'd given me that wedding eve talking-to.

"Which is why we are here." Rogue picked up the conversational ball. Gone was the disinterested mien that he normally affected. "Blame me if you will, but you are cornered. Fight Titania you will. We all will. None of us has a choice any longer."

"Because of *your* game," Lady Healer pointed out.

Rogue simply regarded her with a cool stare and she looked away.

"I did not make the game and well you know it. I've simply changed the rules. We must assume that Lady Incandescence has thrown in with Titania. If any of you wish to leave and do likewise, you may go. I'll release you."

They all seemed shocked by that. Frankly, I was also. Rogue's confidence could be daunting.

"Good Titania, man!" One of Fafnir's cabal exclaimed. I recognized his face, though we'd never met before. Titania had been wearing it as a mask for her masquerade ball, blood continuing to drip from the ragged edges. The last I'd seen, it had been gasping on the floor where she'd tossed it aside to attack me. Apparently he'd managed to retrieve it. An image I didn't care to contemplate for long. "You know what she'd do to us!"

That needed no reply. He'd only confirmed Rogue's point.

"General Falcon—are all your forces inside the walls?" Rogue asked.

Mollified by the restoration of his title, Falcon sat straighter. "I sent many of the humans home—they're useless except against other humans—but otherwise, yes."

"Not my monsters," Lady Strawberry sulked.

"Or my sailing ships," said the fae noble I thought of as Navy Man. "We can't possibly have a decent naval battle here. *Unless* we expand the moat!"

Everyone ignored him.

"And General Fafnir?" Rogue pressed. I had to love him for keeping things from devolving into shades of the Mad Hatter's tea party.

Fafnir and his cabal exchanged glances, shifting in their chairs.

Rogue simmered with irritation. "Your plans to abduct and employ Sorceress Gwynn are done for. Your simpering war with Falcon over. You either join forces with us or leave."

"You kept me prisoner until now." Fafnir looked at me as he said it. "I sought only to save you from disaster."

"Not only." I stroked a hand down Darling Hercules's back and he purred. "You hoped for my help with something else too."

He sucked his thin lips against his teeth, the gray scale

pattern on his face glittering like the undulating coils of a snake. Oddly, instead of triumph, I caught a flash of hope from him. Perhaps he'd stolen Cecily's corpse not out of a morbid determination to succeed, but out of real attachment. She'd believed he loved her. Perhaps he had.

"If you throw in your army—the cabal's forces—with ours, I'll do my best to help you."

Rogue covered my hand with his, though I already had the strum of warning from him. I knew it would be tricky and very possibly traumatizing for me. This was important. The silent hum of his agreement confirmed that.

Fafnir shook his head. "I do not forget—even if you do— that I owe you a favor still. I will add my forces to yours and we can finish with the bargains between us complete."

He had his brand of integrity and, though he wouldn't care, I felt sorry for him and his aloneness. "I'll help you anyway," I added on impulse. "If I can."

His gray-dust gaze met mine. "My army is yours, Sorceress."

"They're useless," Mask Man complained bitterly. "On the other side of Titania's forces. We cannot get them here. We may as well send them home."

"Same as my monsters," Lady Strawberry glumly sympathized. They all sighed in their dismay.

Feeling like the kid seeing the emperor was naked, I looked around the table, totally bemused. Walter, though, met my gaze and rolled his eyes.

"Are you all idiots?" he exclaimed.

Marquise yanked his leash and he subsided, with a strangled squawk.

"Stop that," I told her. "Everyone here gets to talk. What's your point, Walt?" Though I knew, of course.

"Duh." He rubbed his throat under the collar. "Basic strategy. You bring those forces in from behind and trap Tit—the great bitch's army between them and ours. Then we pick them off."

"Doesn't sound very glorious," Falcon sniffed and Fafnir nodded.

"It's not," I chimed in. "It's effective. And, Lady Strawberry—you could do the same with your monsters."

She cheered considerably.

"Agreed then." Rogue stroked the back of my hand thoughtfully. "Once Titania and her army convene, we shall bring in the rest behind."

"They still haven't?" That seemed so odd to me.

"You hadn't looked?" Rogue raised an eyebrow at me.

I hadn't. I'd stayed off the mind web as much as possible. Taking a quick survey, more like running a search term than delving into the files, I found her forces scattered about. Close enough to threaten, but not immediately outside.

"What are they waiting for?" I asked, more rhetorically than anything.

Now it was my turn to receive incredulous looks. As if in response, the baby kicked for the first time, a jab of reminder from within.

Oh yes. They were all waiting on me.

And, at the bizarrely advanced rate this pregnancy was progressing, we would not be waiting long.

"So." I tapped my fingers on the table, not sure how I'd come to be leading this meeting. "I go into labor and she makes her move—then we go into pitched battle?"

"I suspect nothing less will draw her out," Rogue agreed. They all looked uncomfortable, twitching like kids kept at the adult's table too long. If we'd made this a feast, they would have sat and talked all day and night.

"The big problem with that plan is that I'll be somewhat preoccupied," I pointed out to him.

"The Brownies will come to assist," Larch intoned from behind me, in his surprisingly deep voice.

I turned in my chair to look at him. "They will? From the villages nearby?"

He puffed out his chest, purpling with pride. "From all of Faerie. All who can escape service to the queen stand by to serve you, Lady Sorceress Gwynn."

"My kind, too," Athena averred, deftly spinning her dagger. Someone snickered and she stared them down, sweet lavender eyes filled with defiant malice. "We can be taught. Who do you think has been chasing down and destroying all the spider spies?"

That hadn't occurred to me. "Thank you, Athena. And pass along my gratitude." Rogue shifted at that, but I didn't care—I owed them and that deserved voicing. Darling Hercules added that he'd been helping as well, and I scratched his ears, pausing at his further promise.

"Darling Hercules promises to stay with me when the time comes. With his immunity to the Queen Bitch, he'll make an excellent bodyguard."

Decisions reached and roles decided, we adjourned the meeting. I stood and stretched, rubbing my lower back. Was my stomach rounder than when I sat down? If the pregnancy progressed too unnaturally fast, my body might not be able to stand it. Deep in my heart, the cat stretched, too, offering to take my flesh if I wasn't going to be using it. I promised that the time had not yet arrived and maintained calm until she settled again.

Rogue observed the interchange somberly, the Dog having risen in his core as well. Tied in tandem, we were. I gave him a confident smile, which didn't fool him for a second, but he touched my cheek in acknowledgment of all the trepidation I hadn't voiced.

I started to take his arm and became aware that Starling was still sitting in her chair. She looked much recovered— enough to dress and come to the war council, as she'd insisted she should, as my seneschal—but now she seemed listless and weary, her hair tinged with brown. I brightened it for her, though she didn't notice. Rogue discreetly moved away to confer with Lady Healer, who had pointedly waited for him.

"Are you all right, Starling?"

She shrugged. "I'm worried about Mother and Father, though I know they'll be fine. It's nothing." She straightened her skirts, slapped her knees and stood. "Nothing to be done and there's work awaiting me. Seneschal work," she emphasized.

Oh, right. "You're upset that you don't have a job to do in the battle."

"Well, that's my lot isn't it? I can't complain."

"But you'll be with me when I go into labor. Mistress Nancy will need help." Darling Hercules clawed my ankle in reminder. "Help with hands," I modified. "Please say you'll be there."

"Of course, Lady Gwynn, but—"

"There is no *but*." I took her hands. "I need all the friends I can get. I'm afraid, Starling."

"Oh, Gwynn. It will be a beautiful experience that—"

"No." I laughed and it came out a bit hysterical. Rogue was occupied in conversation. I lowered my voice. "I need you there and Athena. Just in case. Remember what happened with Cecily."

Her brown eyes widened, flew to Rogue. "Surely you don't think—But you're married! True love changes everything."

I only hoped she was right. Nevertheless, when the time came, I would not be defenseless.

CHAPTER 25

OMENS AND VISITORS

I think it may be a mistake to conceptualize Faerie as its own universe or world. Perhaps it's more of a microcosm, a bubble of alternate reality stemming off another.

~Big Book of Fairyland, "Notes for Further Research"

"So," I SAID to Rogue, a few days later, "I need to go to Fafnir's castle."

He'd been broodingly staring out the dome, surveying the deceptively peaceful countryside while I worked in my grimoire. I'd been going through my catalogs of the fae species, still working on a reasonable evolutionary tree for them. With the very strong likelihood that one species could eventually become another, it made for a messy diagram. I'd also tried to work out a way to indicate longevity, without much progress.

"What a brilliant idea," he replied without looking at me, his profile sharp against the radiantly blue sky. "Or perhaps I should just deliver you directly to Titania and save her the trouble of fetching you."

I closed the grimoire. "You know, before the wedding, it was that I couldn't leave the castle because of Fafnir's cabal. Now it's because of Titania."

He turned to survey me, not without sympathy. "Feeling imprisoned in my tower after all?"

"The eerie similarity to my hasty prediction has not escaped me."

"The waiting is difficult for me too."

No news there—he practically oozed restless impatience. Especially since sex was suddenly quite uncomfortable for me. I suspected my nervous system had become overly sensitized with the massive changes to my body. My hip bones practically creaked as they adjusted to the rapid expansion of my uterus. Mistress Nancy simply shook her head and did her best to reassure me that, despite the extraordinary rate of progression—she figured me to be in the seventh month now—in all other ways the pregnancy appeared normal.

Small comfort there.

"Nevertheless." I stood and, groaning, braced my hands on the bench to let my body adjust. "I said I'd help him." It went without saying that I might not be in a position to do anything, if the birth did not go well.

"You redeemed your favor. We have his forces without this unwise offer of yours."

"I know." I pressed my fists into my lower back, willing the muscles to relax. "I can't explain it. I just have a feeling I should help him."

Rogue echoed my sigh but didn't argue further. "He cannot bring the corpse here?"

I made a face. "Apparently it has decomposed enough that

he's loathe to move it again. And flesh—so no poofing it here, though I think being inanimate should count. I'm informed that doesn't matter, however."

"I don't like this idea of you going off with Fafnir."

"Jealousy is a sign of insecurity, not affection."

"And your point is?"

I glanced at him. So gorgeous, exotic, powerful. Yet, uncertain of me, after all. "Even if I didn't feel like a cranky hippopotamus, and even if I weren't forever joined at the hip with you, I'd hardly pick Fafnir over you."

"No?" He moved behind me and ran warm, radiant hands down the knotted muscles of my back. I sighed in relief as the vibrating massage lessened their tension. "Why not?"

"I can't believe you're fishing for compliments."

"What an amusing image. You are correct, however. I don't savor the idea of you in Fafnir's home. That said, I'm mainly concerned that he cannot protect you from Titania. In addition, would you take Mistress Nancy with you? What if you should begin to deliver the child? You've made extensive plans to carry that off in the safest possible way." And here he paused, leading me to think that he might know that I'd taken measures against him turning on me, as well. He found the sorest point on my back and worked it loose. I nearly purred. "Why would you jeopardize that? Staying here is the wisest course."

He was right. I just felt so confined. No wonder people used to refer to pregnancy as "confinement." Imagine if I'd had to experience nine real-time months of this.

"There's a reason I never wanted babies," I muttered.

"So you've mentioned." More than once, he didn't say.

"Fine. What's your solution?"

"I'll go with Fafnir and we'll bring the corpse here. You can experiment with it in the safe hall."

I unbent and faced him, suddenly fearful—and hating how dependent I felt. "What if you don't come back?"

"Ah, Gwynn." He stroked my cheek. "Where else would I possibly want to be?"

"Don't say that."

Not only cranky, but superstitiously worried. The closer the time came, the more I saw Cecily's fate and imagined it mine. I knew better than to dwell on the images, not to detail the scene of Rogue striding in under Titania's control, silver-blue sword in hand to cut the baby from my belly. I reached for the icy control Marquise and Scourge had taught me at such great pains to my mental health and managed to dissolve the thought.

Don't make it real.

"Perhaps it would be better for you if I'm not here." Rogue withdrew from me mentally, just enough that I noticed.

I rubbed my forehead. "No. That's not better. I want you here. I need you here."

"We'll be all right." He said it with his usual certainty. But I knew the inside of his heart well enough to know how much of that was bluff, gamble and his excellent poker face.

"Has it occurred to you that we're relying heavily on me and our bond with each other to keep Her from making you act against me—and I'm the one who's most likely going to be out of commission? What if I lose too much blood and pass out? All the stories say it's ungodly painful—what if I'm so distracted by the pain that I can't muster the concentration to help you?"

He gave me a crooked smile. "Are you saying that the training you survived did not put you through painful and distracting trials?"

I shuddered. Pushed those memories back down. "Right. Can childbirth be any worse?"

"Exactly. I shall assist Fafnir and be back directly. You'll hardly know I was gone."

I hated that his words sounded like an omen.

෴

ROGUE'S ABSENCE, HOWEVER, brought me a visitor.

"Yoo-hoo, Lady Gwynn." Puck popped his head through the doorway. "Are you decent? Please say you're not."

"I am," I replied, "and not someone you'd want to see indecent in my current state anyway."

He waltzed in, wearing an eye-jarring shade of cherry, with a train of ribbons that had clearly been co-opted from the wedding decorations. With a dramatic pause, he surveyed me. "Good Titania—whatever have you eaten? You're positively *engorged*."

"Gee, thanks. And it's the kid. This is how it works."

"Reeeallly." He drew out the word in musical astonishment. "I've only ever seen them after they've hatched. It seems so...bestial."

Oddly, I laughed. Maybe it was Puck's solid good spirits. I smoothed my hands over my straining belly. "That's not a bad word for it—pretty close to how I feel."

"You always did feel more than the rest of us," he observed, prancing closer, his fascinated gaze following my hands. "May I do that?"

"What—touch my belly? Sure."

He held out his hands but didn't quite close, as if afraid to touch a flame. Taking his wrists, I pressed his palms against me. His eyes—one grass-green, one sky-blue—opened wide. "It's...moving," he whispered.

"Yes." I couldn't help myself. I added in a creepy tone, "It's aliiiive."

He laughed and booped the tip of my nose. "I told you so, Sorceress Gwynn."

"Told me what?"

"That it would be grand fun. Didn't I say so? And it *has*." He spun off, dancing around the room in an abandoned jig.

Bemused, I shook my head at his antics. "Why are you here, Puck?"

"Instead of there? Now that's a very good question to ask. One you should consider." He picked up the rubber ducky off my workbench. "Do you like it? I always liked the toys best. Your world comes up with the most delightfully absurd ideas. Or absurdly delightful ones—whichever way you prefer it."

"You've been there." Well, boy howdy. This explained so damn much.

"But you knew that. You recognize me."

"I feel sure I would have remembered you." I swept a hand at his outrageous appearance. Nothing like an inhumanly tall, gangly and fundamentally clashing fae to draw attention in the human world.

"I am that merry wanderer of the night." Puck singsonged the line. "Now do you remember?"

Oh, he meant not personally, but in the way he surfaced in the plays and stories. "But you brought me this rubber ducky."

"You were so sad. I thought it would please you. People like to have things to remind them of where they were born. And where they grew up. Which aren't always the same place."

"It did. It does. How can you go back and forth, though? Can you do it at will? What's the mechanism?" I looked for my grimoire, wanting to get the details on this. Puck laid his hand, festooned with glittering rings, on the book. Holding it closed.

"It's who I am. It's what I do." He sounded uncharacteristically serious. "Do you understand what I'm telling you?"

"No." I had no compunction admitting that. "Can you explain?"

"You can put a pig in a pond, but you can't make him swim."

I tried reassembling the sequence of images in my head and still came up with nothing.

"You can bake a pie with four and twenty blackbirds, or only one. When you open it, they'll sing."

"Blackbirds? Do you know where Blackbird and Fergus are?"

"You have the answers," he insisted. "You must only remember." He made a great show of digging in his pocket and pulling out an invisible watch. Making a comical face, he exclaimed, "Oh dear! Oh dear! I shall be too late!" And he dashed off, dropping through the opening to the stairs as if it were a rabbit hole.

"That's another story entirely!" I called after him, torn between amusement and aggravation. In the ticking moments after he left, the frustration won out. "Always with the riddles," I muttered to myself and went to the grimoire to write down what he'd said. Clues to something. Had Blackbird and Fergus somehow gotten through to my old world? It would explain their absence. There'd been no word, and Starling grew more frayed by the day. Rogue flat refused to give the scepter to me or Walter and had buried the knowledge of where he'd put it so deep even I couldn't get at it.

Of course, I hadn't *really* tried to dig it out of him, unwilling to upset our current harmony. I respected his reasons for not wanting either of us to have it.

But he also didn't care so much about the fate of Blackbird and Fergus. He'd been focused on me. Which I appreciated on one level, but he'd hardly let me out of his sight. In fact, I hadn't been alone like this in days and days. I maybe didn't need the scepter—the dome might be enough. Something I'd never quite mentioned to Rogue.

I moved to the center of the dome to do a light test, my thoughts carefully shrouded just in case Rogue returned unexpectedly. The cat stirred in me with interest as I gathered power and focused it. She seemed fairly docile lately, as sedated by copious food and long naps as I'd been. Like an egg, myself, I'd become simply a shell for gestation. If only my shell had similar flexibility.

Easing into the mind web, I virtually tiptoed in, using the vast curvature of the crystal dome to diffuse my impact. As always, the network sang with life, an energetic reflection of a tropical jungle night, dense with the chorus of insects, amphibians, birds, reptiles and the occasional predator slinking through the shadows, leaving hush in her wake.

I steered clear of those, skimming the surface, staying well clear of Titania's icy supernova. What I sought wouldn't be central to this network of beings, but rather at the perimeter. So I went away from Titania, farther from the vivid stars of the noble fae, with their complex tumbling surfaces, off to the edges. It felt almost like those graphics of leaving the solar system, the planets falling behind and the brightness of the center fading to a pinprick as I plunged into depthless space.

Had I expected to hit a wall? Perhaps so. The way the fae spoke of the division between my old world and Faerie implied a barrier. The old tales mentioned the Veil, and when it might be thinner or more penetrable. Gateways, such as standing stones or darkly magical places like Devils Tower, also suggested a passage through a wall. But when Rogue had shown me my old world on another occasion, we hadn't traveled any sense of distance.

In fact, if the Castle of the Dark Gods truly did mirror Devils Tower, then physical distance meant nothing. I lived on top of the gateway.

Not out, but in.

CHAPTER 26

IN WHICH I HALFHEARTEDLY ATTEMPT A RESURRECTION

❦

"You can put a pig in a pond, but you can't make him swim." I have no idea what this means.

~*Big Book of Fairyland,* "Notes for Further Research"

I OPENED MY eyes with a snap, the world outside sharp and bright. I really needed to get over this idea of distance. No traveling vast distances through a solar system of life-forms. It took no time to be back in my body because I'd never truly left it.

Moving to the curved transparent wall, I surveyed the countryside. Any of those green rolling hills—more vividly emerald than ever in the wake of the melting snow—could be the one I had landed on. Did *that* sort of physical location matter? Perhaps Blackbird and Fergus, on their way to the castle had somehow found the gate I'd used. The temptation for both of them to take the opportunity to search for Baby Brody would have been too great to resist.

Or maybe it had been more deliberate. Blackbird had discovered something on her journeys—the very answers Rogue and I planned to seek on the sea voyage she undertook instead. If only I'd paid more attention when I glimpsed them through the scepter and discerned more than that they were headed my way. The scepter might let me reach through the Veil to find them, if I could figure out what Rogue had done with it.

Rogue's hand fell on my shoulder and I emitted a startled squeak, full of guilty surprise as much as anything. "Deep in thought?" he asked, blue eyes as dark as the throat of one of his lilies.

"Yes." I stood on tiptoe to slide my hands behind his neck. He returned my kiss with interest but brushed through my mind at the same time. "How did it go?"

"We have retrieved the corpse," he replied, a lingering shadow of distaste in his words, like the scent of rot. He ran his hands down my sides and snugged me against him as best he could with the iron beach ball of my belly between us. "I wish to extract a promise from you."

Uh-oh. "I thought we were done with bargains. Fully in sync, one with each other, what's mine is yours and so forth."

"I think you know full well what I'm asking. Seeing that human woman..." He looked over my head, out to the meadow of Stargazers.

"The whole mortality thing got to you, huh?"

His gaze shot back to me. "Will you mock even this?"

"Death? Yes. Humankind has a rich and varied history of mocking death because we have no other choice. It's the one guarantee we have, that we all die. I tried to make the point previously that you were in denial over this."

The left side of his mouth, entwined with the black lines of the Dog's presence under his skin, lifted in an unamused smile. "I preferred to focus on other topics at the time."

"Yes, well—then you've clearly mastered the art of it." I started to step away, but he held me in an iron grip.

"Your promise," he reminded me.

I couldn't quite meet his gaze anymore, though surely he sense how my heart pounded. To soothe myself, I released the band holding his hair and twined my fingers in the silky texture. "The terms?"

"You will not attempt to retrieve and use the scepter."

"How could I? I don't know what you did with it."

"Gwynn." He pronounced my name in warning.

"I can't promise that." I risked a look at his face. As I'd suspected, the inky lines writhed, a manifestation of his deep upset. "What if I need it...*after*."

His hands tightened on me and he dropped his forehead to touch mine. Even now, dim as thunderclouds barely cresting the horizon, the black cord of his tether to Titania snaked through the back of his mind. "Should things become that dire, not even that will save me. Promise me you won't use it."

"Why not just destroy it, as you threatened to?" I stroked the back of his neck, soothing him.

"I tried." He sounded both grim and chagrined. And need- ed to say nothing more. The fact that he couldn't affect the thing spoke volumes.

"How about if I promise not to attempt to use it until after the baby is born?"

"I don't want you to use it at all."

"Believe me, I'm clear on that point. I promise not to use it before the baby is born or in any way that will jeopardize our child. That's as good as you'll get."

"Or for my benefit."

"No dice."

"Stubborn Gwynn, you—"

"That's right. I am stubborn and you know full well that I'm better at it than you are. That's my offer. You can't ask me to love you with one breath and then expect me to stand by and not do whatever I can to protect you. This is my version of fighting death."

"I cannot die."

"No. But, as you've pointed out to me, there are far worse things than death." I kissed him and his lips were cool, unresponsive. So I deepened the touch, reaching in and caressing him emotionally, pouring love and desire into him. With a gasp, he opened his mouth to me and drank me in with fierce need. I pressed tightly to him, entwining my own arousal with his, wanting his skin against mine.

And the baby kicked, hard enough for Rogue to feel and for my bladder to protest fiercely. He looked with bemused consternation at my belly and I laughed at his expression.

"I guess that's a no," I told him ruefully.

"Just as well. Cecily's corpse grows no fresher. We may as well deal with that."

ڡﭏ

HE WASN'T EXAGGERATING. They'd created a table in the middle of the magic arena that looked much like my workbench. I would have made something more like the metal tables we used in anatomy, but I supposed it didn't really matter. Besides, it touched me that Rogue tried to make things the way he thought I liked them, so I didn't want to impugn his choice by changing it.

As he'd implied, Cecily's corpse had long passed any sort of freshness. Contained in a close-fitting bubble of Rogue's stabilized magic, the body looked almost mummified rather than decomposed. It had been wrapped in a blanket—Nancy's doing, no doubt—with a withered blossom clutched in the hands folded over her collapsed chest. If I looked, her abdomen would be emptied, carved open by Fafnir's blade.

Fafnir himself hovered over the body, as if he might protect it. The stabilizing shield of Rogue's magic kept him from touching her. Otherwise I thought he might be holding her as close, with as much fearful love, as Rogue had just held me. The usually grim fae wore an expression of tender joy and he looked at me with such hope that I banished my uneasy thoughts that whispered nastily of necrophilia.

"You see?" Fafnir gestured at the corpse with a grand flourish.

Taking some time to gather my thoughts, I edged up to the table and studied her more closely. I'd seen corpses plenty of times in anatomy teaching labs and done more animal necropsies than I could count, so the sight didn't make me squeamish at all. The flesh had decayed remarkably little, though I had no idea how much subjective time had passed for it and I wasn't at all familiar with what to expect for an unembalmed human body buried in dirt.

Still, her saucy curls still clung to the desiccated skull more than seemed likely. And I made out no sign of the insects, nematodes and bacteria that made their living in my world by recycling no-longer-living flesh. Ashes to ashes, dust to dust.

Not for Cecily's abandoned flesh.

"What do you want me to see?" I finally asked Fafnir, glancing up at his lined face.

He gestured at the table. "She's still here. She's not gone at all."

Was that an insane glint in his eye? His thoughts roiled with jumbled excitement, hope and dread, making it difficult for me to sort.

Treading carefully, I said, "The flesh she wore remains, but it no longer lives. The person she was, the life that occupied this flesh, has gone."

Rogue's hand trailed lightly down my spine. In comfort or warning, I wasn't sure.

Fafnir cocked his head in that listening way. "I don't understand."

"This is simply a...leftover. It's not *her*."

"I know it's not her," he replied, full of impatience. "That's why I need you. Remake her."

"It doesn't work that way." My own impatience simmered up. "Look—what happens if one of the lesser fae die?"

Fafnir gave me that look, like I'd said something absurd, and Rogue's thoughts tracked along with curiosity. I wasn't making any more sense to them than they were to me.

"Back when I was at Falcon's camp, a page caught on fire. He was too damaged to survive and his body stopped functioning. What do you say would have happened to him?"

Come to think of it, I didn't know, myself. I'd observed his lifeless body, just as I'd seen Dragonfly's, which Rogue had sent out to sea. But what of funerals and so forth?

"They…" Fafnir seemed to be searching for the words. "Go into the water and come back out again."

"How?" I pounced on that, thinking of the hatching cavern and how that cycle might work.

"By swimming." he answered, clearly pleased to give me a finite answer. I wanted to clutch my skull in frustration, but that would get neither of us anywhere.

"Let me try this—let's say that page who burned went into the sea and reemerged alive again. Would he remember what had occurred?"

Fafnir gazed down at Cecily's mummified corpse with utter adoration. "I don't need for her to remember. Perhaps it's better if she does not. We'll make a new life. Without…" His gaze shifted behind me to Rogue. "Perhaps we shall triumph and we can simply live."

"Perhaps so," Rogue answered.

"All I ask, Sorceress, is that you try." Fafnir transferred his urgent gaze to me, silver-gray eyes tumbling with a dust storm of long-dry feeling. "I beg of you. If not for me or for her, then for your own future." In his mind, he held an idea, of a time and place that could be real for us all, free of the horrors he'd suffered. Of a kind of paradise.

He didn't have to explain more. Rogue held his mind closed, but in the core of him, where we seemed to remain entirely open to one another, his quiet dread grew like a mold over Fafnir's image of paradise. He hated that it could be me on that table. Not like I hadn't tried to warn him.

Still, I sighed and stretched out my senses. The cat, interested, flowed along too and I didn't dissuade her. She liked the arena and remembered the fun we'd had play-fighting here. As

long as she behaved, I didn't mind her being awake. In some
ways, it seemed her presence helped buffer the nagging pains
in my body.

The bubble of Rogue's magic, a seamless field of black-
edged blue, resisted my efforts with a sense of inertness that
reminded me of the dragons' null magic. Interesting. "I need
you to drop the field," I said to him aloud, so Fafnir would
know I made an effort.

"Not the whole thing," he murmured, sliding his hand
back up my spine to settle at the nape of my neck. "But a
window. Where do you want it?"

It didn't matter. I picked anyway. "Over her forehead."

The ancients might have thought the seat of the soul resid-
ed in the heart or the center of the body. I, however, was a
neuroscientist and I believed in the brain.

I almost saw the hole open. Very small, a pinpoint flaw in
the shield. Slipping a mental probe in the opening he made, I
quickly agreed with Rogue's reasoning. The corpse tasted of
ash, indeed. The tissues fluttered in the slight breath of my
thought's passage as dried leaves stirred by autumn winds,
losing their tenuous hold on the branches that once gave them
life.

Nothing of life remained in the dried corpse of Fafnir's lady
love. No cords of life bound her to him or to anything in the
world.

Except.

Anchoring myself to Rogue, like grabbing his hand so I
could lean over the edge of a cliff, I looked not out, but in.

There, deep in some internal dimension, something remained. An echo that connected forward in time instead of

repeating the voices long past. As if the essence of Cecily, the mitochondrial-powered vestiges of her DNA, lingered on in some pool of racial memory, feeding forward to something else. No, to some*one* else. Someone who yet lived.

Her child.

Fafnir's child.

Lit with excitement, I followed the trail down a tunnel that blazed with light at the end, to something familiar. As I moved, though, my steps slowed, my mind tugging me back. Rogue pulling on me, mental hand firmly in mine. Keeping me from going over the edge of the cliff.

Right. Don't go into the light.

I withdrew from Cecily's corpse and leaned back against Rogue, soaking in his relieved gratitude that I remained with him. I would, I let him know, as long as I could humanly manage.

Fafnir watched me with guarded hope.

"Cecily—the woman you knew—is beyond reach," I told him, as gently and firmly as I could. "She is gone. I'm sorry for it."

His face crumpled, the hope fleeing and leaving dust behind. "I felt so sure. There's still a connection…"

"There is," I confirmed. Rogue's hands stilled, every cell of him listening. "I think the connection is to—" Now his fingers flexed in definite warning. How to say it without speaking the words?

But I didn't need to. Fafnir's gaze sharpened, gray dust forging into steel. "Where?"

"I don't know. No." I put up a hand to stop whatever he might be about to harangue me with. "I have an idea. And that's what we'll work on next." A wave of dizziness washed over me. The cat purred as I drew on Mother Earth's font through the dirt beneath my feet. The baby kicked, hard, and I gasped, abruptly breaking out into a sweat. "Though I think I may have been standing too long."

A wash of fluid poured down my legs. Oh, dammit all to hell and gone.

"Or not." I looked up at Rogue. "Time to pay the piper."

CHAPTER 27

IN WHICH THINGS PROCEED EXACTLY AS I SHOULD HAVE SEEN THEY WOULD

ৎ⯑ৎ

Be careful what you wish for.
~*Big Book of Fairyland,* "Rules of Magic"

I PROTESTED WHEN Rogue swept me up into his arms, hating that my skirts were soaked through with amniotic fluids. Then I wised up and wished them clean and dry. Not like the dress could be ruined more and I figured Starling would forgive me in this extremity.

"Not that I care for such things anyway," Rogue reproved me, carrying me with his long, ground-eating strides toward our tower.

"I can walk. It's probably better for me, from what I hear."

"Indulge me," he gritted.

Coming as we did from the gruesome great cautionary tale of Cecily's corpse, I figured I could give him this. Still. "We don't need to hurry," I pointed out. "This will likely take hours and hours." If not days, but no use contemplating that possibility. On the tail end of my words, as if to put lie to them, a major contraction seized me, squeezing the breath out of me on a long wheeze of surprised pain.

I sent a mental note of apology to all the women I'd thought had been exaggerating with their labor war stories.

"This is why you can't walk," Rogue informed me and I realized I'd rather convulsively grabbed on to him, my face buried in his chest.

"We would have stopped walking and waited it out." I had to measure the words around my breaths, since the contraction had left me panting. No Lamaze classes for me. Was I supposed to pant or not? Seemed like the movies showed people breathing deep during contractions and panting between. Or vice versa—I hadn't really paid attention.

"I suspect that, as long as you continue to breathe, that will suffice," Rogue said, beginning the circular ascent up our stairs. I'd be happy when this was over and I could stay weakness-free long enough to climb the steps myself. If I lived through this.

I gazed up at Rogue, his perfectly carved face set in sharp lines like porcelain. A long lock of his still-loose hair was wound around my hand, where I'd reflexively grabbed hold of him. This was it. The moment of destiny. What I'd been rocketing toward all along, knowingly or not.

"I've really loved you, you know," I told him.

"Don't talk that way." He sounded harsh, almost mean.

"I just want you to know that I didn't have to. The rest of this might be fated or manipulated or whatever, but that part is real for me."

"I know why you're telling me that now, my Gwynn. Because you think this is the end of our story. I refuse to accept that."

My megalomaniac.

The birthing team had assembled in the bedroom already, with Starling finishing up preparing the bed as Nancy provided instructions. I'd successfully won the argument for having at least *this* human in my tower. Rogue set me on the bed with infinite gentleness, leaning me against the piled-up pillows. I kept my grip on his hair as he started to pull away.

"Don't go," I told him.

He searched my face, for once deeply uncertain. "It might not be a good idea for me to be in the room."

"If you're somewhere else and…take it in your head to come here, does anyone have the power to stop you?"

His mouth twisted in a self-deprecating smile. "You, if anyone."

And Titania, of course, but that went without saying, since we knew where she fell out on this.

"Then you might as well stay, since this is where I'll be. I need you to stay."

He caressed my left cheek, tracing the twining path of silver. "I really have loved you, too, my Gwynn. I never expected to feel anything for you. It's made everything different."

"Maybe true love will win the day after all," I quipped, amused at myself and yet also, for the first time, maybe kind of believing that.

"If you're staying then, milord Rogue," Nancy inserted, her tone making it clear she didn't approve in the least—and who could blame her?—"then you must needs stay out of the way. You can sit over there."

"No. I need to be in physical contact with him." I wasn't sure why I decided that, but this was my party now. I could be unreasonable if I wanted to. "Rogue can sit behind me."

"Boots off then, milord." Nancy huffed about it, but didn't argue further. Rogue settled himself behind me and I leaned gratefully against him, drawing on his strength as another contraction grabbed me in its merciless fist. Nancy held my hands and my gaze, supporting me though it. "I hope you know what you're doing," she said to me, as if Rogue weren't right there. To his credit, he didn't snarl at her.

"Nope," I replied cheerfully. "Winging it, as usual."

"Gwynn's best guess is more reliable than certainty from anyone else I've met," Athena added, coming back from her station by the glass wall, spinning her dagger thoughtfully. A new one. Pure silver, by the looks of it. She gave me a little nod and smiled sweetly at Rogue, her pansy face radiantly lovely, her sharp gaze full of menace. "And I'll stop you, if I have to."

"And I." Starling set down a stack of towels. "Do you recall, Lord Rogue, that you owe me a boon?"

"Owes the both of us," Athena corrected.

Darling Hercules came bounding into the room, leaping onto the bed, offering chagrin for being late, as he'd found a lovely spot in the sun to sleep in that he'd been loath to leave. He settled against me—my many muscle aches subsiding immediately—and fixed Rogue with a green gimlet stare, adding his demand.

"How could I forget?" Rogue answered them all in a dry tone, sliding his hands down my arms in a soothing caress. "Do you all intend to redeem them now?"

They exchanged looks and turned back to him. "Yes," Starling said, in her firmest tone. "The same for both—oh, yes, Darling Hercules—all of us, to triple the power."

"We want you to promise you'll do nothing to harm Gwynn." Athena spun her dagger meaningfully. Darling Hercules set a paw on Rogue's bare foot and flexed his claws.

"He can't promise that—" I started to say.

"Agreed," Rogue said at the same time.

Dammit. He knew as well as I did that his promise wouldn't hinder Titania if she took control of him and then he'd be forsworn as well, doubly in her power. Or sextupled, if the promise to all of them counted three times.

"Don't fret, my lady Gwynn." Rogue cupped my jaw, turning my head so I looked up at him. He kissed me, long and with great care. "Perhaps it will help."

I made a wish then. One that Marquise and Scourge would have punished me for, with its vagueness. The kind that all the tales warned against—bargains with the devil that turned back to bite you, the monkey's paw that fulfilled the letter of the wish, but in the most dreadful way possible.

I knew better. *Be careful what you wish for.*

But I couldn't be specific this time. I made a wish that I might have made in my old life, full of formless longing for something I couldn't quite define. Like writing it on a piece of paper, I folded it up, filled my little wish-boat with all my hope, with all the love and desire Rogue brought out in me, and set it to sail on the vast ocean of the universe.

Let everything come out okay.

§⁊

I LOST TRACK of time. Even more so than usual. Never again would I turn a deaf ear when women complained about childbirth. The inevitability of the progression of it over-whelmed me. No matter how I might wish to call a halt, my own body dragged me along, unstoppable, grueling, exhaust-ing.

Fortunately I had Darling Hercules to absorb the pain—without the invasion of an epidural, too—and Rogue to press kisses to my sweating forehead, offering me comfort and strength in equal doses.

Like commentators at a baseball game, Athena and Starling narrated the progression of the siege, which had commenced in earnest pretty much the instant I went into labor. Lest anyone doubt that Titania knew exactly what went on with us.

Larch was indeed off leading the Brownies, who had con-vened at the Castle of the Dark Gods in force, both in front of Titania's troops and behind. Rogue had to magically shore up the dragon-perch on our tower, as at least a dozen convened to witness the birth, a pair of lantern eyes occasionally peeping up over the edge to check on me.

"It's not like I'm giving birth to the Christ Child or any-thing," I muttered, after one dragon hovered overhead for a better look.

They all ignored me. Or, at least, ignored my words. I likely wasn't making much sense and really, it didn't matter. They were all doing their part to take care of me and that meant the most.

After a particularly brutal contraction that, though it didn't hurt, left me drained, I closed my eyes and rested against Rogue. Though he fed me energy, as did the cat and Mother

Earth, it felt like pouring water down a bottomless well. Magic into a mortal body. Some of it simply wouldn't stick. Coming back to myself, I happened to glimpse through my lashes a concerned expression crossing Nancy's face.

"What?" I asked her and, though she tried to dissemble, I held her gaze. "Tell me."

She scrubbed her hands on a towel. Soaked with bright red blood. My blood. "The babe is big and you are not. With the pregnancy advancing so quickly, your hip bones haven't adjusted. Though it's tearing you apart, I'm not sure the birth canal will expand enough. In time."

And me without a cesarean section.

"Get Lady Healer," Rogue snapped.

Unbidden, the image from Nancy's story rose in my mind. Fafnir slicing Cecily open. He and Lady Incandescence taking the child. As if on cue, Nasty Tinker Bell poofed into the room. So much for her not being able to do magic.

Under me, Rogue tensed and Darling Hercules growled low in his throat.

"That won't help the child," Incandescence told him in her silver-bell voice. "Lady Healer can stand by to repair your sorceress afterward, but the babe must come out first."

Starling and Athena flanked the bed. For the first time I noticed that Starling had a rapier. She looked proud. "Officer Liam's been teaching me." She pointed the weapon convincingly at Nasty Tinker Bell. "It's silver. You won't get close to Gwynn."

Incandescence kept her smile focused on Rogue. "I don't have to. Lord Rogue will do it. Or they both die. Do I need to explain what that means?"

"No," Rogue replied in a quiet voice that belied his emotional turmoil. Dread, terror, desperate hope. I listened to his internal debate with a sense of exhausted inevitability. Of course it had come to this. As with it all, every portent, each step of my journey had led to this exact scenario. My energy flagging, for a hallucinogenic moment I imagined I still stood in that aspen grove, the bloodied knife in my hand, tying a lock of my hair to the tree, Devils Tower running with blue-black magic like blood from a wound. Almost as if I existed in both realities at once.

Nancy was right, though she hadn't said the words. I was dying.

I clutched at Rogue, forcing him to look at me. "You have to do it. Cut the baby out. It's the only way."

He stared back at me, agonized. "Mistress Nancy shall do it."

"No. It's meant. She can guide you, but it should be you. Just, um—don't use the sword, okay?"

He didn't laugh. "Will you place the knife in my hand then, my Gwynn?"

"Don't be dramatic." I gathered my tattered magical energy and wished up a surgical scalpel. "Use this. Much more precise."

"You undo me." He was tired too, feeding me so much of himself only to have my weakening mortal flesh gobble it up and continue to fail.

"I know." I wrapped his fingers around the handle of the scalpel. "But I trust you more than anyone. Do this for me."

He pressed a fervent kiss to my temple and said nothing more. He didn't have to.

Starling helped me lie back, so I didn't have to see, while Athena kept a wary eye—and dagger point—on Incandescence. Darling Hercules lay on my chest, his purring thrumming through me with comfort. At least he didn't have to put me out entirely this time and I stroked his velvety fur, grateful that he saved me from feeling the piece-by-piece destruction of my body.

Dimly I listened to Nancy instruct Rogue on where to cut while I watched a red-tailed hawk circle lazily over the tower. No—it was a dragon, high above Rogue's castle.

Something gave in my body, a kind of snapping that seemed ominous. Then a baby cried. Rogue stood, the infant kicking in his large hands, her face screwed up in indignant rage.

"A girl," I breathed and reached for her.

But, his face remote, his mind withdrawing from mine, he turned away to show Incandescence.

"You know what you have to do," she told him.

And he handed her the baby.

PART V

FINAL THESIS

CHAPTER 28

DEATH COMES TO THE ARCH-SORCERESS

With magic the guiding force of Faerie, "fate" is not theoretical, but becomes binding law.

~Big Book of Fairyland, "Rules of Magic"

PAIN EXPLODED AS Darling Hercules leaped off me onto Rogue's back, clawing him as he'd attacked Titania for me. This time I wasn't bound to the bed, but I might as well have been, the agony of the incision and my broken body sapping my strength, dragging me into a black well of unconsciousness.

I managed to stay conscious by drawing powerfully on Mother Earth, the cat rising up with her, offering to take my shredded flesh and put it to better purpose. I held her off for the moment, reaching out to Rogue with all my might. Incandescence held my daughter in an uncaring arm, idly backhanding Nancy who, with a scream of rage tried to grab the child.

As if in slow motion, Rogue turned his head to look at me,

befuddled. The black oily whip of Titania's control throttled his thoughts. Athena plunged the silver dagger into Nasty Tinker Bell's slim thigh, pulling it out, neatly pirouetting out of the way and stabbing her in the kidney. As if they'd rehearsed it—maybe they had—Starling stepped up, driving the rapier through the noble fae's throat and catching the infant up to her chest.

Outside, the dragons roared and the scorching heat of Titania's imminent arrival seared the room.

I drew hard on every resource available, focusing it through the dome and on to the bond I shared with Rogue. The one we'd forged together through love and persistence. Weaving my magic through his, I burned away Titania's grip.

"Save our daughter," I commanded him. "You must. You know what to do. Leave me. Leave me to save us."

Understanding rattled through him, saturated with regret. Sending me a burst of love that I wrapped up and tucked into my heart, his image flickered. Darling Hercules went flying as Rogue transformed into the Black Dog.

My internal cat leaped to follow, and how I held her back I didn't know.

Except that she accepted my promise. *Soon. Very soon.*

Starling shrieked as the Black Dog knocked her over, seizing my daughter, still squalling, in his massive jaws.

And disappeared.

I wished with all my heart I'd done the right thing. Anything was better than giving her to Titania, wasn't it?

As if called by my thought, Titania flashed into the room like flame catching on lighter fluid, sucking out the oxygen and replacing it with raging heat. Athena, her dagger still trapped under Incandescence's thrashing body, scrambled away as Titania stomped her dainty foot through the other woman's face.

"You had one job!" Titania shrieked. "And you let these *insects* distract you."

She advanced on me, and Starling, her rapier shaking alarmingly, thrust herself between us. Titania sneered at her. I took the moment to call Darling Hercules to me, praying Starling would survive the blow Titania dealt her with a candy-pink twist of her pretty mouth.

Darling Hercules gave me surcease long enough to focus my thoughts. I had my wish for him ready and, for the first time, I reached voluntarily into the morass of Titania's mind. She seethed, a cauldron of insanity, the magma of power having burned away anything that made her more than pure hunger. I rifled through her thoughts, finding the thing she didn't expect me to look for.

And I broke the spell she'd laid on Darling.

Abruptly, my feline Familiar became the young man he'd so often imagined, with the lithe limbs of the noble fae, an expression of astonished and transported joy on his face as he examined his hands. It really sucked not to have thumbs, I knew.

"Get 'er, Goliath," I whispered. Because I had nothing left.

Tall and strong, Goliath faced Titania down, blasting her with the cool numbing of his magic. She withered under it, her fiery power quenching under the vast reserve he'd accumulated from all those years of powerlessness.

She collapsed, but she wasn't out, no. Instead her mind wormed away, darting off to burrow through the tunnels she'd made through the Veil, to find the changelings she'd seeded.

To pull the trigger.

She had to be stopped.

And I was dying anyway.

The cat inside me welled up and I fed her everything I had. My screams rang in my changing ears as she took shape from my failing flesh. Once and for all, I became the cat, leaping onto Titania, slicing her with lethal claws and piercing fangs. Crunching her bones with my powerful jaws as Goliath drained away her ability to heal.

Between us, we dragged her down the stairs, to the doorway to the dragon perch. My particular dragon friend waited there, as if we'd planned this. And maybe, on some deep unspoken level, we had.

The dragon took the screaming Titania from me like a sweetmeat offered on my palm. And ate her, swallowing her and her dreadful magic into her nullness.

Destroying her forever.

§⁊⸏

I PACED THE room, sniffing the towels soaked with blood I recognized vaguely as my own. It felt good and right to be in my meant body. The ready response of quicksilver muscles, the flex of claws and my long tail adding balance. Gone were the pains the woman had suffered.

We were clean and whole. Strong. Invincible.

The noble fae conferred, watching me warily, uncertain if I understood their conversation. Afraid that I might attack.

I might, at that. Their fear pleased me.

Mostly I heard their words, but it bothered me most that the kitten seemed to be missing. I prowled, looking for it, while a human-smelling woman wept.

"Can't you all combine magic to turn her back?" A human man wearing the stink of silver was arguing. "I can do it but I need the damn scepter, whatever she did with it."

"We have more pressing problems. With Rogue gone, his lady incapacitated and Queen Titania destroyed, the magic grows unstable. The lesser fae and the humans are revolting. Someone needs to take control. Reestablish order."

"The lesser fae and humans have always been revolting." They laughed.

"Without Sorceress Gwynn, none of us can reach our children. Nothing else matters. You're fools to worry about anything else." The fae who spoke stepped into my path. He smelled of snake and something else familiar. Had he taken the kitten? I growled at him and he edged back in a satisfying way.

A little fae girl wrapped her arms around my neck. I didn't want to eat her so much. "Don't hurt him, Gwynn. He knows how to help you."

"Goliath, come here," the snake man ordered.

The one who helped me destroy the evil one with his magic sat down next to me, scratching my ears in a delightful way that made me want to purr. He seemed familiar to me and, in my mind, I saw us playing like kittens together.

"Inside out," the snake man instructed. "Show her. If I can do it, she can."

Kitten-man showed me how he'd been inside a cat—so funny!—and then came out. But no. I didn't want to. This was *my* turn. The woman could stay inside. Besides, she'd lost the kitten. I would not have.

"It's not working. She's gone."

Another tall fae strolled up. I flattened my ears. We hated her. Sure enough, she smacked us on the head. I swiped at her but she danced away and the fae girl I didn't want to eat held me back.

"Wake up, Gwynn!" The mean woman snapped her fingers. "Or will you prove yourself the fragile human we all knew you to be? Our greatest failure."

Her I wanted to eat. I shrugged off the little fae, her strength no match for mine, and stalked after the cruel one.

"You can't best me," she taunted. "Not like that. I doubt you could in your sorceress form either. You always were too meek."

Old rage flickered into life from some deep corner of me. She had not been meek or fragile. She—no, I—I'd done my best and, more, I'd survived and overcome what they'd tried to do to me. Hell, I'd sacrificed my life to stop *their* queen. And now she wanted to make out like I was the meek one? Fuck that.

I flexed, stretching my own being outward, folding the cat back into my soul and reassembling my flesh back from hers.

"Fuck you, Marquise," I said, straightening and dressing myself with a thought, making sure my ring and earrings made it back with me, from whatever singularity of mass and space we'd been tucked into. "And your perverted brother too."

Starling, sobbing, launched herself at me. "You're okay! How can you be whole again? Gwynn, you were—"

"I know." Torn asunder. Dead. And yet, here I'd managed to reassemble myself in total health. Surely that wasn't possible. And yet, clearly it was.

I surveyed the room.

Athena, undaunted as always bounced up and sheathed her dagger. "Welcome back, Gwynn. About time."

Goliath, a gangly young fae with Darling's green eyes, gave me a happy smile and a bow. A purr filled my head.

"You're welcome," I told him. "And thanks for the help with the Queen Bitch. We're even."

He nodded, beaming.

"He's not talking." Fafnir eyed him with speculation. "It's possible he never will."

Too long with a cat's brain. I viscerally got how that could happen.

A boom shook the castle. Something like fireworks shot overhead.

Walter craned his neck back. "Shit's getting real."

"What's going on?" I could rewind some of the conversation, not all. I understood now more of what Rogue meant about being the Dog. What you did and didn't know.

"Gwynn." Starling wiped her tears and squared her shoulders. "The baby—"

"I know about that part," I interrupted. And couldn't think about it right then. Time for mourning later. Rogue would expect me to step up and defend his—our—castle. I seriously doubted he'd be coming back. "We're under attack still? By whom?"

Marquise, Scourge and Fafnir stared back at me. Goliath wondered if we'd have mice for lunch.

"Pretty much everyone not in this room," Fafnir told me in a dry tone. "It seems the…gap in leadership proved too great a temptation."

"Fortunately," Scourge put in, "they've been busy fighting each other."

"What about Puck?"

"That one." Marquise shook her head over his imagined antics. "Who knows? We haven't seen him in some time."

"And Lady Healer?" She should have been here long ago. Mistress Nancy lay on a pallet of blankets on the floor. I didn't need to look at the blood-soaked bed to understand why. "Nancy needs her help."

Starling and Athena exchanged unhappy looks, while Goliath growled and Fafnir nodded. "One of the first to throw in with General Falcon." Apparently she'd taken the opportunity to ignore Rogue's summons in favor of her own ambitions.

"Take the silver off Walter," I ordered.

Scourge opened his mouth to protest, but Marquise stopped him. "He's ready enough. He's not like *her*. Not nearly so stubborn."

"I'm standing right here," I reminded them and they blew me kisses.

"We can't help that you're our favorite sorceress." Scourge gave me a lascivious grin. "Now that Rogue is out of the picture, perhaps we—"

"No. Never. Walter, would you see what healing Nancy needs and—what?"

Walter looked deeply uncomfortable and Starling burst into tears.

"Oh no." Not Nancy.

Athena put a hand on my arm. "I think she died the moment Titania struck her."

All my fault. If I'd left her at the inn, she'd be fine still. Happily making her very fine beer. And we hadn't even saved my child. All for naught. Oh, God. Billy. Orphaned now.

"What about her son? Does anyone—"

"Safe with my kin," Athena supplied.

"He always has a home here. Make sure everyone knows it."

"I'll look after him." Starling firmed her chin. Then took Walter's hand. "We both will."

"If I may point out," Athena inserted, "if we don't secure the castle, none of us will have a home here."

Time to mourn later. For them, not for me. "Walt's right. We need the scepter." Where the hell would Rogue have hidden it?

"I know where it is," Athena said. Then shrugged, maybe a little guilty. "Seems like once I keep track of something, part of me always knows where it is." Another boom shook the tower.

"Sooner might be better."

"Yeah. On that." She dashed off.

I assessed my energy levels. Surprisingly good, though I felt curiously unstable, as if half of me had been torn away. The Rogue half. And our daughter with him. Maybe that left me only one-third of a person.

Should be enough to finish what I needed to do.

Mentally, I checked in with Larch. The Brownies were still fighting for me. The humans appeared to be conscripted. Falcon, Incandescence and Healer had them throwing themselves at each other. Fafnir's army had been divided up among his erstwhile generals, each of those having helped themselves to Titania's crew.

Not surprisingly, Rogue's cyborg army had vanished with him, as I imagined many of his defensive spells had. With battles raging both inside and out, the castle wouldn't last long. Utter chaos.

"Seriously—don't you people have *anything* better to do than fight amongst yourselves?"

Walter shook his head. "Yeah, like we're any different."

He had a point. And it made me think. What exactly had Titania's plan been? If she'd intended to sow dissension in the human world in some way, it would likely be easy to accomplish. Not that I could do anything about it, if she had managed to pull the trigger. The world would have to save itself.

I knew my limits.

Athena, a streak of blood on her check, skidded back into the room. "I got it out of hiding, but I didn't want to risk carrying it past any of the others, just in case they could glom on to it. Figured you could, you know, suck it to you and then give it to—"

Indeed. The magic rose cleanly in me. It made a difference when you didn't plan to keep any in reserve. I'd already died once today. It would make no matter if I did again. I really had nothing to live for at this point. Trapped in Faerie without Rogue or our daughter sounded like the worst of prison sentences. The scepter appeared in my hand. Walt whistled in appreciation. "Nice trick, Gwynnie."

Athena dug her fingers into my forearm. "I was *saying* 'and give it to Walt.'"

"I can handle it." I yanked my arm from her grip.

"Like hell you can—you're obviously crazed from losing

both Rogue and the baby. You're upset about Nancy. You couldn't handle the scepter when you were in good shape."

"She's right, Gwynn." Starling stood, wringing her hands together. "If you use it now, you could—"

"What?" I laughed and I did sound more than a little crazy. "I could die? Been there, done that. Frankly it didn't suck. It was...restful." It sounded so much better than facing the alternatives. "All of you stand back."

Unleashing the magic and pouring it through the scepter and thence in a focused arrow through the lens of the crystal dome, I sought whatever might help. Using my wish like a net, I gathered reinforcements to me.

The flying monkeys arrived first. They swirled around the dome, bat wings blackening the sky and I laughed at the sheer power of it. Dragons roared, landing on every tower and a cry of battle fervor rattled through the mind web.

Finding Incandescence, Healer and Falcon, I knocked the unholy trio on their asses, sending dragonfly girls to alert some humans to put them in silver until someone had time to deal with them.

The rest fell like dominoes, frightened of the power I wielded. Titania's erstwhile army erupted into chaos, regaining themselves as I ruthlessly emptied myself of power to burn away the last dregs of her control. I followed the oily lines through the mass mind, burnishing and purging as we'd done for our injured, but on a grand scale. At the ends languished those captive fae she'd fastened in place. Them, too, I liberated, setting them free to make their way as they would, giving them each a boost of power to do it with.

None of them knew I used the last of my life energy to put

things in order. Tying up my affairs, as it were.

Even as I collapsed to my knees, the scepter eagerly drinking from me, I made one last effort, however. Maybe they had crossed the Veil. If I could only see...

I looked for Rogue. For the Black Dog.

For my daughter.

Nothing.

Nothing.

Nothing.

CHAPTER 29

IN WHICH I TIE UP MY AFFAIRS

༃

The report of my death was an exaggeration.
~Big Book of Fairyland, "Immortality"

NOTHING.
The emptiness of the word reverberated through my mind.

What I had left. What my life had become. What I had become.

I could let go now. Give up the struggle. All this time, I thought I'd been fighting Rogue, but it had never been him. Just the inevitability of this moment.

Like Cecily, I could let myself dry up and dissolve into dust.

Ashes to ashes.

Someone tugged at the scepter and the pain penetrated my fog. I tried to hold on but the flesh tore from my palms as it was wrenched away from me. Then blessed cool healing replaced it, tasting oddly of hot chocolate and warm cinnamon rolls.

I opened my eyes and Walt grinned crookedly. "Sorry, Gwynnie—no noble self-destruction for you. And it's *my* staff. Ha-ha."

The blue sky, deeper sapphire than Rogue's eyes, arched overhead in deceptive flawlessness. No booming or shouting. No wheeling dragons or flying monkeys. The castle had settled into something resembling peace.

"Just leave me be." My voice came out in a whisper, creaking over abused vocal chords. I seemed to recall shrieking as I called the monkeys, like some demented version of the Wicked Witch of the West. Which was redundant, most likely. I should be the Wicked Witch of the East, since I felt as though a house had fallen on me. Rogue would tease me for thinking so much instead of being dead. "Why am I not dead?" I wondered out loud.

"Because you're not mortal."

I struggled to sit up at the sound of Puck's amused voice. "What?"

He strolled into the room, hair cut short, Wall Street-style, and wearing, if I wasn't mistaken, an Armani tux. "I told you. You can put a pig in a pond, but you can't make him swim." He waggled a finger at me. "Or her."

"Of course I'm mortal. I was born to human parents." Wasn't I? A sensation of falling gripped my stomach as my reality fell into pieces, reassembling into a different picture. "I don't understand."

"Don't you?" Puck's mismatched eyes sparkled and he danced over to kiss me on the cheek. "I carried you over myself. You were such a cute baby."

Carried me over? My mind reeled. "I was—I am

a...changeling?"

Puck nodded. "I couldn't tell you before, but I truly thought you'd remember. I visited you from time to time. That was one of my jobs, checking up on all of you. We had terrible problems with failure to thrive." He waved at Walt. "Remember me? Your imaginary friend."

I'd had an imaginary friend too. I'd called him Casper and he'd had mismatched eyes, one grass green, one marble blue. Walter made a choking sound, half laugh, half sob that managed to articulate exactly how I felt too. "You mean *that's* why I felt like an alien my entire life? Because I'm actually a fae baby?"

"More than half, at any rate," Puck qualified. "At least your parents are still alive. And your sister."

Starling realized first, horror, chagrin and astonished joy comingling in her being. I felt bad for her, but happiness seemed to win out over losing the possibility of romance. "Baby Brody?" she asked Walt and he winced.

"Bad luck for us, eh?" He tugged on her hair. "But it explains why we get on so well."

"Not to make this about me..." I turned back to Puck, frenetic dread crawling up my spine. Though I knew. It explained so much. The formless longing. The never fitting in. I couldn't look at Fafnir. "But..."

He cocked his head at Fafnir significantly and winked. That cord leading from Cecily out and back in. No wonder I couldn't find the end. It led to me. From my birth mother.

Had I wept for her in my heart before? For that baby, ruthlessly wrenched away and consumed? I wanted to weep now. Or to shatter the dome in my rage. It felt possible and real in a way nothing else did. My human mother and father, my family—no blood relations of mine.

I had no family.

Fafnir cleared his throat and I stared at him, a bit wild, remembering dancing with him, slicing him apart with my claws. My mother's mummified corpse drifting into dust before me.

"I'm not sorry," he got out. "I know you may be, but I can't. I'm proud to call you my daughter. Cecily would be too."

He'd transformed in those brief minutes, the sense of time and defeat flaking away. He was no longer the one with nothing left to lose—and he shone with new life. As for me...I had no idea how to feel. Never in my whole life had the man I'd thought was my father said that he was proud of me. In fact, he'd always been vaguely disappointed in me.

I had to turn away, blindly anchoring to Puck. Deeply ironic that only he made sense in this vortex of kaleidoscopic uncertainty.

"She—Cecily—" I couldn't call her my mother. "She was also a changeling?"

"Yes, but with none of your magic. She passed for human quite nicely though." Puck pondered. "Some thrive. Some die. The ones who need to make their way back here. But really, it was a bad plan all along. Eggs are better. Isn't that what you discovered?" He waved at the bloody bed with distaste.

"What about the baby my mother gave birth to—her human child? What became of her?"

"She's around here somewhere." Puck shrugged. "Not my job to track the human ones. I mean, who really cares—"

Athena coughed ostentatiously and Puck shrugged. "Not my job."

This, no doubt, was where the human population in Faerie came from then. How many centuries had Titania been running her breeding plan? And Puck—carrying the babies for her back and forth.

Back and forth.

"Where have you been?" I eyed Puck's suit with suspicion.

He grinned sunnily at me and executed a little jig. "Babysitting. That Dog is terrible at it. And Blackbird and Fergus are too busy."

I stared at him, assimilating my sudden and desperate hope.

"What about my—our—parents?" Starling glanced at Walt. "Is that where they went—across the Veil to find Brody?"

"Oh." Puck rolled his eyes with grandiose melodrama. "Fergus is ever the hero, isn't he?"

"What does he mean by that?" Walter demanded.

"Fergus—your father—has an interesting magic." Amazing how collected I sounded as I ran the possibilities through my mind. "He's not a sorcerer like you, but he instead acts as a kind of conduit. It actually transforms him into a champion who can't be defeated. If my theory is correct, then Tita—" even with her theoretically destroyed, I didn't like to speak her name, lest it evoke her, "—our late, unlamented Queen Bitch had plenty of changelings still in the human world. Sleeper spies who would...what, Puck?"

He gave me a weak smile. "Much mischief."

"An ominously vague assessment."

Puck nodded vigorously. "Oh yes. Very ominous."

Afraid to ask. Desperate to know if I might yet have found a loophole. "How did they cross?"

Puck laid a finger alongside his nose like Old Saint Nick did in those rosy-cheeked paintings of *The Night Before Christmas*, mismatched eyes twinkling. I fingered the dagger I'd wished up when I dressed myself, taking Liam's advice to keep one near, and contemplated stabbing Puck with it. Which would accomplish nothing.

"Okay—can you take me? You took me over once before, right?"

Puck clapped his hands and squealed. "Oh, pretty Gwynn, I thought you'd never ask!"

CHAPTER 30

IN WHICH I FINALLY FIGURE OUT
HOW TO USE THE RUBY SLIPPERS

*There appear to be at least three ways to cross the Veil: via
the Wild Hunt, the elemental spirit animals and with
someone who can open a gate. So self-evident it kills me to
write it.*

~Big Book of Fairyland, "Rules of Magic"

I LEFT STARLING and Walt in charge of the castle, with the
others—including Larch's amazingly effective army of
Brownies—to assist.

Marquise and Scourge offered to take the rebels into custody and I agreed, to their delight. A reward for their loyalty
and a bit of payback for the others.

Puck and I left by the front door.

Why that seemed odd to me, I didn't know. Probably partly that there even *was* a front door, the gate no longer
magically spinning. Grooms had to bring our horses around to
us, walking them through the halls. Other parts of the castle
were manifesting the signs of Rogue's nonpresence in this

universe. I only hoped the towers would all hold. We crossed the drawbridge, the moat monsters leaping happily and spraying water. I was glad to see they'd survived.

The field of blue Stargazer lilies had not. Trampled by armies of fae and withering without Rogue's sustaining magic, the meadow had become a sludgy mess of decaying vegetable matter. It hurt my heart to see it—which amazed me that I could still feel anything—and I had to look away. Maybe I'd instead passed into this state where I felt everything, my own self pushed to the Technicolor extreme that Faerie induced.

Felicity, happy to be freed of the castle, tossed her mane and kicked up her heels. Puck sang me songs of pigs and rain barrels and other nonsense. It didn't surprise me one bit that we rode into the pathless countryside, back toward the hills like the one I landed on.

We turned the horses to roam free and I poofed their tack, so they'd be comfortable. The hair prickled on the back of my neck as we approached the spot. I might well have known it, if I'd chanced to walk near this particular hill. It carried the same chill as the path near Devils Tower, the sense of an open door and the draft wafting through.

Puck looked at me expectantly.

"What do I do?" I asked.

"I know what *I* do." He laughed, carefree. "What do *you* do?"

"Can't you carry me over—like when I was a baby?"

He looked aghast, sizing me up as if I'd asked him to carry an elephant. "No. That only works with babies. They're different, you know. Babies. And pigs."

"Great. Why did you say you could take me then?"

"I said I thought you'd never ask. You got yourself here. Why can't you go back the same way? You're the sorceress. I'm just..." He shrugged. "My gift is travel."

"And mischievous obstinacy."

He spun in a circle, a manic, Armani-clad Julie Andrews with arms outstretched. "I am alive with mischief." Then he stopped on a dime and winked. "See you on the flip side."

Then he walked through a doorway and was gone.

Of course I tried to follow. Which meant I ended up walking back and forth across that hilltop about a dozen times, feeling like a complete idiot. I'd done it before, yes, but on impulse. And in an aspen grove. There was no convenient totem tree here for me to tie a lock of my bloodied hair to.

Still.

You got yourself here. Why can't you go back the same way?

Okay, time to replicate as many variables as I could. I wished up the black Anne Taylor cocktail dress I'd been wearing. Or a version thereof, as the original had long since been destroyed. I added my heels as best as I could remember them. That would have to do. The Black Dog had been present then, and no way to add in that brand of magic. The cat, smug, stirred inside. Okay, I did have her.

I reached under my hair, cut a lock from as near the same spot at the nape of my neck as I could manage. With the dagger, I sliced the tip of my finger and wiped the blood on my hair. Separated from me, the hair changed back from my favored shiny black to the dull, dark blond I'd worn most of my life. It seemed appropriate—looking just as it had that day at Devils Tower.

With nothing to tie it to, I held my hand over the draftiest point and let the hair go. It caught in the unseen wind and spiraled up.

Pulling at me. Taking me with it.

꿈

INTO A BLIZZARD.

"Well, shit!" I exclaimed, clapping my hands to my bare arms. You'd think I'd remember what Wyoming winters were like, having lived most of my life bitching about them, but wow—that wind cut like a dagger.

I wished up a cloak. And nothing happened.

Goodbye, powerful sorceress Gwynn. Welcome back, Dr. Jennifer McGee, PhD in being an idiot. I did the only thing I could do. I started walking.

That first morning, I'd made it most of the way around the tower, starting at the west end near the parking lot, passing around the sunny southern face before rounding to the shadow side. So, I kept going that direction, completed the circuit I'd started so long ago. Really wishing I'd been smarter about what I'd worn.

Of course, in this world, wishes did little good. Evidenced by all those beggars not riding horses.

My heels skidded on the slick path and my skin went numb, stinging only when a sheet of ice pellets bulleted against me. I suspected that, in this realm, even my whatever percentage of fae blood wouldn't lend me any level of immortality. Otherwise we'd have changelings living forever. Hmm.

I knew—really I did—that my Honda would not still be sitting in the parking lot where I'd left it. Who knew how many years had passed in my absence? Plus, my car keys had stayed behind. Still, I felt a stab of disappointment when it wasn't there. When no cars were there.

Because who visits Devils Tower in a blizzard? Probably the park was closed. I couldn't possibly walk out, dressed like this. I wasn't even sure I could get back to Faerie, which was the wrong direction, anyway.

The whistling wind let up briefly and the buzz of a snowmobile drifted through the pause. Or was that more wishful thinking?

No—there it was. Puck on a snowmobile, wearing a sandstone Carhartt insulated coverall, strawberry-blond curls whipping behind him, tangling with an improbably colorful and long scarf.

"Finally!" he exclaimed. "I don't know why you people keep it so cold here. I guess it doesn't bother you though."

To my credit, I didn't throttle him. But I did make him give me his coat. Hopefully I wouldn't lose any toes to frostbite. I climbed onto the snowmobile behind Puck and tucked my skirts under my thighs, pressing up as tight against his back as I could to protect myself from the wind chill, wishing it was Rogue instead.

Wondering if I'd ever see Rogue again. My longing, no longer formless as it had been that long-ago day, now squarely centered and focused on him and our daughter.

"Where are we going?" I shouted in his ear.

"To fetch what's yours."

It didn't surprise me a bit to pass the sign I remembered from before. Devils Tower Lodge: Friends and Guests Only. For the owner, Frank, the distinction wasn't a tautology. We pulled up in front, disembarked and I rushed inside, forgetting my manners and that I wasn't—on this occasion—anyone's guest. Perhaps Puck and I could skate by on the technicality of putative friendship.

A woman stood in the center of the room, Devils Tower looming blackly dramatic out the windows, dramatically framed by the billowing snow. She whirled in surprise at my bursting in on her.

And the baby in her arms wailed.

"Oh my God!" The words wrenched out of me on a sob and—I knew this was exactly the wrong thing to do, but I couldn't stop myself—I tore my daughter from the woman's grip. Only after seeing who it was. "Blackbird!"

"There, there, Lady Gwynn. Don't fret. Sit yourself down and comfort yourself that your child is all right. Here now." Blackbird adjusted my grip so that I cradled the baby more gently and my daughter stopped fussing, staring owlishly up at me with deep, sapphire-blue eyes. She waved a little fist, with perfect tiny fingers when one of my tears splashed on her cheek. My heart cracked open and I wept harder, barely noticing when Blackbird urged me into a chair.

I'd never quite gotten why new mothers did this, but I couldn't stop myself. I unwrapped her, laying her on her blanket on my knees and inspected every bit of her. Her round belly with the raw end of the umbilical neatly tied off was otherwise perfect. All her fingers and toes. No bite marks. I placed my cheek against her velvet-soft chest and the 3/4 rhythm of her heart answered.

Mine. My family, forever.

"See there?" Blackbird set down a cup of steaming tea.

"She's just fine. You did the right thing, to send her away." She touched the baby's cheek. "I remember how it feels. I never did get to hold little Brody."

"You remember?" The baby started to fret, so I wrapped her up and cuddled her. So happy to hold her. So at a loss at what to do with her.

Her snapping black eyes flashed up to mine, filled with rage. "Yes. Once I arrived here, the memory spell stopped working. It's a cold place you're from though."

I had to laugh. "It isn't always. But I have news for you. Maybe Fergus should hear it too."

Blackbird shook her head. "He's gone off with Frank, once they saw the news on the magic box."

Shit. The image of aging-hippie Frank taking off in his Jetta with a centuries-old Irishman who'd been trapped in Faerie amused me, despite my stomach's clench of warning. "What news?"

The baby cried harder and she raised her voice a bit. "Seems that Titania contacted some of our children here, set off messages in their minds. What did Frank call it? Brain-bathing?"

I realized then that she was speaking English to me. And so had Puck. Of course they would be, for me to understand them. Something to puzzle over later.

"Brainwashing."

"That's it." She looked pleased, then frowned. "I don't quite understand it, but apparently some of the changeling children did...*things* to open the gates. One stole a flying machine and flew it into a stone ring. Other places, too—many humans in huge villages dead. Frank was beside himself."

Frank. Still alive and kicking, so it hadn't been that long since I left. "What were they planning to do about it?"

"Fergus wanted to visit one in custody, to see if he's Brody, and Frank said something about saving the world."

Of course he had.

"He won't have the magic here, to give him any advantage. Did he think of that?"

Blackbird smiled with exasperated affection. "He told me not to fash meself about it, so I haven't. I was to wait here for you and then shut down the gate after you go back. Before the terrorizers find it."

"Terrorists," I corrected absently, jiggling the crying baby. "I don't know what to do for her." If I'd had any kind of normal life, I would have taken parenting classes and been prepared for this. Surely there was some sort of checklist for dealing with crying babies.

"She's hungry," Blackbird said in a gentle tone. Hesitated. "Do you have milk?"

"Milk?" Why would I have milk? It wasn't like I carried groceries around and coming through—oh. "No, I don't. After the birth I was pretty torn up and I, um, changed into the cat and back." Erasing all effects of the pregnancy. *Stupid, stupid, stupid.*

My little daughter squinched up her face and turned hot pink with crying. Already disappointed in me. "I'm a terrible mother," I realized. "I can't even feed her."

"Oh, stop it," Blackbird snapped. "I've got some goat's milk that we've been giving her. Once you cross back, you can wish up your own milk or feed her a combination of magic and other sustenance. No mother knows what she's doing at first.

We all learn as we go."

She handed me a bottle and I popped it in the baby's mouth. The ensuing quiet did a great deal to steady my nerves. I would need to name her, which I hated to do without Rogue's input. Why had we never discussed it?

"Two things—first, this might be a shock, but remember Walter?"

"How could I forget?" Blackbird replied in a dry tone, shaking her head a little. So odd not to hear her thoughts, sample her feelings. Where Faerie had once seemed over-the-top to me in every way, my old world now felt sterile and one-dimensional. Walt wasn't the only one who'd changed.

"He's come a long way. Very manly and a great help during—all the stuff you missed—which is good, because, surprise! Turns out he's Baby Brody."

The news electrified her. At first she nearly protested, but then frowned, puzzling it through. "It makes sense, doesn't it? We asked you to help find him and you led us right to him. We just didn't recognize him."

I nearly said it hadn't happened that way, but—when she phrased it like that—it kind of had. Magic worked in mysterious ways.

Another thought occurred to her. "Does Starling know?"

"She does now. And, don't worry, things didn't progress far between them, if you know what I mean."

Blackbird sighed. "I wasn't a fan of the old Walter, but I was willing to go along, for Starling's sake. She wants to find love so much."

"I know." We all did. The baby had stopped suckling and looked drowsy. I might be a terrible mother, but she'd have to put up with me, because I'd never let her go. No chance of wandering off into the desert without me again. "You'll like the new Walter, I think. You'll be proud."

"I always pictured Brody like this." Blackbird stroked a hand over the fuzz of black hair on my daughter's head. "Though I knew he must have grown, I never... Ah well, time enough to adjust."

Not much to say to that. I took a deep breath, dreading the answer to my next question. "Okay then, where is Rogue?"

CHAPTER 31
THERE'S NO PLACE LIKE HOME

If I've learned nothing else from this adventure, I know now that what I love is what I value. And vice versa. It needs no more quantification than that.

~*Big Book of Fairyland*, "Personal Observations"

B LACKBIRD RAISED ELEGANT winged eyebrows. "He's where you might expect."

She walked to the window and I followed. Outside, the Black Dog—absurdly large in this context—played in the snow with Puck. He had hold of the long scarf and tugged at it while Puck flailed in a snowdrift. I sighed, torn between laughing at their antics and fear that Rogue might be lost to the Dog forever.

"Why hasn't he changed back?"

"He can't. Not here." Blackbird looked, not at the pair in the snow, but out at the looming Tower. "You have to take him back. Take them both back. But I understand if you want to stay here, in your home. I can go instead."

I was already shaking my head, mildly surprised at myself.

"This isn't my home anymore." If it ever was. *That's why I felt like an alien my entire life.* Walter had summed it up well. Changelings out of place.

"Will he change back, once we get through? Will he...be himself again?"

"I don't know," Blackbird replied, regret in her voice. "We've been here for days. That's a long time."

"I gave Darling Hercules Goliath his fae body back."

She blinked at me, long and slow. "Did you now?"

"But he still thinks like a cat."

The Black Dog tackled Puck, tumbling him through the drifts, snow flying everywhere. Would I be able to stand it, having Rogue's body back powered by the mind of a dog? Was it even fair to him? I imagined the alternative. I could load up a car and the three of us could drive down to Laramie once the storm cleared. Maybe I could get my job back. Maybe I could find Isabel and rescue her from whatever had become of her. Eventually I'd have to face my mother. But could I?

I'd either have to continue to pretend to be her daughter or tell the truth. It would be far easier if I could tell her where her true child was, what kind of life she lived. That meant going back to Faerie to find her.

I could make a life here again, with my very smart Dog, my daughter and Isabel. Or go help Frank and Fergus with saving the world.

It sounded empty.

I'd never believed in true love and now I thought I might wither away without it.

And you can't save everyone. Maybe it would be enough to get my own family to the watering hole. I could maybe come back later. Especially if some of the gates had been blown open. The world would undoubtedly still need saving tomorrow.

"Would you hold her?"

Blackbird smiled and took the baby. "Always."

In the mudroom, I found a pair of boots to fit, along with a parka, hat and gloves. Frank hadn't changed, always prepared for lady visitors. In fact, he had even hung a mirror, for someone to fix her hair or freshen her lipstick on the way in or out. I made myself look, to see who I might be in my old world.

No longer myself, for sure.

The silver pattern on my face didn't glitter, but stood out like the raised lines of scar tissue, the skin twisted and puckered beneath. I might have gone through a car's windshield sideways. Oddly, it didn't bother me. After all I'd been through, I deserved a few scars, a lasting testament that I'd been wounded unto death and healed.

Outside, the Dog spotted me immediately, leaping through the snow with glee and knocking me back into a drift. He licked my face while I sputtered and thrashed. Puck threw a snowball at me, then sang "Sing a Song of Sixpence."

I looked into the Dog's eyes, seeing and feeling nothing of Rogue. Staying here would be a safe choice, but I had to take the chance of saving him too.

"Puck—we're going back."

"Won't that be a pretty sight to set before the king?" He replied, kicking up snow.

"There is no king. Just us chickens."

Puck laughed gaily, as if I'd made an excellent joke. "Do

you know what you're doing, powerful sorceress Gwynn?"

"Absolutely not." I grinned at him. "I figured I'd wing it."

༄

BLACKBIRD SENT HER love to Walter, but elected to stay behind and mind the lodge for Frank until she heard from him and Fergus. I wasn't surprised by her choice. And it amused me that she'd found her role so easily, even in my more mundane world, always the one to keep things running smoothly.

I chickened out and sent my mother an email, amazed that my Gmail account still worked. The password was easy to recall—too easy, really—"Isabel," my treasured cat. Lousy encryption. Perfect reminder.

Keeping it brief, I told her that I'd traveled overseas and that it was impossible to explain—ha to that!—but that I was well and in love. And that she had a granddaughter. I also said I'd be in touch, that we'd visit. I made a wish that it would come true.

We wrapped up the baby and Blackbird assured me that she'd explain to Frank why I'd had to take his things. He'd consider it a fair trade, she thought, for us sealing up the gate and saving this place that was sacred to so many.

"I don't know that I know how to close it," I told her as she folded up my Anne Taylor dress, as she'd done for me before, so long ago.

"If you know how to open, then you know how to close."

"A nifty saying that ultimately means nothing."

She winked at me and handed me a bag with my dress, shoes and things for the baby. "You'll figure it out. You always do."

Puck took us on the snowmobile, much more slowly after I thumped him over the head and told him I'd turn him into a pink chipmunk if he made me drop the baby. The Black Dog romped alongside, big as a pony, but otherwise like any other dog.

I couldn't contemplate that Rogue wouldn't come back from it.

He had to.

We left the snowmobile in the parking lot and walked the reverse path to the aspen grove. I superstitiously almost insisted that we take the long way around, circumnavigating the sunny side first, but practically it wasn't good for the baby to be out in the cold longer than necessary.

Maybe I could make a list of motherly habits and start practicing.

Meanwhile I worked out my wish, aligning the components like an integral equation. Each piece needed to work in sequence and, if one bit failed, it couldn't jeopardize the others. Simple, precise and with all variables eliminated, that I could foresee. An elegant design, even. One, two, three.

So much rode on this.

Puck held the baby while I found the totem tree and got the things ready and the Dog sniffed around, flushing out a squirrel. I wasn't sure how to manage them all at once. "Can you..." I started to ask Puck, then hesitated, worrying about the potential bad juju. Fuck it—I couldn't do it all myself. "Can you carry my daughter through?"

"Of course." Puck bounced her in his arms and made silly noises, sprinkling her face with kisses. "I love to carry the babies. She looks just like you did."

"Really?" That gave me pause. "Except for the eyes, which are all Rogue."

"True. Perhaps the next one will have your green."

"Save your curses, imp," I growled at him and he giggled. "Rogue!" I called the Dog, feeling silly, but what else could I call him? The Dog bounded up and I held up the handle of the bag of things. He took it in his mouth, clamping gently with those white fangs that had carried our daughter miraculously without harm. I cut the hair, bloodied it and tucked the knife away. Putting a hand on the Dog, I gestured at Puck to come close. Then I looped the hair over the tree limb and executed my wish.

CHAPTER 32
ONCE UPON A TIME

Understanding why I was drawn into all of this may change nothing, but it's good to know.

~*Big Book of Fairyland*, "Rules of Magic"

I AWOKE ON soft grass.

Then sat up with a stab of panic. The extraordinary emerald green of Faerie greeted me, the same view as that first time and, for a horrible, endless moment, I thought none of it had happened. That I'd never left this hill or that I had been trapped in some sort of psychotic fugue state.

One that had just looped around and started again.

A baby's cry wafted up the hill and Puck appeared, somehow carrying my daughter while dancing a complicated jig. "Oh good, you're awake. She's hungry as a pig in a poke."

"I think that's a very messed-up metaphor." I levered myself to my feet, sweating in the winter clothes, shouldered the bag and took my daughter. "Welcome home, sweetheart," I murmured to her and kissed her on the forehead with love and relief. At least she'd come through fine.

That was one. "And the Dog?"

"Chasing the cat." Puck shrugged elaborately. "You know how dogs are."

Then he was not himself. I steeled myself against the reality that I might never truly have him back again. As a form of insurance, of fulfilling all my promises, I felt through the gate I'd gone through so long ago. It anchored to me in that way, to my initial entrance to the other side. I pulled it gently closed behind me, locking it to me, to the girl in my arms.

With a pointed wish, I imagined Stonehenge and created the ring atop the hill, the gate itself beneath the capstone. That should hold it.

And if not, I would know.

I could only hope I could do right by Rogue as well.

"Show me?"

We walked down the hill, then up another, me sweating bullets. Kicking myself, I tested the magic. It flowed in with a rush, green as the hills. My daughter waved her fists, blue eyes sparkling. "You like that? Me too." I vanished my winter clothes and replaced them with a sundress and did likewise for her and her blankets. I sent the bag of things to our bedroom along with a mental message to Athena that we'd returned and would be home soon.

Home. It sounded like where I wanted to be. With my family.

Holding on to hope that my dying wish—it counted as that, right? Since I fully believed I'd die when I made it—would come true, in all the best ways.

Let everything come out okay.

Two hills over, the Black Dog saw us and came leaping

over, then ran back to show us our other traveling companion. Isabel had made it through. Hissing and thoroughly unhappy, but just as she'd always been. I handed the baby back to Puck and crouched, letting Isabel catch my scent. Suspicious, she sniffed, then a purr welled up and out. She pushed her head against my hand and I rubbed her blue-smoke fur, tears dampening my eyes. Happy ones, for once.

There was two.

Finally, I turned to the Dog, capturing his great head and staring into his amber eyes, so unlike Rogue's. But I'd pulled Rogue back from this before, when we had far less connection.

I reached for it, throwing my faith and belief into the hope it would be back, the strong golden cord of our connection. So much had changed in the mass mind. As if the absence of Titania had reworked the system, causing all the connections to reset. Like a brain recovering from injury, releasing bad synapses and recreating new ones.

So, when I found it, it had moved some.

But there it was. I poured all the mental magic I could muster through it.

Rogue.

Rogue.

In my mind, a boy swam to the surface, hopeful, seeking light and life. He struggled for shore and I fed him the magic he needed. Anything and everything for him. Had I done this before? Not possible, and yet...

He made it to the beach, running. I took his hand.

And the fur under my hands changed to skin, the black of the Dog condensing and intensifying into the inky lines embedded in Rogue's skin. Amber eyes deepened to midnight, then sharpened with intelligence. Rogue gazed back at me with some bemusement, then growing insight and remembrance.

"And you said you couldn't bring someone back from the dead, magical Gwynn."

"You promised me you couldn't die."

He stood, pulling me into his arms and I reveled in being able to simply be close to him again. "It's good to know you'll hold me to my promises," he said against my hair. He cupped my chin and raised my mouth to meet his. I kissed him back full of happy greed for him and everything about him.

"I have someone for you to meet," I told him.

I took the baby from Puck, who gave me a jaunty salute and wandered off to tempt Isabel with a yellow flower. Our daughter, who'd been working her way up from fussing to the full-blown bellow I now recognized, stopped in midcry and stared at Rogue with fascination. The two pairs of unearthly blue eyes met and fused.

"Your firstborn child, Lord Rogue," I said formally. "As *I* promised."

He smiled, in pure delight, and caressed her cheek with one finger, just as he did with me. "She's perfect." Then his gaze flashed up to mine. "But don't think this finishes things between us."

"No?" I kept a straight face, though I bubbled over inside, with love. With joy. With utter relief that everything had come out okay—at least for this moment. "I'm quite certain this means all bargains between us are settled."

He snagged an arm around my waist and pulled me close, the baby between us making happy noises. "Then I shall have to trick you into new bargains."

"You can try." But I couldn't keep my arch attitude and gave in and kissed him. "We need to name her."

"Yes. Names are powerful things."

"You were well named, it turns out. The rogue, the wild card that brought a tyrant down."

"And you, my queen for a new and golden era."

"I can only hope. Though ours are portentous names. It might be nice for our daughter to have a simple one."

"That's easy. She is what I hoped for all those long, empty years. What you have brought to me."

"Oh yes?"

"Eden."

"So be it."

And that made three.

TITLES BY JEFFE KENNEDY

༄

FANTASY ROMANCES

BONDS OF MAGIC
Dark Wizard
Bright Familiar
Grey Magic
Familiar Winter Magic (In Fire of the Frost)

HEIRS OF MAGIC
The Long Night of the Crystalline Moon
(also available in *Under a Winter Sky*)
The Golden Gryphon and the Bear Prince
The Sorceress Queen and the Pirate Rogue
The Dragon's Daughter and the Winter Mage
The Storm Princess and the Raven King (May 2022)

THE FORGOTTEN EMPIRES
The Orchid Throne
The Fiery Crown
The Promised Queen

THE TWELVE KINGDOMS
Negotiation
The Mark of the Tala

The Tears of the Rose
The Talon of the Hawk
Heart's Blood
The Crown of the Queen

THE UNCHARTED REALMS
The Pages of the Mind
The Edge of the Blade
The Snows of Windroven
The Shift of the Tide
The Arrows of the Heart
The Dragons of Summer
The Fate of the Tala
The Lost Princess Returns

THE CHRONICLES OF DASNARIA
Prisoner of the Crown
Exile of the Seas
Warrior of the World

SORCEROUS MOONS
Lonen's War
Oria's Gambit
The Tides of Bára
The Forests of Dru
Oria's Enchantment
Lonen's Reign

A COVENANT OF THORNS
Rogue's Pawn
Rogue's Possession
Rogue's Paradise

CONTEMPORARY ROMANCES

Shooting Star

MISSED CONNECTIONS
Last Dance
With a Prince
Since Last Christmas

CONTEMPORARY EROTIC ROMANCES

Exact Warm Unholy
The Devil's Doorbell

FACETS OF PASSION
Sapphire
Platinum
Ruby
Five Golden Rings

FALLING UNDER
Going Under
Under His Touch
Under Contract

EROTIC PARANORMAL

MASTER OF THE OPERA E-SERIAL
Master of the Opera, Act 1: Passionate Overture
Master of the Opera, Act 2: Ghost Aria
Master of the Opera, Act 3: Phantom Serenade
Master of the Opera, Act 4: Dark Interlude
Master of the Opera, Act 5: A Haunting Duet

Master of the Opera, Act 6: Crescendo
Master of the Opera

BLOOD CURRENCY
Blood Currency

<u>BDSM FAIRYTALE ROMANCE</u>
Petals and Thorns

Thank you for reading!

ABOUT JEFFE KENNEDY

Jeffe Kennedy is a multi-award-winning and best-selling author of epic fantasy romance. She is the current president of the Science Fiction and Fantasy Writers Association (SFWA) and is a member of Romance Writers of America (RWA), and Novelists, Inc. (NINC). She is best known for her RITA® Award-winning novel, *The Pages of the Mind*, the recent trilogy, *The Forgotten Empires*, and the wildly popular, *Dark Wizard*. Jeffe lives in Santa Fe, New Mexico.

Jeffe can be found online at her website: JeffeKennedy.com, on her podcast First Cup of Coffee, every Sunday at the popular SFF Seven blog, on Facebook, on Goodreads, on BookBub, and pretty much constantly on Twitter @jeffekennedy. She is represented by Sarah Younger of Nancy Yost Literary Agency.

jeffekennedy.com

facebook.com/Author.Jeffe.Kennedy

twitter.com/jeffekennedy

goodreads.com/author/show/1014374.Jeffe_Kennedy

bookbub.com/profile/jeffe-kennedy

Sign up for her newsletter here.

jeffekennedy.com/sign-up-for-my-newsletter

www.ingramcontent.com/pod-product-compliance
Lightning Source LLC
Chambersburg PA
CBHW030547020726
47494CB00005B/1513